Also by Lucy Score

LUCY SCORE *WITH* CLAIRE KINGSLEY

Bloom books

*To Claire Kingsley for walking this journey with
me. You're my soul sister and my book bestie
and I'm so thankful for your friendship.*

Published by Bloom Books, an imprint of Sourcebooks
P.O. Box 4410, Naperville, Illinois 60567-4410
(630) 961-3900
sourcebooks.com

Cataloging-in-Publication data is on file with the Library of Congress.

Originally published in 2019 by That's What She Said Publishing, Inc.

Printed and bound in the United States of America.
POD

Chapter One

Jonah

Activate those glutes," I told the nineteen-year-old star of his college baseball team.

"Dude, if I activate them any harder, they'll turn to stone," Eric complained, hefting the bar off the floor.

"Looks like he's doing just fine from where I'm standing," Mrs. Morganson observed from her vantage point directly behind him.

It was deadlift day.

Once a week, I turned the weight room at Bootleg Springs High School into an open gym for all ages and abilities. The room was crammed full of equipment and smelled like sweaty, unshowered youth. The short windows just beneath the drop ceiling were stingy with the sunlight they let in.

But we made it work.

It should have been a disaster. I was coaching kids on their summer break from college, middle-aged newbies just starting their fitness journey, a few long-time lifters, and a couple of senior citizens. Some were actually here to work out. Others were in attendance primarily for the eye candy.

But somehow, no matter who showed up, we all had a damn good time.

"Nice job," I said, slapping Eric on the back when he dropped the weight bar with a resounding clang. The kid was a hell of a lot stronger than his long, lanky frame let on.

"Woowee!" Mrs. Morganson cheered.

Minnie Faye, owner and operator of Minnie's Meow Meow House, elbowed her friend. "Don't get us booted out of here like you did the football team's car wash," she cautioned.

Both ladies bent to pick up their significantly lighter bars. I winked at them as they made an energetic show of practicing the lift.

"How you doing, D?" Doris to her family and D to her gym friends was glaring at her barbell.

"I wanted a PR today." Frustrated, she swiped the sweat off her forehead with the hem of her t-shirt. Doris was fifty-six and three years on this side of a heart transplant. She'd tracked me down about a whole day after I decided to bring my personal training business to Bootleg last year.

In a town this size with residents this close, news traveled fast.

She'd told me since someone had to die for her to be here, she didn't want to let them down. We had our first workout together that day. A walk through the lakefront park.

We started small and slow, but her commitment never wavered. She'd already quit smoking before the transplant. After, she'd taken up walking. Soon I had her jogging and hanging around my pop-up boot camps. Then she'd discovered a deep love of heavy lifting. Somewhere along the way, she'd dragged her husband, Josh, into it. Josh had lost twenty-five pounds and started rowing. Doris added ten pounds of lean muscle and was currently glaring at the weight plates on her bar that stood between her and her new personal record.

"How much you got on there?" I asked, already knowing the answer.

"Two hundred. Can't get the dang thing off the ground." She kicked at the bar with the toe of her sneaker.

"Tell you what. Go grab a quick drink. I'm gonna take some of the weight off, and we'll check out your form at eighty or ninety percent of your max. Okay?"

She sighed, shrugged. "Yeah. Okay."

"Not every day is a PR," I reminded her.

"Yeah. Yeah."

"She went to bed early last night so she'd be rested for lifting," Josh told me when Doris walked away. "Gonna be pissed if she can't beat her last."

"Don't I know it," I said, pulling a plate off each side of the bar. I swapped a couple out and reassembled the rig.

"That looks like more than—"

"Zip it," I warned him as Doris came back. Josh busied himself with his own bar and played it cool.

"Ready?" I asked her.

"Yeah. I don't know what my problem is. Just feeling weak, I guess. Maybe it's allergies?"

"Maybe," I said, gesturing for her to step behind the bar.

"How much is this?" she asked, adjusting the headband that tamed her wild, curly bob.

"Don't worry about the number. I just wanna check your form. We'll get you to where you want to be when you're meant to be there," I promised her.

"I know. I know. It might not be today, but we will get there." She recited one of my many pep talks with a sigh. "I just really wanted it to be today. Today's *the* day, you know?"

"Your anniversary?"

"Three years ago, I was on death's door and woke up with a new ticker." She thumped a fist to her chest. "Kinda wanted to be able to email the donor's family and tell them I hit a big PR today. Let them know that part of him is still living on."

I put a hand on her shoulder, squeezed. "Hey, I know that's the ideal, but let's work with the reality first. Okay? Maybe it's something simple." It was relatively simple. The anniversary, the wanting to report to the family of the man whose heart she'd received.

Doris had psyched herself out.

We were four weeks out from our last deadlift day, and I *knew* that she could hit 200. *She* just wasn't sure.

She nodded, still disappointed. "Yeah, yeah. Okay. Let's see if you can wave your magic trainer's wand."

She hinged from the hips and reached for the bar.

"Use the over-under grip," I instructed. "It'll keep you from feeling like the bar's going to roll out of your hands."

She nodded again, adjusted.

"This is gonna be a little easier because it's not your max. So focus on the form. Count of three. One, two, three!"

The class, sensing something big was happening, stopped what they were doing and ranged themselves behind Doris. Watching, holding their breath.

She pulled. Face tight, the cords of her neck straining. The bar raised. Slowly, slowly it inched higher.

"Go! Go! Go! Pull!" I shouted.

"Pull!" The rest of the class echoed in varying pitches.

Doris straightened, fully extended and red-faced, the bar clenched in her hands. The class cheered behind her. She dropped it and bent at the waist.

"Why the hell are you guys making all that racket?" She blew out a breath, swiped her arm across her forehead. "Holy crap. I must be getting sick. That felt like a thousand freakin' pounds."

"That's because it was 215," I told her.

"Two what?" She blinked.

"Two hundred and fifteen pounds."

"215? I lifted 215?"

I nodded, grinning.

"215," she said again, a whisper to herself.

Josh grabbed her from behind in a tight hug. "215," he repeated.

She squeezed his hands and calculated the weights in front of her. "Oh my god. That *is* 215! I lifted two hundred and fifteen friggin' pounds!" She escaped Josh's hold, turned, and threw herself at him. "I did it! Holy shit!"

"You did it!" He squeezed his eyes shut tight as he held his wife who'd not only survived but was *living*. I felt the arrow to my own heart and distracted myself by digging out my phone to commemorate the moment.

The celebration was Super Bowl-winning touchdown worthy.

The class passed her from lifter to lifter for a round of back-cracking hugs and celebratory high fives. All celebrating like it was their own personal victory while music thumped in the background.

"You lied to me," Doris said, returning to me, hands on hips. Her face was flushed with happiness.

"Just a little," I told her.

"You knew I was psyching myself out, and you mind-tricked me into making it happen," she insisted. Her eyes were getting misty.

I shook my head. "*You* made it happen. Now, go stand with your bar so I can take your PR picture. You can send it to your heart's family."

Her lower lip trembled.

There were more than a few pairs of glistening eyes surrounding us.

"Don't do it," I said, pointing at her. "If you go, we'll all go, and then it'll be all over Bootleg that I make my classes cry. You'll ruin my business if you cry."

A tear slipped out of the corner of her eye as she came in for a tight hug.

"Thanks, Jonah," she whispered.

"I'm really fucking proud of you, D," I whispered back.

"Me, too."

It was a good way to kick off the weekend. D's personal record cheered me enough to temporarily forget about my own personal life for a moment.

The body that investigators had found and the questions it represented. Was my DNA tainted? Had my father murdered a teen girl? And what did that mean for those that came after? Me. My brothers and sister. What kind of legacy had he left us?

This was the good in the world. The Dorises and the Erics and the Mrs. Morgansons. They were the good. I'd spend some time enjoying instead of worrying about the things I couldn't fix.

"You know, Jonah," Mrs. Morganson said, sidling up to me as I wiped down the bars. "You really ought to think about opening a gym space. Set up shop, plant some roots."

"I bet that June Tucker would be more than happy for another local investment," Minnie Faye added, looking innocent.

"Is that so?" I said easily.

The thought had occurred to me.

But the bottom line was, I hadn't decided if I was staying in Bootleg Springs or not. I'd been here a year. I had family here, a fledgling business with classes and personal training. But that didn't mean that this West Virginia town was home. Once the Callie Kendall case was resolved, then I would decide.

Stay or go.

"Think about it," Mrs. Morganson advised. "Your own space to set up any way you want. A set schedule. I bet a gym would do real well in Bootleg so folks could work off all that moonshine."

"I'll take it under advisement," I promised. "Now, if you ladies will excuse me, I'm gonna go celebrate D's victory with an egg white omelet before my next class."

Chapter Two
Shelby

The Brunch Club served up fancy breakfast with steaming sides of hot gossip. Bootleg Springs residents bellied up to the restaurant's sleek concrete bar or leaned forward in cushioned booths to catch up on the town's latest rumors while enjoying goat cheese frittatas and fried chicken biscuits with mango chia smoothies.

As a natural observer, I couldn't get enough of the crowd.

"Did y'all hear that Moe Dailey's bloodhound got loose again? Knocked up Lacey Dickerson's purebred Shih Tzu," Mrs. Varney shouted over the restaurant din. In deference to the sunny late spring morning, she was decked out in cropped black elastic waist pants that stopped just short of her boobs.

There were seven of us squeezed into a big corner booth at the back of the restaurant. I was the youngest by at least three decades.

"There's something for your notes, Shelby." Old Jefferson Waverly, the only male member of our gathering, poked a fork in my direction. "Bootleg Springs has a long memory and a fine appreciation for karma."

"Mm-hmm." The group nodded enthusiastically. They waited for me to write it down, and I obliged. I'd been adopted by the Breakfast Club—not to be confused with the Brunch Club—a collection of Bootleg elders who generally doled out advice and caused mischief. Especially on bingo nights.

I'd come to town with a very specific objective and quickly came to the realization that I wouldn't be able to simply hang out on the sidelines and observe. No, this small town required full-contact participation before it would open its arms to an outsider. It was participant observation at its finest. I was Jane Goodall, and Bootleggers were my subjects.

They had tentatively accepted me as one of their own. Well, most of them had. There were a few outliers still holding out on me. But I'd wear them down. I always did.

By involving myself in town life, I'd gained more than just the insight I was looking for. These crafty neighbors took my original plan and narrow thesis, doused it with moonshine, then set it on fire.

At their behest, rather than conducting a few dozen or so face-to-face interviews, I'd built an online survey and made it available to the entire town as of two days ago. It included brief personality assessments, questions around how residents related to the larger community, as well as role identification tags and rating systems for compassion, social justice, and participation.

Essentially, my little nerd survey was designed to pick apart exactly who Bootleg Springs was made up of and why they worked so well together. The most recent shiny example of their community activism occurred when the town banded together to evict a crowd of overzealous, disrespectful journalists.

Those same residents were now helping me earn my doctorate one survey answer at a time.

"Guess they'll have a litter of shithounds on their hands," Granny Louisa mused. Her life partner, Estelle—black to

Louisa's lily white and genteel South Carolina to Louisa's rough-and-tumble West Virginia—high-fived her.

"Better than havin' bloodshits," Jefferson cackled.

All around the table, good Southern ladies threw their napkins down and glared. Jefferson snickered.

"Anyway, serves her right for dumping that poor Jonah Jr. at the prom," Gertrude, AKA Gram-Gram, commented while scooping up grits.

The rest of the table clucked their sympathy, voicing their concerns that the man would never find a decent mate. I made a few notes in my notebook. The elders of Bootleg Springs shared an interest in the love lives of what they deemed the "youngins." Apparently with the pairing off three of the five Bodines, they were itching for a full house resolution.

The "poor" Jonah Jr. they were discussing was Jonah Bodine. Illegitimate son of the deceased Jonah Sr. and one of the holdouts who still didn't think highly of me. He'd shown up in town days after his father's funeral upon discovering from the obituary that he had four half-siblings. Jonah was, according to Myrt Crabapple, "the spittin' image of his father and brothers."

Which meant Jonah was very, very attractive.

He was tall. Lean. Strong. Muscular, but not in a steroidal way. He had an easy smile and eyes the color of the grass after a good rain. He was—here.

"Well, speak of the handsome devil," Estelle said, pointing her bacon in the direction of the door.

My little nerd heart beat out an approving tempo.

He strolled inside in shorts and a sweaty t-shirt. I magnanimously decided not to take offense to the fact that my brunch companions had complained to high heaven about me showing up for our meal in my running clothes and my aches and pains that I tried to cover. They obviously didn't have the same qualms about post-workout Jonah.

Every woman in the restaurant held her breath as he used the hem of his shirt to mop at his brow. That flash of abs had me bobbling my coffee cup against the saucer. The resounding clash tore eyes off Jonah's very nice eight-pack and delivered them to my flushed face.

He dropped his shirt and looked at me. The friendly smile faded to stone. Strong jaw, subtle hollows under the Bodine cheekbones. Those eyes were cool, annoyed. My table mates took notice.

"Brrrr. Is it just me, or did it get real cold in here?" Mrs. Varney said in what she thought was a whisper.

I met Jonah's blank stare with a bright smile. It said a lot for the man that he could dislike me intensely but still not bring himself to be rude.

Myrt waved him over, and I saw him hesitate for a moment. His negative feelings toward me seemed to be strong enough to make him consider avoiding the town elders. Interesting. The analytical part of my brain wanted to test which situations were more or less distasteful than a civil conversation with me. I scratched out a quick note in the margin of my notebook to consider it later.

He ambled over to the far end of the table. "Ladies. Jefferson," he said with a nod, pointedly avoiding further eye contact with me.

"We were talking, and we think it's time you find some gym space," Louisa announced.

The rest of the ladies nodded their heads emphatically.

"That seems to be the sentiment of the day," Jonah said cryptically.

"I know not a one of us looks a day over fifty," Gert said, patting her white hair. "But we shouldn't be tripping over tree roots and free-range chickens to get to our Happy Hour workout."

Happy Hour was the name residents over the age of sixty voted to call Jonah's senior fitness class.

"Mona Lisa McNugget Number Five sure is more adventurous than Number Four," Jefferson commented.

"Now, you wouldn't just be trying to get me to settle down, Gram-Gram. Would you?" Jonah asked with a wink. Gosh, his smile was nice. No wonder the ladies loved him. Heck, I liked him, and he wasn't even nice to me.

Gert, Cassidy and June's grandmother, feigned innocence

and pathologically lied her cute little butt off. "I have no clue what y'all are talking about. I'm looking out for your welfare. Why, imagine if Estelle here took a header over a chicken in the park and broke a hip."

Everyone at the table, except for me, knocked on wood.

"What about the high school gym?" Jonah prodded. He was a personal trainer, and I doubted there was a single lady within town limits who wouldn't be interested in him personally training her. I'd taken one or two of his boot camps before he became woefully misinformed and decided to dislike me. It was a shame. He was an excellent teacher, and I was in need of some athletic guidance.

"We just think you would do a better business, especially with the summertimers, if you had a dedicated gym space," Mrs. Varney insisted.

"I'll think about it," he promised, smiling at the table. His gaze skipped over me.

I wondered if he would think about it. The man had come to town to get to know siblings he had never met only to find out that his biological father was the primary suspect in a years-old missing person case. Growing up without a father and *then* discovering the man might be a criminal? Unless he cemented his bonds with the rest of the Bodines, Jonah wouldn't have a reason to stay in Bootleg. No reason to own real estate.

"You do that, Jonah," Myrt insisted. She batted her lashes at him, and her glass eye glinted under the table's chandelier.

"Care to join us for brunch?" Estelle offered.

"I'd love to ladies—and Jefferson—but I've got a family thing to take care of. You all have a nice weekend," Jonah said and headed up to the counter where his to-go order was waiting for him.

I bet it was egg whites and veggies. *Gross.* The man was a paragon of health, and it showed. Rumor had it a pork rind had never crossed his lips.

"Henrietta Van Sickle is due in for supplies," Jefferson announced, restarting the gossiping portion of the meal.

"Think Gert will get her to talk again?"

"You mean force the poor woman to demand to be left alone?"

"I am a delightful conversationalist," Gert sniffed.

"You blocked the woman's exit from the grocery store with your cart until she had to ask you to move," Louisa argued.

"Still counts. She talked to me."

I'd grown up in Charlotte and spent the last several years in Pittsburgh. The idea of a hermit sneaking into town once a month for supplies piqued my interest.

To be fair, just about everything in Bootleg Springs did. Including Jonah Bodine, I thought, idly watching him hustle out of the restaurant. He shot me a parting look before disappearing into the spring sunshine.

"Shelby, honey. Don't you think it's time to come clean with that boy?" Estelle asked.

I shrugged, tucking back into my eggs Benedict.

"I agree. The Bodines are practically the heart of this town. You need them if you're going to write your fancy paper," Mrs. Varney piped up.

They had a point. A small one.

"Your brother cracked the door open by moving in with June Tucker," Jefferson noted. "Use that to your advantage. Show the Bodines they were wrong about you."

"And I know just where you need to start," Gert said slyly.

Q. What's the most neighborly thing you've done for someone in your community?

Jefferson Waverly: I rear-ended Wade Zirkel last year at a stop sign to show my support for that Scarlett Bodine girl. Told the sheriff it was an accident cause of my bifocals. But that Zirkel fella knows the truth.

Chapter Three

Shelby

The sounds coming from inside the cottage suggested I'd arrived at a bad time. Someone was swearing. Something was ringing. And something else was yowling.

I rapped briskly on the cottage door and pressed the doorbell.

There was a crash followed by a lot more swearing, and then the door opened.

"Well, what in the hell do you want?"

Scarlett Bodine glared at me and puffed out a breath to blow the mahogany hair out of her face. There was a cat attached to the leg of her jeans.

I flashed her my friendliest I'm Not a Threat smile and held up the platter of donuts and breakfast pastries I'd ordered to go from the Brunch Club. "Hi," I said chipperly.

Scarlett detached the cat from her leg and nudged him back into the house with her work boot.

I could hear her boyfriend, Devlin, on the phone somewhere behind her.

"I repeat. What in the hell do you want?" she demanded coolly.

But I noticed how her eyes tracked to the goodies which, after my horrific run this morning, were starting to weigh heavily on my weakened arms.

"Scarlett, I think we got off on the wrong foot," I began cheerfully.

"If you mean you being a low-down, no-good, dirty, gossip-mongering, she-devil of a reporter trying to infiltrate *my family* and dig up dirt on us as the wrong foot, then yes. Yes, we did."

Undaunted, I removed the plastic wrap from the tray of carbs so the scent could escape and overwhelm her brain. Olfactory function was on my side. No one could stay angry when they were sniffing sugar. "I'm not a reporter. I'm not writing about Callie Kendall. And I promise I'm not trying to infiltrate your family."

Scarlett looked at me with suspicion. But the scent of French cruller was distracting her. It smelled like victory to me.

"You write for magazines," she pointed out. "You showed up in town with the rest of your soulless, heartless, loafer-wearing journalistic weasel friends. I don't care if your giant brother is dating one of my very best friends in the whole wide world. That does not require me to be nice to you."

She snatched a pastry from the tray.

"I do freelance write," I agreed. "For academic psychology journals. I'm writing a thesis involving field study on the bonds that exist between neighbors in small communities and how these relationships can often be as strong as and as binding as actual biological or romantic relationships."

Scarlett bit off a corner of the cruller and blinked. "Say what now?"

"I'm getting my doctorate in social work. I'm writing my thesis on Bootleg Springs. On how your town chased off a pack of soulless, heartless, loafer-wearing journalistic weasels. GT can vouch for me," I promised, hoping my brother wouldn't mind playing character witness for me if need be.

I was staying in Bootleg Springs until I had everything I needed for the best damn thesis ever written on small-town psychology. And the Bodines might as well get used to the idea. Because I wasn't leaving town without their input in my survey.

Scarlett was still eyeing me like she didn't trust me any farther than she could pitch me off a dock. "You may come in," she said finally. "But one wrong move, one word that I don't like, and I will chase you off my property with my daddy's shotgun. It's not loaded, but it still looks real scary. And I can swing it pretty damn hard."

"Fair enough."

I followed her inside. The cottage was adorable, tiny, and…stuffed to the rafters. Boxes lined one wall of the skinny hall. I turned sideways and edged past them holding the tray aloft, making my back and shoulders scream in protest. The space opened up into a minuscule kitchen and teeny tiny living room. Both of which were overflowing with stuff. There were more boxes, some labeled, some open with their contents spilling out.

Two clothing racks of smart suits bookended the small couch. Plastic totes and file boxes were built up in a wall in front of the TV.

The cat zoomed in and out of stacks of books and magazines before sinking his claws into a cardboard box labeled Case Files 2010.

"You stop that, Jedidiah," Scarlett ordered, whipping out a spray bottle and aiming it at the cat.

The cat looked at her, and I swear it grinned. He continued shredding the box until Scarlett sprayed him right in his little face.

He yowled and sprinted off down the hallway.

"If you'd just listen the first time, I wouldn't have to do that to you," she called after him.

Devlin, tall and impeccably dressed, was standing in the kitchen with a phone pressed to one ear and a finger in the other. He spoke attorney fluently into the phone and gave me a distracted smile. He dropped a kiss on Scarlett's head and ducked into the bedroom shutting the door.

"I'm pouring you some sweet tea. But only because it's polite. Then we can go out on the porch where you can attempt to win me over, at which you will undoubtedly fail, leaving me no choice but to escort you from my property." She sniffed.

I wasn't a fan of sweet tea. It made my teeth hurt. But I didn't feel safe admitting that to her.

"Sweet tea would be so nice," I said cheerfully.

She glared at me and stomped into the kitchen where she produced glasses and a pitcher of sugar. She put it all on a tray and carried it to the sliding glass door. I pulled it open for her, earning a curt nod, and followed her outside.

This was the kind of experience I needed to absorb and somehow translate in my dissertation. This adherence to tradition and etiquette while still being borderline rude. It was fascinating.

I found myself in a cozy screened-in porch that faced the sparkling waters of the lake that kissed the end of Scarlett's land.

My hostess dumped the tea on a small table for two. I added the pastries, and we sat.

"So, what the hell do you want?" she asked, pouring the tea. "And don't even think about asking me one single question about that body those folks in New York found this week."

"Like I said, I'm not a reporter." Scarlett was a no-nonsense kind of woman. I liked that about her.

"The hell you say." She reached for another pastry.

"I'm a grad student, not a journalist," I told her. "I'm working on a thesis for my PhD in social work."

She chewed and studied me with suspicion. I felt compelled to keep talking.

"Those writing credentials that Deputy Tucker found? Those are all articles for psychology journals. The academic world puts a lot of weight on being published."

"So you're *not* a weasel reporter?" she clarified.

"I am not," I promised.

"Well then, what are you doing here?" Scarlett asked, relaxing perceptibly.

"Bootleg Springs managed to eradicate a predatory crowd of journalists in a time when sensational headlines are the only thing that matters for most news organizations. This tiny little town in West Virginia took on some of the biggest publications and blogs in the tri-state area and won."

"Hell yes, we did."

"I'm here studying how your community came together, how you're socially structured. I'm writing a paper about it. One that should earn me my doctorate."

Scarlett sipped the tooth-hurting tea thoughtfully. "Then why exactly did you turn tail and run out of town when Cassidy broke the news that you were a reporter?"

I blinked, not expecting that question. I wasn't big on lies. But I also wasn't looking to spread my personal life all over town. "I had some academic things to take care of." It wasn't exactly a lie. I *had* visited my advisor. It's just there were other things on my to-do list. Things I didn't think Scarlett Bodine needed to know. On cue, my back began to ache. I shifted on the seat trying to alleviate the discomfort.

"Mm-hmm," she said, still watching me carefully. "Then why were you cozying on up to Jonah? What were you trying to get out of him if it wasn't some exclusive on our daddy?"

My laugh surprised us both.

"I just thought he was cute," I confessed. *Really, really cute.*

"Of course he is. All of my brothers are. So you're just saying you were flirtin' for the sake of flirtin'?"

I nodded. "Well, yeah. He's so tall, and he has those green, green eyes. And his smile is really nice."

Shut up, Shelby, I ordered myself. I could feel my cheeks flushing. I had a big, fat crush on Jonah Bodine. Fortunately, he thought I was a low-down, no-good, something or other Southern insult. So there was no requirement to *actually act* on the crush.

I wasn't exactly in the position to get myself a boyfriend.

After my degree. After I got the rest of my life in order. After I handled this latest round of bad news. But for now, I could enjoy admiring Jonah from afar.

"Fair enough. So why are you here today? Besides tellin' me how pretty my brother is?" she asked, kicking back in her chair. The lake sparkled through the trees behind her. The late spring breeze blew warmly through the screens.

I took a deep breath and plunged. "I need a place to stay. The inn is great and all, but I need something semi-permanent with room to spread out a bit for the summer."

Scarlett snorted. "Tell me about it. Crews just broke ground on our new house two weeks ago, and I am countin' down the days until Devlin has a closet as big as a shopping mall so I don't have to trip over a dozen suits on my way to the coffeemaker."

"Congratulations," I said. "Since you brought it up, ask anybody in Bootleg Springs about real estate and rentals, and they'll tell you Scarlett Bodine is the woman to see."

"I *might* be able to help you out," she said cagily. "But first we should make small talk. It's the polite thing to do."

―――――

Scarlett: Quick question for y'all.

June: Why do you announce the fact that you have a question? Why not simply ask the question?

George: What can we do for you, Scarlett?

Scarlett: Your sister, Shelby. Is she a homicidal maniac or a compulsive liar or a real bad person?

June: I find these questions concerning.

George: Shelby is none of those things. I think if you'll just give her a chance, you'll really like her.

Scarlett: Would I like her as a potential sister-in-law? Like could I stomach seeing her at the Thanksgiving dinner table for the rest of my life?

June: I am uncomfortable with this line of questioning.

Scarlett: Are you two sitting on the couch next to each other texting?

June: We are attempting to take advantage of our hot springs time slot. You are interrupting.

Scarlett: Sorry, JuneBug! I just had this idea, and I need to know if I'm gonna have regrets.

George: I've never regretted having her as a sister, if that helps.

June: Which brother are you planning to mate her to?

Scarlett: Who says I'd do such a thing? Now if y'all will excuse me I have a new tenant to orientate.

Chapter Four
Jonah

"What do you think? Is it big enough?" Bowie asked.

I peered over his shoulder. Bowie and I were the same age, half-brothers who shared a father who'd disappointed us in different ways. I'd have expected him to have the biggest problem with me when I'd showed up in Bootleg Springs last year.

But it had been Gibson, the oldest of all of us, who'd had the hardest time warming up to me. At least Gibson didn't seem to warm up to anybody, so I couldn't take it too personally.

His usual cheerless mood had taken a nose-dive in recent days. He hadn't wanted to come on this outing and was scowling over Bowie's other shoulder.

"Can you go bigger?" he asked, rubbing a hand over his forehead like he'd rather be anywhere but here.

"Size definitely matters," Jameson agreed, leaning his elbow on the glass. "You want one that could take an eye out."

"Yeah, but Cassidy isn't gonna want to have to push some mammoth thing around in a wheelbarrow. Not with her line of work. You need to get her something she can have at work. Something that won't hinder her from chasing down a drunken lawn mower driver or locking up Gram-Gram," I pointed out.

Devlin leaned in on my right. "I agree with Jonah. That one sticks out too much."

"You're the expert here," Bowie said to the woman in front of him. "Is it too big? Not big enough? Does it stick out too much?"

The jeweler was staring at us with wide eyes. "Uh, what does your fiancée-to-be do again?"

Bowie sang Cass's praises as sheriff's deputy, and the jeweler took in the new information. She nodded. "I've got some ideas. If y'all will sit tight, I'll be back in a minute."

"I can't believe you're finally buying a ring for Cassidy Tucker," Jameson teased his brother.

Gibson snorted. "I thought you two idiots wouldn't make it down the aisle until you both were in your eighties."

I looked around the store, hands in the pockets of my shorts. We'd made the trip into Perrinville so Bowie wouldn't get ratted out by any big-mouthed Bootleggers.

Devlin was peering into the case at a bunch of the sparklier rings a few feet away. "Scarlett said not until she's thirty," I reminded him.

"My plan is the second that woman turns thirty, I'm putting a ring on her finger," Devlin said, still eyeing the diamonds in the case.

"Couldn't hurt to look at a couple," Bowie told him.

"Maybe they'll give you a discount if you buy in bulk," I offered.

"You want in on this engagement action?" Devlin asked me.

"No thanks. I'll leave it you all." After a year here, I was constantly battling the contagious "y'all."

"What's your deal? You haven't dated since you showed up here," Gibson demanded, crossing his arms and turning his back on the case full of futures.

I couldn't say that Gibs got nicer to me the longer he knew me, but he did get more aggressively curious.

I could have answered the question, but I'd learned a lot from the Bodines. "Could say the same about you," I shot back.

Bowie snickered. "Gibs doesn't date. Once every couple of months, he picks a lucky lady up at one of his shows, bangs her until she makes noises about commitment, and then shows her the door."

"You don't even do that," Gibson pointed out, ignoring our brother's criticism of his sex life.

My face must have done something stupid because they all zeroed in on me.

"You're into guys?"

"You're married but secretly running from your shrewish wife?"

"You're monastic?"

"Those jeans do highlight your ass," I told Jameson, who snorted approvingly. "But none of those creative scenarios apply."

"What's the deal then?" Bowie asked.

This was not a discussion I wanted to have. Especially not with a man buying an engagement ring to seal his future. "I was seeing someone and thought it could be serious, and then it…ended."

"She dump you?"

"You chickenshit out?"

"She crawl out of bed in the dead of the night, steal your wallet, and leave town?"

That last one was from Gibson, and we all gave him a good long look. He shrugged. "Not sayin' it happened to me."

"It was oddly specific," Devlin put in.

"Can we get back to grilling Jonah?" Gibson asked.

"Right," Jameson said, warming to the game. "One brother at a time. Was she a mail order bride that took one look at your ugly face and ran screaming back to Russia?"

"You're all the worst. Literally terrible human beings," I insisted.

"I've got a few options that I think you might like," the jeweler said, returning with a velvet cushion of sparkly rocks.

"Hang on a sec," Bowie told her. "We're interrogating our brother. It'll just be a minute."

"Take your time," she said sweetly. She took her glasses off and started polishing them as if used to ring shoppers pausing to perform interrogations.

"You might as well confess," Devlin warned me. "They'll just pull out the single lightbulb, bag over your head routine otherwise." He sounded like he spoke from experience.

But I didn't like talking about Rene. It opened up too many feelings that would never have closure. "You guys don't really want to hear about this," I insisted.

"Now we really do," Gibson insisted. He took one of the chairs in front of the jewelry case and spun it around backward, planting himself on it to wait me out.

"Her name was Rene," I said reluctantly.

"Did she dump you for your best friend because she was pregnant with his baby?" Jameson asked.

"No. I mean, she did dump me, but she didn't dump me for someone else."

"Ouch. That's the worst. Was it the whole 'I need to focus on myself' speech?" Bowie asked.

"No. She uh…we'd only been dating a short time when she found out—"

"That she was actually a man in a woman's body?" Gibson filled in. "That did happen to me once. We didn't sleep together, in case you were wondering. Just had a few drinks."

"How is Tony?" Bowie asked.

"Doin' great. Lives in Boise. Fishes every weekend. Two kids. Still get a Christmas card every year."

"Back to Rene," Devlin said, guiding us back to the topic I'd rather avoid.

"Can we come back to Tony?" I asked.

"Why'd she dump you?" Jameson asked.

"We'd only been dating a couple of weeks, and she found out she was sick."

"Like a head cold or maybe herpes?" Bowie asked hopefully.

I shook my head. "No. Like cancer."

"Shit," Gibson said succinctly.

"Said she didn't want me to have to take on her illness," I said, trying to shrug off the memory. "Said she'd feel better if she didn't have to worry about me worrying about her."

"Man," Jameson said.

"You never tried to talk to her after?" Bowie asked.

I wet my lips, hating this part of the story. "She, uh…she died. Five months to the day of our first date. We didn't live together or anything. Didn't even say I love you. But I really thought there was a future there, you know?"

They all nodded somberly.

The jeweler blew her nose noisily behind the counter. "I'm sorry for eavesdroppin', y'all. But that is the saddest story."

"I just haven't felt like getting to know anyone since. I'm waiting 'til I feel better about it," I told them.

There was more to it. My anger at her shutting me out. The helplessness at not being able to do a goddamn thing. The fact that the only thing I could do was respect her decision. The last time I saw her was for coffee right before her first last-ditch treatment. She'd held my hand and wished me "luck with everything" like I was little more than a stranger to her. The next time I'd laid eyes on her, she was in a church looking like she was asleep.

Two weeks later, I'd seen Jonah Bodine's obituary, and Bootleg Springs started to sound like a good idea.

"Can we get back to buying rings?" I asked, my voice hoarse.

Devlin gripped my shoulder. Jameson punched me in the arm. Bowie pulled me in for a one-armed hug before releasing me again.

Gibson gave me a tight nod and some advice. "You might not want to tell Scarlett any of that. She'll get it in her head that you need a woman."

They all shuddered. "If she even gets a whiff of you being this sad, loveless puppy, she'll be throwing every bachelorette in town at you," Bowie agreed.

"I'm not a sad, loveless puppy," I argued.

"Do you want to go grab a drink?" the jeweler asked me, her eyes glistening behind her glasses. "My place is just a couple blocks away, and I have a real nice box of wine."

"Uh, thanks. Maybe some other time?" I told her.

Bowie took pity on me and changed the subject. "Jame, you want in on this action?" he asked, waving a hand toward the rings on the counter.

Jameson shrugged. "Nah."

"You're not thinking about proposing?" I asked, surprised. The way he looked at his girlfriend, Leah Mae, suggested otherwise.

"Oh, I'm proposing. And I'm doin' it better than these two rookies. I've been working with a goldsmith. She's helping me custom design a ring. I'll actually do some of the work."

"Well, fuck me," Bowie complained. "Can we get some bigger diamonds here?"

————

Q. During a party, do you prefer to be in the center of the room or on the perimeter?

Opal Bodine: Depends where the bar and snacks are.

Chapter Five

Jonah

H ey, Mom," I answered the call, steering my car into the town limits.

"Well, if it isn't my long-lost son finally answering his phone," my mom teased through the car speakers. She hadn't been exactly thrilled with my sudden desire to move across the country to meet my half-siblings. But her desire to support me won out. She'd accepted my move reluctantly, but I'd been here so long she was starting to make noises about me coming back.

"I emailed you yesterday," I said dryly.

"A lot can happen in twenty-four hours. You could have met a girl. You could have finally given up trying to speak Southern and decided to move home. You could have saved an elderly grandmother from a purse snatcher."

"Zero of those things happened, Mom."

I came to a stop for Mona Lisa McNugget, who sashayed her way across Rum Runner Avenue. I lived in a town with its own free-range chicken. The novelty still hadn't worn off.

"What are you doing right now?" she asked.

"Watching the town chicken cross the road."

She laughed. "I can't decide if you're pulling my leg with half the things you tell me or if Bootleg Springs is as crazy as it sounds."

I watched as Minnie Fae, dressed in a green sweatshirt embroidered with cross-eyed kittens, dashed after a stray cat as it skirted two parked cars.

"Come back here, you fluffy feline," she yelled, puffing past me.

"I heard that," Mom said. "And I don't even want to know."

"A wise decision. What *do* you want to know?"

"Your email said you moved again. Where to this time? A cardboard box with a hobo on the town square? Into a mansion with an eclectic millionaire who only speaks Pig Latin?"

"Funny, Mom. I have my own place this time," I told her. I didn't tell her that I was living out of boxes. There was no point unpacking when I'd just be packing them back up for whatever reason.

"No roommate?" she asked.

"Just me, myself, and I. I can floss naked at the dining room table if I want to."

"Dental health is important," she said mildly. "Send me pictures so I can be sure you're not living in a locker in a bus station. Of the house. Not you flossing naked."

"Will do," I promised. "What's new with you?"

She told me about the customers who came into the diner today and filled me in on the new yard decor her across-the-street neighbor Phyllis put up in honor of Flag Day.

We spoke once a week either by phone call or video chat and by email more often. My mother was funny, smart, and, in my opinion, entirely too good for the life she'd been saddled with. My father, may he rest in peace as they say reflexively in Bootleg Springs, left college student Jenny Leland pregnant and partnerless. She'd given up her dreams of a degree in psychology and started waiting tables. She shopped garage sales and thrift stores, clipped coupons, and built a happy paycheck-to-paycheck existence for the two of us.

She'd ended up waitressing at a diner where the owners treated her like family. I'd spent a good portion of my childhood tucked away in a booth or curled up in the closet-sized office. She was an assistant manager now but still took shifts to keep her regular customers happy. It was a respectable living. But I wanted more for her. She deserved more.

And as soon as I landed wherever it was I was supposed to be, I'd see about getting that more for her.

We hung up after she extracted another promise from me to send her a picture of my new place. I grinned to myself knowing how she'd fall for the Little Yellow House. Scarlett Bodine was quite real estate mogul and shrewd negotiator. I'd had to check to make sure I still had my shirt by the time we were done arguing over the lease.

The arguing had made me feel like family. And so had the invite for ring shopping, I realized as I turned onto the gravel lane that wound its way through the woods. Devlin and Bowie had picked out rings with diamonds big enough to compete with the idea of Jameson's custom design. The jeweler had chipperly rung up the sales while Jameson showed off a sketch of Leah Mae's ring. Gibson and I, finding common ground of being happily unattached, grunted and nodded our approval.

Commitment wasn't something I actively avoided. But looking at my lifestyle—a business with no home and a three-month lease on a rental I'd negotiated down from six—it did make a man think.

Most of my half-brothers seemed hell-bent on planting roots. To marry, settle down. But I was still waiting for… something.

The house came into view through the trees. It was a two-bedroom cottage with tiny rooms and big windows that invited the woods inside. On a breezy day, I could catch glimmers of the lake through the foliage. The best part was the lakeside trail that cut right through the property, making it convenient for my runs.

I thought about hosting a post-run cookout here for the trail running group I'd organized. Decided it wasn't a terrible idea. Some beer, a grill, good times, and good people.

When I pulled around to the house, I realized I wasn't alone. The front door was wide open, and there were two vehicles parked on the gravel circle by the porch. One of them was Scarlett's pickup truck.

I pulled in behind her and got out just as she skipped down the steps of the front porch. She waved cheerfully. "Hey, Jonah! Was wondering when you'd get back."

She pulled a box out of the bed of her truck, and I took it from her. "You moving in?" I asked.

"Not me. Although if Devlin thinks he can bring one more pair of shoes into the house, I might give him the boot until construction's done." She winked, and I knew there was nothing but love behind her teasing. I had a feeling she'd be ecstatic over that diamond he'd pocketed today.

She hadn't answered the question I hadn't asked directly.

"So what are you doing?" I asked, picking a box from the truck and following her up the porch steps with it.

"I'm helping your new roommate move in," she said cheerfully.

I missed a step and smashed my shin on the porch. "My what?" I winced.

"Hey, Scarlett, do you want the security deposit now or—oh, hi, Jonah. Come on in."

Shelby Thompson—or, according to Cassidy Tucker, *sneaky-ass reporter* Shelby Thompson—was standing in my doorway, smiling at me, inviting me inside *my own damn place*. She was short and curvy and always smiling. She had thick brown hair with a heavy fringe of bangs that framed out her wide eyes. Green and brown that made me think of the forest floor. Creamy skin, thick lashes. She was pretty in a girl-next-door kind of way.

Until she smiled, and then people tended to take notice of something that went deeper than pretty.

Of course, none of that made up for the fact that she was one of the horde of journalists that had descended like a biblical plague on Bootleg Springs to get a piece of the Bodine family over the whole Callie Kendall case. She'd flirted with me, and I'd flirted back. It pissed me off that she thought she could get to the rest of my family through me. That I was the weak link somehow.

It also pissed me off that she'd somehow wormed her way back into the town's good graces, that we were all just supposed to forgive and forget.

"Now that you're both here, we can talk arrangements," Scarlett said, leading the way inside.

Shelby frowned. "Arrangements? I thought everything was settled."

"What are you two doing in my house?" I demanded, dumping the box on the porch.

"Your house?" Shelby blinked and looked at Scarlett.

Scarlett grinned her diabolical Southern girl master of manipulations smile. "This is such good news for you both," she said, clasping her hands in front of her.

I knew this was going to be bad.

"Jonah, remember when you signed your lease you agreed that, if I needed, I could rent out the second bedroom?"

I vaguely remembered something about that. But Scarlett had been pouring celebratory moonshine when she went over the documents, and things had gotten a little bit fuzzy. Fuzzy enough that Devlin had to drive me home.

"I don't recall," I hedged.

"I'll email you a copy of the lease and highlight the pertinent section," she promised. "In the meantime, say hey to your new roommate!"

"Wait, a minute," Shelby began. "He *lives* here?"

"And now so do you," Scarlett said, tossing her a key. "Isn't that great?"

She bobbled the key and seemed slow to lean down to pick it up. "You didn't say Jonah lived here," Shelby began.

"I have a feelin' you two are gonna get along like two pigs in a blanket."

"What the hell are you talking about, Scarlett? Also I should have a say in who I share a house with," I cut in.

"Well, you see pigs in a blanket are—"

"Scarlett Bodine, you're up to something," I said, pointing a finger at her.

She was immune to my sternness. "I thought you two would be pleased as punch. Now you're only responsible for half the rent."

"I'm not living with *her*," I said.

"*Her* has a name. It's Shelby, and I didn't ask to be your roommate either," Shelby said, crossing her arms. She gave me a disapproving look through her glasses.

"Scarlett, can I talk to you outside?" I said, taking my sister by the arm and dragging her toward the door. She must have been feeling friendly since she didn't take a swing at me or try to kick me in the balls.

I let the screen door slam behind us. "What game are you trying to play?"

"Game?" She gasped. "Why, Jonah Bodine Jr., how dare you insinuate that I'm playing some sort of game when I gave you this house to live in at a discounted rate. I put *family* before *business,* and you're expecting me to just what? Stop making money altogether? Will that make you more comfortable, Jonah? Will it?"

She poked me in the chest, and I backed up a pace.

"I'm not asking you to not make money—"

"Because that's exactly what it sounds like. It sounds like you're trying to take advantage of my generosity. I didn't have to rent this house to you, did I?"

"No, but—"

"And you don't expect me to stop running my business of putting paying people in my rentals, do you?" She took another step forward into my space. I had close to a foot on her, but I was man enough to admit that my sister scared the hell out of me.

She was unpredictable. And that made her dangerous. She was also a biter.

"No, however—"

"I'm so glad we have that settled. Now, you and Shelby will share the Little Yellow House for the next month. After that I'm sure I can juggle some of my renters around at great expense to myself and get one of you into a different damn place. But until then, I expect you to say, 'Thank you, Scarlett.' And pay your damn rent, which is now half of what it was before I so generously bestowed a roommate on you, on time."

"Th-thank you, Scarlett."

"You're welcome, Jonah," she said, batting her lashes at me from under her Bootleg Cockspurs ball cap. "See ya around, Shelby," she called into the house as she tromped down the stairs.

———

Me: Which one of you dumbasses opened your big mouth to Scarlett about me being a sad puppy?

Bowie: I was planning on it tomorrow. Why?

Gibson: We all would have. No one's had the chance yet.

Me: She just gave me a roommate.

Jameson: Of the female persuasion?

Me: Shelby Thompson, GT's little sister.

Devlin: Scarlett works in mysterious ways.

Gibson: You can do better than that, McCallister.

Devlin: Your sister amazes and terrifies me. I fully support whatever scheme she's concocted.

Bowie: Amen.

Me: I hate you all.

Chapter Six

Shelby

I 'd been Scarlett Bodined.

And I hadn't seen it coming. I'd heard rumors of such things. I'd been warned. And I'd still been steamrolled by a tiny Southern belle whose master manipulations deserved to be immortalized in the annals of psych journals.

I was tempted to throw out my fifty-percent done paper and start all over with Scarlett as the star.

Then Jonah walked back into the house.

Our house.

This was not the ideal solution I'd thought I was engineering for myself. And now I was stuck in a house with Jonah "Eight-Pack" Bodine.

"Um. So hi," I said when he came to a halt and just stared at me with those green eyes. *Smooth, Shelby. Super smooth and casual.*

I was a nerd and as a nerd, I excelled in flirting with nerd men. My interactions with tall, lean, frowny athletic types were slightly less natural.

He was dressed in workout gear. Shorts, a t-shirt, sneakers. And everywhere I looked, I saw things I liked. Muscle. Stubble. Sharp green eyes that looked as though they could peel my skin back and look inside me. He had a breathtaking smile that I'd spotted a time or two, but he definitely wasn't aiming that particular weapon at me now.

He gave me a long blank look.

Nervously, I smiled wider.

His brows knit together.

Our facial expressions were carrying on different conversations.

I knew there was a simple misunderstanding at the heart of Jonah's barely concealed contempt for me. But I also knew he wasn't exactly amenable to clearing the air right now.

"I'm sure we can work this out," I said cheerily.

"I don't know what you did to make my sister think this was a good idea," he said calmly. "I don't want to know. You stay out of my way, and I'll stay out of yours." With that, my new roommate somberly climbed the stairs to the second floor.

A moment later, I heard a door slam and music kick on somewhere above me. Scarlett's abbreviated tour hadn't actually included the upstairs. But I'd get to that. For now, it was imperative to establish a territory.

I was in a hostile living situation. And I was not about to let the enemy corral me into a bedroom. With him pouting or manscaping or learning to play death metal on the ukulele—whatever attractive, athletic types did in their spare time—I was free to assert myself downstairs.

It would be too easy in this situation to retreat. To ensconce myself in a bedroom and stay out of Jonah's way. He'd been here first. But I was sticking. I was staying in Bootleg Springs until this dang dissertation was finished. And I was going to be comfortable while doing it, gosh darn it!

Glancing around, I tapped my fingers to my lips. The kitchen was a galley setup with the back door at the far end. Not enough room for me to spread out in there. Heck, there was barely enough room to open the refrigerator door. And forget about opening the refrigerator and the oven door at the same time.

The dining room was on the other side of the kitchen wall. It had a funky wallpaper mural of birch trees and a battered and charming table that overlooked the scrap of backyard. But the high-backed chairs would be too uncomfortable for me to spend long hours in them.

The living room would do, I decided, testing the overstuffed beige couch. It was comfortable and angled toward the fireplace and the TV mounted above the mantel. There was a big window looking out onto the porch, and a shabby chic occasional table and two chairs tucked into the corner. I could confiscate that area and use it as my office.

Back out on the porch, I grabbed my most important belongings. My laptop bag and my box of research. Nothing was going to derail me this time. Nothing was going to stand between me and my degree. I plopped everything down on the table and lowered myself back onto the couch.

Decision made, space claimed, I closed my eyes for a minute. The backache was sharper today, and I regretted carting all of my belongings onto the porch. Now, they'd need to be hauled upstairs, and I lacked the energy for it. I was toeing the line already. Much more, and I'd shove myself right over the edge.

I'd focus on the essentials. Everything else would be safe on the porch. It was covered.

I wondered if there were bears in Bootleg Springs. I wasn't exactly the outdoorsy archetype. I was the stay inside and read a book type. Living in Pittsburgh for the past few years had limited my wildlife experiences.

I dozed off, imagining a fat bear pawing through my box of academic journals.

———

I woke up to a fierce frown and green, green eyes.

My first thought was *bear!* Flailing, I rolled right off the couch cushion.

But I didn't hit the floor. Somewhere in my nap-addled brain, it registered that my new safety net was a pair of hands.

"What is wrong with you?" Jonah grumbled, rolling me back on the couch. I flopped gracelessly like a walrus.

"A lot of things. You don't really want to know. Are there bears here?" I shouldn't have flailed. Research recommended playing dead in a bear attack.

"Bears?"

"I thought you were a bear when I woke up. Did you know that there are Timber Rattlesnakes and Northern Copperheads in this part of the state? That probably means there's bears too."

He was making me nervous. Looking at me all grumpy and confused. And so close. I could reach right out and touch him. Not that I would. I was an academic, not an idiot.

"You were moaning in your sleep," he said, ignoring my bear question.

"That happens sometimes." I sat up, managing to keep my old lady noises to myself.

"Your stuff is still outside," he pointed out. I felt like he was running through a list of my most immediate flaws. Sleep moans and disorganized porch hoarding.

My back sang the first few bars of "O Fortuna." "Yeah, thanks. I'll get it." I stepped stiffly around him and headed for the door.

"One month," he said.

I paused. "What?"

"Scarlett said in a month she could move one of us to another rental."

That wasn't so bad. I could spend a month staring at Jonah's sweaty back muscles. "We can handle a month, can't we?"

"I guess we don't have a choice," he said, clearly not thrilled at the idea.

"That's the spirit!"

"Do you seriously have to cook dinner right now?" Jonah growled as I ducked under his arm to get at the oven.

The kitchen was small under the best of circumstances. But put two adults intent on cooking at the same time while avoiding each other in it and it became a shoebox.

"Since you're the one with the problem, maybe *you* should cook your dinner later." I pointed out the logic of the situation.

"I don't have a problem," he argued.

Jonah Bodine was turning out to be as temperamental as his half-brother Gibson.

"Are you always so moody, or is it situational?" I reached into the oven and flipped my chicken nuggets over, blowing on my fingers. "Ouch."

He grabbed my hand and slapped a pair of tongs into it. "Use the right tools for the job." It wasn't his intended effect, I was sure, but I felt a little shiver of biochemical reaction work its way up my spine.

Jonah was not my type.

I liked the academic, glasses-wearing, "let me tell you about my research" type. But the fact that I was reacting to Mr. Frowny Jock on such a physical level was…interesting.

"Thanks." I flipped the rest of the nuggets without scorching off my fingerprints.

"I'm not moody," he grumbled, pushing the handle of the frying pan out of my way when I stood up. He was sautéing vegetables. A whole bunch of them. I sniffed at them with suspicion. I'd been born a picky eater. And, to my parents' undying embarrassment, I was still a picky eater at thirty. I kept waiting for this adventurous palate that everyone assured me would come. But sushi grossed me out. Mushrooms made me gag. And don't even get me started on lunch meat. Or mayonnaise.

"Are those nuggets shaped like dinosaurs?"

"They are." I beamed at him, rewarding him for his attempt at polite conversation. I could spend a month positively reinforcing him.

"That's not food."

I looked at the cookie sheet. "Of course it's food. I cook it. I put it in my mouth. It's food."

"Food is fuel with nutrition."

"It's meat. Meat is nutritious." At least I assumed it was.

Jonah looked at me like I was the dullest crayon in the box.

"Look. We don't have to be friends, but we don't have to be enemies," I told him.

"You *are* the enemy," he said.

I could have corrected him. But his attitude was annoying. I didn't care if he liked me, I decided. I wasn't here to make friends or develop a crush. I was here to work. And maybe I would take just the tiniest bit of pleasure in letting Jonah act like an idiot for a while.

"Do you really think your sister would make you share a house with a sworn enemy?"

"I haven't known her that long. It's a possibility."

My annoyance inched up into irked territory. "I'm *not* your enemy. Let's just be adults about this. How bad could the next month possibly be?"

Chapter Seven

Jonah

It was horrible.

The house that had seemed reasonably sized just days before was getting smaller by the minute.

She was *everywhere*.

I was an early riser by nature. I enjoyed the dawn of the day with its reverent silence and quiet potential. There was nothing reverent or quiet about Shelby dancing around to Maroon 5 and Panic! At the Disco while making those god-awful sugar bomb toasted pastries.

She wanted to make small talk about the weather while I laced up my running shoes.

Then she was singing in the shower. Or leaving bras in the bathroom. Or snort-laughing over reruns in the living room. The woman *snorted* when she laughed. And I hated that some dark corner of me found it kind of cute.

She'd taken the guest room and had made herself at home. I was the one who felt like I was intruding. Like I was a guest in *her* home. But, dammit, I'd gotten here first. I belonged here more than she did. I was building a relationship with family. She was just trying to exploit a scandal. Wasn't she?

I made it a point not to let her chase me into my room. Made a big deal out of being "home" as much as she was.

We both had jobs without a consistent nine to five. Most of the classes and training that I did were in the mornings and evenings. Which left me in the house with her during the day while she muttered over reams of notes and typed like her fingers were on fire.

Every time I turned around, she was there. So I fought back.

Whenever she sat down to work in the living room, I turned on the TV and settled on the couch.

Whenever she got in the shower upstairs, I ran the hot water in the kitchen sink until she yelped from the cold.

Whenever she "cooked"—the woman lived off canned food, nuggets, and peanut butter and jelly—I made a production out of my superior meal prep.

And judging by her bubbly morning greetings every damn day, I wasn't bothering her in the least.

Unless it was all an act, Shelby was the happiest damn person I'd ever met. It was like she was hosing down the house with fairy dust.

It made me irrationally angry. Something I hadn't felt for a long time.

I pushed harder in my workouts, focusing my energy on them. But every time I came home, there was Shelby. Perky and happy, giving me a little wave from her corner of the living room or shoveling canned ravioli into her smiling mouth.

I needed to have some words with that half-sister of mine.

"I hereby call this Bodine Family breakfast to order," Bowie said, smacking the bottle of syrup on the table. Kitchen renovations were almost finished for him and Cassidy. They'd lived in two halves of a double for years before ceremoniously knocking down the wall between them and plotting out a new future together.

When it was done, it would be a great gathering place. But right now, there were construction tarps and drywall dust everywhere.

Cassidy was dressed for work in her deputy uniform, and I had a sinking feeling this breakfast was part of her official business.

Gibs was bleary-eyed and knocking back coffee like it was his job. I got the feeling the guy wasn't sleeping much. If he'd been remotely human, I'd have asked him about it. But the way he snarled at Jameson when he asked about the softball lineup clued me in that it would be a wasted question.

"Where's Leah Mae and Devlin?" I asked.

Scarlett was already working her way through a stack of pancakes and checking her calendar on her phone. "Dev's in the office today. Had some client meetings to take care of. I think Ol' Judge Carwell's paying him a visit, too."

Devlin had traded in his political aspirations to fall in love with Scarlett and open a private law practice in Bootleg Springs. Judge Carwell was about ten years past retirement age, and rumor had it, he was looking to get Devlin elected once his Olamette County residency was official.

"Leah Mae and June are checking out the shop. Juney finally stopped winding up the landlord over the rent, and they signed the papers last week." Jameson grinned.

"How's construction coming?" Bowie asked Scarlett.

"Hallelujah, thank you, Lord! We have a basement," she sang. "Or at least a hole in the ground. I'm thinking about taking some of Dev's law journals over and throwin' em in the mud to celebrate."

"Maybe you could take your new tenant over with you and leave her there," I suggested.

"Now, Jonah. I thought for sure you would be mature enough to share your space with a roommate," she said, batting her eyelashes at me.

"Are you trying to fix me up with Shelby?" I demanded.

Gibson dragged himself out of his grumpy stupor. "Damn, Scar. We didn't even get a chance to tell you all about poor Jonah's broken heart."

I glared at him. "Never should have said a damn thing to you assholes." I wanted to say that I never should have shown up in Bootleg. But, even mad, I wouldn't have meant it.

"Tell me what? What broken heart? Was it that Lacey and her dumping you at the prom?" Scarlett demanded, flinging her fork down on the table.

George had thrown a prom re-do when he found out Cassidy's sister, June, had missed out on hers. Under duress to pick a date, I'd invited Lacey Dickerson, who left with Amos Sheridan. I hadn't advertised the fact that Lacey had *asked* me to go to help her make Amos jealous or that her plan had worked perfectly. I'd had a "date" that kept my elderly clients from matching me up with any number of their single—or, in Myrt's case, unhappily married—relatives. And Lacey got her Amos. It was a win-win.

"No. I have no hard feelings toward Lacey. I do, however, have hard feelings toward you forcing me to cohabitate with a reporter who came to town just to get dirt about our father." I was yelling now. I blamed it on my overexposure to the Bodines. None of them could speak at normal volume for longer than a minute or two.

"First of all, have you even tried talking to Shelby? Because you, brother dear, are sorely mistaken about Shelby's line of work. Though that's mostly Cassidy's fault," Scarlett said, joining me in shouting range.

"Hey!" Cassidy complained at being thrown under the bus.

"Secondly," Scarlett continued, ignoring her best friend's outburst, "I didn't force you to cohabitate with anybody. I have a business to run and a house to build. I don't know why you feel like you should get special treatment at my expense—"

"Admit it, Scar. You put us in that house together on purpose."

"How *dare* you, Jonah Bodine! I did no such thing!" Scarlett's gasp moved paper napkins across the table. She was lying. We all knew it. Except maybe Scarlett.

Cassidy groaned, and Bowie leaned in to give her shoulder a fortifying squeeze. "Okay, listen up," she said. "This fight is super entertaining, but I've gotta be at the station in twenty minutes, and I thought y'all would want an update on the body."

That shut everyone up.

"Did they identify her?" Scarlett asked.

Gibson's hands were fisted on the table, his knuckles white.

"Well, it's not gonna be that easy," Cassidy said, slipping into official mode. "The skeletal remains were found during excavation for a new housing development. As of right now, they still haven't found the skull."

I pushed my eggs around on my plate, not so hungry anymore.

"What in the hell happened to her head?" Scarlett asked.

"Jesus, did someone decapitate her?" Jameson asked looking a little green around the gills.

Cassidy shrugged. "It's unlikely. It was a shallow grave, so things like predators are a factor. It could be there. Investigators are goin' through the site with fine-tooth combs. But basically, without dental records, it's gonna be damn hard to identify the body."

"What about DNA?" I asked.

"With remains that have been exposed to the elements that long? It's unlikely at best," she predicted.

"But they think it's her," Gibson said flatly. "They think that body is Callie Kendall."

"According to the reports the locals are sharing with us, the approximate age of the remains and size are a potential match for Callie," Cassidy admitted. "They can tell she was somewhere between fifteen and eighteen years old at the time of death and died somewhere between twelve to fourteen years ago. So it's a possibility. Given the fact that the remains were found less than twenty miles from where your father got the speeding ticket, it takes it from possible and nudges it on up to the edge of probable."

Scarlett crossed her arms but remained silent. She'd staunchly believed in and loudly defended our father's innocence. Gibson, however, was equally stubborn in his belief that Jonah Sr. was a murderer. The rest of us fell somewhere in the middle.

"I'm sorry, Scar," Cassidy said, squeezing her shoulder.

Bowie leaned over and patted his sister's knee. "It's gonna be all right. No matter what," he promised.

"Anyway, I know this isn't great news. And I know y'all are damn tired of the whole thing. But until investigators find the skull, we won't know anything. So just hang in there. Stick together. We'll get through this together."

Scarlett shoved her half-eaten pancakes away. "I don't know about y'all, but I'm sick and tired of bein' sick and tired."

"I hate waiting for the other boot to drop," Bowie agreed. "We find the sweater in Dad's stuff. The blood is Callie's. Then she's alive and all 'Oh, hey, I was just living with a weird boyfriend and his cult family for the last decade.' And Dad was just a guy trying to help a girl out. Then Mom's accident might not have been an accident. Now there's a dead body. How much not knowing can we all take?"

I only shared some blood with them. I was free to leave at any time. But my brothers and sister had planted their roots deep here. They didn't have the option to go and start over. To escape.

"What do you suggest?" Jameson asked wearily.

"You know what we're gonna do?" Scarlett said, rising out of her chair. "We're throwin' the biggest shindig Bootleg Springs has ever seen, and we're going to eat, drink, and dance ourselves stupid."

"You're damn right, we are," Bowie said, throwing his napkin on the table. He stood and pressed a kiss to Cassidy's mouth. "Deputy Tucker, will you do the honor of being my date?"

"How is any of this going to help figure out what Dad had to do with Callie or what happened to Mom?" Gibson asked, more wearily than angry.

Scarlett circled the table and put her arms around his neck. "It isn't gonna do a damn thing other than remind us that we're still here. We all survived."

Gibson reached up and squeezed Scarlett's hand tight, and I saw something that looked like grief flicker over his face.

"If you think you're gonna talk me into taking Shelby to this party you've got another thing coming, sister dear," I said, pointing my fork at Scarlett.

She snorted smugly, and I realized I'd just stupidly thrown down the gauntlet.

———

Q. How have your neighbors shown their support for you?

Gibson Bodine: By leaving me the hell alone. Not everyone needs a hand to hold or a shoulder to whine all over. Solitude is the best medicine.

Chapter Eight

Shelby

Moonshine Diner was my absolute favorite place in Bootleg proper. It served up good food, new rumors, and an opportunity to chat up half of the town on their way through the front door.

I waved at GT in the back booth. My brother, the football hero, was a head and shoulders taller than just about everyone else in here. He was also beaming like a man in love, I noted, sliding in across from him.

"Hey there, Shelby sweetheart," Clarabell—the waitress, owner, and flesh and blood of the institution—called from behind the counter. "I'll be right over with your ice water."

"Thanks, Clarabell!" I turned my attention back to my brother. "Can you believe we have a place where the waitress knows our names and our drink orders?"

GT smirked. He'd spent the last several years living in Philadelphia, playing football and the field. At least until a career-ending injury brought him here. The healing powers of the hot springs and one June Tucker had lifted him from his forced retirement funk. "It's a far cry from the big city," he agreed.

He studied my face. "You look tired."

I bit back a sigh. We weren't biological brother and sister. I'd been adopted as a toddler by James and Darlene Thompson. Young GT and I had instantly bonded, or so the story the eight thousand pictures of our childhood told. Family didn't require blood. We were living proof of that.

Even now, we were close despite the fact that we'd lived in different cities for the past several years. That distance hadn't dulled my brother's intuition when it came to me.

"I'm fine," I assured him.

It was a fib. I'd been keeping a secret. GT had been a little distracted the past few months, what with his career ending, his assistant embezzling from him, and then falling in love with the quirky actuary, June. Now that he was happy and healthy, I should have known he'd zero right in on my problem.

"I just moved into the cutest little cottage," I said, sidestepping his comment.

He held up a hand. "Shel, we live in Bootleg. I already got the low-down from Jimmy Bob Prosser and Sallie Mae Brickman yesterday. June filled me in on the rest and drew me a floor plan to scale. You and Jonah Bodine are roommates."

I laughed. "Don't even think about going big brother on me. I'm thirty freaking years old."

"I didn't say a word," he said, feigning innocence. "But I have to wonder why you haven't told the guy you're not a journalist. Don't you think he'd be a little nicer if he knew the truth?"

I rolled my eyes heavenward. The truth often had unintended consequences. I wasn't a liar by any means. But sometimes it was better, or in this case, more fun to withhold information. "I'm just giving him line and letting him swim himself tired."

"A fishing analogy already?" he teased. "We need to make a pact to urban heritage or we'll be hoe-downing all over the place."

Clarabell arrived with my water. She had two pencils stuck in her impressive coppery beehive. They were there as accessories since she never seemed to write down any orders.

"The usual, sweetie?" she asked me.

"Yes, please," I said, sliding the menu toward her.

"And, George, your order will be right out. Threw me for a loop today changing it up like that." She winked and disappeared back into the late breakfast crowd.

Watching my brother eat with his football player appetite was one of my favorite forms of entertainment. The man could easily eat half a turkey by himself on Thanksgiving. And since his career had ended, I'd noticed he'd put on a few comfortable pounds. It looked good on him.

"She probably had to go buy more chickens just to get enough eggs for your breakfast, *George*," I teased. His whole life he'd been GT, but come to Bootleg and fall in love and the whole town weighed in on what they should call him. The last poll in the Bootleg Springs newsletter showed it split down the middle.

"Back to you looking tired," he said.

I groaned. "It's nothing. I'm sleeping in a new place and getting used to it."

"You're not having nightmares again, are you?"

At least that was one lie I didn't have to tell. "That was years ago, and I haven't had a nightmare in ages."

He nodded, accepting. "You know you could stay with me and June," he reminded me.

"I know, and I appreciate it. But I really prefer our relationship to not require me to put a pillow over my head and sing Alanis Morrissette for an hour or two every night."

"The walls are thin," he agreed with a smug grin.

I was happy my brother was happy. "Okay. I'm getting grossed out. Can we talk about something other than your sex life?"

Clarabell returned looking like the cat that ate the canary, and I knew she'd heard every word. "Chocolate chip pancakes for Shelby. And an egg white, pepper, and mushroom omelet for George."

I tried not to gag looking at his plate. "What the heck happened to your usual tower of waffles with a side of six plates of bacon?"

It was GT's turn to wince. "Stepped on the scale a few days ago."

"And?"

"And it broke."

I snorted out a laugh and reached for my water.

"I'm working with your roomie on some weight loss goals."

"You look great, and you're happy," I reminded him. "There's no need for you to stay in playing shape."

He leaned in. "I know you don't want to hear about my sex life. But if I gain another ten pounds, June will be in danger of being suffocated."

I choked on my pancake, turning bright red until Millie Waggle jumped up and smacked me between the shoulder blades. The pancake went down, but the pain in my back exploded. "Thanks, Millie," I rasped. She was a few years younger than me, but she dressed like she was going to a church bazaar every day. I didn't know what her religious beliefs were, but the woman could bake absolutely sinful desserts.

"Anytime, Shelby," she said cheerfully before tottering back to her table.

"Well, speaking of being physically fit," I told him, "I did it. I signed up."

GT reached across the table for a high-five, his hand engulfing mine. "Seriously? That's awesome! Is Jonah going to help you train? He's a smart guy. Knows his shit. A triathlon's a big deal. You can't just half-ass it."

"I've already started my research."

He snorted. "Shelby, there's a hell of a lot more work than just research that goes into an event like that. Speaking of research, how's your survey going?"

"First of all, the survey is great. As of this morning, I've had almost eighty responses, thanks to the Breakfast Club badgering everyone to fill it out. Secondly, it's not an Ironman. It's a normal person triathlon. They call it a sprint triathlon. It's going to be great." Exercise therapy was supposed to become an important part of my life now. While the idea of regular PT appointments bored me to death, the challenge of an event that I had to study up on, train for? That was my kind of jam.

"What are we high-fiving?" Leah Mae, pretty as always in a cute pink button-down and those fashionable high-waisted jeans, slid in next to me.

"Hello." June, my brother's girlfriend and the woman he was worried about squishing, appeared at his elbow. GT lit up like a Christmas tree, and it made my heart sing. This was better than any victory he'd had on the field. That kind of bone-deep happiness I felt radiating off him every time he looked in June's serious green eyes. I adored her for making my brother so happy.

He pulled June down next to him and laid a PG-13 kiss on her. "This is a nice surprise," he said, sliding back.

"Yes. It is. Leah Mae is pleased with the progress on the renovations at the shop, and we were both hungry," June explained.

"JuneBug, Leah Mae, y'all want your usuals?" Clarabell called.

"Yes, ma'am," Leah Mae said.

"That's a silly question," June said with a small frown. Deviations from routine were baffling to her.

"Back to what we're high-fiving," Leah Mae said, scooting in closer to me.

"My little sister here just signed up for her first triathlon," GT said proudly.

I hadn't been an athletic kid. I'd spent more time falling out of trees than climbing them. There had been entire semesters of gym class when I'd prayed the volleyball would never come near me. It was out of character for me to throw myself into an athletic endeavor. Especially one this competitive. But it was

50

just the kind of project I needed to turn the focus away from the limitations of a diagnosis and onto the possibilities of a life.

Well, that's what I told myself every time I started to get anxious about it.

"That's so exciting," Leah Mae approved.

"Why would you do that?" June asked, legitimately confused.

June's bluntness was one of my favorite things about her. She wasn't tethered to social norms like the rest of us. And there was something refreshing about her reactions.

"I know. I'm not the athletic type. But I need to do something besides sit on my butt and write a dissertation. I want to work toward something with measurable goals that will keep me focused on the prize." I had no visions of grandeur of an age group medal. But I did want to finish. Even if I crawled across the finish line. I wanted to do it under my own power. If I could tackle something as big as a triathlon, the other challenge I faced would be manageable.

"Is Jonah going to help train you?" Leah Mae asked. "It's so convenient that y'all are living under one roof."

"I don't think Jonah is looking for any new clients," I said diplomatically.

"He still thinks she's a reporter," GT explained.

"Why don't you simply cease your falsehood?" June asked.

"It's kind of more fun watching him be all puffed up and mad over nothing." It sounded just a little stupid when I explained it.

"That sounds manipulative," June pointed out. "I can see why it would be entertaining."

"Maybe we should feed him a few more little fibs," Leah Mae mused. "Let it slip that you shoplifted from the Pop In?"

"Or how about you stabbed someone with a knitting needle at Yee Haw Yarn and Coffee?" GT suggested.

"Perhaps it would be more believable if we told Jonah we saw Shelby interrogating Mrs. Varney regarding the Callie Kendall case," June suggested.

I laughed. "Isn't Jonah your friend?"

They all shared a baffled look. "He's practically family," Leah Mae said.

"Then why would you go to all the trouble to mess with him like this?"

"*Because* he's practically family," GT said, as if that explained everything. "Also, the guy threw me in the lake."

"How did Jonah Bodine throw you in the lake?" Jonah was strong. But it would take more than one man to lift my brother.

"He used a trebuchet," June said.

"What a weird, wonderful town you have here," I marveled.

Chapter Nine
Shelby

My research suggests that Southerners in small communities are more likely to volunteer, even in unofficial capacities," I said. "Can you ladies confirm that?"

My unofficial adoption by the Breakfast Club included the members taking a personal interest in me and my little survey. A few of them had invited themselves over for tea and to "sit a spell." Meaning, they were pumping me for information on what their neighbors were saying under the guise of being helpful.

Mrs. Varney, Carolina Rae Carwell, Maribel Schilling, and Myrt Crabapple were rocking away in the pretty little rocking chairs Scarlett had on the front porch of the Little Yellow House. I'd bribed Leah Mae to make the sweet tea for me, and I'd bought cookies and cupcakes in town.

"Where do you get your information, girl?" Maribel giggled. "We don't call helping neighbors *volunteering*."

"What *do* you call it?" I asked, scribbling notes with one hand while licking pink icing from the other.

"Bein' neighborly," Mrs. Varney cackled. "You big city folk try to make being nice a big deal. Like it's some kind of disease. If I give Myrt here a call on my way to the grocery store when I know she's feelin' poorly, it's in my DNA to pick up whatever she may need. I'm not calculating favors or keeping track of whether or not she owes me."

"It's the neighborly thing to do," Carolina Rae said, sipping her sweet tea and rocking.

"'Less of course it's someone who's constantly riled about somethin' acting all ornery," Mrs. Varney put in. "Then there's some score keepin' or maybe we don't bring her the name brand butter. Or we give her the frozen batch of okra rather than makin' it fresh."

"So you're even nice to people you don't like?" It wasn't really the questions that mattered. It was the information dump that occurred whenever more than two good Southern ladies got together.

It was warming into summer temperatures today, and I was sprawled out on the porch with my laptop, my notebook, and a glass of—don't tell anyone—unsweetened tea. Asking questions, getting answers, organizing the information in my mind. This was my happy place.

"Now let's take a little break from the work and talk about how you're doin', Shelby," Mrs. Varney suggested sweetly.

"You seen that young Jonah naked yet?" Myrt cackled, leaning forward in her rocker.

"Um. No. Jonah and I are just roommates." Though I'd seen him sweaty and breathless several times as the man was constantly coming and going from workouts and training sessions. That was almost as good as naked. Probably.

"Youth is wasted on the young." Carolina Rae sighed. "If I were in your shoes, I wouldn't let separate bedrooms hold me back."

The other ladies nodded and rocked vigorously in agreement.

"I'm not here to find myself a boyfriend," I reminded

them. "I'm here to learn why it is that the residents of Bootleg Springs work so well together. You've got people of all ages and backgrounds banding together for a common cause, and you succeeded spectacularly."

"Shelby, there's no secret there," Mrs. Varney insisted. "We're neighbors. That makes us family."

In nearly every other part of the country that was not true. I remembered the next-door neighbors we had growing up in Charlotte. They blared rock music until 2 a.m. and got in loud arguments over who was going to clean up the dog poop in the backyard. My parents ended up building a ten-foot-tall privacy fence and threw a party when the couple divorced and sold the house.

In Pittsburgh, I knew some of my neighbors' names. At least their last names according to labels above their mailboxes. But living together didn't automatically foster any sense of community.

"Let's talk about the history of Bootleg Springs," I said, changing the subject. Perhaps their heritage played an important role in why residents felt like they all belonged here.

"Well, you can't talk about Bootleg Springs history and not talk about Jedidiah Bodine," Myrt cackled.

"Oh, that Jedidiah was a handsome one," Mrs. Varney said, fanning herself with her paper plate.

"You aren't *that* old, Ethel," Carolina Rae pointed out.

"Old enough to remember him tearin' through town in his hot rod the day before he up and keeled over from a heart attack."

"May he rest in peace," the women chorused.

They launched into Volume One of Jedidiah Bodine's colorful history, and I scribbled furiously trying to keep up with their back and forth. I was so engrossed in the story that I didn't hear Jonah until his foot hit the first porch step.

"Ladies," he said. He didn't sound happy.

He was sweaty from his personal training session. I liked the idea that he worked out with his clients, suffered with them, not just told them what to do. I had to force my gaze away from that sweaty patch over his chest.

"Why, Jonah Bodine. You're looking handsomer every time I lay eyes on you," Mrs. Varney said flirtatiously.

"Thank you, Mrs. Varney," he said. He was probably used to the embarrassing attention by now.

"We were just telling Shelby here all about your great-granddad Jedidiah," Myrt cut in. "I bet you'd like to know a thing or two about him, seein's how you grew up fatherless thanks to that no-good Jonah Bodine Sr., may he rest in peace."

"May he rest in peace," the ladies echoed.

"It's so nice to see you ladies," Jonah said, pinching the bridge of his nose as if he were warding off a headache. "Shelby, can I have a word with you inside?"

"Ladies, if you'll excuse me, I'm just going to go pour Jonah a nice glass of sweet tea," I said, climbing gingerly to my feet.

He grabbed my wrist with his sweaty hand and dragged me into the house. He opened his mouth to start in on me then and there, but I shushed him and pointed to the screen door where four ladies had their ears wide open.

"I don't like sweet tea," he snapped when I pushed him into the kitchen.

"Preaching to the choir on that one," I said, filling a glass from the tap. "Why not just eat seventeen packets of sugar instead?"

I handed him the glass. He hesitated for a fraction of a second before chugging it.

"Thank you for the water," he said. "But I don't like you bringing *my* clients to *my* house to grill them about *my* family. I'm trying to make this ridiculous living situation work, but you're making it impossible, Shelby."

I got goosebumps when he said my name.

He sounded a little close to the breaking point. "I asked them about the history of the town. Apparently, you Bodines are a big part of that story," I explained.

He set the empty glass down with a hard click. "Stop asking questions about my family."

I'd had just about enough of the Jonah Hates Shelby show. "Oh for Pete's sake—"

"June said that you cornered some senior citizen at Yee Haw Yarn and Coffee and demanded they tell you everything there was to know about Callie Kendall. Then I heard through Jameson that you threatened the mayor with a Freedom of Information Act request to get your hands on the police records. And *then* your own brother starts telling me today in the middle of his workout how you're thinking about producing a documentary."

His voice wasn't calm or annoyed right now. He was bright, blazing mad.

"And no one but me seems to give a damn!"

I laughed out a sigh. "Jonah, they're teasing you."

He was too mad for my words of wisdom to sink in.

"I don't know what your game is or why my sister thought it was a good idea to have us live together, but if you're stupid enough to think you can take advantage of me—"

"I'm not a reporter, you mule-headed moron!" I shouted. It took a lot to get me going. Calling me stupid was one of those triggers, and Jonah had just pulled it. Unfortunately for him, there was no safety.

"The entire town knows that I'm not a reporter. Yes—" I held up a hand when he tried to speak. "I write freelance articles for scientific publications and research pieces for academic journals. I couldn't care less what happened to Callie Kendall or whether or not your father had anything to do with it. I'm here to write my dissertation for my Ph-freaking-D and find out how an entire town banded together to evict a bunch of journalists who were making their lives miserable."

He blinked, then frowned.

"They're all just messing with you because you're showing signs of that world-famous Bodine stubbornness. Do I *look* like I would hold a senior citizen hostage with a knitting needle? Do I *act* like I'm writing a crime-of-the-century article on your damn father?" I gave a bitter laugh and didn't even care that all four of my guests were pressed up against the screen door catching every word.

"Here's a news bulletin for you, Jonah Bodine: I'm not interested in you. Or your family. I'm here for this town. And if you don't believe me, well, then you can just go bless your own little heart!"

"Close enough," Myrt called approvingly through the screen.

The ladies on the porch erupted into applause.

"Now if you'll excuse me, I'm going to go back to my friends who have been kind and welcoming unlike *some other* people in this house," I shouted.

———

Q. How do you most often communicate with your neighbors?

Cheyenne Hastings: I just holler out my window! Sooner or later everyone in town walks by.

Chapter Ten

Jonah

Shelby stomped out of the kitchen, her long dark hair swinging in its ponytail, leaving me staring after her.

I couldn't trust her explanation…*could I?* Not when she'd waltzed into town under false pretenses. Not when my entire family had tales to tell about her. They wouldn't set me up like that. *Would they?*

I pulled out my phone and called the one person I was sure wouldn't lie to me.

"Hello, sir," Devlin said. "How can I help you?" He had his business professional voice on. I'd probably interrupted him in the middle of being a lawyer.

"Is Shelby really a reporter? Or is she a student working on some kind of degree?" I demanded.

He sighed into the phone. "In this case, it would be the latter," he said.

I tipped my head back and stared up at the ceiling. "And everyone knows except me?"

"That is accurate."

"Well, fuck." I swiped the sweat out of my eyes.

"I think a jury would certainly understand those sentiments," Devlin said mildly. I heard a door close on his end. "Okay, Scarlett can't hear me now."

"Are you hiding from my sister?"

"She's chasing me around with tile samples. Then when I have an opinion on one, she tells me I'm wrong."

I laughed despite myself. "That sounds about right."

"You should have heard her when I suggested we hire a designer."

"I'm surprised you're still alive."

"Sorry for the tirade. No, Shelby isn't a reporter. She freelances for publications in her field. Psychology or social work, along those lines. She's studying the town, not the Bodines. And from what I gather, everyone really likes her except—"

"Me." I sighed.

"Yes. It's been a bit of a running gag since she explained her situation to Scarlett and Scarlett decided to play matchmaker."

I leaned against the fridge and closed my eyes.

"Her heart's in the right place," he said preemptively.

"I've been incredibly rude to this woman for days now because someone thought it would be funny to keep me in the dark?"

"If it makes you feel any better, Shelby was in on it."

"No. That doesn't make me feel any better."

"It wouldn't make me feel better either, but now you have all the information."

"My own brothers, my sister, this whole damn town." I was the butt of the joke. The odd man out. And I hated how I sank into those long-dormant feelings of not belonging. The kid with no dad.

"Do you want me to let Scarlett know that you know, or would you prefer to administer your own Bootleg Justice?"

I took a shower and stayed under the water hoping it would wash away the anger and embarrassment I was feeling. I heard Mrs. Varney's muffler-less sedan fire up and drive away. Undoubtedly to spread the word to the rest of town that I'd gotten into a screaming match with my roommate.

There'd be more laughs at my expense, I thought. Resigned myself to the fact that even after a year, I was still nothing more than an outsider to them. *And why did that bother me?*

Hadn't I healed those wounds into tough scars?

I twisted the faucet off, frowning at the cheerful, sky blue tiles and sliding the flowered shower curtain aside. The room was "charming" and "fanciful," and I was feeling pissed off enough to be annoyed by it.

The anger was familiar. An old friend from long ago. When a teenage kid started noticing what other guys his age had. Fathers who showed up for their games and took them fishing or bowling or sat through chess tournaments and poetry readings. Men who talked to their sons about girls and school. Taught them to drive and swing a golf club. To mow the lawn and make waffles.

I'd had my mother. A woman who had changed her entire life because of me, for me. But what choice did she have since *he* hadn't been there for either of us?

Now I was in my father's hometown, trying to forge connections, and I was still left out in the cold. It chafed enough that I was embarrassed by it.

I stepped out of the shower stall and swiped a towel over the mirror. I looked like him. That, too, annoyed me. For a brief, temperamental stage in high school, maybe I'd acted a bit like him.

But I was my own man now. I didn't have to prove my worth to anyone, least of all the family I hadn't known I had.

I probably owed Shelby an apology. I'd been rude at best. An asshole more realistically.

But she'd played a role, hadn't been an innocent victim.

I wrapped the towel around my waist and headed into the hallway.

And ran right into her.

"Holy mother of pizza," she shrieked as she stumbled backward. Her eyes widened behind her glasses. I caught her before she could take a header down the steps.

"Calm down before you throw yourself down the stairs."

"Before *I* throw myself down the stairs?" she scoffed.

Apparently, she was still mad. Good. So was I.

She seemed to notice my lack of clothing and made a sound like a balloon deflating, her eyes going wide.

Her hair was still in that long tail. The color of chestnuts and copper pennies. She was wearing those glasses, the thick, tortoiseshell ones in blue. She had more than a dusting of freckles on her fair skin, I realized. And those eyes, even bigger than usual, looked just like the browns and greens of the forest.

She had a small scar on her chest, peeking out of the scoop neck of her tee and a fading bruise in the crook of her elbow. I felt like I was seeing her for the first time. I recalled seeing her at the Black Friday Boot Camp, thinking she was cute, bubbly, attractive.

Maybe now I was seeing her for the second time. And maybe that first impression wasn't so off, after all.

"What are you looking at?" she grumbled, stepping out of my grip.

"You."

"I liked it better when you acted like I was invisible."

Feisty. Mean. And a little hurt. Maybe I did owe her that apology after all.

"Don't even think about apologizing," Shelby sniffed as if reading my mind. "I don't want to hear it."

She paused, bit her lip.

"Also, I'm not sure I deserve it since I was a willing participant," she confessed.

"Let's agree to not apologize and to move on," I suggested.

"Fine," she said crisply. Her gaze traveled my chest and torso and seemed to get stuck somewhere around the towel. "I'd offer to shake on it, but I don't want you to lose your terrycloth."

As a show of good faith, and maybe to tease her just a little, I took my hand away from the towel and offered it to her.

She shook it slowly, fighting to drag her gaze to my face.

"You're still mad," I noted, seeing the flash in her green and brown eyes.

"Yeah, well, so are you."

"It's our own fault." I'd been too busy feeling hurt to get to the truth.

"That's part of what I'm mad about," she said. We were still shaking hands, but now we weren't glaring at each other. In fact, that looked like the beginnings of a smile touching the corners of her rosy lips.

"Do you want to tell me about your dissertation?" I asked.

"No. I don't want your pity interest." She pulled her hand out of my grip. "Just because we're not enemies doesn't mean we have to be friends."

"Fair enough," I agreed.

"I'll have you know that I'm a very nice person," she insisted, stepping around me to get to her room. "It's not my fault that you had the wrong idea about me."

"No, but it *is* your fault that you let me continue to believe the wrong idea."

"I don't know about you," she said. "But I'm really looking forward to the end of this month."

Mrs. Varney: Woooo Weee! Sparks are a flyin' at the Little Yellow House!

Estelle: Dang it! I can't believe Louisa and I missed it! Catch us up!

Myrt: Don't know what all the fuss is. Shelby still hasn't seen that boy naked.

Carolina Rae: But the way they hollered at each other? Either love is in the air or there's gonna be a crime of passion in Bootleg Springs!

Chapter Eleven

Shelby

I should have picked a different athletic endeavor. Like curling. Or badminton. Or literally anything other than a triathlon. My swim that morning had been okay. I hadn't drowned. So that was a plus. But a fish did touch my leg, and I didn't much care for that. Also, I got a cramp in the arch of my foot and went down like a ton of bricks.

Now I was running or, more accurately, *plodding* my way through the woods while gasping for air.

I prayed that any bears in the vicinity would decide today was not the day to eat a person. I doubted my self-defense classes would be of much help against a bear. Besides, if one lumbered out of the woods into my path, I'd probably just lay down on the ground and wait for the mauling. I was *that* tired.

I wheezed, sucking in a breath and something that felt like a bug.

I spit it all out and cursed the $300 registration fee I'd already paid. It was a lot of money for a grad student. A grad student without an actual job lined up yet. A grad student whose half-finished dissertation and new medical diagnosis battled each other for priority.

"I hate everything," I proclaimed to the majestic trees lining the path. "Every damn thing."

I should stop talking. I needed oxygen for things other than complaining to nature.

I heard footfalls behind me and whirled around, hands up.

"Not a bear. I promise." Jonah jogged toward me. The man was bare-chested and more majestic than any of this nature stuff.

I turned my back on his sweaty glory and made a good show of jogging. Until my foot caught on a tree root.

He caught me by the elbow.

The guy kept catching me.

And while the squealy teenage girl inside me thought that was worth a journal entry, the adult female felt like I should be graceful enough to not need catching. I'd been in this body thirty years. I should know how to operate it by now.

"Hi," I said, continuing my awkward lumber. I was so winded I sounded like a phone sex operator with a serious smoking habit.

Please keep running, I silently begged him. *Just run right past me, give me a glimpse of your sweaty back musculature, and I'll go back to thinking about bear maulings.*

But Jonah fell into step with me. He could have walked faster than I was running right now. I wanted to kick him.

"How's your morning?" he asked, annoyingly unwinded.

"'S great. Fabulous," I gasped. Spots danced in front of my eyes. "Oh for Pete's sake." I gave up all pretense, stopped, and bent at the waist.

"You okay?"

"No! I'm not okay. I'm dying. I'm going to hyperventilate and die right here and then be eaten by bears or skunks or timber rattlers."

His feet came into my line of sight.

"Go on. Leave me here. I'll crawl home," I heaved dramatically.

"You need to change your stride," he said.

I glared up at him from my hunched over position.

"I *need* to not have registered for a triathlon," I countered.

He didn't react to the information. Which either meant he was disinterested or my big mouth brother had already told him.

"You're taking too much impact on your heels. It'll tire you out faster. Land on the balls of your feet. It's springier. Easier on the joints."

He demonstrated for me while my joints voiced their displeasure at me. "I'll consider your suggestion," I said stiffly.

"Your wind leaves a lot to be desired, too," Jonah observed. "How far did you go today?"

I straightened, pleased when I didn't vomit all over him. Peering over my shoulder, I gauged the distance. "At least six miles," I guessed.

His lips quirked. "If you started at the house, you're only about a mile out."

"Are you kidding me?" Screw it. I'd kiss that $300 goodbye and find a better way to prove to myself that my body was capable of more than just deteriorating.

Was competitive napping a thing?

"Maybe a mile and a half."

"I don't want your pity measurements!"

"Relax, Shelby," he said lightly. "You're doing fine. When's your triathlon?"

"Six weeks." He didn't outwardly flinch, but I was pretty sure the words "*Oh, boy*" flitted through his mind.

"Six weeks? Okay. We can work with that if you're not setting unrealistic goals."

"We? Unrealistic?" I really needed some water. My mouth felt like I'd licked a bag of cotton balls. Longingly, I stared at the water bottle in his hand. Why hadn't I thought to carry a water bottle? Rookie mistake. "I just want to finish."

"Finishing we can work with." He put his hands on his hips and stood there looking like a romance cover model.

"You keep saying 'we.'"

"I'm a personal trainer. I coach people for athletic events."

"I have zero money. Your mercenary sister's rent isn't exactly bargain basement."

"Scarlett is a shrewd businesswoman," he agreed.

I was being grumpy and petty.

"I'm feeling overwhelmed and exhausted," I said by way of an apology.

"And I can help you with that. Free of charge," he offered.

My eyes narrowed as I attempted to assess his motives. But his handsomeness kept getting in the way. "Why?"

He shrugged. "It wouldn't be very neighborly of me having all this knowledge and not share it with you, now would it?"

"Bootleg Springs sure is rubbing off on you," I observed.

His smile faded.

"What?" I asked, intrigued by his sudden shift in mood.

"Nothing," he said, staring out ahead. He reached up and across, grabbing his shoulder. Jonah Bodine was feeling vulnerable. *Interesting.*

"Are you still upset with everyone over the whole 'me being an evil reporter' thing?" I hazarded a guess.

He shrugged carelessly. "No one really loves being the laughing stock of an entire town."

"That's not what they were doing," I told him. "At least not *only* what they were doing."

"Really? Because that's what it felt like," he said.

"Jonah, don't you see what that was?"

"Everyone making sure I remembered that I'm the outsider. I should probably get back to my run," he said, jerking a thumb over his shoulder.

"Don't you dare move," I threatened. If he started running, I'd never catch him. "Your family was welcoming you into its ranks."

"By making me the ass of a joke?"

I rolled my eyes. "Ever pledged a fraternity? Or joined a sports team? This was their way of recognizing you as one of them. You've been initiated into Bootleg Springs."

"Initiated? Feels like they're pushing me out," he said, a little crack in his cool showing.

I saw the flicker of hope shine through. If shirtless Jonah was physically attractive to me, vulnerable, shirtless Jonah was practically catnip. I was a sucker for authentic vulnerability.

"Think about it. How do your brothers interact? Are they cautious with each other? Sensitive to each other's feelings?"

"Uh. No." He laughed.

"They harass each other constantly, right?"

"Yeah. I guess," he said.

"And now they're harassing you. Because you're one of them."

"That's kind of bittersweet. 'You're one of us. Now we're going to emotionally torture you.' Couldn't they have just gotten me a card or something?"

I snorted and died a little inside. I'd spent entire years in junior high school wishing I had one of those adorable, bubbly laughs. But hey, I had the wind back to snort-laugh, so it wasn't a total loss. "Culturally speaking, you've been initiated. And now a lot is riding on your reaction to the initiation."

"In what way?"

"What if you let your hurt feelings steer you out of town, out of this family? Turn tail. Pull up stakes. Insert the appropriate Southernism here. You'd be rejecting their invitation to join their ranks."

"Okay. What's the better option?" Jonah asked, interested now.

The man had to have issues with belonging considering he grew up rejected in a very real sense by his biological father. It only made sense. And the fact that he was listening told me he cared very much.

"If you react in a way they'll understand and appreciate, you'll prove that you deserve to be welcomed. You deserve the place they've offered you."

A slow grin spread across his face, and I had to turn away from the wattage. It was like staring at the sun. The handsome sun that was making my core temperature rise and causing a hormone dump in my brain.

"Shelby, how familiar are you with Bootleg Justice?"

I decided not to mention that nearly every participant in my survey waxed poetically about the merits of an off-the-books "legal" system.

"Vaguely, in that I watched Rhett Ginsler cover Rocky Tobias's pickup truck in shaving cream bumper to bumper after Rocky ran a stop sign and nearly chased Rhett's granny off the road," I said. "What do you have in mind?"

"Are you coming to the deck party Saturday?" Jonah asked.

Was this a date? Was Jonah asking me on a date when I was sweaty and wearing a tank top that said "*Everything Hurts and I'm Dying*"?

"I hadn't planned on it," I said weakly.

I'd planned on spending the day and evening binge-watching a new horror show on Netflix. But if the sweaty god before me wanted a date with me… Okay. My brain was oxygen deprived. I'd already established that. Jonah hadn't asked me to go to the party. He'd asked me if I'd pick up celery at the grocery store. Or wondered what kind of laundry detergent I used. Also, just because he was revealing his mushy center to me didn't mean I had to fall into the trap.

"Well, I was thinking, the party might be the perfect time for our feud to explode," he mused.

Ah. I was a tool for revenge. Not a hot date. I was more comfortable with that.

"So you'll train me if I help you get revenge on your family?" I clarified.

He nodded. "I know it sounds stupid, but around here—"

"Bootleg justice," I filled in for him.

He grinned, and my knees went a few degrees weaker.

———

Q. What institutional resource do you find most helpful in your community?

Hung Kim: I had to Google "institutional resource," Shelby. Might wanna dumb these questions down a little. I can probably speak for most of the community when I say Bootleg Justice, or the authority to solve most problems your own damn self, is helpful and liberating and an important "institutional resource."

Chapter Twelve
Jonah

Hurry up, Bodine!" Scarlett hollered from the dock. Because I thought things like "hollered" now.

I raised a hand and jogged across her yard to where it kissed the lakefront. It hit me. The quiet waters lapping at the pebbled land. The scents of deep water, sunscreen, and beer wove together to create that perfect early summer smell.

The sense of déjà vu was almost overwhelming.

We'd met this way. Scarlett and her brothers returning from a day on the water, and there I was, waiting on land to introduce myself.

In one year, I'd been absorbed into the community. Into the family. I'd been accepted by them. Well, most of them, I thought, eyeing Gibs where he tinkered with the motor on the floating deck. The deck was a floating monstrosity with railings, seating, built-in cooler holders, and speakers big enough to entertain half the lake.

"All right, let's talk about the rules," Bowie said, his arm slung around Cassidy's shoulder, when I hopped aboard the floating party island. "Number one: No talking about anything related to the investigation."

"And if y'all do," Scarlett said menacingly.

"We throw you in the seaweedy part of the lake," Jameson and Leah Mae said together. They were cozied up on lawn chairs, beers already cracked. The artist and the model, looking cool and happy and relaxed.

I felt an unexpected twinge of...envy? Maybe. Leah Mae reminded me a little bit of Rene. Something about her sunny smile, the little gap between her front teeth. Rene never had the chance to be that happy with anyone, let alone me.

"Are we all agreed?" Bowie asked.

I dragged myself out of my melancholy. I had revenge to extract today. There wasn't any room for sadness.

"One rule?" I clarified. "That's it?"

"I'd like to submit for consideration that all the usual state laws should be observed today," Devlin said. "You know, just to cover our bases. Keep us all out of jail."

"Fine." Scarlett sighed like he'd taken some of her fun away. "But if you start sayin' things like 'slow down' or 'maybe don't drink two beers at once' we're gonna have words, McCallister."

My sister was all bluster. The second our attention was caught by the approach of someone else from the lawn, Scarlett jumped into Devlin's arms and wrapped her legs around his waist. She gave him a smacking kiss on the mouth.

Love was in the air.

"What are *you* doing here?" I bumped up the harshness in my tone when Shelby approached. The girl was a born actress. The smile evaporated right off her face, and I felt actual guilt.

"Oh, I'm sorry. I didn't realize. Scarlett—"

"I invited her," Scarlett said, hopping out of her boyfriend's arms. "And you, brother dear, had better behave. You're both my guests."

I gave Shelby a good glare, and she flipped me the bird as she stepped aboard. Something I realized no one else knew was out of character for her.

"Maybe it's time we clear the air," Scarlett suggested.

"Nothing needs clearing in my opinion," Shelby said primly. "Jonah is welcome to be an ass to anyone he chooses."

Devlin choked on his beer and abruptly looked anywhere but at me.

"But, Shelby, don't y'all think—"

Shelby cut Scarlett off with a shake of her head. "It's fine. Let's just leave it alone."

"Juney and George are catching a ride with Opal," Cassidy said, changing the subject and snuggling under Bowie's arm. "I didn't think your deck could handle the weight of a pro football player."

"Good thinking, Cass," Gibs said.

"We're already over the limit," I muttered mostly under my breath while shooting a pointed look at Shelby.

"I, ah, take it your living arrangements have been a little rocky?" Bowie said quietly, offering me a beer.

"Understatement. I came home the other day, and she was interrogating half the town elders—some of them my clients—on the front porch trying to get the dirt on your family."

"Maybe it wasn't exactly what it seemed." Bowie was the good guy. The peacemaker. And he was starting to sweat.

I felt pretty good about that.

I shook my head. "Oh, it was exactly how it seemed. I gotta tell you. I think it might be time for me to be moving on."

Bowie had his beer in a stranglehold. I noticed that Cassidy was on the other side of the deck huddled together with Scarlett and Shelby.

"You put a ring on her yet?" I asked Bowie, changing the subject before he could get himself worked up about my announcement. I gave it about thirty seconds before he excused himself to go spread the word.

"What? Oh, uh. No. But real soon. As in maybe tonight. Jameson and I were fighting over who got to do it first. I won though. I've waited longer, and my ring's already done.

Apparently Jame isn't as talented at goldsmithing as he is with everything else." He nodded in his brother's direction.

Jameson had small bandages all over both hands.

"Real soon though," Bowie repeated himself, and I noticed he slid a hand into the pocket of his shorts.

We cast off from the dock, motoring across the lake in the direction of what sounded like one hell of a party already.

The better part of Bootleg Springs was waiting for us around a bend. Rocks jutted out into the warm water, creating a harbor of sorts. There were a dozen other decks already tied together. Girls in bikinis were lounging on pool floats. Guys were tossing beers and firing up grills. The more adventurous of the crowd were climbing the boulders and jumping off.

The scene smelled like sunshine and sunscreen.

This was why I loved Bootleg. It was also probably part of what Shelby was looking for in her research. These were people who lived their lives entwined. Neighbors who brought chicken noodle soup over when the flu was going around. Friends who would pick you up and drive you around when your car was in the shop. They'd spent all week together. Working, raising kids, shopping. And they chose to spend their Saturday having a good time.

I spotted June and George on Opal Bodine's—no relation—deck. June was sitting with her feet in his lap, a book cracked open in her own.

While the others busied themselves tying off the deck to the two closest ones, I sidled up to Shelby. She looked like a kid on Christmas morning.

"This. Is. Amazing," she breathed.

"I had a feeling you'd like it."

"I can't believe a place like this exists. People like this." She shook her head in wonder. She was wearing cutoffs and a pink tank top that said, "I Have No Life. I'm a Psychology Major." Her dark hair was tied in its usual tail and fed through a ball cap with her brother's football number on it.

She was cute. Like friendly, girl-next-door, "always has a

nice word to say about everyone" cute. I was surprised by the urge to reach out and wrap my arms around her, to make her laugh.

I hadn't felt that urge in a long, long time.

I remembered the plan and schooled my features into a disgusted sneer.

"I'm glad you came," I said.

She lowered her sunglasses and glared at me. "I am, too. Thanks for asking me."

"They're all looking at us," I said quietly, doing my best to look defensive.

"Of course they're looking at us. Their plan is about to blow up in their faces. Mass casualties. Oh, the humanity," Shelby said, jutting her chin out.

"Should we fight now?" I asked her, suddenly a little anxious to get the fight scene out of the way so we could kick back and possibly even enjoy the day together.

"Let's give it another half hour. We need to time it just right," she reminded me.

"Fine. If that's the way you want it," I said, raising my voice.

"If I had my way, I'd be enjoying this day without someone being a giant turd!" she snapped.

I had to turn away and bite the hell out of my lip to keep from laughing. "Giant turd?" I whispered.

"Shut up. I spent a lot of time working with kids. The swearing vocabulary went to my brother."

"Heeeeeey, guys," Leah Mae said, easing between us. "So, Shelby, I love your shirt. Let's go show it to Nicolette way, way over there. She loves funny shirts."

Devlin wandered up when they left. "I've been ordered to keep you under control. You're making my girlfriend nervous."

I snuck a peek at Scarlett who was watching us like a hawk.

"What a shame."

"I assume there's a spectacle coming?"

"Twenty-eight minutes and counting."

He nodded. "You coming to the Cockspurs game next week?"

I played nice for the next half an hour. Making small talk and taking a turn at the grill. Between the partygoers, there were hot dogs, hamburgers, chicken breasts, and even a few grilled pizzas. It was a beautiful early summer day with a soft breeze and cloudless blue sky mirrored on the lake.

The music was upbeat and country. I'd never listened to country music before moving here. Now, I was half considering buying a pickup truck to haul my boot camp and training gear. There was something contagious about this town, these people.

The whine of a boat motor carried over the Chase Rice song. Hell, I could even identify the artists now. I needed an urban vacation somewhere before I was completely absorbed into country culture. Sheriff Harlan Tucker and his wife, Nadine, approached in a small fishing boat. Cassidy waved to her parents and guided them in.

"Are those pepperoni rolls?" Devlin asked, scenting the air.

While the sheriff eased the boat alongside, Nadine handed over the container of what indeed was fresh, hot pepperoni rolls. Devlin, his love for the West Virginia specialty wider and deeper than the lake, nearly shoved Gibson overboard in his quest to get the first one.

I spotted Shelby, and she nodded. It was showtime.

We met halfway.

"You are the *worst* human being I've ever met," she shouted.

"Right back at you, sweetheart," I countered. "At least I'm not an opportunistic bottom-feeder."

"*Opportunistic?*" Her gasp could have filled a sail. "You are irrational, unreasonable, and downright misogynistic. You hate women!"

"No, I just hate you," I roared.

Chapter Thirteen
Jonah

W ell, go screw yourself then!" She shoved me as hard as she could. Which moved me not an inch. I realized it was the first time she'd initiated any physical contact between us. Every time I'd touched her before, it had been to catch her or stop her from falling.

"Is there a problem here?" All three hundred pounds of George Thompson was headed in my direction. I'd seen the man flip a tractor tire like it was a child's toy. I didn't want to give him a shot at me.

Gibson stepped in George's path. Not so much to stop him but more to slow him down a bit.

"The problem is that my roommate is a nightmare, and I can't live like this anymore," Shelby screeched.

"The real problem is I've been saddled with a vulture circling around trying to tear off pieces of the carcass of my father!"

"Okay, now, that's enough airing of the grievances," Sheriff Tucker said, ambling into the fray.

The music cut off, and every single Bootlegger gave us their full attention. I heard beers popping open everywhere.

My brothers were trying to ease their way in between us. Scarlett was climbing over deck railings to get closer.

Shelby stepped in closer so we were toe-to-toe.

"You know what? I'd like to press charges, Sheriff Tucker. I've been verbally assaulted and emotionally attacked."

"Well, now, Shelby, I can understand why you're feelin' what you're feelin'," the sheriff said, trying his best to placate.

"Screw this," I bellowed. "You want the house to yourself? Well, you can have the whole damn town, too. I'm leaving."

"Jonah Bodine, you're not going anywhere!" Scarlett howled.

"Listen, man, we can work this out," Bowie said, laying a hand on my shoulder. I shrugged him off.

"I want you out of my life," Shelby said. She gave me a solid push, both hands to my chest, and I went from standing on the deck to falling backward. I waved my arms like a bird trying to take flight, but the blue bathwater of the lake enveloped me.

I stayed under long enough to let the scene play out a bit on the surface.

When I surfaced, it was to pandemonium.

Sheriff Tucker was slapping handcuffs on Shelby while Cassidy looked on horrified. "Dad, what are you doing?"

"That was assault, clear as day," Sheriff Tucker insisted. "And according to Ordinance 417.2, journalists that assault any resident are required to leave town immediately."

"How dare you!" Shelby said, making a good show of trying to kick him.

"Oh my god. Don't assault an officer!" Cassidy went low and tried to hold Shelby's legs.

June stood in front of George, looking vaguely concerned and trying to keep him from jumping in the water and drowning me. Gibson was helping June.

"Let's all calm down here," Jameson said, standing on a beer cooler.

Scarlett had her hands to her face. "This is all my fault!"

"You're damn right this is your fault," Shelby howled as Sheriff Tucker tried to perp-walk her to his waiting boat.

Scarlett jumped in front of them, waving her arms like an inflatable car lot balloon. "Wait! Shelby's not a journalist! It was a misunderstanding! We were just teasin' Jonah, and maybe I was playing a little matchmaker, too. And it got out of hand. You can't throw Shelby out of town and, Jonah, don't you even think about moving away!"

I swam toward the nearest deck and let Nash Larabee and Opal Bodine pull me out of the water. George picked June up and physically moved her out of his way and then barreled in my direction. The deck swayed as the ex-pro football player charged.

Gibson slid between me and George's helmet-sized fists at the last moment.

"No one treats my sister badly," George insisted.

"Yeah, and no one pounds my brother into oblivion," Gibson said quietly.

Shelby quit screaming and started laughing. I sloshed over to her and threw an arm around her shoulder.

"Think. that about does it?" Sheriff Tucker asked, his mustache twitching.

"I'm happy," I said. "Shelby? How do you feel?"

"I feel real good, sheriff."

"What in the good goddamn is happening?" Scarlett asked from the prison of Devlin's arms.

"It appears we've been had," Bowie said.

Cassidy let go of Shelby's legs. "You two planned this?"

Shelby nodded, still grinning. I gave her a soggy, one-armed hug.

"Of all the low-down, sneaky, underhanded..." Scarlett escaped Devlin's grip and advanced on us. Devlin made a slashing motion across his throat, clearly not wanting any credit for being in the know. "*Brilliant* schemes! You really are one of us!"

Scarlett gave me a tight hug, not caring that I was wetter than the lake.

"I'm so proud right now," she sniffled in my ear.

"I learned from the master," I said, tweaking her nose.

"Sneaky son of a bitch," Gibson said, no longer busy holding back George.

"I can't believe this place rubbed off on you so fast," George was saying to Shelby as the sheriff unlocked the handcuffs.

"I can't believe you were in on this," Cassidy said, shaking her head at her father.

"Can't let you kids have all the fun."

"Say what you will, Gibs, but you put yourself between Jonah and one pissed-off football player," Jameson pointed out.

"You loooooooove him," Scarlett crooned.

Gibson looked as though he was going to toss Scarlett in the water. And then he did just that.

Her shriek was cut off as the water closed over her head.

"Damn it." Devlin sighed. He gave Gibs a shove from behind and sent him into the lake after Scarlett.

Shelby let out a snort-laugh that set everyone else off.

Gibson and Scarlett surfaced, spitting water and splashing each other.

"Can we all just agree to stop messing with each other and enjoy the rest of the day?" I suggested.

"I'll drink to that," Shelby said cheerfully, pulling a Mountain Dew out of her backpack.

———

We soaked up the sun and swam and ate. Late morning gave way to lazy afternoon. Folks coming and going. Because I said things like "folks" now.

I kicked back in a lawn chair, my feet up on the railing of Sonny Fullson's deck. Shelby plopped a chair down next to me.

"You did good," she said, grinning up at me.

I *felt* good.

"Thanks for talking me down before," I told her.

"My pleasure." She reached into her backpack and pulled out a bottle of sunscreen. "Here, you're looking a little pink."

"What else do you have in there?" I asked, squirting the SPF 50 into my palm.

"Well, picky eaters can't go to a floating deck party and expect to have their special dietary needs met," she said, warming to the topic.

"Of course not."

"I've got two peanut butter and jelly sandwiches on white bread. Two bags of sour cream and onion potato chips. Another Mountain Dew." She dug deeper, rummaging. "Oh, and some bug spray, spare sunglasses, and another shirt in case this one gets wet or stained."

"You're a party professional," I observed.

"I also have this," she said, looking furtively over her shoulder.

Rather than pulling it out, she tilted the backpack in my direction to show me a very nice bottle of gin, tonic water, and a bag of sliced limes.

"Have bar, will travel." I approved.

"There are no better moonshine makers in the country. But I still prefer some Bombay Sapphire once in a while. Besides, I like to enjoy a beverage with my show," she said, nodding to the next deck.

Misty Lynn, who'd just got done adjusting her pink leopard-print bikini top over her very fake, slightly lopsided breasts in Gibson's face, was now sobbing as Rhett Ginsler accused her of trying to get in Gibs's pants yet again.

"We might need Sheriff Tucker's services after all," I told Shelby.

She snickered. "You seem like a refined urbanite. At least, more so than our pal Misty Lynn over there. Can I make you a gin and tonic?"

"I'd be honored."

She dug deep, producing two Solo cups. "I've only ever seen you drink beer," she said, helping herself to ice out of the nearest cooler. I noticed a long, jagged scar on her thigh and wondered what had caused it.

"You've seen me hungover on moonshine," I reminded her. I held the cups while she poured the gin.

"The Black Friday Bootcamp," she laughed, remembering. "Half the town turned out to see how hungover you'd be. They really do love you here."

Scarlett's voice carried from where she perched on the rocks with Cassidy.

"What do you mean you don't get it?" Scarlett demanded. She'd mostly dried off, but my sister hadn't dried out.

"I mean, how would letting Jonah believe that Shelby was still an evil reporter get him to start crushing on her?" Cassidy frowned, dipping her toes in the water. Unlike her best friend, Cassidy wasn't one to overindulge often. Though I'd been entertained by drunk Deputy Tucker recently.

"Pfft," Scarlett snorted, obviously having no idea how far her voice carried. "Don't you know anything about matchmaking?"

"You know my dating app history. Of course I know nothing about matchmaking."

"Well, the proximity of them living together with strong feelings toward each other created sparks. I created an obstacle—Shelby being a low-down, no-good, dirty reporter— that I could remove at the opportune moment to best ensure sexy times. Sparks plus no obstacles means those two will be knockin' boots in no time."

I met Shelby's gaze over the cups as she opened the bottle of tonic.

"Your sister is one in a million," she whispered to me.

"That's a nice way of saying she's a manipulative little schemer," I said fondly.

"Maybe you should keep it down. They keep looking over here," Cassidy said.

Shelby snickered next to me.

"Just smile and wave," Scarlett said at full volume. "They have no idea what we're sayin'."

They waved and smiled, and we did the same in return.

"They're all invested in you," Shelby said. "I get the sense that the whole town feels responsible for making up for your father."

"They seem to be fans of you, too," I observed.

Shelby gave a sassy little shrug. "Yeah, I'm kind of hard to resist."

I was starting to see that.

"I guess we can be friends now," I said.

She put the top back on the tonic and took one of the cups from me. "To friendship."

I clinked my cup against hers. "To friendship."

Chapter Fourteen

Jonah

Bootleg Springs had trouble ending a party. We'd stayed out on the lake until the sun kissed the water in a blaze of pinks and reds.

And just before all the decks motored home, Scarlett and Devlin announced a bonfire at their new place. Bootleg apparently also didn't mind a party at a hole in the ground.

Shelby rode with me, and we gave Bowie and Cassidy a lift. Something else neighbors and family did for each other when everyone lived five minutes from everyone else.

My car bounced down the dirt path that cut through the land leading us toward the lakefront.

I felt a burst of pride for my sister. Scarlett hadn't had the advantage of college, and she hadn't needed it. She'd taken over our father's handyman business before she should have had to. By the time she graduated high school, she'd saved the flagging business and started saving for her first real estate rental. Now, she was building a home and planning a future with the man she loved.

It was probably time for me to start weighing my options, thinking about my future. It had been a year since Rene. A year since I'd arrived in Bootleg as a stranger. I was healing here. But that didn't mean that I had to stay.

And even though when I'd said I was leaving it had been a lie, the words still struck a chord within me. A decision needed to be made. *Stay or go.*

Here, I had brothers and a sister. I had friends. Would those relationships survive if I left? Were they real if they didn't?

I spared Shelby a glance. She was in the passenger seat, quiet. Her eyes looked heavy, shadowed.

My headlights caught the ghostly skeleton of construction. "Look at this," I said.

Bowie and Cassidy reluctantly unlocked their lips in the back seat.

Under the light of the moon, we could see the beginning of a real house. The basement was poured, and the first floor was already partially framed. The bonfire was just getting started down on the shoreline. A dozen pickups and SUVs were already there. People were carting food and chairs and even a keg down to the fire. Music played through someone's portable speakers.

When we parked, Shelby peeled off to talk to Hester Jenkins and Penny Waverly while Scarlett and Devlin gave the rest of us the grand tour.

"This here's where we're going to snuggle by the fire in the winter," Scarlett said, pointing at the plywood. She grinned up at Devlin, who leaned in to wrap her up. Their future shined so bright. And again, I felt that sharp reminder that I was missing out on something. That I could have had something like this but it was taken away from me.

They'd positioned the house to take advantage of the lake views. What would be tall windows looked out in all directions, framing in trees and water and rolling hills. I could imagine them here. Could imagine Kitten Jedidiah skidding on the hardwood of the first floor in his reign of terror. I could see Christmas mornings here and birthday dinners.

Would I be here to see them?

Would Rene have liked it here? With her brunches and her cycling classes. Her art gallery visits. Would she have been happy here with me? With my family?

My throat felt tight.

While Gibson admired the quality of the construction, Jameson and Leah Mae asked a dozen questions about the floor plan. Bowie and Cassidy made out in a dark corner. Making up for lost time, I guessed.

I took the opportunity to slip out. I was happy for Scarlett and Devlin. Really happy. But I was also aware how far away I was from a future like this.

The night air was cooler now and scented with the hint of wood smoke.

I wandered in the direction of the flames, the chatter. Tried to find the party mood again.

I spotted her. Even in the dark, I could pick her out.

Shelby was standing on the outskirts of the fun, observing.

"Hiding out?" I asked, stepping up next to her.

She startled and slapped a hand to her chest. "Are you professionally trained as a ninja?"

"Order of the silent-footed," I said seriously.

She nudged me with her shoulder. "Funny guy."

She still looked tired.

"Everything okay?" I asked.

She lifted her lips in the ghost of a smile. "Everything's just about perfect," she confessed. "I really like this place."

I crossed my arms so I wouldn't give in to the urge to pull her into my side. Apparently, I was a mess of feelings today.

"It's one of a kind," I commented.

"I think I like it so much I'm avoiding my dissertation. I have all the research I could possibly need. The survey answers are pouring in. The outline and hypothesis are set in stone. But every time I sit down to write it, I get wrapped up in the fun of collecting the information."

"What are you going to do when you're done with it?" I asked.

"I'm not really sure. I'm hoping to get a research job with a university or some academic organization."

"Will you go back to Pittsburgh?" I pressed.

"I hope so. But I'm open to someplace new if the job fits. I don't want to make any plans until I know where the job is, what the work is. What about you? Are you sticking around here?"

"I was just thinking about it. I haven't decided. I have family here. But I don't know if that makes it home."

"What makes a place a home?" she asked.

"Are you analyzing me right now?" I teased.

"Aren't you adorable? I analyze everyone."

I nudged her, and we started for a pair of chairs on the edge of the action. "Well, don't keep me in suspense, doc."

"Don't even jinx me like that, Jonah. That doctorate is within reach, but I sure as heck don't have it yet."

"Stop stalling. Tell me everything that's wrong with me."

She snort-laughed, and it chased the shadows out of my chest.

"First of all, there's nothing *wrong* with you. You're remarkably normal."

"Considering?" I prodded.

"Considering that you grew up without a father," she said.

That was probably high praise from someone with a background in psychology.

"Judging by how you interact with women," she continued. "I would guess that your mother was strong, independent, but also loving. She taught you respect and didn't let you feel like you were missing out on too much. How am I doing so far?"

I nodded slowly. "So far pretty spot on."

She smiled smugly. "I thought so. Now, let's dig below the surface." She was warming to the topic.

"You show up here a week after the funeral of Jonah Bodine Sr., which suggests you were peripherally aware of him. Which in itself suggests you weren't interested in developing a relationship with him. However, you were very much interested in meeting your half-siblings."

"I spent most of my life hating Jonah Bodine," I admitted. "In my mind, he ruined my mom's life. She was working toward a degree. She could have had a career. Met a nice psychologist or lawyer or bartender. But he took that away from her."

"He or you?" Shelby asked astutely.

"You're annoyingly perceptive."

"I do what I can," she joked airily.

"Anyway, I hated my father for a long time. But at some point, I realized it had been the pregnancy and the resulting baby—me—who had derailed Mom's life. She sacrificed it all to keep me."

"And when you voiced this to your mother?" Shelby asked.

"How did you know?" I shook my head. "Never mind, creepy psychic woman. It gave me a few rough years in high school thinking that I was the problem. I had some anger issues. Acted out. Acted like a teenage asshole. But she never gave up on me."

"Of course not. Probably because—and I'm just guessing here—she felt that her decisions had lessened *your* life in some way," she mused.

"This is creepy. Is this what you do all day?"

Shelby laughed, and I liked the sound of it. "The reasons why people do things are fascinating. So tell me about your mom and your rocky teenage years."

I was proud of how the two of us had come out of it. The choices we'd made. "She saw right through me, kept pushing until I blurted it out that she'd have been better off if I'd never been born."

"And what did your mom say to that?"

"She called me a 'sweet, kind-hearted idiot.'" I smiled remembering it. "Told me she would do it all over again because I was the best, brightest thing in her life, and she wouldn't change a thing."

"Now, that's a good mom," she said with satisfaction.

"The best. Once we had that out in the open, she dumped me in this teen weight-lifting program at a local gym. I found working out drained my anger, helped me focus. And the rest is history."

"Oh, I doubt that," she said, calling my bluff. "You went from an angry teen to a man who makes a living fixing people. What I want to know is what made you come here? You had to know for a long time there was a possibility that you had half-siblings. Something you easily could have discovered with the bare minimum of research."

The subject of Rene sure was coming up a lot lately as if the universe was intent on making me work through it again. "There was a girl," I said slowly.

"Aha!" she said triumphantly.

"Oh, you're going to regret that preemptive victory," I predicted.

"Spill it, my friend. Tell me about this girl."

"Rene was pretty and interesting and smart. She was in commercial banking. Driven, focused. She knew what she wanted and how she was going to go get it. We met online, got paired up on a dating app, hit it off. She was into fitness and museums and had a whole Pinterest board dedicated to her future wedding. After a while, I could maybe start to see the possibility of me as the groom."

"Sounds serious."

"It was heading in that direction. We were still getting to know each other. And the more I got to know her, the more I liked her. And then she got sick."

"Sick?" Shelby tensed beside me.

"It was a pretty aggressive cancer. And Rene didn't want to divide her focus between a new relationship and a new diagnosis. One that didn't have a positive prognosis. She told me she really liked me and she appreciated the time we'd had together but that she needed to put her energy into her health."

"She dumped you because she had cancer?" she clarified.

I nodded. "Like I said, she knew exactly what she wanted and how she was going to get it. And I let her go."

Shelby slumped in her chair. "Wow. And you're using the past tense so…"

"The next time I saw her was at her funeral." I could still see her, lying there looking perfect. But she was a stranger. And she was gone.

"Oh, Jonah," she said softly.

"It's fine," I said, waving away her concern. "I let her push me away. She passed away. And then I saw my father's obituary, saw that I had brothers and a sister."

Shelby got out of her chair and slid neatly into my lap.

"What are you—?"

Her arms went around my neck.

"I'm so sorry that happened to you."

I let her hold me tighter. The tighter she held on, the looser the knot in my chest got. "Yeah, me too." I sighed into her hair.

She held on for a while, and I wrapped my arms around her. We sat in silence. Listening to the crackle of the wood and flames, the laughter of friends, the symphony of the crickets and tree frogs.

The music changed again. Country still, but something slow about first-time love.

"Jonah?"

"Yeah?"

"Do you wanna dance?"

Chapter Fifteen
Jonah

She'd left her hair down and loose tonight. The tips of it brushed my hand where it rested on her lower back. The firelight was soft on her face, flickering us into and out of shadow. Her eyes were more brown in this light, framed by the thick shock of bangs.

I let her lead me toward the fire, into the light and the warmth. Into the crowd of people who had once been strangers and were now friends, clients, neighbors.

"Do you miss her?" Shelby asked. "Your mom, I mean." She slipped her arms around my neck.

Grateful that we were done talking about Rene, I nodded. "Yeah. We're close. I need to think about flying home. Spending some time with her. What about you, your parents?"

"I miss them," she confessed. "They're kind of the best people."

"You were adopted, right?" I asked.

She nodded and grinned. "Mom says they took one look at me and knew I was theirs. Sometimes adults who were adopted as children can feel a kind of crushing sense of abandonment. Or a driving need to find their biological parents either for closure or to discover something about themselves… And I am talking your face off."

I grinned. "I kind of like it. You don't, do you? Feel abandoned I mean."

She shook her head. "I was chosen because I was the missing puzzle piece, and I was loved just for existing. That's a pretty great start to life."

"Did you ever look for your biological parents?" I asked. I had. Even though I'd already known that Jonah Bodine was the kind of man to cheat on his wife and abandon a child.

"I did. I met my biological mother when I was seventeen and going through a 'Yeah, but who am I really' phase. I exchanged emails with my biological father, too. But there was no connection. There was no history between us. Nothing like what I share with my parents and GT. That history means a lot."

"I don't have a history with the Bodines," I said, slowing our sway down to match the beat of the song.

"You're building one. You've been here, what? A year? How many memories do you now have tied up in your brothers and sister? You've been here with them, facing the problems they're facing. You helped them scare off the press, you gave the whole town something else to gossip about besides your father and his connection to a missing teenager."

"Jonah Bodine's bastard son," I said. But the bitterness wasn't as flavorful in my mouth anymore.

Shelby grinned. "There's nothing more fun than an illegitimate child no one knew about showing up in town after a funeral. Not in Bootleg Springs."

We laughed together. The shame of my background, my father, it had somehow lessened in the time I'd been here. Everyone here knew my secret: Rejected by my father. And everyone accepted it, didn't blame me for it. There was a balm in that.

"So you fixed me. Whose left?" I asked, twirling her around and pulling her back into my arms. I liked this, I decided. Shelby Thompson in my arms was a new favorite thing for me, and I hadn't the slightest idea what to do about it. I was so rusty at romantic feelings that I wondered if there were any salvageable moves left in me.

She glanced around the fire. "Well, there's always Misty Lynn."

The woman in question was currently wrapped around Rhett Ginsler like a poison ivy vine. Apparently, they'd made up.

"But you know, some people just shouldn't be unraveled," she amended.

"What about you?" I asked. I slid my hand down her back, pressing her just a little closer. Her fingers toyed with the hair at the back of my neck. I wondered if she knew she was doing it.

"Me? Oh, I'm easy," she said cheerfully.

Her eyes widened. "Oh, gosh. I mean. Not *that* way. Not that I'm a prude. I like sex. Sex is great. I think I'm going to stop talking immediately." She was talking fast, words tumbling out of her mouth in a torrent. She dropped her forehead to my chest, and I let out a quiet laugh.

"You're quite a girl, Shelby Thompson."

"Oh no. Don't start with the first and last name thing. Did you notice how everyone is all 'Scarlett Bodine' or 'Nash Larabee'? The only way you get out of it is if you already have two first names."

"Gotta be a country thing."

"There are *so many* country things." She glanced around us, making sure no one was listening. "Sometimes I feel like I'm observing an entirely new culture."

"Maybe you shouldn't spend so much time observing," I said.

She leaned back, looked up. "Huh?"

"You spend an awful lot of time watching."

"It's called research, smarty pants," Shelby argued.

"Research all you want. Just don't forget to participate."

"I'd be remiss if I didn't point out that I'm currently dancing with a very attractive man next to a bonfire under more stars than I've ever seen in my life. It feels quite participatory."

"Very attractive, huh?" I teased.

"I had a feeling that part would stick."

"Tell me something about you, Shelby. Tell me and the stars something you've never told anyone."

She hesitated, and for a minute I thought she'd make another joke. "I work hard to be good enough."

"Good enough for what?"

"Good enough so my parents never regret adopting me. Good enough so my biological parents might be sad that they missed out on me. Good enough that George is proud of me even though I'm not a well-compensated professional athlete. Good enough to finish a triathlon."

Surprised, I nearly stopped the slow swaying of our bodies. "You know you're good enough, don't you?"

She grinned. "Most days. Other days I feel like I'm never going to finish my paper. Or I'll never be able to run a faster mile."

"If anyone can accomplish those things, it's you, Shelby."

She went wooden in my arms. "Jonah Bodine, are you seducing me?"

"I don't really know. It's been a long time for me, and I'm not sure I'm ready to jump in with both feet. Also, you called me by both names."

"Gosh dang it, it's contagious. You know I had to glue my lips together yesterday when I saw Granny Louisa and Estelle at the Pop In? I wanted to ask them 'How's y'all's day?' Is y'all's even a word?" She shook her head and started swaying off beat again. "Forget all that. You caught me off guard, and so I verbally exploded on you. Are you trying to seduce me?"

"I'm saying nice things. That doesn't have to mean seduction," I hedged.

I liked the way she felt in my arms. Liked the heat of our

bodies as they pressed together. I could tuck her under my arm or rest my chin on her head.

"You're looking at me like you're thinking more than just nice things," she breathed.

"Maybe I am."

"Maybe it's the gin."

"Maybe it's the girl."

"Can someone cut the music?" It was Bowie yelling as he dragged Cassidy toward the fire. "I got somethin' to say."

Shelby and I paused mid-sway.

"What are you doing?" Cassidy demanded.

"What's going on?" Shelby whispered.

"It looks like 'real soon' is happening now."

"What?"

"Shh. Just watch."

The crowd converged on the fire, ringing the couple. Whispers and expectations rose up like the smoke that curled into the night sky.

Sheriff Tucker, a smile under his mustache, wrapped his arms around his wife.

"Hit it, Gibs," Bowie said, pointing at his brother perched on a stool with his trusty guitar.

Gibson started to play a soft, nimble melody. Devlin tightened his grip on Scarlett. "It's happening. It's really happening," she squeaked, her eyes glistening with tears in the firelight. That happiness, that absolute joy for another human being, was one of the things I loved most about my sister.

"Cassidy Tucker," Bowie began, taking her hand. "I've been waiting a long, long time to ask you something important."

Her free hand flew to her mouth in a very un-Cassidy-like move. Deputy Tucker was almost always dignified, never surprised, and rarely speechless.

"Now, timing's never been one of my strengths." Bowie grinned. "But I'd like to make up for all that right now." He held out a hand, and Sheriff Tucker stepped forward, dropping a small black box into it. "Thank you, sir."

The sheriff gave him a hearty slap on the shoulder and returned to Nadine.

Tears tracked their way down Cassidy's pretty face.

I felt goosebumps rise on Shelby's arms and laughed softly. Women and other women's proposals. It was a natural phenomenon.

"Is this really happening?" Cassidy whispered to Bowie.

Devlin clapped a hand over Scarlett's mouth before she could give a good "Hell yes."

Jameson and Leah Mae edged over to us. I gave my brother a nod.

He grinned back at me, and in that smile, I could see the anticipation for his own moment with Leah Mae.

Bowie lowered to the ground on one knee. "Now, as I was saying, I've been waiting to do this for a long time, Cass. I thought about all the right things to say. All the ways to tell you that you're so much a part of me, I feel like I carry your heart in my chest."

The women in the crowd sighed collectively, Shelby included.

"But I realized that it doesn't matter what words I use. Or how I ask the question. It just matters what your answer is. And that we're not going to waste another second of our lives."

Cassidy was nodding and nodding.

"It all went real wrong for us at a bonfire about a hundred years ago," he continued. "And now I'm gonna make that as right as I can. Be my wife, Cassidy Ann. Be my partner. My lover. The mother of my kids. Be the keeper of my heart and the bright spot of my every day for the rest of my life."

"Yes, Bowie Bodine. Yes!" she croaked, dragging him to his feet as the crowd cheered.

"Cass, honey, I didn't even get the box open."

"I don't care! I don't care if it's a damn bat in the box. We're getting married!"

He picked her up and twirled her in the firelight, in the circle of the people who'd loved them best their whole lives.

Shelby sniffled in front of me. And damn if my throat didn't feel just a little tight.

"This is the most romantic thing I've ever seen," Leah Mae sighed as a tear slipped down her face.

Bowie and Cassidy sealed the deal with a kiss that garnered hoots and hollers of appreciation. Cassidy hugged her parents while the Bodines converged on Bowie, and the lovefest was on.

———

Q. Do you ever feel lonely?

Jimmy Bob Prosser: Unfortunately, I am one to succumb to the draw of loneliness. I get to interact with family, friends, and neighbors all day long in the store. But along comes closing time and I know there's no one waiting for me upstairs. I hope someday there will be someone again. I miss having someone. I don't need much. Just a hand to hold while the TV's on or someone to pick up flowers for. Someone to fix a leaky faucet for. I'm hopeful. A little lonely, but mostly hopeful.

Chapter Sixteen
Shelby

The stars were bright, the flames were high, and I was dancing with Jonah Bodine. And dang it, now *I* was doing the first name last name thing. But the moment called for it. It felt momentous and ordinary. Intimate and somehow distant.

The music was low and slow. People surrounded us, all in their own little worlds.

I hurt everywhere. I'd overdone *everything* today. The food and the sun. The fun. I was exhausted and knew I'd pushed too hard. But I wasn't going to let it make me miss out on Jonah.

He was looking at me. Focusing in like there wasn't another thing in the world that deserved his attention.

I wanted him to kiss me. But that was old-fashioned, wasn't it? Waiting for the hero to bestow a kiss. Couldn't I be my own hero?

I wet my lips and noticed Jonah noticing.

"You're a great guy." The words escaped before the thought was fully formed.

We stopped swaying. "Is this a brush-off?" he asked.

"Oh, God no. It was just a thought that popped up. Considering we've spent the last week or so in a rather contentious situation. I'm noticing now that you're pretty great and was just trying to work up the courage to kiss you. Not tell you that you have a nice personality. Which you do. I'm not saying you don't." *Shut up, Shelby!*

"Shelby?"

"Huh?"

"Maybe just don't talk for a minute?" he suggested.

"Yeah, okay. I can do that. No problem—" He pressed a finger to my lips, sealing them. Everything that hurt stopped hurting. My body stopped telling me how exhausted it was and started reporting in how Jonah's finger on my mouth was the most important thing in my world.

I'd kissed and been kissed before. But I'd never hung as much expectation on a first kiss as I was piling on this one.

Was it because he was so blatantly male? So physically appealing? Was it because his green eyes had flecks of gold in them? Or that there was a picture of him grinning, surrounded by weightlifting senior ladies, circulating on social media? Or maybe it was that he cared enough about his family to be hurt when he thought they were rejecting him?

The balance of strength and vulnerability in Jonah was extremely attractive to me. And so was everything else about the tall, leanly muscled man before me.

Or maybe it was just the romance of witnessing the happiest day of another woman's life that was confusing things for me.

He removed his finger from my mouth and slid his hands along my jawline and into my hair, tilting my head up, up, up.

Our eyes locked, breath mingled. I was no longer sure that the heat on my skin was from the bonfire alone. Using his thumbs, Jonah nudged my chin up, and I watched him lower to me. Whisper-soft, his lips brushed mine. Once, twice, before landing lightly. I sighed into him, melting. And the kiss changed. He was still gentle, still slow, but now he was tasting me. Thoroughly savoring every breath, every sigh, every second.

I wanted to watch him kiss me, wanted to keep my eyes on his face so I could see how he looked as he breathed me in, lapped me up. But my lids were heavy, and the sensation of his mouth on mine, his tongue against mine, was too decadent to be dissected and analyzed. A first.

The kiss stretched on and on. My hands fisted in his shirt at his waist, my body pitching forward into him. And still he kissed me.

This wasn't an appetizer, a teaser to sex. This kiss was the main course. A living, breathing chemical reaction.

After an eternity that was entirely too short, he eased back ever so slightly. "I wondered how you'd taste," he said quietly.

His lips were millimeters from mine. Our breath, heavy and hot, mingled in the tight space between us. He threaded his fingers through my hair combing it back and sending a delectable shiver up my spine.

"That was a movie-worthy kiss," I breathed. "That was—that was really good. *Really* good."

We were swaying again somehow. Dancing and kissing under the stars in West Virginia. Who was I? Jonah toyed with the ends of my hair as I clung to his shirt. The kiss was still a palpable thing between us. It was movie perfect.

"I'm probably going to want to do it again," he said, the corners of his mouth turning up.

I nodded, still breathless. "I don't have a problem with that." Oh my god. If he kissed me again, I might accidentally tear my own clothes from my body and insist on sex.

"Is this a mistake seeing as how we live together?" he asked gruffly. His nose nudged the tip of mine, and then his lips were in my hair.

"Seems pretty convenient to me," I said breathily. Move over, Marilyn Monroe. Shelby Thompson is in the house. "It's a kiss, or possibly several, or maybe even sex. Which is all very biologically healthy. Humans complicate sex with expectations."

"What are your expectations, Shelby?" Jonah asked me.

Orgasms galore? Spending long hours staring at the perfection of Jonah's body while he slept naked next to me? Falling in love with him and then being devastated when the time came for me to move on to whatever job I'd land? Or worse, falling in love with him and then being devastated when he decided to leave town and pursue Shelby-less dreams?

"I don't know. I don't know what's next for me," I confessed.

"Same here. So what does that mean?"

"Well, with no set future, maybe we could still have a really good time in the present? Kind of like no strings?" I suggested. I could balance this. My dissertation, my research, my training. I could squeeze excellent sex into my schedule. It would be easier than trying to wedge a romantic relationship into the mix.

"See where it goes with no demands? No expectations?" he asked.

I was hypnotized by the firelight on his face. He could have asked me to donate both my kidneys to a black-market health scam, and I would have dumbly handed him a scalpel.

"No demands. No expectations. A fling." *I'd never had a fling before. And I liked the idea of one day reminiscing about my summer fling with the sexy, interesting, sweet personal trainer.*

"A fling," he repeated.

I couldn't tell if he liked the idea or was horrified by my suggestion.

"Think about it," I said.

"I will." A smile curved his lips. "I have a feeling I'll be thinking about it a lot."

"There y'all are!"

I jumped, trying to extricate myself from Jonah. But his hands were caught in my hair.

"Ouch!" I yelped as my head whipped backward. The pain returned and roared through my system.

"Am I interrupting?" Scarlett asked smugly. I'd never had murderous thoughts before, but if my eyeballs could shoot teeny tiny daggers, Scarlett Bodine would be bleeding from a million wounds.

"Need something, Scarlett?" Jonah asked, extracting his hands from my hair.

"I thought I'd give you your birthday present early," she said.

"Now?" he asked. He glanced at me and reached for my hand. I swooned like a lovesick nerd drooling over the star quarterback. "We're kind of in the middle of something." I mentally swooned again, harder this time.

"While I'm real happy about what y'all are in the middle of, seein' as how this was my plan all along, this present can't wait," Scarlett insisted. She jerked her thumb over her shoulder.

"Hello, Jonah."

"Mom?"

Chapter Seventeen
Jonah

Happy early birthday." My mom grinned and opened her arms.

Jenny Leland was tall and lean with a short cap of blonde hair. She had a dimple in one cheek that was perpetually visible because she was always smiling.

I had my father's coloring, but I had my mom's green, green eyes.

"What are you doing here?" I hugged her, lifting her off the ground. She laughed just like she had when I'd hugged her like this at my high school graduation.

"Surprise. Scarlett called and said it was high time I came to Bootleg Springs for a visit," Mom said, looking fondly at my sister. "And I couldn't say no."

"Not many people can," Shelby said.

Great. My mother crashed my first kiss with Shelby. Maybe Shelby could explore the possibility of operating with no expectations. But judging the sparkle in my mom's eyes—mirroring the one in Scarlett's—there were other expectations on the line.

"Mom, this is Shelby," I said, making the introduction quickly.

"Shelby, this is my mom, Jenny. Shelby is my—"

Scarlett leaned forward expectantly.

"Roommate," Shelby supplied quickly. "Scarlett was kind enough to rent me a room in Jonah's place."

"Well, isn't that nice," Mom said with a big smile.

She'd definitely seen the kiss. Shit.

She looked good. Tall and trim with her sunny hair sweeping low over her forehead. She had faint lines next to her eyes and mouth that, in my biased opinion, made her look even softer and lovelier.

"I can't believe you're here," I confessed. "I missed you."

She hugged me again, tighter this time. "I missed you, too. Now, who's going to introduce me to all these other Bodine boys?"

"Scarlett, why don't you round up your brothers, and I'll get Jenny a drink," Shelby offered.

"That would be lovely, Shelby," Mom said.

Shelby and Scarlett hurried off in opposite directions. "Now, I see why you didn't want to fly home for a visit," Mom announced. "She's gorgeous and polite. I give you my blessing."

"That was literally our first kiss that you barreled into, Oh Ye of Terrible Timing," I warned her. "Don't start putting together a wedding guest list."

"You never know where you'll find love," she said airily.

"I can guarantee it won't be in Bootleg Springs. I'm not here permanently. Nether is Shelby. If anything, we have the summer."

"A summer fling then." Mom sighed.

Even after everything, my mother was a romantic at heart. And maybe I had inherited a bit of that, too. But there was also the piece of me that wasn't sure if I was over Rene.

I sighed. "I promise you. Eventually I'll settle down and give you as many grandbabies as you want. Just not right now."

She squeezed my hand. "I'm only mostly teasing you. You

look happy, Jonah. And I don't want to derail that. You deserve to be happy."

"Jonah Bodine, is this your mother? Your mama? Maaaa-maaaa." Newly engaged off-duty Deputy Cassidy Tucker was three sheets to the wind and sloshing beer out of her cup down her arm.

"Cassidy, meet my mother, Jenny. Mom, this is Scarlett's best friend and town deputy when she's not half in the bag."

"Pfft," Cassidy said. "I'm *whole* in the bag tonight, smarty pants. But I am so excited to make your acquaintance. Your son has just been a delight. Everyone in the whole town loves him, and no one holds the whole illegitimate son of Jonah Sr. against him at all."

My mother blinked. "Oh, well. Isn't that nice?"

Cassidy leaned in and grabbed her for a sticky hug.

"Around here, everyone knows everything about everybody," I cautioned Mom.

"Apparently so," she said, looking a little dazed.

"Bowie Bodine! Get your fine ass over here," Cassidy bellowed. "I'm so sorry. I rarely drink my face off, Jonah's Mama. What was your name again? But you see, I don't have to work tomorrow, and my best friend in the whole wide world, Scarlett Bodine, is building this beautiful house, and we're gonna get married and have babies together and be sisters just like we always planned. And I'm just so happy I could burst."

"You'll get married and be sisters?" Mom asked, clearly entertained.

Cassidy closed one eye. "Hang on. I think I got that wrong. Don't wanna be giving West Virginia a bad impression to you. On you? For you?"

"Cassidy and Bowie just got engaged tonight," I explained to my mom.

"I've loved him my whole entire life." Cassidy sighed, holding up the ring an inch from my mother's eyes. "And it's all really happening. All I had to do was stop being a chickenshit and admit what I really wanted."

It should have been weird. My mother introducing herself to the children of the man who'd derailed her life. My half-siblings. Meeting half of the town that knew she'd had an affair with a married man. But it was remarkably civil. Friendly even.

Bootleg loved a friendly scandal.

Bowie was nearly as inebriated as his fiancée and kept hugging my mom. Jameson beamed at her when my mother told him she'd looked up his art and loved his installation in Charlotte. Gibson brought her a second drink after she finished the gin and tonic Shelby made for her. And while Gibson and my mom discussed the finer points of fast-pitch softball, I pulled Shelby aside.

"I'm beyond sorry about the interruption."

She gave me a wan smile. "It's fine. Your mom is great."

"You look tired. Are you okay? Do you want me to take you home?" She was pale, and those shadows under her eyes concerned me.

"I'm fine. Just a long day," she said. "GT and June are going to drive me home. Juney's hit her wall of peopling for the day."

"You sure you're okay?" I pressed. "I want to talk more about...before."

Her smile was a slow burn. "I would also like to do more 'talking.'"

"I would, too," I admitted. "Scarlett might be a problem," I warned her.

"We can handle her," Shelby predicted.

I laughed. "Have you met my sister?"

"I believe we handled her just fine today," she reminded me.

I remembered Scarlett's face when Sheriff Tucker slapped the cuffs on Shelby. "We make a good team."

"You ready, Shel?" George and June approached. June had a book under her arm and a head lamp on.

"Ready," Shelby said, looking several degrees more energetic than she had a minute ago. I wondered if the show was for me or her brother. "I'll see you back at the house."

I wanted to kiss her again, but not with her gigantic brother, my paying client, hovering. It didn't feel professional...or wise.

Shelby and June headed in the direction of the car.

"Funny joke today," George said. He still didn't sound like he thought it was very funny.

"Thanks for not pounding my face in."

"As long as you're good to my sister, that won't become necessary," he said, crossing his arms in front of his chest.

"Good to know. Appreciate the heads-up."

He slapped me on the shoulder. It stung. "Now that that's settled, we can return to our previous dudebro relationship. See you Monday?"

"Looking forward to it," I told him, rubbing my shoulder.

"You better get back over there. Scarlett's trying to talk your mother into doing shots."

"Fuck."

———

Me: My mom has officially been inducted into Bootleg Society.

Shelby: How drunk is she?

Me: She's laying in the back seat singing Lady Gaga songs. I'm driving her to the inn and pouring her into her room.

Shelby: FYI. They have a hangover room service package.

Chapter Eighteen
Shelby

The pain in my back was a wildfire that existed to drive me insane. I couldn't sleep. I'd known I'd overdone it. The whole day on the water, the party, the sun, the gin…the *kiss*.

Everything hurt. My back, shoulders, hips, wrists.

The only thing that temporarily blurred the pain was remembering every second of that kiss.

I'd kissed Jonah by a bonfire on a clear summer night.

I'd also discussed the possibility of a no-strings-attached fling with the man.

And then his mother and my pain brought everything to a screeching halt.

I'd had to grit my teeth to keep from groaning when I got out of GT's car. My brother didn't know. No one knew. And no one was going to know until I had it under control.

I tried to roll over, looking for a comfortable position on my mattress, and a pathetic moan escaped.

My room in the Little Yellow House was small. The bed was wedged in between cute little bookcases that doubled as nightstands. Not that there was a need for two of them. It would be impossible to fit two adults on this mattress.

I groaned again and winced. Fatigue, aches, discomfort. It was like a never-ending case of the flu. Which sucked because at least when I had the flu, I knew there was an end in sight. Not with this.

"Shelby?" It was followed by a light knock.

Oh, crap. Jonah. Oh my god. Was he coming in to kiss me again? Was he expecting more? Not when I was curled in a ball with all my synapses lighting up with pain.

The doorknob turned.

Maybe if I pretended to be asleep? I closed my eyes.

"I know you're awake," he said, amused from the door. "I've seen your sleeping face. Now, you look like you just ate a lemon."

I opened one eye. "Oh, hey, Jonah. How's it going?" Playing it cool. Casual.

"I heard you moaning. Thin walls. You okay?"

I winced as turning my head delivered a new shock of pain in my neck. "Must have been dreaming."

"Or you must be lying," he said, taking stock of me. I was curled in the fetal position, stiff as a board. Even I knew this didn't look natural.

"I'm just coming down with something. Maybe I had too much sun," I said lamely.

"Can I bring you some water or ibuprofen? A hot pad?"

The sweet, sexy man in my doorway thought I was getting my period.

It made me laugh, and that made me suck in a sharp breath when my back spasmed.

He was all the way inside the room now reaching for me. He laid a cool hand on my forehead and one on my back.

"It's nothing," I said through clenched teeth.

"You take meds every day on a schedule. Meds that you keep hidden in your room. You hold yourself like your back hurts all the time. And now you're curled up on your bed in the middle of the night moaning in pain, Shelby. Don't lie to me."

"Look, there isn't anything anyone can do," I said, sharper than I'd intended. "Don't think you can dig into this and fix it." That's what he was: A fixer.

"Talk to me," he ordered.

"I don't want anyone to know," I confessed, squeezing my eyes shut again.

"Roommate confidentiality," he said, his hands still on me. It was so different from the way he'd touched me earlier, still gentle but now almost clinical.

I cursed my stupid body. He'd never look at me the same now.

"I have a…condition," I said, exhaling slowly when the spasm lessened.

"Okay," he said, waiting for more.

"I was just diagnosed this spring, and it's manageable and annoying, and I hate it, but I'm dealing with it, and it's my body, so I don't have to tell my whole family and have them worrying."

"Shelby."

"Ankylosing spondylitis." I blurted the words out.

It was the first time I'd ever said them out loud. And that was weird. It wasn't like saying it made it more real. Or did it?

"Bless you," Jonah joked.

"Har. Har. It's a form of arthritis. Spinal arthritis. I could end up bent in half." I joked, but the thought of it was still terrifying.

"Arthritis. Inflammation," he said.

I nodded into my pillow and tried not to whimper like a big, dumb baby. I hadn't had a flare since just prior to my diagnosis. I'd thought there was something very, very wrong. Now, at least I had a name for it, and I knew it wasn't some kind of rare form of meningitis devouring my innards. Small comfort in the moment though. With Hot Roommate Jonah sitting on my bed looking at me at my sweaty, pained worst.

111

He got up and walked out.

"Great. Just great. Thanks a lot, stupid garbage arthritis," I muttered into my pillow.

"I can still hear you," he called dryly. "I'll be back in a minute."

I heard the water running in the bathroom and then his quick stride on the stairs. True to his word, he returned a minute later.

"Here. Take this," he said. Grumpily, I opened my eyes. Jonah was standing before me. A glass of water in one hand, two caplets in the other.

"What is it?" I asked.

"Naproxen." He dumped them in my hand and helped me into a seated position so I wouldn't choke and die.

"Thanks," I said, slugging the water back. "You look mad."

He did. His jaw was tight, lips pursed.

"I'm not mad," he insisted.

"Now which one of us is lying."

"I'm not mad," he said, taking the glass of water from me. "I'm annoyed that you're selfishly keeping this from everyone. What good is that doing anyone?"

"I'm going to tell my family. I just want to get a handle on it first. Geez. Cut me some slack. This is my first flare since the rheumatologist put a name to it."

"Was this when you left town a few weeks ago?"

"Yeah. I knew something wasn't right, and I had to meet with my dissertation director anyway to make sure I was headed in the right direction with my research."

"It's not right that you're keeping people out of this part of your life. Now, get up," he said.

"Why? Everything hurts, and I'm whiny. I'm not going to be less whiny someplace else," I warned him.

"Up," he said, gently tugging me to my feet. He guided me out of the room, and I limped across the hall to the bathroom.

The tub was filling with hot water. "Sit," he ordered, pushing me down on the toilet lid.

I gaped at the tub. "You're drawing me a bath?"

He pulled a carton out from under the doll-sized vanity. Epsom salts. "Yes. You shared your situation with me. I'm helping take care of you. You got a problem with that?" He dumped the salts into the tub.

I shook my head.

"Good. Now, do you need help getting undressed?" he asked, testing the water temperature with his hand.

"Nope," I squeaked, clutching my shirt to my chest. I was still wearing the clothes I'd been in all day, too tired to change. His first glimpse of my naked body was *not* going to be helping me into a hot bath like an invalid. If he still wanted to move forward with a physical relationship, I would be draped in suitable lingerie, shaved, lotioned, and ready for action.

"Call me if you need help getting out," he said and shut the door with a decisive click.

I would most certainly not need help getting my wet, ouchy body out of the tub. "Thank you," I called weakly.

Alone and embarrassed, I stripped and eased my way into the water, sliding in up to my neck. God bless Scarlett and her deep tubs. It soothed instantly, and I decided to spend the night submerged if it meant feeling degrees better.

Then I remembered every celebrity bathtub death and pushed myself a little higher out of the water.

I heard Jonah on the stairs again, the bathroom door opened a crack, and I made a move to cover myself. But he merely dropped shorts and a tank top through the opening and then shut the door again.

I sighed and leaned back again.

My secret was out. I had a rare-ish disease that, if left unmanaged, would turn my spine into a question mark. It caused back, muscle, and joint pain. Fatigue. And, on occasion, not very attractive skin reactions and eye irritation. Now, the ball was in Jonah's court. Would he still want to roll around naked with me? I didn't think the odds looked good.

Pouting in the tub long enough to wrinkle like a raisin,

I did feel marginally better. At least physically. I made a note to make warm baths a part of my "screw you, inconvenient disease" routine. Carefully, I climbed out of the tub, dried off as best I could, and pulled on the fresh clothes. I opened the door a crack. There was no sign of Jonah.

I stepped out into the hall and looked in my room. The pillows were arranged in a weird configuration. There was a fresh glass of water, two hot pads, and a portable fan.

"Get in," Jonah said, appearing in my doorway and gesturing toward the bed.

"You don't have to tuck me in. I'm not four."

"You're acting like it," he reminded me, reaching out to hook a finger over my protruding lower lip.

"Hey. I'm the one with the incurable disease here. Doesn't that earn me some slack?"

He sighed. "*Please* get in bed."

Too tired to argue, I obliged.

Then got less tired and a lot more defensive when he leaned over me.

"Do not even think that you're going to give me a pity kiss," I said, slapping a hand to his chest.

To my humiliation and physical relief, he moved the first heating pad so it was under my shoulders and then tucked the second one under my low back. He arranged the extra pillows so that my knees were open to the sides, supported in a pose I recognized from yoga class.

"Oh, that's kind of nice," I murmured.

"It's no pity kiss," he quipped, but I could tell he was still annoyed.

"Remind me to talk to you tomorrow about why you're exponentially madder than you should be, 'kay?" I yawned.

He angled the fan toward me and pulled the blanket up, the slightest of smiles on his perfect lips.

"Goodnight, Shelby."

I kissed my hopes for a smoldery summer fling with my handsome roommate goodbye.

Chapter Nineteen
Jonah

I just have to put my contacts in and find a clean sports bra. Then I'll be ready to run," Shelby promised with a yawn from the top of the stairs. She was still in the clothes I'd laid out for her last night, her hair in a messy tangle on her head. And her glasses were crooked. She looked tired but less pained.

I shook my head. "We're not running today, Shelby," I told her as I laced up my shoes.

"I knew I shouldn't have told you," she complained. "Now you're going to be all 'You can't compete in a triathlon. You're too feeble and pathetic to do anything athletic.'" Her baritone impression of me was mildly offensive.

"Shelby—"

"No! I'll continue my training even if you refuse to help me. I'm doing this with or without your permission." She actually stomped her foot.

"Are you done?" I asked mildly.

"I think so," she said.

"We're not running *today*. We're going to breakfast."

She looked at me with suspicion. "You still want to hang out with me?"

I nodded.

"And you're still willing to train me?"

"Yes. And now that I know more about your health, I can do a better job of coaching you, you stubborn, secretive pain in my ass."

The insult seemed to have the opposite intended effect. She looked downright happy. "Okay! Let me find a regular bra, and I'll be right down."

"Maybe run a brush through this?" I suggested waving a hand over my own head.

"Don't be silly. Your hair always looks great."

I couldn't tell if she was joking or not.

––––––––

We decided on Moonshine Diner for our breakfast and chat. I had a lot of things I wanted to say to her. But I'd wait until we had some coffee and food first.

I took the menu from her when she slid into the booth across from me. Shelby was moving a little gingerly but leaps and bounds better than last night.

"How are you feeling?" I asked her.

"Fine. Can I have my menu?" she asked, stretching her arms across the table.

"No, you can't."

"Mornin' Jonah. Mornin' Shelby," Clarabell greeted us with a smile and a pot of coffee. "Interest y'all in some caffeine?"

"Yes, please," Shelby said, offering up her mug.

"Thanks, Clarabell," I said as she filled mine.

"Shelby? The usual?" she asked.

"I'll have the pancake stack—"

I cut Shelby off. "We'll both have veggie omelets with cheese and a side of fruit."

Clarabell's red, red eyebrows climbed toward her hairline. "Is that so?"

Shelby wrinkled her nose but nodded reluctantly.

"You haven't kidnapped this nice girl, and she's sending me an SOS?" Clarabell asked me.

I grinned.

"Whatever Jonah here says," Shelby said with zero enthusiasm.

"Comin' right up," Clarabell promised and disappeared with her coffee pot.

"Veggie omelets? *Fruit*?" she scoffed at me.

"Your diet is horrendous. I'm saying it as your trainer and your friend. With your condition—"

"Lower your voice. Fifty percent of the people in here are just waiting for some tasty niblet of gossip," she hissed.

"Fine," I said, leaning in. "Diet is one of the most important components of managing your condition. Which, judging by the look of disgust on your face, is something your doctor has already explained to you."

"My rheumatologist may have mentioned something about nutrition," she grumbled.

"And?" I pressed.

"And I didn't hear what she was saying since I was too busy inhaling a bag of pork rinds on the exam table."

I wasn't sure if she was joking.

"Oh, come on." Shelby rolled her eyes. "I'm kidding. It was a six-pack of Slim Jims and a carton of chocolate milk."

I didn't want to smile, but I felt one working its way up.

"There's the smile," she said, pointing at my face. "Now, let's talk about why you're having breakfast with me and not—as they say 'round these parts—'your mama'?"

"We're talking about *you* right now," I reminded her. "And you're valiantly trying to use your adorably weird sense of humor to deflect."

She leaned back against the booth. "You're trying to turn this into a professional relationship, aren't you? We have a kiss that knocks my socks off, and then you find out I have a little bit of arthritis, and it's all business now," she complained.

She delivered it like a joke, but I could hear the disappointment.

I reached across the table and squeezed her hand. "Shelby, there's nothing professional about my feelings for you. But I've never slept with a client before."

"I'm not a client, and we haven't slept together *yet*," she pointed out.

"I'm trying to explain this is new territory for me. I want to help you train. It's my area of expertise. But I'm also attracted to you. I'm also a little surprised you haven't analyzed the hell out of all this."

She gave a dainty shrug. "It's harder to find perspective when it's my stupid feelings of inadequacy."

"Why would you feel inadequate?" I asked, stretching an arm across the back of the booth.

"I'm flawed," she said with a small frown. "Duh."

Now I laughed. "Shelby, of course you're flawed. We're all flawed. Let me be clear, I have a bigger issue with you asking forty million questions to dissect something than I do with you having ankylosing spondylitis."

"You looked it up?" Surprised, she picked up her coffee and sipped.

"I did. You got a problem with that?" I teased.

"I don't know. I haven't decided," she said primly.

"Well, you think on it."

Clarabell returned, a steaming plate in each hand. "Enjoy, y'all."

Shelby stared down at her plate like it was fresh roadkill.

"Back to your diet and nutrition," I said, sliding the napkin-wrapped silverware in her direction. "We're going to find healthy foods that you'll like to eat. You don't have to eat anything you hate."

"Good. Because I think I'm going to hate this." She poked at the omelet with her fork.

I pulled the containers out of the carrier on the table. "Let's cut it into thirds. One with just salt and pepper. One with ketchup. And one with hot sauce," I suggested.

"Okay," she said miserably.

She was unbelievably cute. Her freckles were rioting after yesterday's sun. She'd scooped her hair back in one of those knots women seemed to favor. Her bangs framed her glasses and those mournful, hazel eyes.

I had the urge to order her a short stack of pancakes with a gallon of syrup just to see her smile.

"What's this?" she asked, spearing a piece of melon.

"It's what they make sangria out of."

"Let's get this over with," she muttered.

———

She liked grapes, pineapple, and honeydew. And she spit out the cantaloupe in her napkin. As for the omelet, Shelby surprised herself and didn't hate it spiced up with hot sauce.

"This isn't awful," she mused, taking another forkful.

"I'm sure the cook will take that as a compliment," I said wryly.

"Coming from me, it's high praise for anything other than chicken nuggets and applesauce."

I winced. "You eat like a picky toddler."

"Believe me, I know it. It's embarrassing when Mom whips up some fabulous chicken parm from scratch for the family, and there I am with my nuggets and ranch dressing," she said, cutting another bite of eggs.

She put down her fork and pulled her phone out to snap a picture of her plate. "Speaking of Mom, I'm going to send her proof that my palate is expanding."

Her thumbs flew across the screen, and I tried to focus on my breakfast. Now that I'd kissed her, well, it was hard to not think about doing it again. And again.

She'd responded to me like I was waking her up from a long sleep. Like I was something special. And I really liked that. But was I ready?

"Okay," she said, dropping her phone back on the table. "Let's cover the following topics. One, do you still want to

119

pursue a physical relationship with me? And two, how do you feel about your mom surprising you, and why aren't you out to breakfast with her?"

"Mom thing first," I decided. "I'm thrilled she's here. I hadn't realized how much I missed her until I saw her last night. As for why I'm having breakfast with you, Mom's nursing a hangover. I'm giving her a grand tour of the town this afternoon when her eyes are less bloodshot and she's done sweating Fireball."

Shelby nodded approvingly and ate another grape. "Go on."

"The physical relationship thing. I'm obviously attracted to you. You know that, don't you?"

She cocked her head, frowning. "I sense a 'but' approaching."

"But I don't know if I'm ready to pursue anything. I've never been a fling kind of guy," I confessed. I liked long-term relationships. Liked building a history with a woman. "However, I don't know what the future holds. I wasn't kidding about missing my mom. We're close. And I don't know if I really want to set up a life on the opposite side of the country from her."

She pursed her lips. "I don't have room in my schedule for an actual relationship. This dissertation is basically haunting every waking moment, and then there's the triathlon training and dealing with this diagnosis thing. And I don't know where I'm going to be by the end of summer. Hopefully juggling well-paying job offers."

"Okay. Where does that leave us?" I asked.

"I think I would be doing a disservice to myself and nerd girls everywhere if I didn't try to enjoy a summer fling with my incredibly attractive roommate. Every woman needs a man she can remember fondly forever. I want you to be that for me."

I nodded slowly. "A physical relationship with no strings or expectations? And you'll look back on this summer when you're eighty-five and wonder whatever happened to that nice trainer you lived with?"

"Exactly!" she said, beaming at me.

I hesitated, and she sensed it. "I appreciate you being so open about it," I began.

"But?" she pressed.

I hated myself for it. "I just don't know if I'm ready yet."

"Because of Rene?" she asked softly.

I set my teeth, annoyed with myself that after an entire year I still hadn't moved on. "Yeah. I guess it still weighs on my mind."

Shelby nodded and scooped up another bite. "The offer is there. You think about it."

I doubted I'd be thinking of much else.

Chapter Twenty
Shelby

Breakfast eaten and physical relationship offer made, Jonah guided me out of the diner with a hand on the small of my back. I approved.

"We're going to take a whole new approach to your training," he was saying.

I wondered if he knew he retreated into professional mode as a defense mechanism. I guessed that with as attractive as his clients were bound to find him, he had developed the defense early on in his career.

It didn't bother me that he was using it against me. I'd rattled him. And presented him with an offer that he would most definitely be considering. A researcher was nothing if not patient. And I could be patient for Jonah. He had things to work through. I respected that.

It was a bright summer day. Summertimers, as Bootleg called them, flooded into town, filling rentals, buying out the Pop In, and splashing in the warm waters of the lake.

Jonah explained how we were going to work more on

endurance and rest to ease my body into the distances required for the triathlon. It sounded well-thought-out, carefully researched. I approved the method.

"Pardon me," I said when Mona Lisa McNugget pranced in front of us. We stopped and gave the chicken on a mission the right of way. "Be careful crossing the street," I warned her.

I felt Jonah stiffen next to me and looked up.

The couple looked familiar. They were older, well-dressed, but unsmiling. There was something about them. Something wounded. Something *wrong*.

"Morning, Judge," Jonah said. "Mrs. Kendall."

The Kendalls. Missing Callie's long-suffering parents. The dark cloud immediately made sense.

"Good morning," the judge said, searching for Jonah's name and coming up dry.

"Hi, I'm Shelby," I said, offering my hand. "Jonah and the rest of the Bodines have been so welcoming to me in town."

The judge looked down at my hand and hesitated briefly. It might have been my imagination, but I thought Mrs. Kendall nudged him before he took my hand. He shook like a limp fish. His palm was soft, smooth like it had never been sullied with manual labor. Mrs. Kendall, on the other hand, had a grip that was firm and bone dry. Her hair was cut in a ruthlessly stylish pixie shape. Her lips were painted a neutral pink, and she was wearing a sedate set of pearls over her ice blue sweater.

"Welcome to Bootleg Springs," she said, her voice quiet yet not soft. "I'm sure you see why my husband and I keep coming back here. It's a lovely escape."

"It's a wonderful town," I agreed.

Inside, I was running through the last updates on the missing person case. These poor parents had been put through the fiasco of having an imposter come forward pretending to be their daughter. And now they were waiting, along with the rest of West Virginia, to find out if the body in New York was all that was left of their hopes of finding Callie alive.

It was miserably unfair. I felt guilty for my knee-jerk reaction to them.

I tried to focus on the tension radiating between Jonah and the Kendalls. Blood of the prime suspect pumped through his veins. The parents wanted answers, and the Bodines were afraid of what those answers might be.

"You're the new Bodine, aren't you?" Mrs. Kendall asked suddenly.

Jonah hesitated for a moment. "Yes. I came to Bootleg last year."

"Did you and your father spend much time together when he was alive?" Judge Kendall asked, interest burning off the coolness in his gray eyes.

Jonah blinked, shook his head. "He wasn't in my life, sir."

Judge Kendall nodded, his expression unreadable. "A sad situation. A child should grow up with their parents."

Mrs. Kendall slid her hand through her husband's arm. It felt as if it was a signal more than a sign of affection. "Every child deserves good memories of their parents," she said. "And every parent deserves a lifetime with their child. Not all of us get what we deserve."

There was an unavoidable bond that linked the three of them together in the summer sunshine. Two people, now long gone, held the answers to the questions.

"I'm sorry for your loss," Jonah said sincerely.

"Thank you," Judge Kendall said. There was something flat about the man's eyes. Empty. Or was it cold?

"Well, it was so nice to meet you both," I said, reaching for Jonah's hand. "But we have a trail to run, don't we, Jonah?" I gave his hand a crushing squeeze.

"Uh. Sure. Have a nice day," Jonah said as I dragged him down the sidewalk.

"What was that about?" he asked.

"If that situation got any more uncomfortable, it would permanently damage our psyches," I whispered, sparing a glance over my shoulder. Judge Kendall was standing in the same spot watching us. A shiver worked its way up my spine. I tossed a friendly wave in his direction.

"Their daughter went missing over a decade ago from this town. And they have to share their vacations with the family of the prime suspect," he said, steering me in the direction of his car. "I think some slack has been earned."

"I get it. It doesn't make it any less awkward," I told him.

The uncomfortable vibe was logical on several levels.

Sometimes people who survived a tragedy were marked by it. There was a distinct Before and After in their family history. Some never returned to the before.

Culturally, there were the psychological constructs of classism to be considered. A judge and his well-to-do wife vs. rural West Virginia. There was an automatic divide between the you alls and the y'alls. The existence of privileges and protections that didn't apply equally.

And of course then came the resulting isolation from a traumatic event that could leave people in their own impenetrable social bubble. No one else could possibly understand how they felt about their daughter's disappearance. And they were surrounded by people here in Bootleg Springs who felt their own sense of ownership over the case.

Walls were necessary for survival sometimes.

I knew that better than anyone.

I slipped. Back to the stairwell, the blood, the sound of footsteps. The razor's edge of fear sharper than any blade.

I felt the slow slide of nausea roll through me. But I brought myself back, calmly. I could tiptoe that line. I could remember without suffering. Much.

"Are you okay?" Jonah asked, concerned. "You went pale."

"I guess I'm a little less steady than I thought." It was the truth, though not necessarily for the reason he suspected.

He opened the passenger door for me, and I gratefully sat.

"I'm taking you home. We're going to work out a training plan that fits your health, and then you're taking a nap."

"No sex? Ten whole minutes, and you're still not sure you

want to consummate our physical relationship? Sheesh. What's a girl got to do?" I teased.

"Don't be a brat. I don't like seeing you go pale like that. You're going to have to get used to having someone care."

Get used to having someone care.

I'd used the physical distance from my family to insulate myself. They'd always worried about me. Adopted Shelby. Nerdy Shelby. I was more interested in reading books on the weekends than going out with friends and kissing boys. To be fair, the boys weren't great kissers. And the friendships I had didn't thrive on conversations about Myers-Briggs personality types that I found fascinating.

I was different, and I fit as best I could by keeping little pieces to myself.

"Maybe it was the fruit?" I mused.

"Your body is detoxing from artificial sweeteners," he predicted.

He looked over his shoulder before easing onto Bathtub Gin Alley, and then he took my hand. Maybe he wasn't ready to make a decision yet, but I could tell in which direction he was leaning. Reassured, I let the memories fade and focused on the feel of the sun on my skin through the open car windows.

———

Q. How do you handle a dispute with a neighbor?

Nadine Tucker: Step 1. The friendly nudge. "I hope you don't mind me sayin', but could y'all do me a favor and not..." Step 2. The gentle warning. "Do you remember how we talked about this or are you touched in the head?" Step 3. "If you do that one more time, I will burn your life to the ground." Step 4. I've never had to activate the nuclear option.

Chapter Twenty-One

Jonah

This is Build A Shine." I pointed to the cedar-shingled building on our right. "You can flavor your own moonshine. Want to give it a try?"

My mother pressed a hand delicately to her mouth. She was hangover chic in khaki shorts, a soft polo, and very large sunglasses. "I think I'll pass on that today."

I chuckled. "You're so hungover right now, aren't you?"

I could feel her glaring through those sunglasses as we continued our stroll. "I'm trying to set a positive example for my son," she complained.

"Mom, I'm thirty-one."

"Not yet. Not 'til Saturday. Don't age yourself faster. It just makes me older," she reprimanded.

"You haven't aged a day," I told her.

"You're a good boy, Jonah."

"I learned from the best."

We wandered up a side street and headed toward Main Street and the park. "This is an adorable town," she observed.

"Even hungover I can appreciate it. Did you know I got a nice little note typed up and slid under my door today?"

I could tell she was gearing up for something.

"They kicking you out already?" I teased.

"No, they just wanted to make sure I knew that my son kissed Shelby Thompson last night."

"Mom!"

"Jonah!" she teased.

"The inn did not hand-deliver a gossip note to you," I argued.

She smiled, and I slung my arm over her shoulder.

"Okay, maybe they didn't deliver a note, but the front desk clerk and the girl who delivered my hangover care pack this morning both made sure to mention it."

"I don't know if it even means anything yet," I said, anticipating the motherly concern. I'd gotten Shelby home, set her up with water and more pain relievers, and tucked her into bed for a nap. It made me feel useful. Being able to do something. To fix something or make it better.

Mom stopped in front of Yee Haw Yarn and Coffee and peered through the window. "I'm just happy that you're happy. Whatever it is. This town." She nodded and said a polite hello to the third person who'd greeted her by name on our walk. "Getting to know your siblings, potentially having protected but expectation-free sex with Shelby. I like seeing you happy."

"You make it sound like I was miserable at home."

"You were grieving. And forgive me for saying so, but part of me wasn't sure if you were grieving Rene or the life you thought you'd have with her."

Was there a difference? Could you love someone and not be attached to how they fit into your life?

"Let's go hit up Moo-Shine and change the subject," I suggested, pointing in the direction of the popular ice cream shop.

"Please tell me they don't put alcohol in their ice cream,"

Mom croaked. "I don't think I can handle any more alcohol in my bloodstream for at least another hour or two."

"I'm sure you can order a virgin butter pecan," I teased. "Now, let's talk about *your* dating life."

"Ugh. Don't even get me started. Have you heard of Tinder?"

"Oh my god, Mom!" I was mildly horrified.

"What I'm looking for is a divorcé with a bunch of grown kids who will give me grandbabies, but all I get are men sending me below-the-belt selfies."

I made an urgent mental note to steal my mother's phone and delete the app just in case she was telling the truth and not just trying to get a rise out of me.

"You always wanted a big family," I said, ignoring the bait.

"Instead I had to settle for my one perfect boy," she said, tucking her arm around my waist.

It was an old routine, but this was the first time I heard the wistfulness in her tone.

Moo-Shine's Ice Cream and Cheese shop was a free-standing building tucked into a copse of trees on one end of Main Street. It had the requisite red-and-white striped ice cream shop awning as well as a collection of picnic tables clustered under the pine trees. There were walk-up windows for warm weather orders on the side. Inside, the floors were black and white tile, the tables were round and red, and the ice cream and cheese selection was unbeatable.

"Ooh. Cheese," my mom cooed, peering into the case.

"We can get some to go," I promised her. "But first, ice cream."

We ordered. Chocolate frozen yogurt for me and Blue Moon with sprinkles for her.

The shop was crowded with residents and summertimers, so we headed back outside and snagged a table.

"Hey, Jonah. Hey, Jenny," EmmaLeigh, pretty and perky, said with a wave as she hustled her four kids through the ice cream shop's doors.

"How does everyone know my name?" Mom asked. "I haven't even been here twenty-four hours yet."

"Give them another twenty-four hours, and they'll have a complete dossier on your life since birth," I teased.

"I'm going to grab a water. Do you want one?" she offered, getting up from the table.

"Sure, thanks."

She went inside, and I gave my full attention to my yogurt. My phone chimed in my pocket. A text from Shelby.

Shelby: Nap complete.
Me: Feeling better?
Shelby: Still sore, but a lot better than last night. I think this is a mild flare. According to my research, I should be feeling significantly better soon.

I hesitated to respond. I liked that she was discussing her diagnosis with me and wanted her to feel safe enough to continue to do so. But I also didn't want to move us into intimate territory before we were ready.

Me: Good. Do me a favor?
Shelby: Sure!
Me: Tell your rheumatologist you're signed up for a triathlon.

And cue the crickets. I waited a minute, noting my mom was holding the front door of the shop open for a man. Jimmy Bob Prosser, hardware store owner and flannel connoisseur.

Me: Stop pouting. Just ask him or her if they have any specific advice on how to proceed with training.
Shelby: Fine.

She included an annoyed emoji.

Me: Jimmy Bob Prosser is putting the moves on my mother.

Shelby: Which Bootleg eligible bachelor is he? Oh no. He's not the one with the taxidermy hobby, is he?

Me: No. Thank God. JBP owns the hardware store.

Shelby: Oh! He's very handsome. I approve this match.

Me: He's also Misty Lynn's father.

Shelby: We don't know for sure if that's a nature or nurture problem. He could still be a nice stepfather for you. What's their body language saying?

Me: What would body language say?

There was another minute of silence from Shelby while I watched Mom laugh at something Jimmy Bob said to her.

Shelby: Uh-oh. George needs me at his and June's place. Some kind of emergency. Keep me posted.

Me: You too.

I looked up from my phone to see Jimmy Bob Prosser give my mother a sample of his ice cream cone.

"What the hell?"

"You glaring at anyone in particular?" Gibson scared the hell out of me, and I almost dropped my frozen yogurt.

"What are you doing here?" I asked.

"You stupid? It's summer. This is an ice cream shop."

"Sorry. I'm distracted. Tell me everything you know about Jimmy Bob Prosser," I said, pointing my spoon in his direction.

Gibson followed my gaze. "Huh. You got a problem with your mom being human?"

I blinked. "No. I wish her a happy and healthy sex life that I hope to never know anything about. I just want to make sure he's good enough."

"He took over the hardware store from his parents. His wife, Misty Lynn's mama, skipped town a few years back to follow her dreams of being a singer or an actress. Some shit like that. Heard she never made it farther than one of those restaurants where the servers sing and dance."

"Is he the reason Misty Lynn turned out the way she turned out?"

Gibson shrugged. "Some eggs are just hatched rotten."

My mom threw her head back and laughed at something Jimmy Bob said. She brushed her hand down his arm.

"Uh-oh," Gibson said. "That's definitely female interest there."

"I want her to be happy," I said, reminding myself it was true. "But is it too much to ask that I get to pick who she's happy with?"

"They're just flirting," he cautioned. "No need to freak out."

"Why is he getting out his phone?" I asked. "What the hell? Did she just give him her number?"

"Okay, a slight reason to freak out. Want me to have Cass run him for you? Background check, known priors?" he offered.

My phone buzzed.

Shelby: Bigger emergency than I thought. Can you get over here?????

"Shit. Five question marks. That's not good."

"What's up?" my brother asked.

"Shelby has an emergency. But I can't leave my mom in the clutches of someone named Jimmy Bob."

"I'll hang," he volunteered. "Keep an eye, make sure she gets back to the inn."

"Alone?" I pressed, already backing away.

He cracked a smile.

"Alone," he promised.

"Thanks, man. I owe you."

Me: On my way.

Chapter Twenty-Two

Shelby

I was wandering around June and GT's front yard whistling and clapping my hands when Jonah pulled up. My body was still stiff, still sore, but at least I was ambulatory. Another hot bath was definitely in the cards for me tonight, I decided.

"What's the emergency?" he asked, climbing out of the car looking six shades of delicious. I'd had breakfast with the man this morning, let him talk me into bed—alone, unfortunately—for a nap before lunch, and I still got the little dip and slide in my stomach when I saw his gorgeous face, concern written all over it.

"Oh, thank God, man," my brother said jogging around the side of the house. "I fucked up. Big time." GT shoved his hands into his hair.

"This doesn't involve a body, does it?" Jonah asked.

"Oh, God. Shel! What if she makes a run for the road?" GT said, letting his imagination off its leash.

"She'll be just fine, GT. Calm down," I said, scouring the underbrush.

"Did you maim someone and hold them captive?" Jonah asked.

"No, she just got loose. Marshmellow scared her, and she just bolted right out the door. Oh my god. June's at the office for a meeting today. What if she finds her on the road? What if June finds her hit on the road? What if June hits her on the road?"

"GT, take a breath. She's not going anywhere near the road, and Juney isn't going to find her."

"Someone please explain so I can decide if I'm helping or avoiding becoming an accessory," Jonah said.

"GT got June a potbellied pig as a surprise," I explained. "His bunny Mellow scared the crap out of the poor pig, and she bolted."

"She doesn't even have a name yet. I mean, I think it's gonna be Katherine. But I didn't tell her yet," GT said. "We can't call her by the name she doesn't have. This was supposed to be the best surprise. Now there's a pig running around becoming a bear snack."

"I knew there were bears here!" I said triumphantly.

Jonah held up his hands. "Let's deal with one problem at a time. Did you see which way Nameless Pig went?"

GT paced. "She ran out the back, and I tripped trying to avoid Mellow." Mellow weighed maybe two pounds in my estimation. The fact that my gigantic football hulk of a brother twisted to fall on his girlfriend's breakfast table—breaking it in half—rather than squish a bunny was adorably sweet and oh so GT.

There were woods behind the house and a trail. It was as good a place as any to start.

"What does she eat?" I asked my brother.

"She eats vegetables mostly and some pig pellets," he said.

"Okay, I need you to put some of the pellets into a container with hard sides. Something that will make noise when I shake it. Got it?" Jonah said, catching on.

"Yeah. Okay." GT nodded. "Yeah, that's good." He charged into the house.

"What's the plan, Inspector Pig Finder?" I asked Jonah.

"Start warming up. You and I are going for a little jog."

We left GT behind us in case No Name circled back. Also, the fact was a 300-pound receiver lumbering through the woods would probably scare the poor creature farther away.

The trail behind the house was rocky and uneven, but the woods were thin enough that we could see in all directions. While we jogged, Jonah shook the container as I called "Here, pig, pig, pig!"

"I didn't think to ask. Is she friendly?" he asked, scouring the tree line ahead.

We were taking it slow, and my joints were grateful for it.

"I think so. GT said she rode like a dog in the passenger seat on the way home. He adopted her from a rescue, and all the staff there just loved her. Here, pig, pig, pig!"

We ran in silence for a few moments, and I had to admit that it felt good to be out and moving in the sunshine. Even though I was hunting for a missing potbellied pig instead of training for a triathlon or, you know, actually writing my dissertation.

"I've had a lot of expectations about my life. This scenario was not one of them," I mused.

Jonah cracked a smile beside me. God, he was good-looking. He wasn't broad like my brother. He wasn't broody like his brother Gibson. He was tall and lean with sharp cheekbones and grass green eyes that looked into you. But it was the smile that took him into the interesting stratosphere.

"Given any thought to my offer?" I asked cheerfully.

Jonah stumbled on the path, and I grabbed his arm to hold him upright.

"Jeez, Shelby. Aren't researchers supposed to be patient?"

"Oh, come on," I said, scanning the field that opened up on my right. "I was kidding, mostly. Besides, what else are we going to talk about on our pig hunt?"

"You brought it up hours ago," he complained. "I said I'd think about it."

I liked seeing him flustered.

"You're not just trying to come up with a way to tell me you aren't attracted to me, are you?" I asked.

He slowed his pace and came to a stop, still shaking the container of pellets. "Look. It's been a while for me," he confessed.

"How long is a while? A month? Six months?"

"Fifteen."

"Fifteen days?" I pressed.

"Fifteen *months*."

That was longer than I expected. That was longer than my longest dry spell. That was longer than most of the relationships I'd been in. "Whoa," I said, catching my breath. "Since Rene?" I asked.

"Yeah. So there's some pressure. Kissing you was the first contact I'd had in a long time, and it was overwhelming. Kind of rattled me," he admitted. "I don't know if I'm ready to explore that."

There was that vulnerability again. And I was a sucker for it.

"As much as I'd like to take credit for an earth-shattering kiss," I told him, "there was ambiance. We were outside under the stars. There was a bonfire and a proposal. It was orchestrated for romance. You were reacting to physical and mental stimuli. That's all. It's biology with some fun chemistry thrown in."

He studied me. "So if we kissed—say right now—it wouldn't be the same 'stimuli' and therefore not the same outcome?"

"We're sweating half to death chasing a pig—which, by the way, only in Bootleg, am I right? I think it's safe to say that, no, it would not be the same chemical reaction. But we could test the theory. We're only changing one variable, the environment," I mused, intrigued with the idea. Also always up for a kiss that would melt my bones.

"Are you suggesting I kiss you right now?" he asked.

"Do it for science, Jonah," I teased.

He laughed softly, stepping in close. My body was already humming at his proximity.

"Hang on," he said, putting the container of pellets on the ground. "Let's do this right."

Instead of threading his hands into my hair, this time Jonah slid them around my waist pulling me in until we were pressed up against each other. My back was sweaty. I hadn't bothered with deodorant this morning. My bangs were everywhere. But his serious eyes demanded my full attention.

He was moving in soft and slow again. "Wait." I put my hand up and held him where he was. "I'll kiss you this time." On the off chance that him slow-motion kissing me was the trigger for earth-shifting-under-our-feet, it would be safer to change up the process.

"Okay," he said, his voice husky.

I slipped my arms around his neck and rose on my tiptoes. "Are you ready for this?"

He nodded, his fingers disrupting the trickle of sweat running down my back.

I skipped the slow motion and went in hot.

It was supposed to be fun and light. Reassuring. Friendly even.

But our mouths met, and everything went sideways. It wasn't the sounds of summer in Bootleg that I heard now. It was his breath, ragged and harsh. The sun disappeared from my skin, and instead I felt the heat and pressure of his hands. The erection stirring in his shorts. The hammer-like thud of my heart in my chest.

I was the aggressor here, opening my mouth and sinking my teeth into that perfect lower lip of his.

"Shelby," he growled.

And then our tongues were tangling, hands roaming, teeth biting. He slipped his hands under my t-shirt, thumbs resting under the band of my sports bra. His broad palms spanning my rib cage.

I went for the gold. I removed my arms from around his neck and shoved my hands into the back of his shorts, squeezing the world's most perfect ass.

His erection was at full attention now, throbbing against my stomach.

Biology was so damn sexy.

The kiss was wildly unpredictable, both of us fighting to deepen it. Both of us fighting to hold back. And I realized too late that this would do nothing to relieve his concerns. I decided to worry about that later.

At least until what sounded like an ear-splitting shriek cracked the cone of sexy that surrounded us.

We pulled back and stared at each other. "I'm very stimulated," I whispered. My lips felt swollen. Jonah's eyes had gone to green glass. His grip on me was deliciously possessive.

"What the hell was that?" he asked, finally breaking through the sexual haze.

One hell of a kiss.

The shriek sounded again. High-pitched and frantic.

"That's a pig! Come on!"

Chapter Twenty-Three

Jonah

That is *not* a baby pig," I said, eyeing the hefty black form that trotted down the path to us.

"Potbellied pigs can weigh up to 120 pounds," Shelby recited. "I'm not sure how I know that."

No Name had to be at least fifty pounds and had black bristly hair and a curly tail that was wagging like a delighted dog. "There's a halter but no leash," I said, the realization sinking in. "How are we going to get her back to the house?"

Shelby gnawed on the lower lip that I'd just kissed. I was still fully hard, the aftereffects of a second world-tilting kiss still occupying most of my brain power and blood supply. I was definitely going to worry about the outcome of our experiment later. For now, I had to figure out how to get a pig home.

"Maybe she'll just follow us?" she said hopefully.

The pig pranced up to us stopping about six feet out. It squealed and danced on dainty hooves.

Adjusting my hard-on, I squatted down and held out my hand. "This works for dogs, but I'm not sure about pigs." If I could get a hand on her, I could pick her up…and then carry her the mile back to the house.

She pranced away and then back again, squealing insistently.

"Am I stupid for saying that it looks like she wants us to follow her?" I asked.

"I'm so glad you said it. I didn't want you to think I was an idiot. What's the matter, piggy? Is someone stuck in a well?" Shelby asked, head cocked.

The pig bowed on its front feet like a dog and then jogged up the path in front of us. She stopped a few yards out and hurried back.

I shrugged and stood. "Looks like a 'yes' to me. Let's see where she's going."

The pig seemed delighted that we were following her. She scurried a few yards in front of us over the crest of the trail before veering off into the meadow. Tall grass tangled around rock outcroppings and trunks of trees.

"Is now a good time to mention I really don't want to step on one of those poisonous snakes that reside in rural West Virginia?" she confessed.

"At least we'll be able to see the bears coming."

"You're so silver lining-y," she said.

We picked up the pace. The pig was on a mission. I just hoped she wasn't leading us to a giant pile of shit or a dead body. If a Bodine was found in the vicinity of a dead body, law enforcement would have a shit fit.

The pig came to a stop in front of a few jagged rocks under a huge hickory tree. The shade was a welcome respite. I swiped the sweat out of my eyes with the hem of my t-shirt. The breeze stirred the leaves over our heads.

The pig squealed and then lay down.

"What's that?" Shelby asked, venturing closer. "Oh my god, Jonah."

It was a puppy. At least I thought it was a puppy. The poor thing's fur was matted with mud and probably shit. It had a dirty rope around its neck. The end of which was tangled in loose branches and rocks.

It whimpered.

"Oh, you poor baby!" Shelby eased in, carefully not to startle the pig or the pup.

The pig nudged her hand, and Shelby gave her a stroke. "You're a hero, little pig. You just saved this baby's life."

I edged in and grimly went to work on the rope. It was filthy, and the dog's neck was rubbed raw beneath it. "Whoever had this dog is not getting him back."

"Oh, he *is* a he!" Shelby said with delight as she lifted him carefully into her lap. Listlessly, he lapped at her hand. It was impossible to tell what color he was through the layers of dirt and mud and God knows what else. But he had the floppy-eared look of the beagle my neighbors had in Jetty Beach.

"He's probably dehydrated and hungry as fuck," I predicted.

"Get the pellets," she ordered. "And bring me the water bottle I dropped."

I did as instructed. Shelby cupped her hands in front of the puppy, and I poured the now warm water into her palms.

If dogs could be grateful, this puppy was worshipping Shelby. He drank deeply, and I refilled her hands.

The pig nosed her way in.

"Are you thirsty, too?" Shelby laughed. "I bet with all that running you did."

We gave them the rest of the water and then the treats. The puppy devoured the pig kibble as if it were Kobe beef.

"Two animals and no leashes," Shelby said, eyeing me.

I sighed. "I'll carry the pig."

———

"Hey, remember that time we kissed and then carried a pig and a puppy all the way home? Talk about a memorable summer fling." Shelby joked behind me.

It was a long, sticky walk back. The pig seemed happy enough to be carried but had to continually reassure herself with glances over my shoulder at the puppy cradled in Shelby's arms. I had the heavier of the two, but Shelby was holding the one that smelled like cow shit.

We were within a hundred yards of the house when George lumbered up the trail. "Katherine!" He ran to us, and the pig scrambled against my chest.

"Katherine?" I asked. It was an interesting name for the pig.

"After Katherine Johnson, the NASA mathematician," he said reaching his receiver paws for the pig.

I handed her over.

"You're a good boyfriend, GT. June's going to love Katherine," Shelby predicted with a grin.

"Why are you holding a lump of dirt?" Her brother moved in closer, caught a whiff, and backed off again. "Jesus, are you carrying a load of shit?"

"Oh, this old thing? This is just the puppy your pig saved," Shelby said.

I slapped George on the shoulder and shook out my arms to get the circulation moving again. "Your pet pig is a hero. She led us right to him."

He ushered us in through the back, this time securing the door behind us.

Mellow the bunny hopped into the kitchen.

"Now, listen, Katherine. You and Mellow have to be friends. There are no other options. Got it?" he explained.

The pig wiggled, and George set her gently on the tile floor. She tiptoed toward the fluffy bunny. The bunny took a tentative hop closer. Katherine's nose twitched as she leaned in for a sniff.

"Huh. Guess you're not scared anymore," George observed.

"Aren't pigs highly intelligent?" Shelby asked from the kitchen sink where she was preparing the disgusting puppy for a bath. "Maybe she knew this little guy was in trouble?"

While Mellow hopped off with Katherine on her heels, George flopped down in a kitchen chair next to the totaled table that lay crumpled on the floor. "You're my fucking heroes."

"You'll be June's hero when she gets home from the office today," Shelby promised him.

I joined her at the sink and dug around for the dish detergent. "This should be safe for him." I turned the water on and let it warm up. The puppy scrambled against the stainless steel, but Shelby kept him contained.

"This is for your own good, little man. You smell like a porta potty," she warned him.

We washed and dried the little guy. And tried to keep him from drinking the filthy bathwater and eating the soap bubbles. He was getting cuter by the minute.

He had patches of brown and black and white with huge velvety ears.

George stopped chasing Katherine around with the big red bow he was trying to affix to her long enough to share some ground chicken and rice with the puppy. His tail wagged while he ate, and the tips of his ears dipped into the bowl.

Shelby interlaced her fingers with mine. "What are we going to do with him? And before you say look for the owner, I'm going to stop you right there. Whoever tied him around the neck with a rope deserves to be run over by a pickup truck and pecked to death by Mona Lisa."

"Agreed. Let's get him to the vet, have him checked out. Then we'll go from there," I said, watching as the little guy fell asleep in his food.

"We can't keep him," she said, staring at the dog with hearts in her eyes. "Can we?"

"Of course not. How would we decide who keeps him at the end of the summer? It would be a custody disaster."

"Right. Of course," she agreed. But the hearts were still there.

The pup sneezed in his sleep, and the sound was just about the cutest thing I'd heard in my entire life. "We'll keep him for now," I decided. "Until we can find him a good home."

"Fostering. Okay." She nodded and squeezed my hand. "Thanks for carrying my brother's pig all the way back."

"Sentences you only hear in Bootleg Springs."

She laughed and released my hand. "GT, we're going to take Katherine's puppy to the vet," she called as she walked into the living room. "What's all this? Is June getting a doctorate, too?"

I followed her into the room. It was a comfortable space despite its over-the-top tidiness. Bookcases jammed with books flanked both sides of the brick fireplace. In front of them were stacks of boxes and a whiteboard with notes scrawled across it.

"That's Scooby June's Callie Kendall research," George said, adjusting Katherine's bow and giving the pig a scratch. "She was convinced there was something wrong with Fake Callie's story and did some digging."

"That's a lot of digging," Shelby observed. I could tell she was impressed.

"When she gets focused on something, she doesn't stop." He grinned, flipping the lid off the top box.

"I need to learn her ways or I'm never going to finish my dissertation," she complained, peering into the box.

Mellow hopped over to me and sniffed my shoe. I leaned down to stroke the bunny's soft fur.

"Don't get her started on research," I warned him. "You'll have two Scoobys in the house."

"What's this file about Constance Bodine?" Shelby asked, her interest piqued.

I made myself comfortable on the couch. Mellow eyed me expectantly, so I picked her up.

"Turns out that Connie Bodine's accident might not have been an accident," GT explained.

I thought of my mother and realized I hadn't had a status update from Gibson yet. Had he left his post? Had my mother been coaxed into a pickup truck by Jimmy Bob Prosser?

"What would that have to do with Callie Kendall?" Shelby asked.

GT shrugged. "Probably nothing. But she died coming back from some big fundraiser thing Mrs. Kendall attended in Baltimore."

"That's an odd coincidence," Shelby mused.

"That's what June thought, too. It's not like they ran in similar social circles."

The puppy woke with a bark and skittered into the room. He stopped at my feet, tail wagging. I leaned down and picked him up. He cuddled up against the bunny, licked Mellow, then me.

"Are you purposely trying to be the sexiest man in the universe right now?"

I looked up and found Shelby watching me, hands on hips. "You're cuddling a puppy *and* a bunny."

She had those hearts in her eyes again, but this time they were directed at me. And I sure as hell liked it. I had a feeling my dry spell might finally come to its official end.

Chapter Twenty-Four
Shelby

I'd thought for sure I'd be getting naked tonight. Especially after that kiss.

Instead I was setting the table for three.

Not that I didn't *like* Jenny Leland. She was lovely and bright and funny. She was also the mother of the guy I was trying to see naked. And as such, she was essentially cock-blocking me. However, given Jonah's uncertainty and all the excitement of the day with pigs and puppies, I was prepared to be patient.

"Aren't you just the smartest little guy in the whole wide world?" Jenny cooed at the puppy, who sat his wiggling butt on the floor when she held up one of the treats Jonah had picked up at the Pop In today. He'd been a favorite at the vet earlier. Malnourished and underweight, covered in fleas. But friendly and sweet. He was given a bag of special dog food, a flea bath, and an optimistic bill of health. We were given a coupon to Pet Paradise, a pet store in downtown Bootleg.

We'd gone on a spree that included food, dishes, collars

and leashes, a crate with memory foam mattress, and an entire basket of toys. For our temporary dog.

A pan sizzled in the kitchen where Jonah was cooking something that smelled suspiciously of vegetables.

"Can I top off your wine?" I offered Jenny.

She held out her glass and smiled. "I'm allowed this refill, and that's it. I don't think I can survive another Bootleg hangover so early in my visit."

She was a pretty woman with short blonde hair and a long, lean frame. It wasn't hard to guess where Jonah got his quick grin and those gorgeous green eyes.

"What are you guys going to name him?" she asked me, nodding at the dog while I poured.

"Jonah and I have gone a couple rounds over it," I confessed. "For two people who aren't keeping a dog, we're putting way too much thought into a name. But we finally settled on Billy Ray, in homage to his country roots."

Jenny laughed and studied the dog as he pounced on a green alligator squeak toy. "Welcome to the family, Billy Ray."

As if in acknowledgment, Billy Ray tipped over on his back and wiggled in delight.

"Dinner's ready," Jonah called from the kitchen.

"Need any help?" I asked.

"Just make yourselves comfortable. I'll bring it in."

"It's probably something healthy," I warned Jenny. "But I picked up a pie from the bakery for dessert, so we just have to make it through the vegetables."

"You're adorable," she observed. "I can see why my son is interested in you."

I felt my face flush with pleasure at the thought. Was this a weird conversation to be having with a potential sexual partner's mother? I was of the opinion that the United States was a bit too prudish about something as natural as sex. And that opinion often led me to make people uncomfortable in polite conversation. For instance, how the physical connection

147

accomplished through sex was often pursued as a way to feel more connected, less alienated or lonely.

Not exactly dinner conversation.

"Ladies, please give my vegetable and beef stir-fry the standing ovation it deserves," Jonah announced from the doorway of the dining room. He hefted a wok, the contents still steaming. And still smelling healthy.

Jenny applauded. I sniffed apprehensively.

"A few bites, and if you hate it, you can nuke your nuggets," he promised me.

"Jonah is trying to expand my palate," I said to Jenny.

"It's stunted in four-year-old territory," he explained to his mother.

"Really?" She asked pulling out a chair. "What's your favorite meal?"

"I rely heavily on small microwavable pizzas and chicken nuggets. If I'm feeling fancy, I go for a box of mac and cheese."

"Jonah tells me you're pursuing a doctorate in social work. Have you experienced any of the phobias associated with being a restrictive eater?"

I lit up, remembering Jenny had been working on a psychology degree when she'd gotten pregnant with Jonah.

He rolled his eyes and dished out the food while his mother and I debated the social stigmas of picky eating.

"Speaking of eating habits," I said, changing the subject before he got bored. "I heard you had ice cream with a few of Bootleg's eligible bachelors this afternoon."

Jenny smiled and looked at her plate. "I met a very charming hardware store owner," she said.

"Jimmy Bob Prosser certainly is handsome," I prodded.

Jonah didn't look exactly thrilled over the turn in conversation, but he didn't get defensive either. *Points for him,* I decided.

"And then I spent some time with Gibson. He showed me his shop."

Jonah looked up from the stir-fry. "Gibson Bodine?"

Jenny nodded, looking amused.

"He willingly took you to his place?" he pressed.

She laughed. "He did. He showed me the cabinets he's working on right now. It's this custom bar for a client in Perrinville. They're stunning. He does incredible work."

"Mom, I lived here for six months before I even saw the man's driveway," he said.

I pushed a snow pea around my plate trying to soak up as much of the sauce as possible to drown out the vegetable-ness. I took a breath and popped it in my mouth. It wasn't my favorite. But the sauce was nice. I could probably choke down a few more bites, make a good impression.

"I think he's kind of lonely," Jenny mused.

I slapped the table enthusiastically. "I think so, too!"

"He's not lonely," Jonah argued. "He's a loner. There's a difference."

"He can be both," I insisted.

"I really like him," she said. "Scarlett, too. It's hard not to fall in love with her. And Jameson and Bowie seem like good men."

"They're a tight family, good people," I supplied.

"Good people waiting to find out if their father was a drunk and a murderer or just a drunk," Jonah said.

I stuffed a bite of beef in my mouth. He never talked about the "situation." Not around me. I knew he was protective toward the Bodines, but I was still curious how he felt about it all.

Jenny reached over and took his hand. "Your father, their father, was no murderer. I'm sure of that."

"That's all well and good, Mom. But opinions won't give either family any peace," Jonah said. "We ran into the Kendalls this morning, and you can just see the toll this is taking on them."

Her eyes widened.

"The investigation has been going on for quite some time since Scarlett found the sweater in her father's things after he passed away," I explained.

I was curious how Jenny felt about the father of her only child and his untimely death, his unhappy life. But, again, the dinner table probably wasn't the place to dig into those questions. "I think everyone is frustrated and fatigued without any firm answers. We may never know for sure what happened to Callie Kendall."

"Jonah's wife, Connie, died in a car accident about a year after the Kendall girl disappeared," Jonah told his mother. "Now they're saying there's a possibility that it wasn't an accident at all."

Jenny fumbled her fork, and it fell to her plate with a clang.

Billy Ray woke with a start from his nap under the table and started barking. Then the barking switched to howling.

"Definitely some beagle in the little guy," Jonah shouted over the ruckus.

"Billy Ray! Quiet down, now," I said, poking my head under the table. The dog looked surprised by his own big voice.

Jonah's phone rang in the kitchen. He glanced down at his fitness watch. "Huh."

"What's wrong?" I asked.

"Scarlett's calling, and I just got a bunch of messages from Bowie."

He left the table and answered his phone.

"Slow down, Scar. What channel?"

From the table, Jenny and I watched him pace into the living room and turn on the TV.

The evening news anchor was talking about Callie Kendall.

I pushed my chair back and hurried to join Jonah in the living room.

"The skull had been missing from the skeletal remains found a few weeks ago outside of Cleary. The human remains were discovered during excavation for a housing development. Experts believe the bones are between eleven and thirteen years old, a timeline that coincides with the high-profile disappearance of sixteen-year-old Callie Kendall. With the discovery of the skull, investigators are confident the remains will be identified through dental records," the anchor said.

"Yeah, I heard it," Jonah said into his phone. "Okay. Thanks." He disconnected the call and tossed his phone on the couch.

He shoved a hand through his hair. "Am I an ass for hoping the Kendalls aren't about to get the closure they deserve?"

"You're not an ass," I assured him.

"Jonah," Jenny began from the doorway.

Just then the doorbell rang, and the dog tore out from under the table, barking his sweet little head off.

"Jeez, Billy Ray," Jonah complained.

"I'll get the door. You get the dog," I yelled over the ruckus.

I pulled the front door open and stopped in surprise. "Mom? Dad?"

Chapter Twenty-Five

Jonah

S urprise!" the couple at the front door sang in unison.
Then Shelby was flinging the screen door open and jumping into their arms.

"That Scarlett sure has been busy," Mom observed behind me. I nipped Billy Ray under his little puppy armpits and picked him up. He licked my face with enthusiasm.

"What are you two doing here?" Shelby asked, pressing a kiss to her father's cheek and another to her mother's. He was tall and broad, and I could tell where GT got his shoulders. She was softer, quieter, and had a good four inches of leg on her daughter. Both had a good amount of silver in their hair—cropped short for him and poker-straight and shoulder-length for her.

Adopted, I remembered when I searched for the familial resemblance that would tie Shelby to them. But there didn't need to be a physical link. Not when they were all so obviously happy to see each other.

"We missed you and your brother," Shelby's mom said, giving her daughter another squeeze for good measure.

"And your friend Scarlett gave us a great deal on a rental for the week," her father said cheerfully.

Shelby turned and met my gaze.

Damn that Scarlett Bodine.

Of *course* my sister had had available rentals while telling us we had to cohabitate.

"Well, get in here! Was GT surprised to see you?" Shelby asked, ushering them inside.

My mom and I shared a short, meaningful look. Both of us wondering why Shelby assumed they'd go to GT first.

"We came straight here," her dad insisted. "Your brother's been good about emailing, but you, young lady, keep trying to disappear off the face of the Earth."

Shelby laughed nervously. "I've just been—"

"Busy," her parents finished for her.

"I can see why," her mom said, eyeing me from the doorway.

Billy Ray scrambled up my chest and stuck his nose in my face.

"Mom, Dad, this is Jonah and not our dog Billy Ray. And this is Jonah's mom, Jenny. Jonah, Jenny, these are my parents Darlene and James."

Introductions were made, handshakes exchanged. "How about I open another bottle of wine?" my mother volunteered.

"I'll get more glasses," Shelby said. The two of them ducked into the kitchen. And the Thompsons watched me expectantly. Well, Darlene watched me. James made kissy noises at the dog.

"Are you two hungry?" I asked. "We've got plenty of stir-fry."

"Stir-fry?" Darlene said, her eyebrows arching. "Chicken nugget stir-fry?"

"Har har, Mom," Shelby called from the kitchen. "Jonah's forcing me to eat better to help my training for the triathlon."

"Triathlon?" James brightened, looking interested.

I assumed the father of a professional athlete probably had an innate enjoyment of sports.

"Triathlon?" her mother repeated.

Shelby and my mom returned with glasses of wine. "I signed up for one at the beginning of August. Jonah is a personal trainer and is helping me get ready for it."

Darlene looked surprised. "Here," I said, handing her Billy Ray. Puppies made everyone happier.

"Oh, look at this sweet face," she said in rapture. "What happened to his poor little neck?"

"Someone tied this poor baby up with a rope." My mom and Shelby filled them in on how exactly we found him.

"An escaped potbellied pig led you to him?" Darlene asked, returning to surprised.

"That escaped potbellied pig is your grandchild," Shelby told them. "So be prepared for that when you get to GT's."

"Welcome to Bootleg Springs," I said, raising my wine glass to them.

———

My mother was with James and Darlene on the front porch admiring the slow set of the sun through the leaves while Shelby and I cleaned up in the tiny kitchen.

"That kiss today," I began, keeping my voice low.

"You mean our interrupted experiment?" she asked, amused.

"Yeah. That."

"Don't worry about it, Jonah," she assured me, nudging me with her elbow. "If and when you're ready to experiment again, you know where to find me. I don't want to rush you into being the most memorable no-strings-attached sexual experience of my adult life."

I appreciated that. "Thanks," I said. "I think I need to go see my brothers, and maybe you want to spend some time alone with your parents."

"I think that's a good idea," Shelby agreed. "Why

don't you take Billy Ray with you? Puppies make everyone happier."

"I like that you think about other people," I said, reaching out and tracing her lower lip with my thumb.

"Well, that was a sweet thing to say," she said, sounding baffled.

I grinned and brushed my lips over her bangs. "I'll see you around, Shelby."

"Bye, Jonah."

I rounded up the pup and packed half of his belongings in case he needed a snack or a drink or a toy or flea medicine. I said my goodbyes, kissed my mother goodnight, and dialed Bowie on my way down the driveway.

"I feel like we should hang out, talk," I said.

"Jameson called me five minutes ago. I was just getting ready to text you," Bowie said. "Gibson's in fifteen?"

"Sounds good to me. I'm bringing a special guest," I warned him.

"Yeah, well, I'm bringing a twelve-pack."

Gibson's house was a good half-mile up switchbacks and hairpin turns. I had no idea how the man made it home in the winter.

I was the first brother to arrive. I ignored the house, an austere log cabin built on land that had once belonged to his grandfather—our grandfather, I corrected—and followed the lights coming from the workshop. It was the large metal pole building that Gibson spent more time in than his actual house.

Snapping the leash on Billy Ray's collar, I put him down. "You'd probably better pee out here before we go in there. If you piss on one of Gibson's custom cabinets, there's no telling what he'll do."

As if not willing to sully his first impression, Billy Ray sniffed and lifted his leg on a sapling.

"Good job, buddy."

He did two more good jobs before we made it to the shop door.

I skipped knocking, since the music was loud, and let myself in. The smells of polyurethane and sawdust melded together in a satisfying scent of manly productivity. Toby Keith belted one out on the speakers mounted in the rafters.

Gibson was at a workbench against the wall organizing hand tools. He had an open root beer in his hand. Gibs didn't drink. Ever.

He tapped his phone, and the music's volume cut in half. "What the hell is that?" he asked, pointing the bottle at the dog at my feet.

"That's your temporary nephew, Billy Ray."

He bent at the waist and slapped his thighs. "C'mere, buddy. Come on!"

The dog perked up and, deciding the big man with the surly expression looked like a good source of attention, bounded across the concrete.

"That's a good boy," Gibs said, ruffing the puppy up. Billy Ray dissolved into ecstasy and flopped over on his back inviting belly rubs.

The door banged open again. Bowie, followed by Jameson, strolled inside.

"I got beer and root beer," Bowie announced, holding up two twelve-packs. "Who wants?"

I caught the can he tossed in my direction.

"What the hell is that?" Jameson asked, looking at the dog now cradled in Gibson's arms.

"That's Billy Ray, my special guest," I told them, filling them in on the day of pigs, puppies, and surprise visitors. They took turns asking questions and calling bullshit on the fact that I walked a mile carrying a fifty-pound pig. Even going so far as to text George for confirmation.

Small talk complete, we drew up stools around a relatively clean work table. Billy Ray contented himself to fall asleep in Gibson's arms.

"So," Bowie said, popping the top on a beer.

"So," Jameson repeated.

"Not much to say," Gibson said, staring down at the puppy. "Either it's her, or it's not."

"What happens if it is?" I asked.

"I talked to Jayme on my way here," Bowie said. "If the remains are Callie's, there's still only circumstantial evidence connecting Dad to her."

"And he's still dead," Gibson said. He sounded more resigned than bitter.

"The Kendalls will get closure," Jameson said. "But we'll have that shadow hanging over the rest of us."

"We've dealt with shadows before," Bowie said. "We'll handle this one, too. It doesn't change who we are." He looked directly at me. "None of us."

I nodded. And most of me believed him. The four of us were already better than the man who'd made us. I just hoped that the rest of the world would see that.

"Now that that's settled, I'd like to ask y'all to be in my wedding," Bowie announced.

Billy Ray woke with a start and sneezed in Gibson's face.

Wiping puppy saliva off his face, Gibs grinned. "What's in it for us?"

"All the root beer you can drink," Bowie offered.

"We can probably make ourselves available," Jameson mused, answering for all of us.

"When is it?" I asked.

"First weekend in August."

"Well, hell. You're not wasting any time," I observed, checking the calendar on my phone. First weekend in August. Shelby's triathlon. That would require some juggling. Two events that I didn't want to miss.

"I've waited a long-ass time," Bowie said. "And if it were strictly up to me, we'd be gettin' hitched tomorrow."

"Suits me," Jameson mused, looking at the bandages on his fingers. "My ring is finally done. Now it's just figurin' how to pop the question. No interference with your engagement or your wedding, of course."

"Appreciate it, Jame," Bowie said, clinking bottles.

"Now that that's settled, let's talk about Jimmy Bob Prosser gettin' all tongue-tied around Jonah's mama today," Gibson said, stroking the puppy's head.

Chapter Twenty-Six
Shelby

"Well, *that* was an eventful day. Puppies, pigs, and parents," I said, passing Jonah in the hallway outside of the bathroom. He was shirtless—did the man ever bother with a shirt?—and his shorts rode low on his delightfully defined hips.

How much half-naked man could a girl nerd take before she snapped?

I made a note to research unrequited lust tomorrow. People could die from broken hearts. What were the side effects of unused, inflamed sex organs?

"Yeah. What's with Scarlett surprising everyone with their parents?" he asked, stretching. The muscles in his chest and abdomen moved hypnotically.

"Huh? What?" I said, trying to snap myself out of the physical attraction fugue state.

"Scarlett. What's with her springing our parents on us?"

Tearing my gaze away from his impressive torso, I bent down and picked up Billy Ray. "Maybe it has to do with the fact that she doesn't have any herself," I hazarded a guess. "Maybe she's curious about them? Or maybe she feels like our family is partly her family, and she's staking a claim?"

Jonah nodded and leaned in to scruff the puppy's head. I caught a whiff of his deodorant and toothpaste.

"He sleeping with you tonight?" he asked me. Billy Ray had barely survived fifteen minutes in the crate downstairs while we swapped bathroom time. His little yips and pathetic howls were too much for either of us to handle.

"We'll give it a try. He's so exhausted he should sleep like a rock," I predicted with new dog mother optimism.

"Night then. Sweet dreams, both of you," he said. One more scruff for the puppy, a long curious look at me, and then Jonah headed into his bedroom.

"Looks like it's just you and me tonight, Billy Ray," I muttered. I knew Jonah needed time to get used to the idea of there being an "us" no matter how temporary. But I hoped I wouldn't spend the entire summer in a state of unrequited lust.

In bed, the novelty of cuddling with a puppy lasted all of twenty minutes. The damn dog seemed to be confused. Nighttime was for sleeping, not for playing and barking and biting the pillows.

It went on like that for another half an hour until Jonah burst in without knocking. Wordlessly, he pulled Billy Ray out from under the bed where he'd begun howling.

Jonah took the dog and closed my door.

Ridiculously relieved, I fluffed my slobbery pillows and settled in for a dog-free sleep.

Then the howling and barking started across the hall.

It was a small, old house. The walls weren't exactly sound-proof. I pulled a pillow over my head. But I was listening now. Some kind of biological motherly instinct had kicked in, and I was rigid with worry that Billy Ray was going to make himself sick if he didn't calm the heck down.

I could hear Jonah talking to him in low tones. He could have soothed me to sleep like that. But the dog was having none of it.

The clock on the nightstand read 2:35 a.m., and I punched my poor, innocent pillow. I had things to do tomorrow—correction, today—that required a good night's sleep. A swim and a bike ride. Lunch with my parents. And four solid uninterrupted hours of working on my paper. I was just on the other side of the flare. One sleepless night and too many obligations would put me right back where I'd been. And I wouldn't be able to hide it from my parents.

"Damn it," I whispered into the pillow.

Billy Ray gave a particularly mournful howl, and my feet hit the floor. I was moving on exhausted instinct.

I opened Jonah's door with a creak. The man was sitting, still shirtless on his bed. The puppy was biting at the blanket, snarling playfully.

Billy Ray spotted me first and gave a happy yip.

"It's not play time," I said sternly.

"He keeps running to the door and whining," Jonah explained.

"Does he have to go outside?"

He shook his head, yawned. And I remembered that Jonah had a 7 a.m. boot camp class at the high school. "I took him out half an hour ago. I think he wants to go sleep in your room."

"Nice try," I said, flopping down on the bed next to him. "He wasn't interested in sleeping in my room either."

Jonah's room was significantly bigger. There was a brass queen-size bed, a dresser next to the closet door, and a tiny seating area with two mismatched armchairs under the saltbox roof that poked out over the back porch. The window overlooked the backyard and woods.

Billy Ray gave up his war with the blanket and trotted over to me. I stroked a hand from head to tail, and he flattened himself like a pancake on the mattress.

"Is he going to sleep?" Jonah whispered.

"I can't tell if he's falling asleep or if he's just gearing up for his next bed linen assault."

The pup's little belly rose and fell.

"You're the damn puppy whisperer," he said.

I yawned. "What were we thinking, rescuing a dog?" I sighed.

"It's just temporary," he said, returning my yawn. "We'll find the cute little bastard a nice family he can deprive of sleep."

I couldn't look at him directly. Jonah's hair was sleep-tousled. The shadow of stubble on his jaw took his sexy factor up another ten points. And those sleepy green eyes did something strange to my chest region. Sleepy, stubbly man and sweet puppy were making me feel…things. Confusing things. Twin pulls of physical attraction and now affection warred for my attention.

"I'm going to try to sneak out," I decided. It was pure torture sitting on a bed with Jonah. Shifting on the mattress, I tried to ease away, but Billy Ray rolled to his feet with a disgruntled yip. I moved to the edge of the bed, intent on getting away from sexy, sleepy Jonah.

But the pup followed me and pawed pathetically at my leg. He cocked his head to the side and gave me *the look*.

"What's happening?" I whispered.

"You're falling in love with him," Jonah yawned. "And he's using it against you."

"I don't think he wants me to leave." I was so tired. So very, very tired. And Jonah's bed was so inviting. So very, very inviting.

"Just lie down for a few minutes. Maybe he'll settle if he's between us?"

Superb idea. I'll just lie down in Jonah's bed and continue not having sex with him.

I woke to the loud blaring of an alarm that wasn't my own followed almost instantaneously by the howl of a puppy in desperate need of the bathroom.

"Shit. Don't pee, dude."

My eyelids sprang open, and I launched woodenly into a seated position.

I was in Jonah's bed. I'd slept *with Jonah*. Also a dog.

The man was scrambling out of bed, and the warmth that was evaporating from my back? The only hypothesis that made sense was that Jonah had been spooning me. I felt my back, hoping for some kind of six-pack ab fossil.

Jonah, in a hurry and very focused on not letting Billy Ray pee in his bed, grabbed the puppy and dashed downstairs.

I flopped back on the pillow, noting that Jonah's pillow was pushed up next to mine. I'd slept the sleep of the exhausted and missed out on waking up cuddled against my roommate's hard body. My roommate that I wasn't having a physical relationship with.

It was a lot of disappointments for 6 o'clock in the morning, I mused.

"Damn it, Billy Ray. You were two feet from the door," Jonah grumbled from downstairs.

Well, since I was awake, I might as well get up and tackle that swim, that run. Get them out of the way.

When I got downstairs, Jonah had a shirt on in the backyard and there was a clump of paper towels soaking up the puppy pee on the kitchen linoleum. Like I said. A lot of disappointments.

Judge Henry Kendall, of missing daughter fame, eyed for federal judge appointment.

Bootleg's own Judge Kendall considered for higher calling.

Father of teenager missing for thirteen years considered for federal judgeship.

Chapter Twenty-Seven

Shelby

The cabin Scarlett arranged for my parents to rent was halfway up the mountain. It had a front porch with a spectacular view of the lake and town. The green siding made the building seem as though it was part of the forest that surrounded it. It was cute enough that I temporarily forgot to obsess over the fact that I'd woken up in Jonah's bed…without having had sex with the man.

I sipped my coffee on the blue plaid couch and listened to my parents as they alternated naturally between their two favorite forms of communication: good-natured bickering and finishing each other's sentences.

In my professional opinion, James and Darlene Thompson were suitably matched.

As their daughter, I thought they were just about perfect. My stint as a social worker had given me an intense sense of gratitude for growing up in the family that I did. My parents were steady, loving, and interested in their kids.

"Begone, woman," my dad said, playfully pushing Mom out of the galley kitchen.

"You're cutting the sandwiches wrong," she insisted.

"And they'll taste exactly the same," he shot back, wielding a container of mustard in her direction.

Laughing, Mom joined me on the couch. Her hair was pulled back in a short tail today, and she was wearing comfortable hiking shorts and a t-shirt. Vacation Casual Darlene also had a tube of Rosy Mauve lipstick in her cargo pocket.

After thirty-five years of marriage, Mom still wore lipstick every day, and Dad still got her flowers on the seventeenth of every month in homage to their first date.

Of course, they weren't perfect. Mom hoarded greeting cards. GT liked to joke that she made new friends just to have more birthdays and surgeries to celebrate. And Dad. Well, Dad considered himself a handy man when, in reality, they would be better off calling in a professional. The coat closet light still turned on every time someone used the toaster in their kitchen after Dad's DIY wiring job.

"So, before GT and June get here, tell me about this gorgeous roommate of yours," Mom said, tucking her feet up under her on the cushion next to me.

"Not only is he gorgeous and built like the human version of a racehorse, but he's also very smart and very nice," I told her.

"And you're sure you're just roommates?" Mom prodded.

I didn't want to get her hopes up and then dash them when I went back to Pittsburgh or on to wherever my career took me. "Just friends," I insisted. *Just friends for now. Hopefully sex-having friends soon.*

"Have you tried pretending you forgot where your room was and walking into his in a towel?" she asked, her face serious.

"Mom!"

"Kidding! Kidding," she promised. "You two looked like you were getting along. And I'd love to see both of my kids living their happily ever afters."

Her heart was in the right place. But her nose could stand to be removed from our business.

"Speaking of," I said grasping for a subject change. "What do you and Dad think of June?"

"She is abrupt. Inflexible. Sharply intelligent. And—"

"Absolutely perfect for GT," Dad interrupted. He joined us in the living room. A mug of coffee in one hand.

My mom beamed at him. "In short, we're thrilled. She's so *different* from the women he's dated the past few years," she said.

My parents were devout believers in karma and tried never to speak ill of anyone. The "women" my brother had dated before June could be neatly labeled attention-seeking gold diggers. But we were too polite to mention it.

"Tell us more about your survey, Shelby," Dad insisted, settling his broad shoulders back into the armchair. He may have been wired to love football, but Dad never shirked his fatherly interest when it came to my studies.

I unleashed the nerd girl in me and filled them in on the responses I'd received so far, regaling them with the nuggets of small-town life.

Before long, we heard a car in the driveway.

I peered through the front window, watching as GT and June got out of his SUV. They raced around to the hatch.

GT carefully lifted the pig out of the back and carefully checked her leash and harness while June gave her a good petting.

"Your grandpig is here," I announced.

My parents burst through the front door greeting GT and June—and Katherine—as if it had been months rather than hours since they'd last seen each other.

It made me want to check in on my own little family.

Me: How's BR?

Jonah replied immediately with a picture of the puppy sound asleep on his back, his paws frozen in the air as if mid-run.

Jonah: Now the little punk sleeps.

I thought of how I'd woken up that morning. With the ghost of Jonah's body heat still warming me. How could I broach the subject without being weirdly clinical about it or awkwardly clingy?

Me: I hope I didn't crowd you last night.

Good! Subtle. Not too pushy.

Jonah: Not at all. Thanks for the co-parenting help.

It was no "You look stunning in the morning, and it took all my willpower not to wake you with sex." Baby steps. The more comfortable Jonah felt with me, the easier this friendship would be. The more potential we had…temporarily, of course.

There was a ruckus when my parents trooped back inside with June, GT, and the pig.

We sat down to a casual lunch of sandwiches and family patter. June, obviously enamored with her new pet, paused every few moments to check on Katherine or take her picture or give her words of encouragement.

My parents took turns shooting indulgent looks at each other, and I was suddenly fiercely glad we were all together.

"There's a woman in the backyard," Dad said mildly, his gaze fixed out the window.

We abandoned our meals and crowded against the dining room window. We observed as a woman of indeterminate age strolled across the backyard. Her clothes were dirty, but her face and the hair under her battered Bootleg Cockspurs cap were clean.

She had an odd hitch in her stride.

"That's Henrietta Van Sickle," June announced, nudging GT to lift up Katherine so the pig could see what we were looking at.

"Really?" I pressed closer to the glass.

"Who's Henrietta Van Sickle?" Mom asked.

"She's the town hermit," I explained.

"I heard she doesn't speak and she doesn't have indoor plumbing," GT added.

"You have a town chicken and a town hermit?" Dad asked.

"Of course. Doesn't everyone?" June frowned.

When Henrietta moved around the side of the house, we followed her from window to window.

"She is most likely heading into town for supplies," June hypothesized. "She makes the trip every eight to ten weeks."

"I should go talk to her," I decided, moving toward the door. I didn't know if Henrietta would have access to a computer, but I'd love her input for my survey.

"Is that a good idea?" Mom asked in her careful, motherly, trying to respect her children's boundaries way.

"It's a great idea," I assured her.

I ducked out the door before anyone else could voice their concerns and jogged down the steps. Henrietta was moving toward the road at a good clip.

"Excuse me," I called after her. "Henrietta?" The woman continued to walk toward the road.

The door opened and closed again behind me.

"Henrietta," June called. "Come meet my pet pig."

The woman paused and turned slowly.

"Come on," June said, nudging me and Katherine forward.

Henrietta ignored us and crouched down to the pig's level. She held out a wrinkled, ringless hand. Katherine's black nose snuffled the woman's skin.

"She's nice," June told Henrietta. The woman nodded slowly.

"Are you going into town?" June asked.

She nodded again, tentatively petting the pig.

"Did you remember your cell phone?"

Henrietta shook her head.

I blinked in surprise.

"She only texts," June said in an aside to me. "Would you like me to call Gibson and see if he can give you a ride?" she offered.

Henrietta hesitated and then nodded.

"I'll do that," June said, pulling out her phone. "This is my friend, Shelby. She is pursuing her PhD in social work. She would like to tell you about her project." For the first time, Henrietta looked up.

She had brown eyes ringed in wrinkles as if she'd spent much of her life smiling.

June stepped away, and I heard her dial the phone.

"Hi," I said, suddenly self-conscious under Henrietta's quiet stare. "I'm, uh, Shelby. Like June said. I'm studying small-town community and the hierarchy of neighbors for my dissertation. I have a survey for Bootleggers. I don't know if you have a computer…"

She continued to stare blankly at me.

"Um, if you do," I fished a card out of my back pocket. "This is the URL, I mean the web address for it. I'd love your input. You don't have to do anything but type," I promised.

Reluctantly it seemed, she took the card.

"It would really help me out," I told her.

There was no response. Just those wary brown eyes.

"Is Gibson your friend?" I asked.

Her unpainted lips curved slightly, and she nodded again.

"I like him, too," I confessed. "He's nice. His brother Jonah is my roommate. And I really like him."

Henrietta paused and then, to my delight, flexed her arms, pointing to her biceps.

I laughed. "Yes. That's Jonah."

She nodded more warmly now. Inspired and curious, I pressed on. "Do you know the Kendalls?" I asked quietly.

The ghost of a smile flickered away as quickly as it had come. She shook her head vehemently. No. No. No.

"Gibson will be here in two minutes," June said, returning to us. "He was out at the lumber mill."

Henrietta, studiously avoiding me now, crouched down again and began to pet Katherine in slow, soothing strokes.

Chapter Twenty-Eight

Jonah

Crickets and tree frogs provided the backdrop to my evening as I pulled up the spreadsheet I was working on and adjusted the number of reps. Once a week I went through all my personal training clients, checking their routines, their results. Reassessed goals. Adapted as necessary.

Lather. Rinse. Repeat.

Victories and failures. Constant adjustments to keep everyone moving in the direction of their goals.

Night had fallen and with it came a crisp breeze cool enough that we'd opened the front and back cottage doors for the air flow.

Usually I worked at the dining room table. However, tonight, I was sprawled on the living room floor with a puppy sound asleep between my legs. Billy Ray had exhausted himself chasing butterflies around the bush in the backyard that afternoon. His chin rested on my shin bone as if he couldn't bear to be separated from me.

Shelby was in her corner of the living room squinting at

her laptop. Headphones at full volume, glasses perched on her nose. Constantly shuffling papers, tapping pens, jiggling feet. I could tell she liked the work, was energized by it.

I liked watching her work. Hell, I liked watching her. There was something about her that drew me in and held me there.

It was a cozy scene. A quiet Thursday night with a dog and satisfying work. I had to admit it was nice having someone to share it with. Nicer still to know that my mom was here in Bootleg Springs, that she'd be here for my birthday Saturday. A quiet cookout here at the house. That was the plan. I'd never been big on parties. Not with a single mom trying hard enough as it was to fill both roles. Even as a kid, I recognized that making sure Mom knew she was enough for me was important. It was easier on us both to keep the celebrations simple.

Turkey burgers, grilled veggies, cold beers on the porch while the sun set. It sounded just about perfect.

For once, everyone that I cared about happened to be in the same spot. I liked that feeling.

Shelby sighed again, and I wondered if her arthritis was flaring up.

I fired off an email to Doris with some cardio and flexibility outlines for the upcoming week. And then started on my newest client. One Shelby Thompson. My gaze flicked back to her.

Her shoulders were tight, hunched. Long hours spent sitting usually led to poor posture. A problem common to most. Unfortunately for my pretty roommate, a hallmark of ankylosing spondylitis was the fusing of vertebrae, which could lead to spinal deformity.

First order of business would be a short stretching routine designed to be inserted into her writing and research schedule at regular intervals. As I toggled back and forth between spreadsheet and how-to videos, she yawned loudly, the headphones muffling the sound to her own ears. Billy Ray let out a corresponding yip in his sleep and snuggled closer to my leg.

I liked getting my hands on a new athlete, liked pointing

them in the right direction. For most people, a few consistent tweaks made vast differences in their lives and goals. And I hoped it would be the same for Shelby. She was a researcher at heart, an observer. But judging by the reams of data she'd collected for her paper and her lack of progress on the actual writing, she had difficulty turning that research into action.

That's where I could come in. She'd read up on triathletes and training. Yet her efforts on her own had been haphazard and inconsistent.

Shelby was on my watch now. It was up to me to give her a program that balanced her work, her training, and her condition. It was the kind of challenge I appreciated. And I had a feeling I would enjoy working with her closely.

While she frowned over interviews and academic journals, I pulled together a schedule for the week. Running. Swimming. A bike ride to gauge her abilities. I penciled them into my own calendar, too, before emailing the finished product to Shelby.

"Did you just email me from the living room floor?" she asked with a laugh, slipping off the headphones. Leaning back in her chair, she stretched her arms overhead.

"All of my clients are getting emails from me tonight," I said, closing my own laptop and sliding it to the floor. Billy Ray grumbled in his sleep.

"I know I'm showing bias, but I find him to be the cutest puppy I've ever seen," she said, staring fondly at the dog.

"I agree with your hypothesis. Did you have a chance to work on his write-up?" I asked.

She cringed. "Not yet."

Minnie Fae had offered to help us find a permanent home for Billy Ray if we were willing to foster him. We were *supposed* to be writing a profile that she could post on Minnie's Meow Meow House's website.

"There's no rush," I said. "It's probably better if he has time to get used to living in a house. Maybe let him get more consistent with not peeing all over furniture."

173

The first few days of having a puppy had been an eye-opening and excessive paper-towel-using experience.

"I think that's smart," Shelby said, brightening.

"How's the dissertation coming?" I asked.

"Ugh. It's like writer's block for academia. I've collected more data and information than I could possibly use. The entire mammoth of a concept is outlined. I just can't seem to write the damn thing," she complained. "Plus, I found another project to distract me."

"Besides me and the dog and your training?" I teased.

"Seeing all that research at June's into the Callie Kendall thing really sparked some interest," she confessed. "First of all, the situation is a researcher's dream. Years of articles and conspiracy theories and the last twelve or so months of developments."

There it was, her disappearance into fact and figures. The distance she put between herself and the people involved.

"There is a lot of material there," I agreed, organizing my own papers and files into a stack.

"Plus, I just got a vibe from the Kendalls."

I stopped what I was doing. "What kind of vibe?"

"I used to be a social worker," she said. "Sometimes you'd meet someone or you'd walk into a home, and it would just have dirty fingerprints. Like appearances were normal, but something beneath the surface was off."

"That's what you felt in the five-second conversation with the Kendalls?" I asked, intrigued.

"It made me wonder. Were they ever suspects? And if they were, what exonerated them in the eyes of the law? I'm hoping it's not just because Judge Kendall is a state judge. Bad people can have good jobs *and* be very good about hiding their bad."

"I'm not doubting your instincts," I prefaced. "But those people lost their daughter in a very public way and have gone through hell in the last twelve months. Maybe that's what makes them a little off."

"A little off," Shelby repeated triumphantly. "You feel it, too. You're just too polite or too guilty to really think it."

"Guilty?"

"Your biological father is a person of interest. You and your siblings all feel some level of responsibility, which, however unnecessary, is understandable. You're all good people. Good people feel bad about things. Bad people don't."

The hair on her arms was standing up, and I wondered if she was cold.

"How about we put it all away for tonight?" I suggested. "It's getting late, and you haven't had dinner. I'll make something. We can go over the schedule I sent you. And maybe watch some TV or a movie?"

Her eyes lit up behind her glasses. "Can I pick?"

"Sure."

Under Billy Ray's watchful eye through the back door, I grilled chicken breasts and roasted a foil pack of vegetables.

While I cooked, Shelby opened two beers and got the plates and silverware ready.

"Did you know Gibson knows Henrietta Van Sickle?" she asked, poking her head out the back door.

I nodded, inserting the meat thermometer into a chicken breast. "Yeah, I think she sometimes cuts through his land on the mountain when she's roaming. Sometimes he gives her rides into town."

"He picked her up at my parents' cabin and took her in," she said.

"Do you think they bond over the whole hermit thing?" I asked, pulling the meat off the grill.

"Maybe," she said. "I gave her the link to my survey and asked her to fill it out."

"Those would be some interesting answers," I predicted.

"Henrietta thinks you're pretty buff," she said.

"I thought she didn't talk?"

Shelby grinned and made a show of flexing her muscles. "She didn't have to."

"Women," I teased.

She sniffed the plate with suspicion when I carried it into the house.

"It's chicken. You like chicken."

"I like breaded chicken with dip that's main ingredients are fancy chemicals," she complained.

"You're doing a great job with your training, but your eating could use that overhaul," I reminded her.

"It's not that bad," she shot back.

"Oh, it is. Just try it." I hefted the fork at her, and she turtlenecked away from it. I stepped in, cornering her against the kitchen counter.

"Come on, Shelby. Just one bite," I said, moving in slower with the fork. "It's just vegetables. Nothing scary."

She pinched her eyes closed and opened her mouth. Before she could change her mind, I swooped the fork into her mouth.

She chewed in tiny, frantic motions, her nose under her glasses wrinkling. Then she cracked one eye open. She looked at me suspiciously. "That wasn't horrible," she accused.

"I know," I said smugly.

"What was it?"

"Sautéed peppers and onions."

"But I don't eat peppers and onions," she argued.

I shoveled another forkful in her mouth while it was open. She chewed, with less haste, then took the plate from me.

"Why does this taste good?" she wondered out loud. "Is it because I'm starving? Maybe because I didn't make it?"

She speared a bite of chicken and popped it into her mouth. I waited.

"Oh. My. god. This is so superior to dino nuggets! What the heck, Bodine? What else have I been prejudiced to?"

I laughed while she shoveled nutrition into her face.

"Slow down there, slugger."

I made up a second plate. "Dining room or couch?" I asked. "Couch. "

We sat and ate our dinners, watching a terrifying horror show. After we finished our food, Shelby slid her feet into my lap. I rested my hand on her smooth shins, resisting the urge to skim higher.

It was comfortable. Relaxed. Even though I was paying more attention to the feel of her legs, the smooth texture of her skin, the way her lips parted in anticipation as she watched TV.

Oh, boy.

Chapter Twenty-Nine
Shelby

If an invitation to a Girls Night Out on a Friday at The Lookout was any indication, I'd been officially inducted into Bootleg Springs society. Scarlett, Cassidy, June, and Lula—the best massage therapist in the county—were waiting around a table near the dance floor for the round of drinks it was my turn to fetch.

I'd spent the morning working out. Then a picnic lunch with my parents and Billy Ray. And wrapped up the day spending hours building charts and graphs for the dissertation that was going to drag on forever and ever. Pushing back gainful employment and essentially wasting all that money I spent on education.

My frustration had risen to the point where Jonah made me go take a nap with the puppy. Tonight was a very welcome respite.

The bar was crowded with regulars and summertimers. Peanut dust rose up from the floor from shells crushed by boots. Good-natured arguments were brewing around the pool tables. I'd been in town long enough to know that the good-nature often turned bad if left alone too long.

"Usual?" Nicolette in her "*I'm fluent in three languages: English, sarcasm, and profanity*" t-shirt asked from the other side of the bar.

"Yes, please. And a round for the table," I yelled. I waited while Nicolette made the drinks and watched the fun unfold around me. It was a rowdy country band on the tiny stage in the back. They had a long-legged blonde fiddler.

Just inside the door were two tables of Bootleg Springs elders gossiping about everyone who walked in. Bar-goers ranged in age from the newly minted twenty-one to the generous side of eighty.

It was an eclectic microcosm of the community. A concentrated drop of everyone that made Bootleg Bootleg. I wished I would have brought my laptop to encourage people to take the survey. I'd gotten over two hundred responses, which was an impressive sample in a town this size. And with every question answered, I learned a little something new about community.

I was still missing the hook for my paper. There was something I was looking for without knowing exactly what it was. But I'd know it when I found it. The thread that would tie all my work together.

"Here you go," Nicolette called, sliding the drinks across the bar to me. Cassidy appeared at my elbow and took half of the bottles and glasses. I followed her back to our table.

"Did we miss anything?" I asked as Cassidy and I passed out the beverages.

"Only twenty or thirty more pictures of potbelly Katherine," Scarlett said with amusement.

June retrieved her phone from her pants pocket. "Would you like to see a timeline of Katherine's first bath?" she asked, already flipping through photos.

"Hang on to those, June Bug," Scarlett interjected. "I've got myself a few questions for Shelby here."

"I've got a question for you too, Scarlett. Why haven't you

filled out my survey yet?" I asked, taking a sip of my fresh gin and tonic. My second and last of the night. Alcohol and inflammation were kissing cousins as Jonah had explained.

"Why haven't you slept with my brother yet?" Scarlett countered. The music was loud, but not so loud that a couple of nearby tables took interest in our conversation.

I leaned back in my chair. "I've indicated my interest," I told her.

"And?" Lula pressed.

"And nothing, yet," I said with a dainty shrug. I kept the kisses to myself. Also the sharing a bed thing that we'd been doing since Billy Ray joined our little family. Sleeping next to Jonah hadn't led to anything besides sexual frustration on my part.

Being in a man's bed and still not having sex made me seem not very efficient.

Scarlett let out a groan.

"What was that for?" I laughed.

"You'll have to forgive our Scarlett," Cassidy said. "She's a little impatient."

"I put two people with tons of chemistry in close proximity, and you're telling me that *nothing*'s happened yet?" Scarlett was incredulous.

"Sometimes it takes more than chemistry," I pointed out.

Someone bumped my chair from behind. A young guy in a hurry to get his pretty girl on the dance floor. I watched his enthusiasm and envied the girl. The truth was, Jonah dragging his feet on my offer was starting to dent my pride a little. He hadn't even tried to kiss me again.

"I just don't understand it," Scarlett complained. "You two like each other just fine. You're attracted to each other. Consenting adults living in the same house, and you still haven't gotten naked. This doesn't make any sense!" She slammed her beer down on the table in frustration.

"Not everyone is as comfortable going after what they want as you are, Scarlett," Lula reminded her.

I watched the young couple two-step their way across the dance floor with eyes only for each other. I didn't need that. Not *now*. Maybe someday. But for right now, I was too busy for those yearning glances and the kind of affection that would eat into every waking hour of my day. But a little healthy sexual gratification? What was wrong with that?

"Maybe I came on too strong?" I hypothesized.

"Did he find you naked in his bed with a can of whipped cream?" Cassidy asked.

I shook my head.

"Then you didn't come on strong enough," Scarlett said, slapping the table.

"I don't know. I don't think that a physical relationship should be this difficult to initiate. Either we both want it, or one of us doesn't, and in this case that would be Jonah."

"Your hypothesis is flawed," June said with a frown.

The band slowed it down with a ballad, and couples melted onto the dance floor and into each other's arms.

"What's so flawed about it?" I asked June.

"Just because an individual doesn't rush into a sexual relationship does not indicate disinterest."

"Juney's right." Scarlett nodded, patting her friend's shoulder. "Is Rene the reason he's not knocking around your bedroom door with his pants around his ankles?"

"Who's Rene?" Lula asked, crossing her long, long legs.

Seeing as how half the town had already heard, I saw no harm in letting Scarlett repeat an abbreviated version of Jonah's story about his former girlfriend.

"That's just about the saddest damn thing I've heard all day," Lula sniffled into her drink when Scarlett finished theatrically.

"And that is exactly the reason why he should be jumping into Shelby's bed," Scarlett insisted. "He needs to get past this quicksand and start opening himself up to new opportunities."

"Perhaps Jonah is experiencing anxiety at the thought of entering into another physical relationship," June mused.

"Well, sitting around thinking on things don't get a damn

thing done, now does it?" Scarlett complained. "He needs a good push."

I thought about that for a minute. I thought about everything. I was a thinker, a data collector. I was not a doer by nature. I didn't *take* action. I observed. And observing wasn't getting me into Jonah Bodine's bed.

I sucked on my straw, surprised when I came up dry.

I'd declared my interest. He'd reciprocated his. Maybe we both just needed a little nudge over thinking and into doing. I opened an app on my phone and typed up a bullet point to remember to research seduction techniques.

On stage, the fiddler kicked up her hand-stitched cowboy boots, flashing her long legs under a short denim skirt, her long blonde curls bouncing under the stage lights. Jonah would've noticed her. Heck, any red-blooded American man would have noticed her.

And then there was me. In my geeky glasses. My lack of makeup. My wardrobe that existed for only two purposes: working out and sitting on my butt in front of a computer. I made it too easy to miss me. To skim over me and see only pretty fiddlers.

"This is giving me a lot to think about," I told the table.

"Are you seriously takin' notes right now?" Scarlett asked, amused.

"Let us know if you make anything happen," Cassidy said with a suggestive eyebrow wiggle.

"Do not feel obliged to keep me updated," June insisted.

"All right. I've answered your questions," I said, tucking my phone away. "Now, tell me when you're going to take my survey, Scarlett."

"I will take your survey when you bag my brother," she said, crossing her arms smugly.

Only in Bootleg Springs.

"Now that Scarlett's done selling off her brother into sexual servitude," Cassidy said with a grin. "I have some news."

We all perked up, leaning in to hear over the sounds of boots stomping and drinks being drunk.

"Bowie and I are getting married, y'all."

We continued to look expectantly at her, waiting for the actual news.

"We made that assumption when you accepted his proposal," June observed.

"Correction," Cassidy continued. "Bowie and I are getting married next month."

Scarlett's screech drowned out June's cordial congratulations and the band itself. "How are we going to find you a dress, a venue, a band, and a bartender in one month, Cassidy Ann?" Scarlett demanded, shaking her friend by the shoulders and then hugging her tight.

"There y'all are," Leah Mae hurried up to our table and drew up a chair. "I had to follow the sound of Scarlett's screams to find you. It's packed in here tonight!"

"What took you so long?" Cassidy asked.

"Oh, nothing much. Just drawing up some sketches for a certain somebody's wedding dress," Leah Mae said smugly.

"Give them to me right now," Cassidy said, making grabby motions with her hands.

We talked wedding plans and futures. Bridesmaids dresses and honeymoon venues. But my thoughts were on Jonah. How I would go from sharing his bed to *sharing* his bed? Did he really want me, or was he too nice to reject me?

Q. Where in your community do you feel the most welcome?

Rhett Ginsler: The Lookout on a Friday night. It's got everything you need. Beer. Pool. Music. Neighbors. Someone's always willing to blow off a little steam with a fight. Good times.

Chapter Thirty

Shelby

H ave any nightmares last night?" I asked, sucking in a breath as we crested a slow rolling hill on the road. My legs were on fire. My hands cramped into claws on the handlebar. I forced them to relax. But it was a good kind of pain. The kind of challenge to push through. I was learning the difference between what to push through and what to acknowledge.

Last night, I'd introduced Jonah to my guilty pleasure: horror movies. He'd been a good sport about it.

"Not unless you count waking up to Billy Ray's cold wet nose in the small of my back," he said.

Fifteen minutes after his rude awakening and a potty break for the dog, I'd woken to Jonah's morning wood in the small of *my* back when he'd climbed back into bed and draped an arm over my waist.

I'd looked over my shoulder, and we'd stared at each other for a long, heated thirty seconds before Billy Ray realized we were both awake and made his desperate plea for attention.

Jonah was annoyingly not winded. He looked like he could

ride for fifty miles without getting tired. Meanwhile, I was struggling with sprint triathlon distances. A 750-meter swim, a 12.2-mile bike ride, and a 3.1-mile run. My illness made me more sore, feel more joint pain than the average healthy adult. But I was learning to pay attention and make better choices, thanks in large part to my sexually unavailable roommate.

I'd slogged my way through a 500-meter swim this morning and was pleased with my improved time. It wasn't going to set a course record, but it was a hell of a lot better than what I'd accomplished on my own. We'd dropped Billy Ray off with Gibson this morning and headed out for a ten-mile ride before Jonah's birthday party tonight.

And after the party?

I was going to seduce the birthday boy. I would be showered, made up, hair styled, and sexed up. He would be putty in my hands. Wait, no. He would be achingly hard—

"How you feeling?" Jonah called over his shoulder.

I dragged my thoughts away from Naked Jonah. Eight miles into the ride and I was starting to think that maybe, just maybe, I had a shot at finishing next month.

"Good," I puffed.

Sweat trickled down my back to the waistband of my shorts. It was a sensation I was learning to get used to and maybe even enjoy. I still preferred the swim. I liked sinking into the water, letting it muffle all my senses. But the bike was fun, too. Unless you took into consideration how much it hurt getting hit with a bumblebee as you flew down a hill.

I had welts.

I took the downhill, intending to be cautious—bumblebees and all, of course—but the speed, the wind that cooled my skin, made me brave.

I let out a whoop of joy and hinged over the handlebars.

Jonah shot a look over his shoulder and grinned at me. Together we raced down the winding hill.

Enjoying the view that unfurled in front of me. Forest, thick and green, rolled out on both sides of the ribbon of asphalt. I caught a glimpse of lake off to the left, saw Bootleg's church steeple in the valley below. Dark clouds crowded in on the blue sky in front of us.

And between me and the clouds was Jonah. He rode in perfect form. His calves bunched, biceps flexed. I couldn't see his face, but I knew he was smiling.

A doer, an adventurer in search of fun. And that's what he wanted to share with his clients, I realized. I wasn't hunched over a pile of research pecking away at the keyboard on a beautiful summer day. No, I was flying with the sun on my face and wind lifting my ponytail.

The road curved gently away from the lake, taking us deeper into the forest. We slowed as valley turned back to hill.

"Having fun?" he asked, slowing down so I could ease up alongside him.

"I was just thinking this was a more enjoyable way to spend a day than sitting in front of my laptop," I confessed.

"Not too shabby." He grinned. "Water break?"

I nodded. I was not comfortable enough on these roads to reach down and make a grab for my water bottle. That maneuver was above my current skill level. I wondered if I could get one of those beer helmets they sold at Build A Shine for the triathlon and fill it with water.

We pulled off the road at a trailhead that led up, up, up the mountain we'd skirted.

"Rain's coming in," he observed before taking a deep drink.

Lord, he was glorious. Sweaty was a good look on Jonah Bodine. His athletic frame warmed by exercise was a sight to be appreciated, swooned over. He wore a short-sleeved training jersey that fit him like skin and bike shorts that highlighted a particular piece of anatomy that I was trying not to stare at.

"Think we'll make it home before that?" I asked, again tearing my gaze away from his crotch.

"Still two miles out. How fast can you peddle?" he teased.

A fat raindrop fell from the sky and landed on my chest. "Uh-oh."

And with that, the West Virginia skies opened up on us.

"Let's go further in," he yelled over the slow roll of thunder. He gestured up the trail.

We pushed our bikes into the trees and away from the road. He found a copse of hemlock trees that formed a low leaky canopy. I crawled in behind him.

"Homey," I said, sitting down on a cushion of lost needles and other forest floor debris.

I unclipped my helmet and pulled my hair free from its low tail. I shook it out, fluffed my bangs. Just because I was stuck in a rainstorm in the middle of a forest didn't mean I shouldn't make a small effort with my appearance.

I was, after all, on schedule to seduce the man tonight.

Shower, leg shaving, unscented lotion so I'd be super soft to the touch. Makeup light enough to look like I wasn't wearing any. And a cute outfit. Not lingerie. Lingerie brought with it expectations. Fun shorts and a daringly low-cut tank would be friendlier, sneakier, Scarlett had assured me.

They were expecting a full report tomorrow. Well, June wasn't. And Scarlett probably didn't want any details seeing as how Jonah was her brother and all. But I was still looking forward to this grand experiment.

I was tired of doing nothing but sleeping in his bed. We had chemistry on our side. And judging from the morning wood Jonah sported this morning we had biology, too. It was time to initiate a reaction.

The rain was slower under the trees, but it was still soaking. My white tank clung to the psychedelic sports bra underneath, and my nipples hardened to points.

"Shelby?" His voice was strained.

"What? Oh my god. Do you see a bear?" I whispered, scanning the forest beyond our bikes.

Getting mauled would seriously hinder the seduction experiment tonight.

Not spotting any forest monsters, I looked at him and noticed he was looking at me.

"What's wrong?" I asked.

He shook his head, smiling wryly. "Nothing's wrong. No bears. I just thought now would be a good time to kiss you."

Another roll of thunder rumbled. This one I felt in my bones as Jonah's mouth, wet and firm, found mine.

There was an urgency here.

A beautiful, painful urgency. And if he was going to back off again or we were going to be interrupted by—God, please not a bear—I was going to develop the equivalent of lady blue balls. I wanted him so keenly it hurt. The ache between my legs went deeper than just flesh and muscle. It was visceral.

I wanted Jonah to know he was wanted. To let me remind him what that felt like.

Nerds interested in sociology and biology and motivation turned out to be rather excellent lovers. I prided myself on being good at sex.

As if reading my mind, he dragged me to him, spreading my legs so I straddled him, his back braced against a tree trunk.

His erection, that biological miracle of blood flow and arousal, nestled between my legs causing the breath to catch in my throat. He felt *ready*. But I needed to know. Needed to hear the words.

"Jonah," I said, dragging my lips from his.

"What?" He pulled me back. Tasted me deeper. His hand fisted in my hair. And when I moaned, I felt the hard length of his shaft twitch against me.

"Are you sure you want to?" I breathed. "I don't want you to feel pressured or to have any regrets afterward."

He eased back an inch, far enough for me to see the amused curve on the lips I'd just voraciously kissed.

"I'm sure, Shelby. I want you."

Hallelujah!

"That's convenient because I really, really want you," I confessed.

He kissed me again, this time his hands skimming the outer curves of my breasts. My flesh, beneath layers of shirt and sports bra and rain and sweat, paid attention. I craved more.

"You know what's not convenient?" I whispered, shifting against him just to feel his hard-on line up with my body.

"What's that?"

"Wet spandex."

Chapter Thirty-One
Jonah

We stripped as best we could out of wet spandex and rain-soaked clothes. We tossed them over shoulders and stood facing each other. It felt hedonistic to stand naked in the forest, to skim Shelby's beautiful body with my gaze.

She looked like she belonged here, her hair long and curling in the damp, the mist that settled over the forest floor. A nymph. Tiny frame, lush curves. Her waist and hips begged for my hands. And her breasts, creamy pale perfection. Lush again, heavier than I expected, forming ideal tear-drops with rosebud nipples.

It speared through me, and I remembered what this felt like now. *To want.*

But it felt sharper, keener somehow.

Maybe it was the scene. Or maybe it was the woman.

She looked her fill, wetting her lips. I felt her eyes roam my body. And I wondered which of us would be the first to cross the invisible line between us etched in the pine needles under our feet.

Me.

I wasn't conscious of moving until I stood before her, until I took her mouth. Only our lips touching. The rest of our bodies a breath apart. Thunder rolled long and low, vibrating between us and through us.

Then she was drawing me closer, her breasts pressing against the muscle of my chest, fingers digging into my shoulders. Now I was free to touch her.

I slid my palms down her neck, over her shoulders and down her arms. Thumbs skimming the delectable curves of her breasts.

My cock, aching and hard, was pinned against the smooth skin of her belly. I wanted so many things in the moment. Too much.

I wanted to feed on her breasts, making her nipples budded against my tongue. To feel her lips wrap around the crown of my hard dick. To slide two fingers deep inside her. To watch her come. To hear my name whispered when she came. To paint her with my own climax.

Fuck.

"Shelby," I said, pulling away from her eager mouth.

"Huh? Yeah? Wha?" she breathed. Easing back, her tight nipples dragged lightly through my chest hair. She gasped.

"I don't have a condom."

Her eyes were wide, dazed. "Me neither."

"We can't—" A lifetime of safe sex lectures from my mother echoed in my head.

"I'm on birth control. You haven't had sex in over a year, and I just had a boatload of blood tests a few weeks ago," she said.

I was afraid to say anything. "I don't want you to feel like you have to," I began.

"Jonah," she said my name in exasperation. "I want to have sex with you. Right here. Right now. It's a green light."

"If you're sure," I said.

She responded by grasping my hand and placing it on her

breast. I felt her nipple bud against my palm, and every rational, cautious thought dissipated from my head. Cupping both breasts, I rubbed my thumbs over her nipples and reveled in the sigh that broke free from her.

The rain was light and cool on our skin, but my blood was hot and roiling beneath the surface.

She used my distraction with her breasts to do her own exploring. She closed a clever hand around the base of my shaft and stroked up. Electric need pulsed through me as she pumped me from root to tip.

I pinched her nipples gently, and she bit my pec. Then she was sliding down my body.

I watched her sink to her knees in front of me, her mouth inches from where my cock hung heavily. My nostrils flared as I forced air into my lungs, and then she was closing those perfect pink lips around the head of my dick.

I'd forgotten this. How slick and sweet a woman's mouth was. Shelby's mouth. Because, again, this was different. Special.

I couldn't take my eyes off her as she, seemingly enthralled with my taste, licked and sucked her way up and down my cock. This was heaven on Earth, I thought, fisting my hand in her hair and fighting the urge to thrust into that sweet mouth.

I held back, knowing if I gave in to the urge to fuck her mouth, her throat, I'd lose myself there. It had been too long. My endurance wasn't what it once was. And Shelby was very, very good at what she was doing to me.

She groaned her disappointment when I pulled her mouth off me. But I silenced it when I took her down to the ground. A bed of leaves and pine needles and discarded clothing. Eagerly, I closed my mouth over a breast sucking, sampling, savoring.

Her knees fell open welcoming me. And with one hand, I trailed a path up the inside of her thigh. She shivered against me, encouraging me with those sexy little moans. How had I thought I wasn't ready for this? I could have missed this. *And this,* I thought, sliding the tips of my fingers through her wet cleft. Every inch of our bodies was wet from the rain. But here where I probed, it was different. Thicker, hotter, and oh so tempting.

I sank two fingers into her as I sucked rainwater off her other nipple, crossing two items off my list. She bowed up off the ground against me, driving me insane with her reactions to me. And when her fingers closed around my cock again, I let myself go just a little crazy.

I thrust into her grip, driving my fingers into her sweet pussy in time.

Our breathing was hard and fast. Her eyes were glassy and half closed. She opened wider for me, inviting me deeper, and I thrust in to the knuckle, holding her there.

"Jonah," her teeth chattered. "I want—I want you," she hissed.

I could feel her muscles tightening around my fingers, felt that ache echoed in my own groin. Fingers and hands were good. But we both desperately needed more. It was biology. Pure, raw, primal.

I pulled out of her and took her hand away from my erection. "Hold on to me," I instructed.

She did as she was told, slipping her hands behind my neck, linking her fingers.

I settled my hips between her legs, the tip of my cock brushing the wet, welcoming folds.

Impatient now, Shelby bucked against me, and I reveled in the feel of my cock slipping over her clit.

Leaning in, I allowed myself another lick at her breast. And when she bowed back, when her knees fell open, I drove myself into her.

Our shouts of triumph, of awe, caught on the rain. I was inside her, gripped by her slick, velvety flesh. Muscles quivering, I dug my toes into the ground so I could stay buried inside.

Her nails bit into my back, and she chanted words, nonsensical sounds, softly as she fought for air. This was Nirvana. This moment of two bodies joining after the teasing, before the fulfillment. This was a recognition of sameness.

She flexed, tightening around me, and I had to move then. Withdrawing, I paused. Savored. Then decadently slid back inside, needing to feel her close like a fist around me.

"How does it feel?" she whispered.

"So good, Shelby. So fucking good," I promised her, moving again. Loving the drag of her flesh over mine. Was it special because it had been so long? Or was it because it was Shelby? My roommate. My client. My friend.

"Don't you dare stop or come to your senses," she pleaded with a laugh.

I flinched as the laugh had her tightening further. Sweat already dotted my forehead, and I knew I couldn't hang on forever. I kept my thrusts measured, controlled. Focusing on the beauty of the joining even as the need to go harder, faster, clawed its way up my throat.

She hitched her legs higher up on my hips and bucked into me.

I wanted to give her what she needed, what she craved, what she chased. I just hoped I could hold on long enough. I thrust harder, and she murmured her approval against my neck. Her breasts, those lush curves, were flattened to me, and I wished I could taste them again. I settled for slipping a hand between our bodies and caressing that soft skin, that taut nipple.

She liked it.

"Yes, Jonah. Oh, yes!" She was breathless.

And I was pummeling into her now, pinning her to the forest floor with fast, vicious strokes of my cock. But she welcomed the speed, the need, the greed. Encouraged it with the way those silky inner muscles danced over the veins of my cock.

She was leading me toward a climax I wasn't sure I could survive.

I needed to get her there first.

With regret, I abandoned her breast and slid my hand lower. As I thrust into her like a warrior, an animal, my thumb slicked over her sensitive bud. Her body tensed, every muscle and her breath stopped.

I bit at her neck, her shoulder, still thrusting, still circling that beautiful little clit. And then she came back to life under me as her orgasm detonated.

I felt her come, closing fist-tight around my cock. Her hips undulating to chase down the waves that wracked her body. I couldn't hold out a second longer. As she clamped down on me again, I felt it race up my spine, stabbing through my balls. And then I was coming harder than I ever had before into her as she teased and squeezed every drop of my release from me. She was still coming in gentle, distant pulses when I collapsed on her, sealing our orgasms together.

Chapter Thirty-Two
Jonah

There are few things more awkward than having sex for the first time and then walking in on your own surprise party.

I was pretty sure what Shelby and I had been up to was written all over our faces—and tangled up in her hair, judging from the dried pine needles that were still shaking free.

"Surprise!" My mother, the Bodines, the Tuckers, and the Thompsons bellowed when we climbed off our bikes.

"Well, there goes Round Two," Shelby said under her breath.

Once the rain broke, once we'd dragged our wet clothes back on, we'd pedaled like hell for home. For a shower and a second shot at each other, this time in a bed.

I stared longingly at the front door. Between it and us were over a dozen people, a pig, and a puppy, ready and waiting to celebrate my birthday.

Shocked, I slapped a stupid smile on my face and waded in to accept the congratulations. I could tell by the smug look my sister was shooting in my direction that she had guessed exactly what Shelby and I had been up to.

After accepting the first round of congratulations, I escaped for a five-minute shower during which I thought of nothing but how it felt to be inside Shelby. I turned the faucet all the way to cold until my hard-on finally gave up. Apparently now that the dry spell was over, I was going to be walking around sporting wood all day every day.

By the time I made it back to our front lawn, the party was in full swing.

They'd certainly put quite the effort into it. Someone had strung lights around tree trunks. Portable picnic tables were set up covered with white tablecloths. Gibson was manning the grill, Billy Ray sniffing around his feet with Katherine the pig.

And Shelby, well, Shelby was relaxing in a hammock with a lemonade just on the outside of the action. I made my way to her and gave the hammock a nudge.

She opened one eye. "Shower free?" she asked.

My back to the festivities, I trailed a finger up the inside of her thigh. There were so many things I still wanted to do to her, with her.

"It is. Did you know about this?" I asked.

"Do you think I would have insisted we come back here for Round Two if I knew there was a yard full of people waiting for us? This is the most disappointing surprise party I've ever been to," she teased.

"We'll make up for it tonight," I promised.

"What's that they say about a Bootleg party?" she mused. "Ain't no party like a Bootleg party?"

"'Cause a Bootleg party don't stop," I finished. "But this one will stop. At a reasonable hour, too, if I have to fake food poisoning to get them out of here."

"I'm looking forward to your fake explosive bowel issues later tonight," she teased.

She held a hand out to me, and I pulled her out of the

hammock. "I'm going to shower. Go make nice with your guests before we kick them out."

"Oh, hey, Shelby?"

She paused.

I took a step closer to her so no one could overhear. "I'm going to make sure I'm the most memorable summer fling you've ever had in your life," I told her.

She grinned and bit her lip. "I just might hold you to that."

Shelby waved over her shoulder, and I wished more than anything that I was following her up those stairs.

"So? Were you surprised?" My mother and Scarlett approached, looking smug.

"Shocked," I said. "I thought this was going to be a quiet cookout." That didn't start for a few more hours and ended at a reasonable hour.

"Your mama was telling me how you never wanted a party or a fuss over your birthday. Why, Jenny, did I tell you that he neglected to tell us that it was his birthday last year?" Scarlett said, dishing the dirt.

"You mentioned that," Mom said, winking at me.

"And I just couldn't let another year pass without us giving Jonah a proper birthday party. He's only owed thirty-one of them," Scarlett said.

It was oddly sweet. Still, incredibly inconvenient. But I guessed I could put forth the effort to appreciate their work.

When Shelby returned, in a frothy sundress that teased the eye as it floated around her thighs, I was engaged in a horse-shoes battle with my brothers.

Someone had turned the music on to, what was that? Eighties rock? I supposed my birthday got a reprieve from the country music so preferred in Olamette County.

We ate—someone had been kind enough to make grilled chicken and provide salad fixings in addition to the standard artery-clogging cookout fare—and drank and shot the shit.

Jimmy Bob Prosser made an appearance, presenting me with a gift certificate for his hardware store and a stolen kiss on the cheek from my mother before he left. She beamed after him, and I found myself unable to be anything but happy for her.

Now, if the guy went and broke her heart, I'd be enlisting my brothers for some Bootleg Justice. It was only fair.

A pickup bounced down the driveway and pulled into the grass next to Gibson's SUV. Jameson and Leah Mae, both beaming brighter than the sun, linked hands and strolled our way. I nudged Bowie next to me, pointed my beer bottle.

"Well, well. Here come the soon-to-be newly engaged," Bowie observed.

Jameson's imminent proposal plans were still cloaked in mystery. But it made my day even brighter, knowing that another brother was marching happily toward his future.

George and Shelby's parents were enthusiastic about the chaos and made plans to attend Tuesday's Cockspurs game. Devlin stepped in when Scarlett batted her lashes and tried to recruit them to the team. He'd fallen for it once before and paid a very steep hangover price.

When evening fell and the string lights twinkled on, Mom and Shelby marched out a cake with sparklers and candles. The Bodines serenaded me with the worst, off-key rendition of "Happy Birthday" I'd ever heard in my life.

Little Billy Ray howled along with them. It was awful and beautiful.

I laughed and smiled. Ate and drank. Embarrassed, I opened gifts, both gag and thoughtful. And I watched Shelby at the opposite end of the table.

I caught her eye, and the slow, sweet smile on her face warmed something in me that had been cold for too long.

And then I took an elbow to the gut.

"Looks like *someone* took his pants off today." Scarlett grinned up at me, a cat that ate the canary.

"I don't kiss and tell," I said, slinging an arm around her shoulder.

"No, but you kiss and moon around with puppy dog eyes. She's a nice girl, Jonah. I approve."

"You practically picked her out for me. I should hope you'd approve," I teased.

"Now listen, I know this is all new to you. But y'all should probably define exactly what this is because news will be all over town by tomorrow."

"You mean, you're going to open your big, fat mouth and tell everyone in town that I'm dating Shelby," I corrected her.

"Dating, huh? I can get behind that."

"Even if it's none of your business."

"Why, Jonah Bodine. You're my brother. Your happiness is my business."

"Just don't start any wedding plans, Scar. Shelby doesn't plan to stick around past the end of summer."

"What about you?" she asked. "And before you even think about answering, you better not be considering leaving. Why, I brought your mama all the way out here to make her fall in love with this town."

"You're a diabolical puppet master, Scarlett Rose."

She beamed up at me. "If it's a crime to want my family to be happy and all together, then put me on death row."

"You're ridiculous."

"I found my happily ever after," she said, eyes flying to where Devlin and Jameson were deep in discussion. "Jameson and Leah Mae, Bowie and Cassidy, they found theirs, too. You can have a good life here."

I nodded. "I know it. But I'm just not one thousand percent sure yet."

"Well, you'll have more incentive once I get your mama married off and moved in here," she predicted.

———

As darkness fell, I noticed Bowie sneak off toward the shadows to take a phone call. I could see the tension in his shoulders, and something told me it wasn't good news.

I excused myself from the table where James and Darlene were recounting one of their recent home renovation horror stories to Scarlett, who insisted that the next time they needed some plumbing done they call her first.

Bowie was standing there staring down at his phone when I got to him.

"What's wrong?" I asked.

He looked up and I knew.

"Fuck," I said quietly.

"It was Jayme. Dental records were a match. It's Callie."

Behind us, laughter erupted as Gibson and Jameson vied to tell my mom about their attempt at ice fishing when they were kids.

"This doesn't change anything," I said, knowing full well that it changed everything. Callie Kendall was dead. And so were the hopes of an entire community.

"It doesn't mean that Dad did it," Bowie said, sounding even less confident than me.

"No. It doesn't."

"Jayme says they're keeping the news under wraps for a few days."

I watched my mom dab tears of laughter from the corners of her eyes with a napkin. Now, Scarlett was slow dancing with Devlin, looking up at him like he was the sun and the moon and everything in between.

Shelby was leaning into her father's arm, laughing at some story he was telling June.

"Let's not ruin this," I said. "Everyone's having a good time. I'd rather keep it that way for another night." It was selfish. But there wasn't anything any of us could do about poor Callie Kendall. And this was my first family birthday party ever.

Bowie squeezed my shoulder. "Happy birthday, brother."

"Yeah. Thanks."

Chapter Thirty-Three
All of Bootleg Springs

D id y'all hear the news?"
"'Course we heard already. Such a shame. I always thought that that Callie girl was traveling in Canada with one of them there acrobatic acts."

"I always figured she was dead. May she rest in peace, of course."

"Why's that?"

"She ain't never come back, did she?"

"How you think the Kendalls are handling the news?"

"Doesn't seem like it's a surprise to them."

"They always figured she was dead and gone. Seemed right sure of it."

"I heard they was planning the funeral. Private. Don't want a buncha looky-loos pokin' their noses around the church and cemetery."

"What about the Bodines?"

"What about 'em?"

"Does this mean Jonah Sr.—may he rest in peace—killed her?"

"Hell if I know. With him dead and gone—rest in peace—I figure we'll never know what happened to that poor girl."

"I reckon Jonah Sr. did it. Who else would have?"

"What about that no-account Lester McCoy from over yonder in Hollersville? That sumbitch would put a rattlesnake in your pocket and ask for a light."

"You know, my Millie was a year younger than that Callie. I didn't let her leave my side for a year after that girl up and got herself killed."

"Everyone was huggin' their kids extra tight after that."

"And to think she's been dead this whole time. I hoped she'd gone off to Hollywood and got herself a star on that Walk of Fame."

"You know they pay for those, doncha?"

"The hell you say!"

"It's the God's honest truth. I was watching Under the Red Carpet, and they said how's the celebrity gets themselves nominated and then coughs up $30,000. Wham bam. Presto. They got their own star."

"That takes some of the fun out of it, don't it?"

"Sure does. I stopped hopin' Callie Kendall would get a star after I found out all about it. Still sad though."

"Quite the rolly coaster. One minute she's missing. Then there's this bloody sweater and she's dead. Then along comes that faker girl… What was her name?"

"Dunno. Fake Callie's what we call her 'round the dinner table."

"Along comes Fake Callie, and we all bust out the celebrations thinking she's alive and well. Now this. I gotta say, this feels like a letdown."

"How you think the Bodines are feelin' today?"

"I'm hoping they're feeling right guilty."

"That's a terrible thing to say! Why should they feel guilty?"

"Their daddy done did it, didn't he?"

"No one knows for sure."

"The evidence is there. In my mind, Jonah Bodine Sr., may he rest in peace, was a drunk and a murderer."

"I for one don't agree with the whole 'sins of the father' bullshit you're selling. That's like sayin' you should be responsible for your papa causing Mott's heart attack when they got in that hollerin' fit over at The Lookout twenty years ago."

"Pfft. That wasn't Pop's fault. Mott was the one who got all uppity about his bingo card."

"Still. I don't think it's fair that people are looking to point the finger at those Bodine kids. They're just as much victims, ain't they?"

"How y'all figure?"

"They grew up with Connie and Jonah, may they rest in peace, for parents. Them kids are lucky they didn't come out more screwed up."

"I bet that Jonah Jr.'ll be moving on now."

"If he does, it's 'cause old biddies like you telling everyone he's the son of a murderer."

"I'm just speaking my truth."

"You're speaking bullshit. There's a difference."

"Speaking of Jonah Jr., did you hear that he's dating that sweetheart Shelby Thompson?"

"Well, ain't that nice?"

"I heard he showed up at Springs Sundries and bought out just about everything in the bath section for her. Put together a real nice gift basket."

"Well, I heard that she went to Build A Shine and made herself up a recipe called Bootleg Boot Camp. Obviously, she was pokin' fun at him for being hungover after the moonshine tastin'."

"Oh, for sure. It's damn adorable."

"They're all puffed up about not being serious and about movin' on at the end of summer. But a lot can happen in one summer."

Q. What is your most reliable source for community news?

Cassidy Tucker: A five-minute walk down the street with your ears open.

Chapter Thirty-Four

Shelby

With a few notable differences, the Bootleg Springs Community Library was just like every other small-town library. Its book stacks were neatly organized in rows containing hundreds of volumes on everything from classical poetry to farmer's almanacs. The children's nook was too noisy. And the whole building smelled like furniture polish and old books.

Where it differed from most other libraries was in the people and the services. The head librarian, Piper Redman, was a pink pixie-haired walking billboard for piercings and tattoos. She was painfully cool. Literacy rates were on the rise just because she made reading look so darn cool.

She'd built programs not just around story hours and book clubs but expanded community services. There was a volunteer squad of tech support teens who every weekend walked some of Bootleg's less tech-savvy residents through problems with their mobile devices.

Then there was the free weekday shuttle that picked up

elderly residents and brought them in to socialize and volunteer. And, of course, the monthly spaghetti dinner, the proceeds of which went toward new books, better computers, and more comfortable reading chairs.

In an age when community libraries were struggling for funding and in some cases relevancy, Bootleg's library was thriving.

There was also an extensive local history section, which I was in the process of devouring.

I'd started out with good intentions. Jonah and my brother were off doing some fat-busting boot camp for two hours today. I planned to use the time to put together a timeline of defining events in town history.

But when I walked through the front door, the community bulletin board was different. There was no missing flyer of Callie Kendall where it always was. I'd guessed that flyer, or one like it, had been at the top of that bulletin board since the girl disappeared.

That made it even sadder, in my opinion. The surrendering of thirteen years of hope.

I pretended it didn't matter and settled in to the matter at hand. But in my cursory search of local newspapers on microfiche, I came across an article about the Kendalls after Callie's disappearance and then another. And another.

The disappearance *had* helped shape the community, I rationalized. I'd be doing a disservice by ignoring the tear that moment and the years that followed had ripped in the town's fabric.

An hour, I decided. I'd spare an hour and do a little digging into the Kendalls. Then I'd go back to my own work.

The microfiche blurred before my eyes as I consumed article after article about the disappearance, the family statements, the investigation. It was interesting that the Kendalls had never wavered from their claim that their daughter was dead, had harmed herself. Not until Fake Callie came onto the scene.

I called up a photo of Callie and another of Fake Callie. There was a resemblance, I thought, squinting at the screen. But more of a "You remind me of a girl I knew" way. The more I looked, the less Fake Callie looked like real Callie. And that bothered me.

Wouldn't her parents have known? If not by physical appearance, then by gaps in the imposter's knowledge of family history. How had Fake Callie convinced the Kendalls that she was their long-lost daughter?

They'd rented an apartment for her in Philadelphia. Far away from their home, even farther from Bootleg Springs.

I drummed my fingers on my lips. If they'd believed Fake Callie's story, wouldn't they have wanted to be close? To make up for all those lost years? The parents had seemingly given up hope of ever seeing their daughter alive again from the beginning, despite the lack of evidence. Wouldn't they have been overjoyed that she was still alive and reaching out to them?

Nothing about the situation sat right with me.

A thought fluttered in, took root.

On a whim, I pulled out my phone and ducked outside. It was hotter today. July arrived in a matter of days. The town was already decorating for the Fourth. Swathing everything that didn't move in red, white, and blue bunting.

Opting for the shade, I walked down the library steps and took a seat on a bench under a yet-to-be-swathed oak. I dialed, waited.

"Shelby Thompson! What are you doing on the other end of my phone?" my old friend and former supervisor from Allegheny County Children Youth and Families demanded.

"I'm doing a little research down here in the great state of West Virginia, Amanda, and I could use a hand with something."

"Name it, sweetie." Amanda had been my supervisor during my brief tenure as a social worker in Pittsburgh. She'd even come to the hospital's emergency department the night my career came to its disastrous end.

"Do you still have friends at the state level in Virginia?" I asked.

"Sure do." I could hear the click of her fingers on the keyboard as she multitasked. CYF's to-do list was never caught up.

"I was wondering if you could have them do a quick case search for me?"

"What county?" Amanda asked.

I screwed up my nose, knowing this was the big part of the ask. "All of them," I said.

Amanda blew out a breath. "It'll take a while." Counties had their own databases for managing children and youth cases. There was no central database connecting them, which made looking for information tedious and time-consuming.

"I know, and I really appreciate it. It's important," I promised.

"Gimmie the names, and I'll see if I can have something for you next week."

"Judge Henry Kendall, Mrs. Imogen Kendall, and Callie Kendall."

"Oh, boy. Sounds like you're down there kicking a hornets' nest." She sighed.

"I don't think there's going to be anything. If there was, the police would have already looked into it. I just want to be certain."

"Just don't go stirring things up by pointing fingers at a state judge."

"He might not be a state judge for long," I told her. "Word has it, our Judge Kendall is first in line for a federal judge appointment." News traveled fast. Especially news that Bootleggers could brag about. *Our Judge Kendall. Finally being recognized for his years of service. A federal judge? Imagine that.*

"Well, that happens," Amanda said, and I could tell she was getting distracted by the dozens of other tasks that required her attention. I gave her the date ranges to check, which posed an additional problem since some of the records from the earlier years still weren't electronic and promised to email her an update about what I was doing in rural West Virginia for the summer.

We hung up, and I stared unseeing across Main Street into the lakefront park where families picnicked and swam.

I couldn't shake the feeling that there was something sinister happening in Bootleg Springs.

"Shelby?"

I jumped a mile, wincing when my shoulder—which had been a little tender this morning—burst into flames of fresh pain. Dang it. I needed some anti-inflammatories STAT.

"Jenny. Hi. You startled me," I told her, pressing a hand over my pounding heart. I didn't like being snuck up on. Had never gotten over the trigger for that particular fear.

Jonah's mother looked pretty and fresh in shorts and a button-down blouse the color of summer skies. "Sorry about that. I was just on my way to meet…someone, and I saw you."

The way her cheeks pinked at the mention of "someone" I wondered if it was Jimmy Bob Prosser. She was headed in the direction of the hardware store, I noted.

"I was on the phone and didn't hear you," I said.

"I hope you don't mind, but I overheard a bit of your conversation. I understand where the interest comes from. It's a fascinating case. But it's closed now. They found her body. What are you expecting to find that law enforcement missed? "

"I'm sure investigators have done their due diligence," I assured her. "I'm just curious. It's a flashy story with a lot of shiny information for a researcher like me to play with. That's all."

Jenny sat down on the bench next to me.

"Men like Judge Kendall have the kind of power that others easily underestimate. Don't forget that. Don't underestimate him." It sounded less like friendly advice and more like a warning.

And she wanted me to hear it, abide by it.

"Do you know him?" I asked.

She shrugged, and the corners of her mouth lifted as she watched a pair of grandparents corral their three grandchildren on the sidewalk.

"Everyone knows people like him," she said vaguely. "Don't underestimate them, and don't do something that could be misconstrued as a threat. Men like that guard their power and their reputations fiercely."

"Like I said, I'm sure there's nothing to find," I said lightly.

"Good. I'd like to think that my son's casual summer fling is careful."

"You heard the news," I said. I wondered if I'd ever had the "so you are engaging in sex with my son conversation" before.

"I think Scarlett took out a billboard," Jenny said with an easy smile. "My son is a good man. And I think you'll treat him right. So don't expect any interference from me no matter how much I'd like to see him married and happy and to have a few grandkids on my lap."

The woman had said no interference. But she hadn't meant no pressure.

"Speaking of dating," I said, changing the subject to something a little safer. "You should probably tell me who you're meeting for lunch so I can do my duty as a temporary Bootlegger and spread the gossip."

We chit-chatted like two old friends for a few minutes until Jenny said she had to go. She was looping her purse over her shoulder when she stopped again.

"You haven't seen Gibson around lately, have you?" she asked.

I frowned, thinking. "No. Not since Jonah's party."

"Hmm," she said.

"Why?" I asked.

"I was just wondering how he was taking the news that the body they found was Callie Kendall. I hope all the Bodines are doing okay," she added quickly.

"They're all probably just waiting to see what will happen next with their father still a person of interest," I guessed.

Jenny pursed her lips and nodded. "Well, you have a nice day. Be safe, Shelby. My son likes you a lot."

There it was again. That vague warning that gave me a little shiver up the spine.

Chapter Thirty-Five

Jonah

Ten more burpees," I said, dropping down into a push-up position.

"I really fucking hate you right now," George groaned next to me.

"No, you don't. You hate that you have to go through this," I said, gritting my teeth through the push-up and hopping back on my feet.

"That, too. And burpees. I fucking loathe burpees," he said, climbing to his feet.

"Where's that jump and clap?"

I was practically begging to get punched in the face. But training George, a professional athlete, was pretty freaking awesome. The man's strength was circus-freak level. And his muscle had already burned off six unwanted pounds since we started working together.

He gave a lackluster bounce on his toes, a sloppy clap.

"Nine more. Let's go."

"I could punch you for these or the fact that you're sleeping with my sister and didn't tell me," he wheezed.

"Yeah, you could," I agreed.

"I want points for my self-control," George said, eyeing me before dropping down to the ground again.

"Consider points awarded."

We bitched and busted our way through them, and when it was over, we both lay down in the grass. Chugging water and swiping sweat out of our eyes.

"You're meaner than any trainer I had when I played," he complained.

"They have to be nice to you in the league. Can't have a bunch of three-hundred-pound babies crying about drills and sit-ups."

"So you and my sister?" George said, picking up the thread I'd let drop.

"Yeah," I said.

"As long as you're good to her, I won't plow my fists into your face," he said.

"Understood." I sat up, grabbed a foam roller, and tossed it to him. "Here, this will help you hate me less in the morning."

He leaned forward and rubbed at the scars on his leg. One bad tendon had brought his career to a screeching halt. "I gotta ask Shelby what she used on her scars to help them heal," he muttered.

I remembered the scar on her chest, the jagged one on her leg.

"How did she get them?" I asked. I'd noticed them, but their origin had never come up in conversation.

He studied me. "She doesn't like to talk about it," he said, taking another swig of water before shoving the foam roller under his hamstrings.

For a minute, I thought that would be the end of it.

"Since you're sleeping with her, living with her, I'd feel better if you knew. Sometimes she still has nightmares about it."

Despite the heat, the sweat, the hair on my arms stood up.

"This was back when she was fresh out of college. A family

Shelby was working with called her one night, late. They had a lot of issues, but the main one was their teenage son. Big sonofabitch, unstable. More than just impulse control shit. He'd taken a shine to Shelby. She could get through to him sometimes when others couldn't. But he kept going off his meds," George said, swiping a hand over his face. "He'd show up at her favorite coffee shop. The grocery store in her neighborhood. She made light of it. Like it was no big deal."

I felt the tension in him as he recalled it.

"She didn't listen to me. I was the overprotective big brother. She had it all under control. She just wanted to help."

"That sounds like Shelby," I said.

He nodded. "She cares too much. Thinks she can fix everything, and there are just some things, some people, you can't fix."

He rubbed his palms together slowly as he worked through his memories.

"One night, he showed up at her apartment. She didn't let him in, and he tried to kick in the door until one of the neighbors called the cops."

"Shit," I said, clenching my fists.

"Yeah. Her supervisor reassigned her. They'd seen shit like this before. The kid was obsessing. He'd do things just to get Shelby to show up at his place. Anything for her attention. So they tried to take her out of the equation. Assigned the family to a guy social worker."

"How did Shelby feel about it?" I asked.

George shrugged. "She keeps stuff private a lot. She doesn't like people worrying about her. But from what I could gather, she thought she failed him. Like somehow she should have convinced him to stay on his meds. They helped when he took them. But he'd forget, or he'd pretend to take them, and then he'd just lose control."

He got up and paced restlessly now. A brother who loved his sister.

I wondered how I'd feel if someone tried to hurt Scarlett. The wave of raw anger, fear, was instinctive.

"Anyway, one night, the mother called Shelby in a panic," he continued. "The son had chased her and the rest of the kids into a bedroom with a kitchen knife. They were locked in, and he was kicking and punching at the door."

"Why didn't she call the cops?" I asked, dreading the resolution of the story.

"Didn't want her son to get taken away. Shelby knew that. She told the mom to hang tight, she'd handle it."

I closed my eyes, took a breath.

"So she goes over there—"

"Alone?" I interrupted.

He nodded. "Like the innocent do-gooder she was."

The past tense got me.

"He was waiting for her. His mom told him through the door that Shelby was coming to help him."

"She knocked on the damn door, but it was already open." George rubbed a hand over his mouth, taking a moment. "It was dark inside."

My hands were clenched again. I crossed my arms over my chest and waited for the words he didn't want to say. The story I didn't want to hear.

"She walked in. All by herself. He came at her with the knife. They struggled. He got in a lucky swipe or two, the whole time screaming about how he loves her and they're going to be together. But his grip slipped because of the… the blood.

"She started to run, and she either tripped or he pushed her. But she took a header down the stairs."

"Jesus," I muttered.

"You know her," George said with a ghost of a smile. "Odds are she tripped over her own feet."

"Yeah, odds are."

"Anyway, another tenant—because everyone was in the hallway now calling 911—picked her up and carried her into his apartment. Another couple of them confronted the kid, got the knife away from him, held him down, until the cops came."

"Meanwhile, Shelby's texting me and my parents all like 'Don't freak out, but I'm heading to the hospital.'"

I could picture it.

"What my idiot sister didn't tell us is that kid nicked her femoral artery and she almost bled out in a stranger's apartment. By the time I flew in and my parents got there, she'd had a transfusion or two and was all smiles. Looked like that fucking vampire from the *Twilight* movie. So damn pale. Insisting that she was fine."

"What happened to the kid?" I asked.

"He was sixteen. He went into a juvie mental facility. I kept an eye on the court proceedings. He was charged as a minor, sealed record."

"So he's just out there now?" I was horrified.

"His family moved out of state. When he got out at eighteen, he moved with them. Shelby had moved too by that time. Different apartment. New neighborhood. Better security. She decided to go back to school and get her doctorate. I think she just wanted to find a different way to help people," he confessed. "Like it scared her bad enough that she couldn't work one-on-one with clients anymore. Moving into research made us all feel better."

"Smart girl," I said.

"That's why she's not on social media. You never thought it was weird that our little social scientist isn't on Facebook or Instagram?"

I hadn't given it much thought. Hadn't thought to ask.

"She cares too much and worries too little," George said. "The whole thing scared the hell out of me and our parents."

"She ever talk about it?" I asked, thinking about her diagnosis, her reluctance to discuss it.

He shook his head. "I think she thinks she's past it, but you'll see that fear every once in a while if something startles her."

I'd seen it and written it off.

"Brave girl," I said.

"The bravest. Sometimes I wish she weren't so brave. That she didn't think she had to handle everything on her own. She was always big on proving herself. And after seeing how worried we were when she was attacked, well, she'd probably never willingly tell us anything again. We hovered and smothered, did the family thing."

And that explained a lot. But it sure as hell didn't excuse her for shutting out the family that loved her.

"Well, she's safe here. She's got you, me, and an entire town of weirdos ready to back her up," I said lightly. But I meant it. I didn't know exactly what was happening between the two of us. But I was invested enough to make sure she never had to face that fear again.

Chapter Thirty-Six
Shelby

The lake was bathwater warm, but I sure as hell wasn't lounging in it. No, I was dragging my butt through it like it was molasses and I was a wrecking ball.

Something grabbed my ankle, and I shrieked under the surface. I surfaced sputtering.

"Shelby, honey, you gotta pull your face out of the water every once in a while. You don't have gills," Jonah said calmly as he tread water next to me. I got a good grip on his muscled shoulder and held on for dear life.

Purposely depriving myself of oxygen while traveling through water that I could have easily crossed in a boat was stupid. *Who invented triathlons anyway?*

"How far did I go?" I gasped, spitting out another mouthful of fishy lake water. I was swimming off Scarlett's dock.

"A hundred yards or so," Jonah gauged. We'd been working on speed to break up the monotony of the endurance workouts. He'd been yelling instructions from the end of the dock until I apparently stopped listening.

He was shirtless. Just the way I liked him. I tried to take a peek beneath the lake's surface to see if he'd lost his shorts, too.

"You're doing great," he said. "You just need to pull up more often. The more oxygen you get, the better you'll feel in the water."

"You jumped in here just to tell me that?" I asked, still breathing heavily. I wanted to try winking at him, but there was too much water on my eyelashes, and I ended up just blinking fast.

His eyes warmed as they skimmed my body beneath the surface.

"Maybe I had a few other thoughts I wanted to share with you," he said.

"I would very much like to hear those thoughts," I said, trailing a finger over his shoulder.

Was there anything sexier than a smiling, turned-on Jonah Bodine? I was willing to do some research, but I had a feeling it wasn't necessary.

"Have you ever gone skinny-dipping?" I asked suddenly.

He grinned at me, and my bikini bottoms got unrealistically wetter. "Not since my wayward teenage years. And, let me tell you, Jetty Beach water isn't nearly as warm as this lake."

"You know, if we weren't swimming off your sister's dock, I'd dare you to skinny-dip with me." I let my fingers take a wet little stroll up his chest and over his shoulder. He grabbed my hand, brought my fingers to his mouth, and sucked.

"Gah!" I forgot to tread water and went under.

Laughing, he pulled me back to the surface. We both looked back at Scarlett's house. It was awfully close to the water. And Devlin's SUV was parked in the driveway.

So much for a skinny-dipping fantasy.

"Let's focus on what we're here to do," he suggested, reaching beneath the surface and skimming fingers over the bottom edge of my bikini. I grabbed onto his shoulders to keep my head above water.

His eyes were watchful, sharp as I wrapped my legs loosely around his waist.

"I like swimming better than running," I confessed. His finger traced over my folds through the bathing suit bottom. My legs trembled. "And I like this better than swimming."

He grinned. "If we weren't in full view of my sister's house." He sighed.

"What about those hot springs everyone's always talking about?" I asked, sliding in for a wet kiss.

"You mean the secret hot springs that only the residents know about?" Jonah teased.

"I mean the hot springs where my brother met June and she asked him if he was masturbating."

He winced. "I really don't want to think about what other people do in the springs."

"But *we* could be doing it, too," I said, looping my arms around his neck.

"I tell you what. After you finish your triathlon, I'll take you to the hot springs."

"What if I don't finish?" I asked, biting my lip.

He spun us around so our backs were to the land and the lake stretched out before us. "You gotta play the mental game, too, Shelby. Don't just focus on the physical training. See yourself running. See yourself finishing."

I released him, rolled onto my back, and looked up at the blue, blue sky.

I tried to picture it. Me being driven over the finish line by a helpful ambulance. No. Me limping and sobbing my way to the finish line. No. Scratch that. I rewound the tape. If I put in the work, if I paced myself and fueled myself properly, I didn't have to limp and sob. I could finish strong.

"What do you see?" he asked, his voice husky. His hand snaking out to hold my ankle. I loved his touch.

I loved that I was still sleeping in his bed, but that wasn't all we were doing anymore.

"I see me," I said, bringing back the picture.

"Uh-huh. What are you doing?"

"I'm crossing the finish line—running, not on a gurney," I added. "People are cheering. Someone has a piece of pizza for me."

Jonah laughed softly.

"How do you feel?"

"Invincible," I whispered.

"Then that's how you'll finish," he promised.

The tips of my fingers brushed his as we floated side by side. Then his fingers were linking with mine. "You can do it, you know," he said.

"I'm starting to think I can."

"I tell you what," he said, releasing my hand and sinking back into the water. "I'll race you back to the dock."

"That's not even remotely fair."

He raised a hand. "I'll give you a head start. If you finish strong, you get to pick your reward."

My reward? *A make-out session with him in the water. An entire 12-pack of Mountain Dew. A whole day without training. More sex.*

I grinned slowly.

"What kind of reward makes you smile like that?" he asked.

"I want to practice the *Dirty Dancing* lift with you in the water," I insisted.

"I really wish I didn't know what that was." He sighed.

"But you do, and you will?" I pressed.

"Two attempts," he offered.

"Two? It's gonna take more than that. Five," I countered.

He eyed me thoughtfully. "Five." He nodded.

"Ready. Set. Go!" I dunked him and, with more enthusiasm than actual grace, swam like hell for the dock.

I cut through the water, remembering to pop my head up and breathe more often. It helped until I heard his approach behind me. Jonah did everything athletic well. And that included things that happened in the bedroom and the forest and the back seat of his car. The man was a prime physical

222

specimen. And my body was on high alert as he pursued me through the water.

I'd been chased before. Had been terrified by it. But this kind of a chase brought out something exciting, something primal in me.

I felt it click. The effort. The training. The endless research on proper form. And suddenly I was a fish. Jonah was closing in, but the dock was in sight. I shut off my mind and let my body do what it had learned to do.

I was the water and the air. I was the sun warm on my back. As the dock speared up in front of me, I reached for it. And felt his hand close around my ankle. He yanked me backward, and I sucked in half a lung of lake water in protest.

"Hey!" I sputtered, trying to swipe my bangs out of my eyes and cough up the lake I'd inhaled.

"Sorry, Shelbs. I won fair and square," he teased.

I fumed, splashing him in the face. "There was nothing fair and square about that! You cheated."

"Damn right I did. Had to! You got fast. Real fast."

I preened at the praise. "I did, didn't I? It all just kicked in at the same time."

"Maybe I should chase you the whole way through the triathlon," he mused.

"I'd have a heart attack halfway through it," I predicted. Though my heart sped up at the thought of Jonah chasing me again. "And since you cheated, I demand my prize."

He feigned a long-suffering sigh. "Fine. But don't knee me in the face."

"Yay!"

"Hang on," he said grabbing me when I tried to turn away from him. "Let's get closer to shore. I need to be able to stand up."

"Oh, right." I plowed through the water toward land, escaping his hands and the heat they scorched me with.

"Okay," he said, stopping me in the water. "You stay here." He backed away from me several paces. "You ready?"

"I was born ready."

He rolled his eyes. "Remember. No kicking me in the face," he called as I started running—or slogging—through the water at him.

Kicking wasn't a valid concern. Our first attempt had me kind of lunging at him. His hands slid under my arms and lifted me straight up.

"This doesn't feel right," he said under me.

"No, I'm supposed to be like horizontal. Our bodies should be perpendicular," I deduced.

"Right. Okay. So come in faster this next time, and I'll grab your waist," he suggested, still grinning up at me.

"If you put me down, I will." I expected him to toss me back into the water like a discarded fish. But instead, Jonah lowered me slowly into the water. Our slick bodies sliding against each other. Oh, I liked that. A lot. Too much.

He liked it, too, I noted with a satisfied smirk as I felt the prod of his erection.

"Okay, faster," I said as though I hadn't just slid down his body like a stripper pole.

"Faster." He nodded.

I returned to the starting place and hurled myself at him again.

The results were the same. "This isn't working," I called down from my vantage point above his head.

"This looks familiar," he said to my navel.

"Let's try going a little deeper. I'll kick off the dock and kind of launch myself at you," I suggested. "No kicking," I promised him before he could remind me.

The next two attempts were closer. Jonah actually fell over backward, which I considered to be respectable progress in our scientific method. We surfaced laughing, and this time he scraped my bangs out of my face.

"One more try," he said with a sexy eyebrow wiggle. I didn't even know eyebrows could be sexy before Jonah.

"We've got this," I said with confidence. "We're a good team."

I swam back and assumed the position. "Are you ready for me? Because I'm coming in hot."

"Oh, I'm ready for you," he assured me.

And he was.

His hands went around my waist, and just like with the swim, my brain shut down, and my body took over. I jumped as he lifted, and then I was airborne. Arms spread, core taut. I was flying, and Jonah was holding me up.

"We're doing it!"

"We are when we get home!"

Scarlett: I'm not sure, but it looks like Shelby and Jonah are practicing the lift from Dirty Dancing off my dock.

Cassidy: So cute! Also, we need to re-watch Dirty Dancing immediately.

Scarlett: Agreed. Hang on. I have to get a picture of this. We can give it to them at their wedding.

Cassidy: I'll go halfsies with you on a frame.

Chapter Thirty-Seven

Shelby

T hat scar," Jonah noted, when I climbed in the car next to him, soggy on the outside yet physically aroused inside. The plan was to go home, enjoy a quickie, as the cool kids called it, then meet my parents who were pig-sitting for June and GT. He trailed a finger over the jagged mark that scored my upper thigh.

It wasn't exactly a question, but I felt like he was hunting for an answer anyway.

"It happened a long time ago," I said. "Hey, have you seen Gibson lately? Your Mom was asking how he was handling this whole 'Callie Kendall is officially dead' thing."

"It looks like it was a pretty deep cut," he said casually, completely ignoring my segue.

I, being a trained observer, was instantly suspicious. "After I graduated with my bachelor's, I worked in the city as a social worker for a while. One of my house calls didn't go well." I said it lightly. I'd earned the right to say it lightly. To not tremble every time I thought of what happened in that apartment.

"Someone did that to you?" His voice was even, but I saw his jaw tighten.

"It's a long, boring story," I sighed airily. "So how is Gibson? Have you talked to him?" *Call me Miss Direction. Ha. Nerd joke.*

"He's not answering anyone's calls as far as I know. We've all taken turns. Probably just holed up with a project. Did it happen the same time as the one on your chest?" Jonah ventured.

He'd taken a very careful inventory of my body. First as a trainer and now as a very thorough lover.

"Okay, which one of my big-mouthed family members opened their gigantic mouths?" I demanded, dropping the pretense.

"Your brother. Why don't you want to talk about it with me?" he asked with that stupid sexy grin.

"It's not exactly the feel-good story of the year, Jonah." The truth was, I was proud I'd lived through it. But when people heard what happened, when they saw the scars, they looked at me differently. Just like I knew they would if they knew about my diagnosis.

I hated the pity, the worry, the whispered concerns.

"I'm perfectly capable of taking care of myself, you know," I snapped at the silent and listening Jonah. I wasn't angry at him specifically, but he was here. He was handy.

"I don't doubt that," he said in that careful neutral tone.

"Yes, you do. Everyone does. I'm too small. Too nerdy. Always have my nose stuck in a book. Too smart for my own good. Too much thinking, not enough doing."

"Has anyone *actually* said those things to you, or are you just putting words in people's mouths?" he asked.

I crossed my arms over my chest, the wet of my bathing suit bleeding through my t-shirt. "Plenty of people have said them, and more have thought them. For instance, if I'd been more assertive about seducing you, you wouldn't have dragged your feet for so damn long."

"You said 'damn.'"

"You're damn right I did." My temper was a hibernating dragon. It rarely reared its fiery head, but when it did, watch out. "That's how mad I am right now. What was GT's reasoning for telling you? Worrying that I couldn't take care of myself? Hoping you'll step up to be my new babysitter?"

"I realize you're the one with a psychology degree and an impending doctorate in social work, so I probably don't need to point out the fact that your anger seems a little reactionary, like I just pushed a button or something."

Gritting my teeth, I let out a throaty grumble. The man had a point. It wasn't exactly his fault that he'd stumbled across the one thing guaranteed to piss me off. "You want to know why I didn't tell my family about this whole ankylosing spondylitis thing?"

"Yes, unless that's a separate conversation. And then I'd like to finish this one first."

"When I was attacked, they descended on me. They moved into my apartment. They cooked my meals, did my grocery shopping, drove me to doctor's appointments. It was like I was a kid again. Like they didn't trust me to handle anything on my own. You know what happened when GT blew out his knee?" I asked.

"What?"

"Sure, Mom and Dad flew out for his surgery. But they didn't smother him to death. They even stayed in a hotel. Treated it like a visit. Because he wasn't me."

Jonah smirked.

"What?" I demanded. "What's that look for?"

"You're upset because you got more attention than your brother. That your parents love you so much they can't help but worry about you after you were attacked and stabbed." The easiness went out of him, and he was suddenly gripping the wheel as if he'd like to break it in half. "Injuring your knee on a football field and almost getting killed are two entirely different things. And you are more than smart enough to know that!"

I knew he had a point. I'd made the same point to myself

on several occasions. But sometimes it didn't stop the rush of emotions.

"You know what I think?"

"I'm sure you'll tell me anyway."

Even angry, I was maybe the tiniest bit curious about what he thought.

"I think that attack made you doubt yourself. You went in there thinking you could handle it, and then you couldn't contain the situation. You couldn't fix it. And that broke a piece off you. It's a piece that gets broken off everyone. But you're using it to think you can't do other things."

"Like what?"

"Like deal with your disease. Like finish a triathlon. Like write your goddamn dissertation. You think if you just put everything off by getting more information, doing more research, that you'll never have to actually see something through. And if you don't finish something, you won't be disappointed in yourself again."

"You know what I think about that, Jonah Bodine?" My voice was entering the Billy Ray howling octave.

"I *live* for your opinion," he said sarcastically as he pulled into our driveway.

"You are absolutely, without a doubt, one hundred percent right." Just like that, the anger burned itself out, leaving behind a lighter, brighter me.

Jonah cracked a grin.

"Have you ever thought about getting into counseling?" I asked.

He laughed. "I'm a personal trainer. It's the professional equivalent of a bartender."

"I don't mean to say this in an offensive way," I pre-empted. "But you are way more than just a pretty face and a six-pack. You are an excellent listener and keenly insightful. And I think I like your brain even more than I like your very nice body. To be clear, I like your body very, very much."

"Sounds like I'm going to be a very memorable summer

fling. Do you think you'll tell your grandkids about the hot, smart guy who talked sense into you?"

"Come sit with Grandma, little Shelby the Third, and let me tell you all about the boy I fell for for a summer," I said, affecting an elderly tone.

Jonah reached out, squeezed my knee. "I care about you, Shelby. Your family cares about you. That's not a bad thing."

"I feel like if they're worrying about me, then I'm not proving that I can take care of myself," I confessed.

"Families worry. Regardless of how well you can take care of yourself. And sometimes we all need a little help."

I unsnapped my seatbelt. "Speaking of families, your mom went on a date with Jimmy Bob Prosser. A proper one with dinner and candles last night. And she's hoping that you'll fall in love, get married, and give her some grandbabies."

I left him sitting behind the wheel, speechless, and went inside to let Billy Ray out.

Chapter Thirty-Eight
Jonah

"A re you sure you don't want to join us?" Mom asked me under the protective arm of Jimmy Bob Prosser as they escorted me toward the fire escape.

They'd invited me over for dinner, which I'd declined since I wanted to make sure Shelby was eating something healthy tonight. So we'd decided on drinks on the rooftop deck of the hardware store. Jimmy Bob lived in the apartment above the store, the back of which opened onto the first-floor roof overlooking the rear parking lot.

It was a cool, functional spot, with some camp chairs and a folding table. I could tell by the way my mom scanned the deck while we talked that she was mentally redecorating the space.

"I'm sure," I told her. "You two have fun with the banjo trio."

"Jimmy Bob's been taking banjo lessons from Mayor Hornsbladt," my mother said proudly.

I made a mental note to remind her of that particular

statement later. And add it to the list of things said only in Bootleg Springs.

"Really? That's great, Jimmy Bob," I said.

The big bear of a man blushed pink, his barn-broad shoulders hunching. "It's just a fun hobby," he said. "Drive safe now, you hear?"

"Will do, Jimmy Bob," I said, stepping onto the fire escape.

My mom gave me a sunny smile, which I returned.

She'd been cagey about when she was returning to Jetty Beach. She'd had a month's worth of vacation days saved up from all the years she'd never taken one. And since the diner where she worked back in Jetty Beach was closed for renovations, there seemed to be no rush to get back. Not when she was enjoying her own summer fling.

"Have a nice night, y'all," I said. "Thanks for the beer."

Shit. I'd said y'all. Bootleg Springs claimed another victim.

I got in my car and headed in the direction of home. My windows were down, letting the evening summer breeze into the car. Fireflies lit up and snuffed out, working out their own kind of Morse code on the humid night air. The crickets and tree frogs were competing for loudest celebration in the woods that flashed past my headlights.

I tapped my hands on the wheel in time to the Darius Rucker song I'd cranked and turned into the gravel drive of the Little Yellow House.

I felt *good*. Better than good. Especially when I thought of Shelby waiting for me at home.

Shelby.

Just thinking about her made me smile, I thought as the back of the house came into view. I knew it was a summer thing. A fling.

And maybe that was part of this feeling.

We were free to have fun, to just enjoy.

We'd developed our own routine. Waking early before any obligations, spending the first quiet moments of the day naked and playful. Learning each other's bodies. Most mornings, we worked out together, and in the evenings, I cooked and Shelby cleaned while we filled each other in on our days. Billy Ray at our feet or in our laps. In a sense, we were playing house without the strain of commitments and responsibilities. Of expectations and futures.

I wouldn't mind summer nights like this in my future, coming home to Shelby. More nights tangled up in the sheets, eating cold leftovers naked in bed while we laughed and talked.

I hoped that was the agenda for tonight.

I wouldn't mind if it was on the agenda every night. The thought, fleeting though it was, caught my attention. Could we find a way to make our own endless summer? Was that even a possibility? Was it something that I really wanted?

There were cars here, I noted, pulling around the front of the house.

My plans for a quiet, naked night evaporated.

I got out from behind the wheel to Billy Ray's excited yips. The front porch was dressed for fancy. Candles winked in the darkness, and a string of lights glowed on the railing, illuminating a linen-covered table set for two, a bottle of champagne in an ice bucket, and…was that a string quartet?

Yep. It looked as though Shelby had raided the Bootleg Springs High School band. The kids were dressed in the teenage version of fancy in jeans and black t-shirts. The cellist had braces.

I took a tentative step forward, and the quartet began to play a quiet country—of course—ballad.

But what caught and held my attention was Shelby. She stood on the top step in a pink party dress with a low scoop neck and a full skirt. She was smiling ear to ear, hands clasped in front of her.

"What's all this?" I asked, climbing the steps to her.

She leaned in and gave me a soft kiss. I tried to be mindful of our underage audience. But I still had a brain full of naked plans.

Her lips against mine, the soft brush of her body, the night air filled with nature's song. It went straight to my head. I wouldn't need the champagne. I was already buzzing.

"You're not the only one who wants to be memorable," she said, pulling back with a grin. The woman could light up a room or an entire front yard with that smile.

"Shelby, there isn't a chance on this Earth that I won't be remembering you when I'm eighty and leading a chair yoga class at the retirement home," I teased.

"Just making sure," she said.

Billy Ray scrambled against my leg, demanding his share of the attention. I leaned down to scoop him up but couldn't resist giving Shelby another kiss. Pretty in pink. Her dark bangs framed those wide eyes that sparkled like all the joy in the world lived inside her.

She took my breath away.

"Come on, dinner's ready," she said, leading me to the table.

I gave the dog a snuggle and a kiss before setting him down in front of his food and water dishes. A family dinner, I realized.

"You cooked?" I asked, trying to hide the apprehension.

"I ordered out," Shelby said smugly. She pointed to the heaping Cobb salads on the plates.

"Hi, guys," I said, giving the quartet a little wave. Fingers on strings and bows wiggled back.

I sat and admired the view as Shelby adjusted her skirts across from me.

"You're a hell of a girl, Shelby Thompson."

"Thank you for noticing, Jonah Bodine." She batted her lashes coyly, and I laughed.

We dined al fresco to live music. And I filled her in on the latest in my mother's relationship.

"It sounds serious," she mused, over her glass of champagne.

"It's just a fling," I predicted. "My mom isn't going to uproot her entire life to take a chance on love in Bootleg Springs."

"In that case, to summer flings," she said, raising her glass to mine.

"To summer flings," I echoed.

Later that night, I tipped the teenage musicians twenty bucks each and then guided Shelby upstairs. And when I settled over her, into her, with the flavor of champagne between us, I wondered again if there was more to this. To us. Than just one summer.

Q. In what ways do you interact with your neighbors outside of societal norms?

Walter Nagley: I play the violin on their front porches while they're on a date. Thanks for the $20.

Chapter Thirty-Nine

Shelby

N ext time you need a favor, can you please make it an easy one that actually pays off in the end?" Amanda huffed into my ear. It was a hot July morning. The park was still decked out from last week's holiday festivities, the breathtaking engagement ring Jameson had slid on Leah Mae's finger this weekend hadn't lost its sparkle, and I was hustling my wayward puppy through a series of training exercises on our walk through town that he was all too happy to ignore.

"I promise you I'll never ask for another favor again," I said, untangling Billy Ray's leash from my legs. Leash manners and walking etiquette were *not* his strong suit. He'd just gotten done wrapping me up with a cocker spaniel named Linda in the lakefront park when Amanda called.

"I'm afraid you might have wasted this one," she said. I heard her bite into something crisp and crunchy. Lunchtime for most social workers happened on the fly.

"No cases?" I asked, disappointed but not surprised.

"There was one."

I perked up and towed Billy Ray toward a park bench, wishing I had a notebook on me. Jonah and I were meeting up after his personal training session to swap dog parenting duties, so I hadn't thought to bring anything with me besides a collapsible water dish for the puppy.

"You're kidding me," I said. I felt the interest hum to life inside me. New information. Something no one else had. It was a researcher's fantasy.

"Unsubstantiated claim in Henrico County. It's an old file, so it looks kind of like someone forgot to enter ninety percent of the information, including what the initial complaint was. Unfortunately, par for the course since the move was made to electronic records. And it was sealed."

That explained why it had never made the news.

"Does it say who reported it?" I asked, drumming my fingers against my lips. The puppy sniffed after a butterfly and then lifted his leg on a pinecone.

"There's a name but no title. I'll send you the particulars. My contact copied me on it, so I'll email you the file. Not much there. It was from back in '98. Odds are it was an elementary teacher, maybe a school nurse or someone along those lines."

"Thanks for the info, Amanda. I owe you big time."

"I don't know what you're up to. But be careful," she cautioned me.

I started dialing the second the call disconnected.

"Hello?"

"Hey, June. It's Shelby."

"I ascertained that fact from my caller ID," she said.

"You tracked down the fake Callie, didn't you?" I asked.

"Yes. Is that all? I'm occupied teaching Katherine to fetch."

"How would you feel about taking a road trip with me today?"

"No, thank you. I prefer to stay here with my pig."

"What if you could bring her along? I'll bring Billy Ray."

"Where are we going?"

"We're tracking down two people who might have information about Callie Kendall," I told her.

"I assume you mean information besides the fact that she is deceased?" she asked.

"Yes," I promised. "I think we could find something that might point suspicion away from Jonah Bodine Sr."

June sighed. "Fine. But I'll want lunch. A turkey sandwich. Turkey Tuesday."

Callie Kendall was dead. But there were still questions. And if I could get a few of them answered for Jonah and the rest of the Bodines, we'd all sleep better.

————————

After another phone call, a handful of texts, and a stop at the Pop In for gas and provisions, I swung by June's house. June hefted the haltered Katherine up and into the back seat. Katherine oinked a greeting at Billy Ray, who bravely licked her face and then cowered in the corner.

June was wearing a ball cap featuring the logo of GT's team rivals. Beneath the brim was a pair of movie star-huge sunglasses.

"Did GT see that hat?" I asked.

She shook her head. "It's part of my disguise. I borrowed it from Opal Bodine. If we're tracking down the Fake Callie Kendall, I've ripped hair from this woman's head. It would be safer for all of us if she did not recognize me."

"Smart," I said, typing in the first address into the GPS program. "First stop: Abbie Gilbert."

"What are we talking to her about? Is there a requirement for good cop, bad cop? I think I could perform an effective bad cop," June said.

"We're asking her why the Kendalls believed that she was their daughter."

She pursed her lips under the glasses. "Do you believe they knew Abbie was not their daughter?"

"It's crossed my mind."

"Then why would they give her an apartment? Why would they publicly claim her as their daughter?" she asked.

"That's what we're going to find out." I pointed to the bag at her feet. "There's a turkey sandwich in there for you."

"Turkey Tuesday."

———

Abbie had been booted from her upscale Philadelphia apartment financed by the Kendalls. She now lived in a squat, gray brick building on the outskirts of Baltimore. The neighborhood was made up entirely of rundown row homes and graffitied convenience stores. Fast food bags and the cardboard from six-packs littered the sidewalks and gutters.

It didn't feel dangerous. Just well past its prime. Like its residents had given up on keeping up appearances.

I put the car in park and cranked up the air conditioning. "Do you want to wait here with the kids?" I asked June.

She looked torn, peering into the back seat where her beloved Katherine was enjoying a snack of lettuce and pellets.

"I should accompany you," she decided reluctantly.

We locked the car and crossed the road to the apartment building. *A. Gilbert* was listed above Apartment B3. I pressed the buzzer and waited.

There were no security cameras here, and some of the mailboxes inside the foyer had their doors broken off. It did not give off a homey vibe.

I buzzed again. Waited.

"Perhaps she is at work?" June suggested.

I shook my head. "Cassidy says there's no job on record for her."

"My sister gave you this address?" June asked, surprised. Cassidy Tucker was straight as an arrow. A good guy to the bone. She took the law and its rules very seriously.

"Of course not," I scoffed. "I had Leah Mae use her super social media sleuthing powers to track her down."

"I just asked Cassidy if she knew if Abbie was employed."

239

"She must have been suspicious," June insisted. On cue, her phone rang, and Cassidy's name scrolled across the screen.

"Maybe don't answer that until we're on our way home," I suggested.

"I believe that is the correct course of action."

I stabbed the buzzer for B2 belonging to an M. McManus.

We waited another minute, the hot sun baking us on the sidewalk. "Maybe we should go back to the car. We have another stop to make. We could try Abbie again afterward."

June gave the front door a hard tug, and we both watched bemused as the door opened.

"Some security system," I muttered.

We took the stairs to the second floor. The paint on the walls and railing was peeling, and the carpet had bare spots, but overall it was clean. B3 was the second door on the left. I held my ear to the door and listened.

"What are you doing?" June asked at normal volume.

I eased back and shushed her. "I'm trying to see if she's in there. She might not be answering the buzzer because she doesn't want to talk."

"This is taking too long. I would like to get back to my pig." She reached around me and rapped her knuckles on the door. "Abbie Gilbert. I would like to speak with you."

A dark head poked out of the door across the hall. "You're going to have to yell a hell of a lot louder than that."

June took a breath. "ABBIE GILBERT—"

I cut her off with a hand on her arm. "That's not what you meant, is it?" I asked the woman.

Her jet-black hair was styled in a pristine bowl cut. She was wearing a purple and yellow housecoat and slippers that looked older than me.

"The poor girl," the woman tut-tutted. "Couldn't catch a break. Said her boyfriend broke up with her and she lost her job in Baltimore."

June opened her mouth to argue, but I squeezed her arm.

"Do you know where we could find Abbie?" I asked.

The woman frowned. "That's what the police called her, too."

"The police?" June asked.

"We knew her as Ashley. Not Abbie. But whoever she was, she was hit by a car and killed last Thursday. Hit and run on her way home from the liquor store," the neighbor said, shaking her head sadly. "Like I said. The girl couldn't catch a break."

Chapter Forty

Shelby

I did not anticipate that," June said when we returned to the car.

Katherine danced on dainty hooves in the back seat, thrilled at June's return. Billy Ray was too busy napping under a napkin to notice that I was back.

"Can you look the accident up on your phone?" I asked grimly as I input the second address into the GPS. "There should be an accident report or a news story."

Dutifully, June performed a search with one hand while scratching Katherine's head with the other.

"Died on Thursday crossing Miller Avenue sometime after midnight," she read. "Struck by an unknown vehicle. There were no witnesses and no suspects."

"That's convenient," I muttered.

Odds were, it was a legitimate accident. A drunk driver fleeing the scene. A kid joyriding in stolen wheels. Abbie's death most likely was not suspicious. And yet it nagged at me.

Loose ends.

"Thursday," I said, opening a bottle of water and taking a long drink. I wished it were Mountain Dew. "Saturday is when they found that the dental records were a match."

"Are you suggesting that those events are connected?" June asked.

"I don't know. I don't see a connection, but that doesn't mean there isn't one."

I drummed my fingers on the steering wheel and thought.

"Abbie Gilbert had a court date for the fraud complaint brought by the Kendalls. But essentially, she was no longer part of the story. Abbie was unveiled as an opportunist, and now Callie is deceased. The missing person portion of the case is closed. Unless Abbie was the one who committed the homicide, I fail to see her connection," June said.

I didn't have an inkling either.

"Maybe someone was worried that the press would come asking more questions once the remains were identified. Like how did Abbie convince the Kendalls that she was Callie? Wouldn't someone be wondering how she fooled them?"

"Perhaps. But why wait until now? Why not run her down with a vehicle immediately after discovering she committed fraud? And are you insinuating that you believe the Kendalls have some responsibility in Callie's death?"

"I'm not insinuating anything," I promised. "I'm just not positive that one of them didn't have something to do with her death."

The sun did little to warm the chill developing in my body as I steered onto the highway and headed southwest. It was too convenient, Abbie's death. The one person who could answer questions about exactly why the Kendalls accepted her as Callie was gone. And I certainly wasn't about to walk up to Judge Kendall and demand an explanation.

"Let's walk through this. What if the Kendalls knew she wasn't Callie?" I said.

"That theory makes no sense. Why would they publicly perpetuate the myth that their daughter had been found?"

I bit my lip, considering. I remembered those cool gray eyes and shivered. "Judge Kendall is up for appointment to a federal judgeship," I said. "A big deal, right?"

"It is a prestigious position," June agreed.

"A lot of power, prestige. He wouldn't want to jeopardize that. Right? He wouldn't want anything from his past coming to light that would cast doubt on his character."

"Investigators always look at the family first. It's standard procedure," she reminded me. "Judge Kendall was never named as a suspect or a person of interest."

Could anyone cover their tracks that well?

"Your expression suggests you are angry," she said.

"This is my thinking face," I explained.

"Where are we going now?" she asked.

"North Bethesda," I told her. "There's another person who might have some insight into the Kendalls' relationship with their daughter."

"What makes you think there was an issue in the relationship?" June asked, fishing in the bag at her feet and pulling out the other half of her turkey sandwich.

"I can't explain it. It's just a hunch, a feeling in my gut. I've met a lot of families, a lot of dysfunctional families, and the Kendalls are ringing that bell for me."

"I do not hear a bell," she said.

I smiled. I loved the literal mind of June Tucker. "You're a fact girl, aren't you, June?"

"I rely heavily on facts," she agreed as she chewed a bite of sandwich.

"As a researcher, I too have to rely on facts. But in my line of work, it was essential to develop instincts as well. And my instincts are telling me that there's something off about this entire situation."

"But nothing you discover will change the fact that Callie is dead."

June had me there.

"If I can find information that will give the Bodines any

hope at all that their father was not involved in Callie Kendall's murder, I intend to do it."

"That makes sense. It's our duty as friends to ease their suffering."

"Then let's find some answers for them."

"Perhaps your instincts are rooted in fact," she suggested. "I was certain there was something false about Abbie Gilbert's story but was unsure what the falsehood was until I did my research."

"Then let's do a little research in Bethesda," I said.

"What is in Bethesda?"

"The junior high music teacher who reported signs of suspected child abuse involving Callie Kendall in 1998."

June frowned. "My research did not uncover any such report," she said.

"It was sealed and recanted," I explained. "It took some digging, and the case file is basically empty. The only thing that exists is the date, the accuser's first and last name, and her written retraction." I really owed Leah Mae for her social media research skills.

"If this teacher recanted her concerns, that means she was wrong." June frowned.

"We're just tying up loose ends," I assured her. "It's probably nothing. Let's go into this with an open mind."

In my time as a social worker in Pittsburgh, I had seen a lot. Not everything, but enough to know that people were capable of just about anything. Including filing false abuse and neglect reports. I'd seen angry exes file reports of child abuse against their former spouses just to get back at them. I'd also seen well-meaning people with genuine concerns file complaints only to have the investigations show the claims were baseless. In those situations, relationships were damaged, reputations tarnished.

But someone at some point looked at Callie Kendall and wondered if someone was hurting or neglecting her. And June and I were going to ask that woman some questions.

We took a break at a rest stop and let the dog and pig

stretch their legs. Both pig and puppy drew a crowd of admirers before we got back in the car and headed south into North Bethesda. Cece Benefiel retired from teaching in Richmond and moved to Maryland to be closer to her children. It also made her conveniently closer to us.

North Bethesda was tidier than Abbie Gilbert's town. Wide sidewalks crisscrossed under canopies of neatly trimmed trees. Red brick buildings lined the trash-free streets. Everything felt well-maintained and proud.

I followed the GPS directions and twenty minutes later, we pulled up in front of a dull gold split-level home. The yard was maintained by an avid gardener, I guessed. Tall spikes of wildflowers and grasses exploded out of tidy flowerbeds. The grass was jade green and cut in a crosshatch pattern that spoke of pride and precision.

"This is much more pleasant than the last place we attempted to sneak into," June observed. "Does this music teacher know that we are coming?"

I shook my head. "I didn't want to scare her off with some cryptic message asking questions about a children and youth report she filed twenty-odd years ago."

"That was probably wise," she said, adjusting her ball cap. "Do you suppose I will still have the opportunity to play bad cop?"

I laughed. "I hope so. I'd love to see it." We left the car running, the air conditioning cranked, and crossed the street.

We followed a winding walk through azaleas and tall fluffy grasses to the front porch. I reached for the bell, but June stopped me.

"If this music teacher is also deceased, then I will start to share your suspicions."

"Let's hope that's not the case."

Chapter Forty-One
Shelby

Mrs. Cece Benefiel was very much alive and thrilled to have the company.

Especially once I told her we were interviewing retired teachers for a grad school project.

Fortunately the woman didn't catch June's "No, we're not," as she ushered us inside.

Her husband, Mr. Benefiel, was on a three-day golf trip with two of their adult sons and three grandsons, she explained. She insisted that she was always happy to talk to fellow lovers of education. I took the information dump as a hopeful sign that she was an over-sharer.

She was just what I would have wanted in a music teacher. Bubbly with short, fluffy hair, reading glasses worn on a chain, and bright smile that insisted we were welcome. My junior high music teacher, Mr. Hendricks, by contrast, was a balding, angry fifty-something going through a divorce and taking it out on his students.

I felt a tiny stab of guilt at misrepresenting our reason

for being there but managed to shove it aside. We were on a mission. Also, it was almost worth it just hearing June introduce us as "July and Sheila."

"I promise we won't take up too much of your time," I told her as she led us into her living room. It was cozy and crowded with furniture that looked as if it had been heavily used and well-tended for at least a decade. I imagined some of the half-dozen grandchildren in frames adorning the wallpapered walls enjoyed bouncing on the overstuffed sofa and mismatched, but equally comfy, armchairs. This was the home of someone who appreciated and enjoyed family.

"It is no trouble at all, Sheila. I'm thrilled to have some company," Mrs. Benefiel insisted. "I was just about to make some tea. Would you like some?"

"Do you have any cookies?" June asked.

I elbowed her.

"Of *course* I have cookies." Mrs. Benefiel beamed. "I'll be right back." The woman disappeared toward the back of the house, and I could hear the sounds of a kettle being readied.

"That was not very polite," June said, rubbing her ribs.

"We're here for information. Not snacks."

"George is on a diet, which means I am on a diet. George isn't here, so I can have cookies. Grandmas make the best cookies." Her logic was flawless.

"Eat as many of them as you can before I tell her why we're really here."

"You got us invited inside on false pretenses. I'll accept snacks on false pretenses," she said. "How will you broach the subject of Callie Kendall?"

I shrugged. "I haven't gotten that far yet."

I hoped she would provide an opening for me. I didn't feel good about being booted from an elderly school teacher's very nice home.

Mrs. Benefiel returned carrying a tea tray. "Do either of you two mind dogs?" she asked.

"Not at all. We both enjoy pets," June said.

"Oh, wonderful! Then you won't mind if Scout joins us. Scout! Come!"

I heard the thunder of what was way too big to be paws tearing down the hall. Pictures in the frames rattled on the wall. Knickknacks on shelves trembled.

The beast that loped into the room wasn't a dog as much as a bull, an elephant, a rhinoceros. She was tall and leggy with blue-gray fur. Her ears were perked up over one blue eye and one brown.

"There's my sweet little girl," Mrs. Benefiel crooned. Scout sat on her haunches and remained at my eye level. "She's a Great Dane."

"My pig is in the car," June announced. Mrs. Benefiel blinked behind her glasses. "I'm sorry, my dear, did you say pig?"

"Yes. Her name is Marie Curie," June said.

I blinked. June had just given her pig an alias.

She dug her phone out of her back pocket. "Would you like to see some pictures?"

"Well, if she's in the car, why don't you bring her inside?" Mrs. Benefiel suggested, putting her reading glasses on to better admire June's pig.

"Sheila's puppy is in the car as well," June mentioned.

"Oh! Scout loves puppies," our hostess exclaimed.

While I was trying to discern whether she meant Scout loved puppies for breakfast or as playmates, June trotted outside to retrieve our pets.

Five minutes later a pig, a dog, and a horse—because there was no way Scout was a dog—were chasing each other all over the first floor of Mrs. Benefiel's home while June and I drank green tea and ate freshly iced sugar cookies.

"Now, tell me about this project of yours, Sheila and July," Mrs. Benefiel insisted.

Scout tore through the living room chased by an ecstatic Billy Ray. Katherine trotted through at a more leisurely pace.

"Mrs. Benefiel I'm sure you've taught hundreds of children over the years," I began. "I'm sure you had a few favorites."

June grabbed a second cookie.

Mrs. Benefiel chuckled. "Well, now dear, we try not to have favorites. But there are always a few students every year that stand out."

"How many years did you teach?" I asked.

"Thirty-two years. And nearly every day was a delight."

"I imagine you've seen it all in your career," I ventured. "Good and bad."

"Oh, certainly." She nodded, her glasses swinging on the chain around her neck. "Teaching is more than just rules and grades and summers off. We're peacekeepers and protectors, too."

That was my opening. I went for it, swinging for the fences. "Do you remember Callie Kendall?" I asked.

A flicker of wariness danced across her face, and her teacup trembled on its saucer in her lap.

"What kind of project is this?" she asked, softer this time.

Billy Ray chose that moment to trot into the room proudly dragging a six-foot-long stuffed snake toy. Scout was on the other end of the snake, putting up a good show of playing tug. I hoped my sweet puppy's antics assured her that I wasn't an enemy.

"Mrs. Benefiel, I am in grad school, but I also have a license in social work. I know that you filed a complaint with Henrico County Children Services in 1998."

She set her cup and saucer down with a definitive snap.

"I made a mistake," she said, coming to her feet. "A terrible, terrible mistake. And I told the authorities that." That was fear etched on her face. Stark fear caused by some unknown threat.

I rose. June's hand snaked out for another cookie, sensing our visit was coming to an abrupt end.

"Mrs. Benefiel, I think that maybe you weren't wrong," I said softly. "I don't know what happened, but I think you saw something, and you were right to report it."

"She was a good girl. Bright and sweet. So quiet. But she came alive in music class. She loved music of all kinds," Mrs.

Benefiel said, her hands bunching into fists at her sides. "But I was wrong."

June stood up, too. "I am confused by this conversation. You say you were wrong, but you are acting as though you are supposed to say that you are wrong."

"Are you working for him?" she whispered, eyes glistening. "Because I haven't done anything wrong. I did what I said I would. I kept my promises."

"Who, Mrs. Benefiel? Who are you afraid of? We aren't working for anyone. No one knows we're here."

"He knows. Or he will," she said flatly.

"I promise that no one knows we're here. We came because our friends' father is a person of interest in her murder."

"Callie Kendall deserved better than what she got in this life," Mrs. Benefiel said, her voice shaking. "Now, please leave."

"We can help you," I said earnestly. "If you need help, we can figure it out together."

She shook her head. "No. Please go."

"I'm very sorry for upsetting you," I said, gathering my purse.

"Garth. Marie Curie," June called. "Come." Pig and puppy jogged into the room, tails wagging.

She showed us to the door, tension in every movement.

"I'm sorry I can't help you." Her eyes implored me, and then she was looking past me and at the family photos on the wall behind me.

Chapter Forty-Two
Shelby

After terrifying an elderly woman in her own home that we gained entrance to under false pretenses, I felt like I'd done enough damage for the day.

We headed home with our exhausted pets, immune to the terror their mommies unintentionally inflicted, snoozing in the back seat.

"I have concerns that Mrs. Benefiel was not being completely honest," June said, polishing off the last bite of cookie.

"I have similar concerns," I agreed, merging onto the highway and pointing us in the direction of Bootleg Springs.

"Who is the 'him' she asked about? Perhaps we should turn around and go back and ask for clarification?"

"I think she's probably had enough questions for today."

"Perhaps I don't read people with any consistency. But I felt her physiological reactions point toward fear," she said, frowning out her window.

"Someone—besides us—scared Mrs. Benefiel, and I think it was tied to that children services report," I said grimly.

I thought of Judge Kendall again. Those flat, cool gray eyes. Was he capable of aggression? Of violence? And if so, could he inflict both on his own daughter?

The sigh escaped me in a whoosh.

"Are you having difficulty breathing?" June asked.

"No. I'm feeling frustrated. I expected to come home with at least a few answers instead of just more questions. And what did we find out?"

"We discovered that the woman who impersonated Callie Kendall, bilking the Kendalls out of money and an apartment, is now deceased. And the accident remains unsolved," she summarized. "Then we questioned Mrs. Benefiel, who perpetuated the existing story. That she made a report and then immediately recanted it."

"Yep. That's what we found out," I agreed, feeling tired and frustrated. I'd forgotten lunch and now wasn't even hungry.

My phone rang, and I winced when I saw the readout on the screen. Jonah.

I hit the ignore button. "We should probably decide on what we're going to tell Jonah and GT about where we were today," I told June.

She blinked and frowned at me. "That we went to Baltimore to question Abbie and found her deceased. Then we drove to Mrs. Benefiel's home where Katherine and Billy Ray got to play with her Great Dane while we questioned her about the sealed child services report."

"We can't tell them that!"

"Why not? It's the truth."

"Do you always tell GT the truth?" I didn't know if I was more nervous about Jonah or my brother discovering how we'd spent our day.

"Of course. What's the point of being in a relationship if you feel it necessary to tell falsehoods?" she asked, looking at me as if I'd just suggested that math was stupid and shouldn't be taught in schools anymore.

"Well, I…" I didn't know what to say to that. It wasn't that I didn't trust Jonah…was it?

Of course not. He was a good guy.

I was just trying to avoid his judgment over what might be deemed questionable behavior. I didn't want to have the argument that would undoubtedly unfold when I explained that I stuck my nose into an investigation without trusting law enforcement to do their due diligence.

"Oh, hell," I whispered. I was doing exactly what he'd called me out for doing. Hiding things from people I cared about so I didn't have to face their reactions or defend myself. I didn't think I'd done anything truly wrong today. Besides upsetting Mrs. Benefiel. I felt terrible about that, and I was planning on sending her a nice fruit basket or maybe a pizza gift certificate as an apology.

"You shouldn't be dishonest with Jonah," June said, pulling her ball cap off and stuffing it into her purse. She didn't bother looking in the mirror to fix her hair.

"I know. I know." I *did* know. But old habits were hard to break.

"Sometimes men surprise you in delightful ways," she said. "Sometimes they accept you for exactly who you are. But the only way you can discover that kind of relationship is by behaving authentically."

"Oh, June," I sighed. "You're a good friend."

"Yes. I am."

I cracked a smile. Maybe it was time to stop shutting everyone out. I was thirty years old and this close to a doctorate. I shouldn't spend my time worrying about having to defend my decisions. If Jonah didn't like who I was, then he was welcome to move on and find someone else less curious, less rash, less creaky in the joints.

I gripped the steering wheel a little tighter. I had to trust Jonah to accept me. I owed that to him.

"I feel that we should bring our findings to my father's attention," June announced as I pulled into her driveway. Katherine, sensing she was home, woke with a snort.

Part of me wanted to retain ownership of the research. But a slightly smarter part recognized that it was a better choice to turn things over to Sheriff Tucker and let him pass them up the chain of command. If my concerns were dismissed, then I'd be free to continue my own investigation.

"I think that's a good idea, June. How about I go home and talk to Jonah? Then we can go see your dad at the station?"

"That will be acceptable."

June and Katherine got out and headed into the house. I spent the five-minute drive home practicing what I'd say to Jonah.

"Hey, so you know how I said I was taking Billy Ray on a playdate with June and Katherine? Well, instead I took everyone on a road trip to interrogate the Callie Kendall impersonator—who by the way is conveniently dead as of Thursday—and a really sweet retired music teacher who I'm pretty sure cried after we left. What's for dinner?"

Billy Ray propped his paws up on the console and yipped.

"It's just a first draft," I explained to the dog. "Uh-oh. Daddy's home." I pulled in behind Jonah's car. He was stretching on the front porch, taking hits from a water bottle.

He looked up, grinned, waved.

My heart did a little thump hop in my chest. Just physical attraction, I told myself. Just appreciating the fine male form.

"Hey there, cutie pie," he said, descending the stairs to meet me in the driveway.

He brushed his mouth over mine in a sweet, lazy kiss.

My cheeks flushed with heat. I couldn't tell if I was nervous about coming clean or if it was something else. Something about coming home to Jonah Bodine who called me cutie pie and kissed me in the front yard.

"Hi," I said breathlessly.

"There's my buddy," Jonah said, kneeling down to rough

up Billy Ray's ears. The puppy looked about as smitten as I felt. Oh, boy. I was in serious trouble.

"We were invited to dinner with your parents, drinks at Jameson and Leah Mae's, and out on a double date with my mom and—God help us all—Jimmy Bob Prosser," he announced, scooping the puppy up under one arm and slinging his free arm over my shoulders steering me toward the house.

"Oh?" Since we'd initiated our physical relationship, we'd gotten awfully popular.

"I told them all we were busy," he said.

"You did? What are we busy doing?" *Besides spending the evening fighting over what I'm about to tell you?*

"Each other," he said with a devilish wink. His hand skimmed my bare arm, and my sensible underwear dissolved.

"Before we, um, participate in that particular activity, we do have to do something fully clothed and socially um... necessary."

————

Scarlett: Has anyone talked to Gibs lately?

Bowie: Gibs who?

Jameson: Does Gibs willingly talk to anyone?

Jonah: Haven't heard from him since the cookout.

Scarlett: I'm getting annoyed with the hermit routine. Y'all think he's wallowing?

Bowie: I'll give him a call and obnoxiously pump him for information. I need a favor from him anyway.

Scarlett: Bless your Bodine heart! Lemme know if the grumpy bastard needs anything.

Chapter Forty-Three
Jonah

I took it as well as I could. Mindful that this was very likely some kind of Shelby test.

So my girlfriend took our dog, our friend, and our friend's pig on an investigation road trip because she was convinced she had a lead that investigators had ignored for thirteen years. And now she needed to go to the sheriff and explain what she'd found.

I took another cleansing breath.

"Do I have time for a shower?" I asked.

Shelby blinked. She'd been twisting her hands together and biting the corner of her bottom lip.

"Uh. Yeah? I mean, sure," she said.

"Okay. Why don't you grab a snack while I shower and change?"

"Yeah. Great. Sure. Wait!" She grabbed me when I started for the stairs. "You don't seem mad."

"I'm not." I wasn't really mad. Mad wasn't the right word. Concerned. Annoyed. Extremely cognizant of the fact that if

I launched into a lecture on what she should have done, I'd be reinforcing the concerns she had about sharing information with people who cared about her. Nothing good would come from me blowing up at her. So I gave her a smile and a gentle shove in the direction of the kitchen. "See you in a few."

I dashed up the stairs and stripped in the bathroom. My face was under the stream of tepid water when the door burst open.

"I'm not buying this 'not mad' thing," she announced, waving a yogurt cup at me. "I did something a little bit on the stupid side today, and you're fine with it?"

I turned to face her. "Stupid is a little harsh, don't you think?" I said mildly.

Her gaze traveled down my body, lingering on the interesting parts.

Not wanting to miss out on the conversation, Billy Ray trotted in behind her and sat down on the bath mat.

"I tried to track down a known con artist and then intimidated a really nice older lady because I had a hunch."

"From the sounds of it, your hunch has some basis to it." I ducked my head back under the water to rinse the shampoo.

She watched me for almost an entire minute, eyes narrowed and calculating. I twisted off the faucet and stepped out. In the bathroom the size of a postage stamp, we were almost touching.

I reached around her for a towel and heard her intake of breath.

"I know what you're doing," she said, spooning yogurt into her mouth, her expression a picture of suspicion.

"What am I doing besides drying off?"

"You're proving to me that telling the truth to people I care about doesn't necessarily have to have the consequences I fear."

Smart, smart girl.

"Is that what I'm doing?" I asked innocently.

"Jonah!"

"Shelby!"

"I'd rather you be honest with me," she said. Then she laughed. "Darn you, June Tucker," she muttered.

"You'd rather I be honest?" I repeated.

"Yes!" It looked like Shelby's answer surprised her, and that took the edge off my frustration. "I was honest with you. Now it's your turn. Jonah, I took our puppy and our friend plus a pig on a road trip with the intention of interrogating two strangers. One of which was under investigation for fraud until she mysteriously ended up *dead*. Then I made a grandma cry after taking cookies from her under false pretenses."

"At least you didn't go alone," I said mildly.

"Jonah Bodine!" She stomped her foot, and Billy Ray let out a joyful bark, certain it was a game.

"Shelby Thompson. What do you want me to say?"

"The truth. What are you thinking right now?"

"I'm thinking that I'm glad you grabbed a yogurt instead of some garbage candy for your snack. I'm thinking you look so pretty right now that it's hard to concentrate on how much I want to yell at you."

"Thank you! Go ahead and yell," she shouted.

I obliged. "What in the hell were you thinking, Shelby? Do you have any idea what could have happened to you or June? That con artist could have been more than a fraud, and you know it. She could have been dangerous. It was irresponsible, and you should have told me. You could have talked me into going with you. You know I would have."

"You would have tried to talk me out of it and then complained the whole time about what a dumb idea it was!"

"That's exactly what I would have done!" I agreed at full volume.

"I really like you! Your opinion matters to me. I didn't want you disappointed that I couldn't just let this go or hand it off. It was a sealed record, but someone with the right authority had to have looked at it and disregarded it. I felt that there was something there, and I wanted to find out!"

"I understand that!" I yelled back. "And I like you, too.

A lot. That's why it matters to me when you do something rash without clueing me in! I'm here because I care about you. So don't do more stupid shit without at least talking me into supporting you first, got it?"

"Fine! This is the healthiest fight I've ever had in my entire adulthood," she admitted, lowering her voice almost to normal conversational level.

"This *is* adulthood. Kinda makes you wonder how your family would react if you finally told them about your health, doesn't it?" I shot back.

"Stop distracting me with your dancing pectorals and put some clothes on," Shelby insisted. She turned for the door. Billy Ray looked forlorn like he couldn't decide which parent to stay with. She paused. "And I'm going to tell them. After my triathlon."

"Aren't they going home before then?" I asked, already knowing the answer.

"A phone call works just as well as face-to-face." She sniffed.

"Does it?" I made my pecs dance. Shelby's gaze was drawn hypnotically to my chest.

She shook her head and turned her back on me. "Please put some clothes on and come with me to the sheriff's office."

———

Not much in this world riled the sheriff of Bootleg Springs. It came with the badge. Harlan Tucker was a calm man used to soothing frayed feelings, smoothing over rough edges.

But hearing his daughter's admission that she willingly hunted down a known fraud had him blinking rapidly for almost a minute straight.

George handled it…less subtly. His big frame was slumped in a chair in the station's conference room, a meaty hand over his eyes.

The room smelled of stale coffee and old pastries.

"I can't believe my sister and my girlfriend thought they'd just take the law into their own hands," George moaned. "Again."

June patted him on the shoulder. "Let's focus on the part where Shelby and I believe we've uncovered important information regarding the investigation into Callie Kendall's murder."

Sheriff Tucker stroked a hand over his white mustache. "Huh," he said.

I felt a little sorry for the man who was being forced to walk the line between family and the law.

"So what do we do next?" Shelby asked next to me.

I saw the sheriff's nearly imperceptible flinch at the "we" part of that question.

"We are going to pass this information on to the investigators," he began, holding up a hand when both June and Shelby started to argue. "And we are going to impress upon them that some of these details might bear consideration."

Shelby sat back and crossed her arms. "In other words, you want us to mind our business."

"Shelby, I appreciate your…initiative," he decided, choosing the word carefully. "And I certainly believe that this information needs to be relayed through the appropriate channels. But I would be remiss if I didn't strongly encourage you all to bring your concerns directly to law enforcement. It's what we're here for. It's job security for me."

"You will look into Abbie's death, won't you?" Shelby pressed.

"I certainly will. I promise you that," the sheriff agreed.

"Good. George and I need to get back to our pig," June announced, rising.

"Sheriff, if you don't mind another request from me," Shelby said. "I think someone intimidated Mrs. Benefiel into recanting her claim. Someone that she is still afraid of. If you do speak to her, can you do it very quietly?"

Sheriff Tucker nodded. "I will definitely do that," he promised.

Some of the tension left Shelby's shoulders. "Okay. Good. Thank you for your time," she said.

We rose and started for the door.

"I'm telling Mom and Dad," George said, pointing a long finger at Shelby.

She scrunched her nose up at him but didn't argue.

"Gee, Shelby, you sure are working hard to win the most memorable summer fling," I told her, slinging my arm around her as we stepped out into the night thick with humidity.

"All part of my master plan to make sure you never forget me."

Chapter Forty-Four
Shelby

I rolled my shoulders and adjusted the volume on Salt-N-Pepa as they warbled nineties vibes in my ears. It was early evening, and I was nearing the end of my allotted work hours. I still had a ten-mile bike ride to squeeze in. Working my way through the most recent survey responses—I'd had 936 so far—I was slowly crafting a structure for my paper. One that felt as organic yet cohesive as the responses I was getting.

I still felt like something was missing. That the key was somehow in the next response or the next. But overall, I was finally making real progress.

I shot a glance at the vase of wildflowers behind my laptop. Jonah. He'd picked them up at a little stand in the park yesterday and brought them home for me. Going for that Most-Memorable-Summer-Fling notoriety. He made it so easy to appreciate him, to fall for him.

I grinned at the whimsical flowers, the chipped pitcher we'd found in the kitchen. And turned back to the next survey.

Q. What factors make you feel as if you belong here as part of the community?

Jonah Bodine: A few months ago, I would have said I didn't necessarily belong. That I was just passing through. That the only thing keeping me here was the family I was getting to know. But that's not the case. I came for the family, stayed for the family. Then something strange started to happen.

I wasn't just new in town anymore. I wasn't just a gossip item or an oddity. I was providing a service, meeting a need. The more I gave to this town, the more they gave me in return. I was alone when I came to Bootleg Springs. But I'm not alone now. I have new family, new friends, interesting clients, a roommate that I can't stop thinking about, and a dog.

Somehow, I accidentally built an entire life here without noticing that I was planting roots. I think part of it is good-natured conspiracy. My family wants me to stay. This town wants me to stay. Every connection I make here binds me tighter to the community. Every class I teach, every client I help is one more root planted. Every bonfire, every kiss, every beer or pepperoni roll or day on the water makes Bootleg Springs more a part of my life. And I don't know if I want to fight it anymore.

My heart did an agreeable little tap dance as several stimuli worked on my system simultaneously.

The woman in me swooned just the tiniest bit at Jonah's admission that he couldn't stop thinking about me. The data nerd tap danced at the fact that he'd willingly filled out the survey.

Attacking me from my romantic and analytical sides in one fell swoop. I approved.

What made the researcher in me push back from my chair and do a little boogie was the idea of the levels of assimilation. It wasn't just one group like a church or an office full of coworkers that did the heavy lifting when it came to providing a sense of belonging. Bootleg Springs was an organism that used multiple prongs of attack.

You weren't only welcome at Moonshine Diner or just

Yee Haw Yarn & Coffee. You were welcome in the park, the church, the police station, Sallie Mae Brickman's kitchen table. They called you by name in the Pop In and were happy to see you at Build A Shine. Jimmy Bob Prosser remembered what kind of a dishwasher you had in your kitchen when you came into the hardware store.

The entire town worked together to entice and welcome and infiltrate every aspect of residents' lives. Until there was no boundary between the individual and the society.

I envisioned vines, all sprouting from the same place, all wriggling and stretching and winding their way in and around the society binding everyone and everything together.

Jonah Bodine had just unlocked my entire thesis. Removed the block. Turned the angel chorus on in my head.

He'd also just inserted a key directly into my heart. And I wasn't surprised at all.

I pirouetted, startling Billy Ray who barked himself awake from under the table. I picked up the puppy, swooping him into the air in a circle.

He wriggled with joy.

"Billy Ray, your daddy is a genius, and your mommy is going to get her doctorate. Doctor Mommy!"

I set him on the ground and tossed a ball for him. He tore after it, little feet scrabbling on the floor. A glance at my watch told me I needed to leave now to get my ten miles in if I didn't want to do the entire ride in the dark.

Good. Exercise seemed to juggle everything that swam in my head into neat and tidy boxes. A nice summer evening bike ride would give me a chance to figure out exactly how to make Jonah's answer the center of it all.

———

With Billy Ray mournfully ensconced in his crate with a handful of treats and his favorite stuffed bear toy, I pulled on my fluorescent green cycling shirt, clipped on my helmet, and set off on the route Jonah had programmed for me.

The crickets were loud, and a few early fireflies lit up over the fields.

A part of me couldn't believe that I, Shelby Thompson, was pedaling a bike over hill and dale in rural West Virginia. Not too many years ago, I'd been convinced that I needed to be in a city, working in the trenches with families and children in need. It was the most direct way to help. Yet even then, with that naïve confidence in the cause, the work didn't sit well with me. I'd sit in my car, eyes closed, taking slow deep breaths to work up the nerve to knock on doors I dreaded.

I felt like a failure giving it up. But I also knew, after the attack, I couldn't knock on another door again. I hadn't exactly embraced the sense of failure. More like tucked it away and tried to think about anything and everything else.

Research was safe. But it was also essential. And it brought me joy—bright, exciting, nerd-like joy—every time I dove into new data. It made me happy. Now, I was on the very early side of accepting that being happy in my life was more important than fulfilling a duty I didn't feel cut out to perform. Maybe I didn't have to feel so guilty about not finding the meaning I'd expected social work to provide? Maybe doing what I enjoyed would still help make a difference in the world?

I juggled gears and came out of my seat. Jonah had, of course, incorporated some of the hillier sections of road around Bootleg Springs. I kept an eye on my heart rate and my speed.

But my mind was racing with all the ways I could thread Jonah's insight into my paper. I couldn't wait to talk to him about it.

That wasn't something new. I looked forward to my time with him every day. I liked watching him cook. Enjoyed playing with Billy Ray in the yard.

He'd accidentally built a life, and I was part of it.

Could I continue to be part of it?

If Jonah was staying, could I stay, too?

The hair on my arms stood up. I needed to look into universities and nonprofits within driving distance. If Jonah was staying. If *I* was staying. If we wanted a future together… Well, it was a lot of ifs. But they excited me rather than terrified me.

Headlights caught me from behind, and I moved to hug the edge of the road. I was a mile out of town on Mountain Road where there was road, guardrail, and then nothing but a steep drop.

I'd gotten more confident biking with traffic. But dusk had fallen, and the car wasn't making any attempt to pass me. I could feel it inching closer and closer.

Maybe the driver didn't feel safe passing me on such a twisty stretch of road. I let off the brake and folded over the handlebars.

Immediately, I picked up speed. So did the car.

I broke out of the turn, pedaling like hell toward the lights of town. Something felt *wrong*. And yet oh so familiar.

I wanted to twist in my seat, to look behind me. But I couldn't do that without falling and probably breaking my neck. The tiny mirror on my handlebars did nothing but reflect headlights. The road was flattening, my speed dropping.

The angle of the headlights changed.

"Oh, thank God," I whispered. The car was going to pass me.

But it didn't. It pulled alongside me. An older sedan. Gray or dark blue. I couldn't tell in the dark. The front wheel was missing the hubcap. I couldn't see the driver. But they were riding the double yellow line keeping pace with me.

Did I know them? Was this just a joke?

But nothing about this felt funny.

I needed to get into town. Needed to be around people. *Witnesses.*

The car swerved into my lane and then back again. Too close for comfort. This wasn't a joke. I wasn't overthinking. I was in danger.

I shifted gears again and focused on form. I didn't need to see the heart rate readout on my watch to know it was stratospheric.

The car slid toward me again, claiming the lane, but there were streetlights now. People ahead. I heard music coming from the park. I ignored my instinct to turn down an alley and try to get away from the car. I needed to lure them closer. Into the light and buzz of town. I needed to see who was behind the wheel.

One block and the car slowed, sliding in behind me again. I pedaled like mad, bursting onto Main Street across from the park. There was a band in the gazebo. A summer night concert I realized. The town square was crawling with people, and I felt tears of relief prick at my eyes.

I chanced a glance over my shoulder. But the car was gone.

I didn't feel any safer.

Jumping off my bike, I pushed it over the curb and into the park, joining the throng of summertimers and residents. But someone was out there in the night. And I felt them watching me.

Chapter Forty-Five
Jonah

"Hey, honey. How was your ride?" I asked, answering the phone on the first ring. Gibson and I had just stopped wedding trellis construction for a root beer break. He'd magically reemerged from his self-imposed exile and demanded I drop everything to help with the woodworking project.

It hadn't exactly been a *fun* evening with Gibson's black mood hanging like a toxic fog between us. But I was here for it. As a good brother would be.

He'd never been the happy-go-lucky type, but I'd also never seen him quite this broody before. Something was going on, but I hadn't been able to pry it out of him. "I'm fucking fine," was his answer to everything.

"It was, uh, eventful," Shelby said.

I slid off the stool in Gibs's shop, clueing in on her shaky voice. "What's wrong? What happened? Are you hurt?"

Gibson was already reaching for his truck keys. We both started for the door, not a word exchanged. But I noticed he'd shed the dark cloud as if it had never existed.

"I'm fine," she said, but I didn't like the nerves I heard in her voice. She was rattled.

"Where are you? Gibs and I are coming to you."

"I feel like a big baby, and it was probably nothing. Just a stupid prank, but I wouldn't say no to some friendly faces. I'm in town in the park near the gazebo."

"I'll follow you in," Gibson said as I yanked open my car door. He locked the shop behind him, Bowie and Cassidy's wedding trellis still on its side inside.

On my short but breakneck trip into town, I got most of the story out of her. I double-parked on the street, Gibson nipping into a space on a side street just behind me.

I stayed on the phone with her until I spotted her in the crowd. She was standing under a lamp on the park path as if she didn't want to leave the protection of the light.

I grabbed her and pulled her in for a hard hug to reassure her as much as myself. "Are you okay?"

"Honestly, I'm probably overreacting. It just felt so…familiar," Shelby said. I could feel her heart pounding against me.

Gibson plowed his way through the crowd, Jameson and George on his heels.

"What happened?" George demanded. "Are you okay?"

When she didn't put up a fuss about Gibs pulling her brother into it, I realized just how scared she'd been.

Shelby ran through it again. I kept her tucked under my arm and scanned the crowd, looking for anyone who seemed out of place.

"I think they pulled out behind me from Chestnut Road," she said. "There was a car sitting there when I rode by. It almost felt like they were waiting for me."

"You would know," George said, reaching out to squeeze her hand.

"What are we missing?" Jameson asked, a frown furrowing his forehead.

"George, why don't you fill them in? I'm going to take Shelby and get some water," I told him.

He nodded.

Shelby stayed cuddled up against me, and to the outsider, we looked like a young couple in love just enjoying the starry summer night.

I grabbed bottles of water for both of us and then on second thought bought two moonshines from the stand.

"Here," I said, holding both beverages out in offering.

She gave me the ghost of a smile and went straight for the moonshine. "Thanks," she coughed as it burned down her throat.

"Are you sure you're okay?" I pressed.

"Physically yes. But mentally… Abbie is dead, Jonah. And someone scared that Mrs. Benefiel half to death. What if they found out that I was asking questions?"

I'd been considering the same possibility, and I didn't like it.

"Shelby honey, I think we should go to the police." I expected a denial, an argument. And when I didn't immediately get one, I pulled her in for another hug. Resting my chin on the top of her head, I wrapped my arms around her.

No one was going to get to her. Not without going through me.

"I'm willing to talk to the police," she said. "Especially if it makes them take the rest of it more seriously."

She took another drink of the moonshine. "Jonah, what if I did this? What if I stirred this up and someone thinks they need to take care of Mrs. Benefiel now? She has kids. Grandkids."

"Let's call the sheriff," I said firmly.

We returned to the Bodines and George. Bowie had arrived with Cassidy in tow. She was in civilian clothes, her new engagement ring winking on her left hand. But her pretty face was all business.

"Let's go somewhere we can talk," she said, putting her arm around Shelby and leading her away.

"I don't like this," George said as the rest of us started after them.

Scarlett leading Devlin appeared out of the crowd. "What in the hell happened? Is Shelby okay?"

News in Bootleg traveled almost as fast as it did within the Bodine ranks.

"Cassidy has her," I explained. "Why don't you two go sit with her?" I wanted Shelby surrounded by people. I wanted to make it impossible for a stranger to get within twenty feet of her.

I needed to move my car. I needed to go find this son of a bitch and rearrange his face. I needed to glue myself to her side. "Gray or blue sedan missing the front passenger side hubcap," I muttered.

"You stick with Shelby," Gibson said. "GT, move the car. Jameson and I are gonna do a few laps around downtown looking for this asshole."

"If you find him, you'll call me?" I said.

"You'll get the first crack at his face," Gibson promised me.

"Dibs on what's left over," George called over his shoulder as he jogged toward where my truck was backing up traffic.

I nodded and clapped my brother on the shoulder. "Thank you."

"Go be with your girl," Gibson said, shrugging off the thanks.

It was good to have family.

————

Cassidy was just wrapping up her questions when I got to them. Shelby looked relieved to see me, and I elbowed Scarlett out of the way to get to her.

"Hey!" she complained.

"Do you know of anyone who might want to hurt you?" Cassidy asked, tucking her notebook into the back pocket of her shorts. She nodded as her father strolled up.

"The only person I can think of is whoever ran down Abbie Gilbert or whoever intimidated Mrs. Benefiel into retracting her claim that Callie Kendall was being abused in junior high," Shelby said. She didn't sound scared now. She sounded downright pissed off.

"The girl who pretended to be Callie is dead?" Scarlett screeched.

"Don't look at me like that," Cassidy insisted. "Dad just told me this afternoon."

"I need to call June," George said, tossing me my keys. "Make sure she's okay."

Gibson and Jameson jogged up. "We saw a dark gray four-door sitting about a block down," Jameson reported. "But when Gibs started running toward it looking like he was gonna bust open the windshield, the driver pulled a U-ey and peeled outta here."

So he'd been waiting. And watching. I pulled Shelby a little closer.

"What's with you, man?" Jameson asked Gibson. "You look like you're ready to either get up and murder someone or give up and pray for the good Lord to take you now."

Jameson's phone rang, saving Gibson from having to answer.

"Leah Mae," Jameson said.

George was on his phone, plugging one ear.

Shelby's phone rang. "Dang it! Which one of you big mouths told my parents?"

My phone vibrated next. It was my mother calling. News traveled fast.

Sheriff Tucker appeared in full uniform, a face etched with concern. "Why don't we all go someplace a little less chaotic and talk this through," he suggested.

———

We descended on the Tucker house. The sheriff felt like privacy was more important than professionalism in this case.

June arrived shortly after with her potbellied pig on a leash. In a much-appreciated moment of empathy, she'd swung by our place and picked up Billy Ray, who was snuggled up in

Shelby's lap in the Tucker dining room while Nadine made tea and put out a buffet of snacks. The lights, the crowd of friendly faces, it all seemed to calm Shelby down.

I, on the other hand, was so angry I could feel it vibrating in my bones.

Sheriff Tucker, with help from June, filled everyone else in on the now infamous road trip and what they discovered.

"I don't know if this is connected," Shelby said. "If it's not, it's an awfully big coincidence that once I start poking around into this case file and the Callie Kendall impersonator, someone just happens to decide to play cat and mouse with me on Mountain Road."

I noticed my brothers and sister sharing a quiet look. Mountain Road was where their mother had lost her life when her car went through a guardrail. Until recently, it had been thought to be an accident.

"Look. I know it sounds all conspiracy-theory-like," Shelby said when silence descended around the table. "And I know that we don't have proof. But how many coincidences have to occur before we start asking questions?"

Sheriff Tucker leaned back in his chair. "I passed the information along to the investigators," he began. "They said they'd look into it."

"Bullshit," Devlin muttered under his breath.

"I also decided to reach out to the Bethesda authorities and raised some concerns with them," the sheriff continued. "They were pretty interested. Went to her house to pay her a visit. A neighbor told them Mrs. Benefiel and her dog left with suitcases at around four yesterday afternoon."

"That is approximately thirty minutes after we left," June said.

"Another coincidence?" Shelby snorted.

"And at around midnight last night, the Bethesda authorities got a series of calls of suspicious activity at the Benefiel house. Seems the neighbors keep a close watch on each other and noticed two people ringing the doorbell and peering in windows. They were gone by the time authorities arrived on the scene."

Shelby's hand tightened in mine.

"So we've got an unsolved vehicular homicide, suspicious activity at a retired teacher's home, and now someone trying to chase Shelby down in a car the day after she goes looking for the dead girl and the teacher," Cassidy summarized. "That's more than coincidental."

"What we've got is a whole lot of suspicion and not one scrap of solid evidence," Sheriff Tucker said.

"What do we do?" I asked.

"We remain watchful," he said, his eyes skimming every face around the table until he got a nod out of each one of us. "We stay together. We let the police do their job."

"Where did Mrs. Benefiel go?"

"We tracked her to a golf resort in South Carolina. Seems her husband and some family are there now."

"They need to be warned," she insisted.

"Already have been. And authorities are watching the house."

"I can't just sit back and wait," Shelby insisted. She got a lot of agreeing nods from everyone else including Nadine.

"If these events are connected to Callie Kendall's murder," Sheriff Tucker said, "we can't afford to let word get out and have a whole town gossipin' about the possibilities. Whoever is behind all of this is already nervous. And because of that, I can't have you, young lady," he pointed at Shelby, "or you, JuneBug, doing any more digging. Do I make myself clear?"

"As long as you and everyone else involved is taking this seriously," Shelby said, stroking a hand over Billy Ray's silky ear.

"This is bullshit," Gibson snapped. I couldn't help but agree with him.

Chapter Forty-Six
Shelby

At first, being surrounded by people was entertaining. But the suffocating *Shelby Watch* soon began to take its toll. Not only was I never alone, but Jonah and I were never alone either. News of the "incident" on Mountain Road had spread. No one outside the Bodine, Tucker, and Thompson clans knew that there might be more to it than a stupid, dangerous prank.

But within our ranks, everyone was aware and vigilant. And very, very present. Babysitting me seemed to have become a new Bootleg Springs pastime. I was looking forward to the triathlon tomorrow just to slip my guards for a few hours.

Right now, Gibson was kicked back on the couch with Jonah's mother, Jenny, watching some diving competition on TV. But even my noise-canceling headphones couldn't block out their presence.

Gibson was pumping off pissed-off vibes while Jenny was curled into herself. She'd tried to draw him out and was rewarded with the patented Gibson brush-off. A combination grunt and shrug that made it clear he wasn't looking to be friendly.

And I was just tired enough of dissecting things to let them both stew.

I was tired.

Bowie and Cassidy's wedding was tomorrow, the triathlon. The end of summer. I'd scheduled my interview with the doctoral program director for a week after the triathlon. The tension in me was taut like a wire.

I wanted to talk to Jonah about us. About the possibility of an "us" beyond August. But it was hard to have the conversation when we were surrounded by parents and siblings. And between the scare on the bike, the training, and polishing my dissertation, I was exhausted every night.

I spared the couch occupants another glance.

Gibson had hardly been seen since news broke about Callie's murder. His brothers said he was locked in his shop. But he had shadows under his eyes and a beard that was days beyond well kept. He'd lost weight as well.

Jonah walked in with Billy Ray on his heels. He paused in the doorway, the tension everyone exuded acted as a forcefield.

"Everything okay?" he asked with suspicion.

"Just great," I lied, tilting my head in the direction of the couch.

A diver on TV executed a perfect maneuver, and neither Gibson nor Jenny reacted.

Abruptly, Gibson pushed off the couch and walked past Jonah into the kitchen. He returned with a beer and cracked it open.

Jonah and I both watched as he sat back down and guzzled it. Gibson didn't drink. Ever.

"Gibs. What's going on?" Jonah asked.

I braced myself for an explosion. A denial.

"Our father's a murdering bastard. And we're all just supposed to be fine with that," he said, his tone flat and dull.

Jenny winced, looking surprised.

Jonah opened his mouth to speak, but I shook my head, warning him off.

"He killed a sixteen-year-old girl who had her whole life ahead of her. We come from that. That's in our blood. He was a monster," he spat out, setting the beer down on the end table with a snap. "How are the sons of monsters supposed to protect someone?"

"Your father didn't kill anyone," she said firmly. Too firmly for it to be parent patronization.

I remembered our talk outside the library. How she warned me about taking on men of power. Specifically Judge Kendall. "Oh God, Jenny," I breathed. "You know something."

All eyes went to her. Now, she looked sick.

"I promise you boys, your father didn't hurt Callie Kendall."

"Mom?" Jonah said his voice low. "What do you know?"

She closed her eyes, rubbed a hand at her forehead.

"I think we're all going to need a drink," she said.

————

We opened a bottle of whiskey and moved the discussion to the dining room. It felt formal. Gibson stared at the glass in his hand while Jonah and I waited.

"I know your father didn't kill Callie," Jenny said, gaze skating back and forth between Jonah and Gibson.

"Why? Because the drunk sonofabitch told you he didn't?" Gibson snapped. There was so much pain in his voice that it hurt me to hear it.

"Your father saved Callie Kendall's life."

Gibson was shaking his head already. Like he was trying to shake free the hope the words sparked.

"Mom, what are you saying?" Jonah asked.

Jenny took a fortifying sip of whiskey and settled back in her chair.

"Jonah was coming home from a late run to the grocery store—"

"You mean the liquor store," Gibson sneered.

Jenny covered his hand with hers, and I watched in surprise when he didn't pull away.

Gibson Bodine needed a mom. A mom like Jenny. And that just about broke my heart for the man.

I reached for Jonah's hand under the table and squeezed.

"The grocery store," she repeated gently. "He'd gotten paid for a big job that day and had some money burning a hole in his pocket. So he got steaks for the whole family to grill the next day."

Gibson sat stonily. But he was listening.

"He was on his way home. It was dark. There was this flash of red crumpled up on the side of the road."

I held my breath.

Gibson pushed away from the table and rose but didn't go anywhere.

"It was Callie. She'd been hurt badly. Jonah thought maybe she'd been hit by a car. Until he got a better look at her. Her face was bruised and cut. There was a lot of blood. She had several cuts on one arm. They looked deep."

Gibson's nostrils flared.

I fought against the memories that threatened to swallow me. I knew what it was like to be bruised and cut.

"He took his shirt off and tied it around her arm. Asked if she wanted to go to the hospital or home. She said neither. Asked him to help her get out."

"Who did it?" Gibson demanded. "Who did she say did it?"

"She didn't. She refused to tell him. Jonah worried that because she didn't want to go home that it meant her father had done something. But when he asked her, Callie refused to answer. She begged him to get her out. To help her leave. To save her life. She was shaking, in shock. And terrified. He said he'd never seen anyone so scared in all his life.

"So he took her to your grandfather's cabin, where you live now. It had been empty for a few years by that point. And he called your mother. Connie called you that night and asked you to take your brothers and sister for the night. Remember?"

Gibson nodded slowly. "I thought they'd had another fight and didn't want anyone around."

"She came to the cabin with first aid supplies, and they did what they could to stop the bleeding and clean her up. She was hurt badly but kept insisting that she needed to get out. That her life depended on it. They believed her, Gibson. So the next day, your father took your mother's car, and he and Callie left town. He drove her to New York. To a friend of a friend of Callie's. Someone she said she could trust. And then he came home."

"None of this makes any sense. Obviously, he didn't save her life. That's still her body they found."

"No, it's not," Jenny said firmly.

"The dental records matched," Jonah chimed in. "They identified the body as hers."

"I'm telling you the dental records are wrong or the report was tampered with. That body is not Callie Kendall's. But someone wants her to stay gone."

The hairs on my arms stood at attention.

"What proof do you have?" Gibson demanded, his voice breaking.

Thoughts whirled around in my brain.

Wordlessly, Jenny reached into her purse and pulled out a stack of postcards. She laid them out one by one in front of Gibson. Blue Moon Bend, New York. Buenos Aires. Tokyo. Atlanta. Los Angeles. London. Seattle. Boston.

There were twelve in total. The first several were addressed to Jonah Bodine in Bootleg Springs.

"I don't understand," Jonah said.

Jenny tapped the first one. Blue Moon. "Flip it over."

Restlessly, Gibson flipped it on the table.

Thanks for everything.

Gibson sank back down in his chair like his knees had gone weak. He looked pale.

Jonah picked up the card and studied it. "The postmark is a week after she went missing."

"Are you saying these postcards are all from Callie Kendall?" I asked, my curiosity getting the better of me rendering me unable to stay quiet.

This was a family matter. But I'd been drawn into it. Or I'd drawn myself into it.

Gibson flipped every card over carefully. "That's her handwriting," he said hoarsely.

I skimmed over them quickly. They were all postmarked about a year apart. The more recent ones included innocuous song lyrics. The last card had been mailed thirteen months ago. To Jonah's mother.

"If she sent these cards," I said, "there's no way those remains are hers."

"And if they aren't hers, who do they belong to?" Jonah asked. "And why does someone want everyone to believe it's Callie?"

———

Q. Bootleg Springs is famous for the disappearance of Callie Kendall. What is your theory?

Misty Lynn Prosser: Why's everyone always goin' on and on about that girl? So she disappeared. Big deal. She didn't even live here. Personally, I couldn't give two shits about what happened. Maybe she up and got herself murdered and dumped in the lake. Maybe she met a boy and ran away and got herself murdered and dumped in a different lake.

Chapter Forty-Seven
Jonah

Out of all the Bodines, I'd been the least affected by the Callie Kendall investigation and our father's involvement. I hadn't grown up here. Hadn't known Callie or experienced the horror of her disappearance. Hadn't been raised by the man that many now considered to be a murderer.

But with my mother's revelation, my head was spinning. Gibson looked like he'd just seen a ghost.

I picked up the postcards again, examining them as if they held the answers.

"I can't believe you never told me," I said to my mother.

Mom winced. "Subjects pertaining to your father were a sore subject for you," she said diplomatically. "And if his suspicions were correct and Judge Kendall had anything to do with Callie's injuries, then that man is dangerous. Your father made me swear never to tell anyone. He didn't want anyone else becoming a target."

Shelby was watching Gibson closely, drumming her fingers against her lips. Her tell for deep thought.

My brother's words echoed in my ears.

That's her handwriting.

There was more to the story. A lot more. I was sure of it. But right now, there was an immediate danger to be dealt with.

"I gotta be honest. This is a lot to process," I said to the room in general.

Shelby nodded, still staring at Gibson. I knew she'd zeroed in on his comment as well.

"You knew this whole time?" he asked my mom quietly.

"Yes. But it wasn't my story to tell. I don't tell stories that aren't mine," she said carefully as if she were delivering a message in code.

"Jonah, can I see you in the kitchen for a minute?" Shelby said suddenly.

"Uh, sure?"

I followed her out of the dining room and into the kitchen.

She turned to face me, arms crossed over her chest. "Are you okay?"

"I'm fine," I said, not quite sure if I meant it or not. My mother had been keeping a secret so big it now involved dead bodies. And she'd kept it for over a decade.

"This is a lot of information," she pressed.

I ran my hand through my hair.

I could hear Gibson and my mother speaking in the dining room. He had questions. We all would. And I had one, too.

"How did he recognize her handwriting?" I asked quietly.

Shelby bit her lip. "I was wondering that myself," she confessed.

"Things are gonna get crazy," I told her.

She nodded. "But I'm here for you. Whatever you and your mom and the Bodines need."

I pulled her into my arms. "Thank you for being so good to my family."

"In a town this small, there aren't many degrees of separation between your family and my family."

"Still," I said, tilting her chin up. "Thank you." I kissed her softly.

––––––––

"So, who do we tell?" I asked.

Everyone around the table was silent. Billy Ray burped under the table, then barked in delight.

"We have to go to the authorities," Shelby said. "They need to know that that body isn't Callie Kendall. That some other family lost a daughter, a sister."

"Bowie and Cassidy are getting married tomorrow," I reminded her. "Your triathlon is tomorrow."

"I realize that. But if this is all connected? If whoever threatened Cece Benefiel into retracting her claim was involved in Abbie Gilbert's death?"

"If the same person is responsible for that car nearly forcing you off the road on your bike," I added.

"If one person did all that, they're also likely the person who hurt Callie in the first place. And they're powerful enough to change a forensics report," Shelby said.

Her statement hung like a cloud over the table.

"This is bullshit. We know it's the judge," Gibson said, slapping a hand on the table.

The puppy barked ferociously at the noise. Gibs had accepted my mother's story as the truth, which told me he either trusted her or he needed Callie Kendall to be alive. Maybe it was a bit of both.

"Sorry, bud," he said, leaning down to pick up Billy Ray. Despite the anger in his tone, he held the dog gently.

"The evidence points in that direction," Shelby began. "But we can't be certain. If we start making accusations—"

"Fuck accusations," Gibson said. "I want a face-to-face conversation with the asshole." Billy Ray took exception to the language and slathered Gibson's face with his tongue. "Get your damn tongue out of my mouth!" he sputtered.

The mood around the table lightened almost imperceptibly.

"This is exactly why we shouldn't tell Scarlett," Shelby pointed out. "Half-cocked accusations aren't going to get us a confession. And if it *is* the judge, he obviously has power and reach. He has access to police records, maybe even a thug or two in his pocket to do his dirty work."

Gibson handed the puppy over to my mother who still looked guilty and dazed.

She and I were going to have a long talk in the near future.

"Why didn't you tell Jonah when he came here?" Shelby asked. It was like the woman could read my mind.

"Everyone was safer assuming Callie Kendall was gone," Mom said. She seemed lighter, too. As if sharing this news had somehow lessened a weight she'd been carrying for a long time.

"Maybe everyone is still safer assuming she's dead," I pointed out.

"What's that supposed to mean?" Gibson demanded.

"Our brother is getting married tomorrow. Do we really want to have a family sit-down and ruin that? Who's going to be paying attention to two people who waited their entire lives for six o'clock tomorrow when the whole world is lit up over Callie Kendall being alive?"

"Still, it would be nice if she could go un-missing to clear this mess up," Shelby mused.

"Call her," Gibson said earnestly to my mom. "Bring her back here."

"I can't do that, Gibs. It was one-way communication. Everything was set up for her safety. I don't know where she is or how to contact her. After your mother died, Callie and your father spoke on the phone. They decided that she would continue sending postcards but to me instead of here, where someone might notice them and wonder."

"Who would see a postcard and find it suspicious enough to raise a red flag?" Shelby asked.

"Seriously, Shelby? How long have you been in Bootleg?" Gibson asked dryly. It was the first hint of humor I'd seen from him in a long time.

She gave a little mock bow. "Point taken. The bottom line is, what if the postcards aren't enough proof?" she said, wetting her lips. "If someone has the power to tamper with a forensics report, they're not going to have much of a problem disproving a couple of postcards that could have been sent by anybody. Without Callie herself, we've still got nothing."

"You have me," Mom said firmly. "Your father's name needs to be cleared. I'll tell them everything I know."

"It's still…what would Jayme call it?" I asked. "Hearsay? So you got postcards in the mail. What are they going to do? Fingerprint them?"

"Maybe. And there's also the fact that I met her last year."

"Mom! Are you fucking kidding me?"

"Holy shit," Shelby breathed.

"Holy shit. Disney princess swore," Gibson whispered.

"Watch your mouth, Jonah. And no, I'm not fucking kidding you," Mom said with a slight smile. "When your father died last year, Callie called me. We met in Seattle for lunch."

"What did she say? How did she look? Could you tell it was her?" Shelby was hinged so far forward her chin was almost on the table.

I stroked a hand over her back, feeling unusually calm. I assumed a complete and total breakdown was in my near future and decided to embrace the calm while it lasted.

"She'd heard your father passed away. With both your parents gone, she felt her debt to them, to make sure they knew she was safe, had been fulfilled. That's why the postcards stopped."

"So we tell the sheriff," I pressed.

"Tomorrow. After the wedding," Gibson decided.

"Okay," I said.

We were all silent for another minute before Gibson spoke again. "She's really alive?"

The hope in his voice made me hurt for him.

Mom nodded. "She's alive, and your father saved her life."

"Why would she have stayed away this whole time?" Gibson wondered aloud, his face broody.

"Only Callie could answer that," Mom said.

Billy Ray tore into the dining room, dragging one of my running shoes by the laces. It got wrapped around the table leg, and the puppy stubbornly tried to tug it free.

We watched him, all a little dazed.

"You know, I thought it would feel good to finally have some answers," Shelby said. "Now, I just have more questions."

"Join the fucking club," Gibson said, pushing away his untouched whiskey.

Chapter Forty-Eight
Shelby

The toe I dipped into Cheat Lake was considering frostbite. I'd done the majority of my training in Bootleg's lovely, heated waters. So normal lake temperatures were cold enough to take my breath away, even in the swelter of the first Saturday in August.

I was standing in the back of the pack of bathing-suited athletes with race numbers written on their arms and legs feeling like there were few places on Earth that I belonged less than right here. Everyone else looked leanly muscled, icily calm like they did this every Saturday on this sliver of beach surrounded by thick trees that sang with cicadas.

According to my fitness watch, my heart was attempting to explode its way out of my chest.

I felt alone. *Lonely.*

It wasn't true, of course. I'd been chauffeured here in Estelle's minivan with the Breakfast Club, my bike on the roof, my gear behind Gert and Jefferson in the back bench seat.

The odds of me being attacked fifty miles from Bootleg Springs in a crowd of triathletes and spectators were low enough that Jonah had settled for me having a geriatric team of babysitters. They were waiting for me at the transition point between the swim and the bike. "To make sure you didn't drown," Myrt had offered helpfully.

Once I returned to start the run, they would drive to the finish line to meet me there.

I wished Jonah could have been here. But I'd been the first person to tell him he absolutely had to focus on the wedding today. Bowie was the first brother to tie the knot. This was big. Huge. Much bigger than my personal quest to compete, to complete.

Still, I missed him fiercely.

But I'd started this process *by myself* to prove *to myself* that I could do it *myself*. And I would. Last night I'd reached another milestone. I'd finished my dissertation. Of course there was a need for another pass at polishing, for perfecting. But the hard work, the bleeding was over.

Just like now. I'd trained, I'd sweated, I'd bled.

I'd ached.

And all that was between me and that finish line was a 750-meter swim and 15.6 miles divided between bike and my own feet.

The hard part was over. This was the fun part.

I hoped.

Best of all, there was no crazy potential murderer here watching me. It was just me and the culmination of my hard work. And I was going to enjoy it.

"First tri?" A man in a very small bathing suit with a rather large belly asked, wiping his nose on the back of his hand.

I nodded. "Yeah. Does it show?"

He leaned in conspiratorially. "You look as nervous as I feel. Hey, Tameka!" He waved over a woman in a sleek blue one-piece. She had silver curls peeking out of her swim cap. "Found us another virgin."

Her face transformed into a smile. "Welcome to the club, honey."

289

"Thanks," I said. "You're both first-timers, too?"

"Yep," the man said. "I'm Gus. I lost fifty pounds this year. Figured I'd put all this energy to good use. Grandkids are waiting for me at the finish, so I gotta finish. This here is Tameka."

Tameka gave me a wave. "I'm here because I bet my twin sister $500 I could finish faster than her. She's running her first tri today in Michigan. We quit smoking together in January."

"What's your story, pipsqueak?" Gus asked, giving me a hard punch in the arm. "Sorry 'bout that. Nerves screw with my depth perception."

"I'm Shelby. And…" I paused, considering my options. "I was diagnosed with a weird kind of arthritis that causes me a lot of pain and might turn my upper back into a question mark. And I thought if I could finish a triathlon, I could probably handle the diagnosis."

"Cool," Tameka said with a grin.

"You don't look questionable to me. Ha!" Gus said, moving to elbow me.

I took a step back to be safe.

"Are you some super-fast athlete?" Tameka wondered.

"Me?" My eyes widened. "No. I'm just hoping to finish."

"We're all gonna finish," Gus insisted.

Tameka jerked a thumb at him. "What he said. Wanna stick with us? Moral support?"

I instantly felt better.

———

The organizers ran us through everything one more time. We'd enter the water and swim parallel to the shore, following the buoys until they brought us back on shore. There were lifeguards in the water and medical boats already on the water. Just in case.

"Please don't let me need a boat," I whispered as we moved closer to the starting line on the beach. Bodies pressing in, energy rising.

Event photographers snapped away.

Gus took my left hand. I took Tameka's. And when the starting gun fired, we trotted forward as a team.

The water was cold enough to take my breath away, but once I had room, I ducked under the surface. Reinvigorated, awake, *alive*, I reached for the surface.

I broke into the light and air, found Gus and Tameka waiting for me. With a laugh, I kicked my legs, and we started swimming. The main crush of bodies was ahead of us, but the water was churning all around us in their wake.

Nerves shifted to excitement now that we were moving. Gus had a slower stroke, but I paced him. Conserving energy now was exactly what I should be doing. I kept my new friends in sight and focused on strong, deep breaths, certain that Jonah would be proud.

We clipped past buoy after buoy. My arms felt strong, my strokes textbook perfect. I wished Jonah could see me. See his hard work pay off.

I was so focused on form that I was startled when my fingers scraped bottom.

"Let's go, Shelby," Tameka called from a few feet away in knee-deep water.

The swim was over, and we weren't even dead last. I felt elated as the three of us slogged out of the water.

"Meet up on the road, girls," Gus called as he jogged toward the parking lot where the bikes waited.

I stripped off my goggles and swim cap like Jonah told me and trotted up the beach in the direction of the transition area. I dipped my feet in one of the kiddie pools closest to my setup and then ran for my bike. I pulled on a pair of shorts over my bathing suit bottoms, prayed my soggy ass wouldn't chafe, and sat to pull on my cycling shoes. My adrenaline was ramping up again. I bobbled my helmet when I reached for it. My sunglasses went flying, and I had to scramble for both.

Relax. Focus. Don't go for speed. Be consistent.

I heard Jonah's words as clear as if he were standing behind me. They steadied my hands. Pushing myself too hard would send my body into a tailspin. I slowed my movements intentionally. I made sure my running shoes and hat were on the towel with the race number belt. I grabbed a quick swig of water, and I was on my way. I plucked my bike off the rail and pushed it toward the start.

Gus was already there. Tameka was ten seconds behind me. We mounted up together and pushed off.

"Yee haw!" Gus hollered.

Chapter Forty-Nine
Shelby

G us's event was clearly the bike. I watched his sixty-year-old butt bob in front of me as he powered up the long, rolling hill. Tameka was a bike length ahead of me on the right. My legs burned, my lungs burned. Sweat sluiced down my back, leaving me sticky and salty.

"Can you believe this is how we chose to spend a Saturday?" Tameka called over her shoulder.

I grinned. Yeah, I could believe it.

We were in the middle of the back of the pack. Surrounded by the non-elite athletes. The real people. The regular people who had something to prove. Not a time to beat. We were sweating and suffering together. And something about that bonded us together as we pedaled our way through hills and turns, trees flashing past us. The stingiest of summer breezes enhanced by our speed.

I thought again of Bootleg Springs and my survey. Bonds. Roots. I was going to remember this hill, Gus's butt, Tameka's sharp laugh for the rest of my life. Because we were bound together now.

The Bodines were tied to Bootleg. Not just because of the history of the generations that came before them. But because of how the town witnessed their pain and arranged itself within it. I imagined the casseroles that would have lined the Bodine fridge and freezer when Connie died, the turnout for Jonah Sr.'s funeral. I'd seen first-hand the gossip stir about Jonah Bodine's involvement in the Callie Kendall disappearance. It was a small town. Gossiping was a professional sport. However, so was compassion.

And as often as a "may he rest in peace" was raised up in atonement for gossiping about the man, there were many more instances of the town stepping up to claim the surviving Bodines as their own.

They hired Scarlett for handy work. Proudly ooh-ed and ah-ed over Jameson's metalwork when his installations made the news. They pushed new clients at Gibson and praised Bowie for his work with the students at the high school. They took their legal issues to Devlin. They sweated with Jonah in the gym or in the park, trusting him to guide their health, their bodies to a better future.

And though they discussed it to death, the town never once seemed to hold Jonah Sr.'s misdeeds against his children.

Love wasn't just being there in the good times. Real love was standing next to someone on their darkest days. Real love was sweating together, striving together. Falling down and getting back up. Hurting, healing. That's where the bond came from. The work.

I felt a new burst of energy wash over me and crested the hill with a big, fat smile on my face.

The miles were ticking by, and I didn't want to miss a single one of them.

I didn't want to miss out on anything anymore. Yes, I was a researcher at heart. But that didn't mean I couldn't get out from behind my data and *live*.

Love.

Jonah.

I almost fell off my bike.

I loved Jonah Bodine. This was no summer fling. This was no temporary stopover before I got on with the rest of my life. This *was* my life.

"Well, I'll be damned," I wheezed. I felt…*free*. Lighter than I had in years. *Happy*.

"Almost there," Gus puffed over his shoulder in glee as we spotted the transition area a few hundred yards ahead of us.

"Oh my god. What is that?" Tameka gasped beside me.

On the side of the road, six elderly Bootleggers hooted and hollered from lawn chairs at racers as they passed.

"And why aren't they wearing shirts?" Tameka asked.

Because they'd painted S-H-E-L-B-Y on their bellies. My neighbors, my friends, proudly displayed their painted torsos. The horror. The hilarity. Now, I was certain I wouldn't forget today. These memories would be etched into my mind like the blue paint on the sweet wrinkled skin of my fan club.

"Shelby! You're not in last place!" Jefferson hollered.

"Great job, Shelby! You don't look like you're going to vomit!" Myrt bellowed. She was wearing an umbrella hat to keep the August sun off her face.

I waved, careful not to veer into the ditch.

"We're real proud of you!" Gert said, hefting a jar of what looked like apple pie moonshine.

"Thank you," I laughed as I zipped past.

"What was that?" Tameka asked still in disbelief. "Or am I dehydrated and hallucinating mirages?"

"You wish! That's my fan club," I told her.

We reached the transition area and high-fived Gus on our way back to our spots. Only 3.1 miles were left in my personal challenge, and I was actually looking forward to them. I hopped off my bike and nearly face-planted when my knees tried to give out. It was either love or exertion that was taking my legs out from under me. I decided it was love.

I was in love. And I finished my dissertation. And I had a

degenerative disease. And I was really, really tired and might have to crawl my way across the finish line.

That was life. The good, the bad, the ugly all mixed together in a special kind of recipe of possibility.

Gratefully, I sank to the ground and swapped out my cycling shoes for my running shoes. I guzzled more water and wished for dino nuggets while I snarfed down a packet of gross energy gel crap for some calories.

My body was so tired. It was tempting to just lay down here on my towel next to my bike. But that's not why I was here. I could nap tomorrow. And eat all the dino nuggets I wanted. Jonah promised. For now, I needed to get up and push for another thirty or forty minutes. That was it.

I'd done worse things for longer. Heck, I'd been stabbed. I could freaking finish this race.

Using the seat of my bike, I pulled myself back up to standing.

I lumbered my way back to the start. My legs felt like overcooked spaghetti.

"The run's my worst," Gus said, appearing next to me. "If you need to leave me out there to finish, you do it."

"Not happening, Gus, my man," Tameka said, between hits from her water bottle.

"Let's do this," I said, putting my hand out. "Three point one miles is the only thing that stands between us and grand-kid hugs and five hundred dollars and all the dino nuggets I can eat."

Their hands joined mine.

"Let's do this," Gus wheezed.

"I want that money," Tameka huffed.

"I want those nuggets."

We started off slowly, and I tried to focus on form. It deteriorated when I was tired, and I was so freaking tired. My legs felt like blobby gelatin in an earthquake. I added Jell-O to the list of things I was going to eat tomorrow.

I should have chosen to prove a point with just a 5k. Or

maybe a nice hike. Then I remembered bears. I glanced around at the scenery. We were on a country road, but the woods were thin enough that I felt confident I could see a large mammal coming at me.

West Virginia really was beautiful. The trees were lush and green. Fields and hills rolled off in all directions in more greens and yellows and browns. This part of the road was flanked by a tidy split rail fence.

I steadied my breath and focused on the rhythm of my foot strikes.

"First mile is the worst," I whispered to myself.

I wished Jonah was here, urging me on. Squirting water on me. Telling me I could do this.

"I don't know if I can do this," Tameka said through gritted teeth.

"You are absolutely doing this," I told her, glancing down at my watch. "Five hundred dollars in exactly two miles." One mile down. The worst mile.

Gus was wheezing on my left. He didn't have the oxygen to spare to complain. So I did it for him.

"It's so hot. Like convection oven broiling a steak hot."

"Like coal-fired pizza oven hot," Tameka gasped out.

I added pizza to my Sunday meal list.

Gus grunted.

I was sweating so much I felt like I might dehydrate into a raisin.

But my legs kept moving.

We all kept going forward. Things were starting to hurt. My shins, my heels, my arches. I could tell I was going to have bra burn from the amount of salt exploding from my pores. But my breath was still there. My feet were still moving.

The crowd around us had thinned.

Some pulling ahead in the run, others slowing to walk. The August sun beat down on us, bouncing back off the asphalt of the road.

I thought about what I wanted after this. Thought about

calling Jonah from the finish line with my medal. Thought about calling my parents. I'd tell them. I could tell them now. Because I'd done this.

We paused at a water station, rehydrating and rinsing the sweat from our faces and necks.

"How much farther?" Tameka asked.

Gus was still too winded to speak.

"One mile to go," the attendant said cheerfully.

We pushed off again without discussing it.

One mile. I repeated it to myself. Chanted it. There'd been a time just a few short months ago when a mile hadn't been possible. When I'd battled pain just from existing. Now, I had one mile left to go, and I was going to finish.

The hair on my arms rose. I hoped it was determination and not a symptom of heat exhaustion.

"One mile, guys," I barked. "We're finishing this!"

It was the longest mile of my life. That ribbon of road seemed to stretch on indefinitely, and I wondered if maybe I'd stumbled into some strange corner of hell where the race never ended. The torture was never over.

Then I heard cheering.

"There! Over the hill," Tameka hissed.

Gus, the workhorse, hadn't lifted his gaze from his sneakers since Mile Two. "Just lead me in the right direction," he puffed without looking up.

The hill, the longest, tallest hill in the history of West Virginia geography, gave way to the most beautiful thing I'd ever seen in my life.

The finish line.

The route was lined with spectators and athletes who'd finished ages ago. I wanted to hate them, but I didn't have the energy.

"It's all downhill from here," I wheezed.

"Let's do this," Gus said.

"I'm definitely puking," Tameka confirmed.

"Do it after the finish line." Together, we took the decline.

The cheers, the flutter of the Finish Line sign drew us in like a siren's song.

It was really happening. I was finishing an entire triathlon with a disease. I couldn't tell the difference between sweat and tears. Judging from the wet snorts coming from my compatriots, they were experiencing the same sense of overwhelm.

The cheers were deafening. I felt them in my blood and bones.

Community. Connection.

"Let's do this, ladies," Gus said, his voice cracking.

Together, we linked hands and, sobbing and sweating, made our way across the finish line.

I. Did. It.

The heartbeat that hammered in my head said it over and over again.

I. Did. It.

There was more cheering. Gus was dragged away by a horde of toddlers chanting "Grampa!" Tameka was bent at the waist over a trash can laughing.

And Jonah was…*here.*

In a suit and tie. Holding the biggest bouquet of flowers I'd ever seen. And a piece of pizza. He was here. For me. With pizza.

These were tears.

He pushed his way through, the crowd parting around him, and I was running again. He tossed the flowers over his shoulder and caught me mid-leap.

"You did it, Shelby! You fucking did it," he shouted over the noise. His joy was palpable. I could reach out and hold on to his happiness for me. "I'm so fucking proud of you!"

I threw my arms around his neck. "I did it," I confirmed with an undignified sob. "And I'm in love with you!"

Q. What's one thing you wish your neighbors would recognize about you?

299

Scarlett Bodine: That I'm a damn genius when it comes to pairing folks up. If people would just stop stickin' to their guns and actin' like they know best I could wrap up my goal of romantic matchmaking domination a hell of a lot faster.

Chapter Fifty
Shelby

I wasn't sure if I'd said it loud enough for him to catch the words over the roar of the crowd. Runners were finishing around us. Spectators were cheering. And I'd just shouted my declaration of love in the middle of it.

He lowered me slowly, gently to the ground, and I was grateful when my legs didn't give out.

"What did you say?" he asked in a half shout. I was getting his suit sweaty, but he didn't seem to notice.

I looked him in the eye, squared my shoulders, and delivered the message again. "I love you, Jonah Bodine."

Something flickered in those sharp green eyes.

"I finished my dissertation last night and the triathlon five seconds ago. Summer's coming to an end. But I'm hoping this is just the beginning for us."

He opened his mouth, but I shut him up with a hard, sweaty kiss. "I sprang this on you, and I'm not expecting an answer. Figure out how you feel and let me know when you're ready."

"You're a hell of a girl, Shelby," he said softly.

"I am, aren't I?" I agreed with a grin that I felt in my soul. "Now, gimmie that pizza."

He handed it over with a grin.

Then someone else was calling my name. "Shelby!"

"Mom? Dad?"

I blinked as my parents wound their way to us.

"What are you doing here?"

Dad snatched me out of Jonah's grasp and squeezed me tight. "We are so proud of you, Shelby!" He had his GT touchdown face on. Only this time it was for me. And I was sweating and crying again.

"We saw you come across the finish line, and I swear it gave me goose bumps," Mom said, leaning in for her hug and kiss.

"I can't believe you're here," I said, my voice breaking.

My parents shared a baffled look.

"Why wouldn't we be here?" Dad asked, looking confused.

"It's just a sprint tri," I said.

"It's *your* sprint tri," Mom insisted. "And it's a huge deal, Shelby."

It was a huge deal. They didn't even know how huge a deal it was.

It made me want to cry…or keep crying. At this point, between the sweat and the tears, my face was a salt mine. Everything was gritty, and I wasn't sure where the moisture was coming from. I thought I'd do this alone. I'd finish this alone. But I'd never been alone in the first place.

"You guys, I'm in love with Jonah," I announced. "And I finished my dissertation finally last night. And I don't want to find a home for Billy Ray. I want to keep him. Also, I was diagnosed with ankylosing spondylitis earlier this year. But it's going to be okay because I just finished a triathlon, so I can pretty much do anything."

My parents shared another one of those baffled looks. "I'm not really sure where we should start with that," Dad admitted.

I pulled him down for a hug. "Everything is going to be great."

"Shelby! Let's get a picture!" Gus and Tameka, re-energized by sports drinks, bananas, and familial accolades, pushed their way into our little circle.

Introductions were made. Photos were taken. Pizza eaten. And I finally got my hands on a finisher's medal. It hung around my neck with a significant weight.

And while all of that was going on, Jonah's quiet gaze never left me.

Steady. Secure. Proud. Amused. All things I loved about him.

I grinned and winked at him. I'd proved to myself everything I'd set out to prove. And now the real fun could begin.

"Yes!" Tameka fist-pumped her phone in the air. "I beat my sister by a whole two minutes!"

"There she is!" The Breakfast Club, thankfully fully clothed now, pushed their way through the finish line crowd. More introductions were made, and I felt thoroughly surrounded by love.

"So, uh, what's with the suit?" Gus asked Jonah. "You proposing?"

I laughed as my parents went back to looking dazed. "He's in his brother's wedding today, but he surprised me here," I explained.

Mom's eyes went misty.

"What time is it?" I demanded.

Dad read off the time from his watch.

"We need to get you to a wedding," I exclaimed.

"What about your bike? The rest of your stuff?" Jonah asked.

"You go," I insisted. "I've got plenty of help. Go."

Still he paused. He had things to say. But I had time to hear them.

I rose on tiptoe and pressed a kiss to his clean-shaven cheek. "We'll talk later. I'm good. I'll see you at the wedding."

He stared down at me, a slow grin spreading across his face. "I'll see you there." He kissed me on the mouth for a few NC-17 seconds before pulling back.

"See you all later," he said. Jonah blew me a kiss as he backed away.

"That boy is head over heels for you," Granny Louisa sighed.

"That would be awfully convenient," I said, watching the suited shoulders of Jonah Bodine disappear into the crowd.

"So, honey, um, back to this ankle-losing thing?" Mom said, trying to draw my attention back.

———

While the Breakfast Club hauled my gear back to Bootleg Springs, I sprawled out in the back seat of my mom's sedan and answered all their questions about my diagnosis. Mom did an internet search on her phone while Dad drove, and I spent the last fifteen minutes of the drive talking her down.

"Never do an internet search on a diagnosis, Mom! You know these things."

She was staring in horror at a worst-case scenario image search. Dad swerved trying to peer at the phone screen.

"You guys! This isn't terminal, but smashing through a guard-rail might be. Can we please focus on the fact that I have this under control, and I'll let you know if there's a reason to worry?"

"I can't tell if you're Pollyanna-ing us again," Dad griped.

"Pollyanna-ing you?" I asked.

"Oh, I'm fine guys! Just a little mishap at work with a very small knife. It's hardly a scratch," Dad said in a falsetto.

"Come on! I didn't want you to—"

"Worry," my parents said together, rolling their eyes at each other.

"What? Is that so wrong?" I demanded. "Isn't part of being a family trying to protect each other?"

"Part of being a family is trusting each other to handle the tough stuff," Mom said, clearly not happy with me.

"So I've heard," I said dryly. I pulled my shoes off and blanched at the smell. I was going to need six showers before showing up at the wedding.

"And if you want to have a real relationship with that handsome Jonah Bodine, you're going to have to figure that out. Isn't that right, James?"

"Do you think Scarlett would have a lead on any fixer-uppers in Bootleg?" Dad mused, having tuned out the meat of the conversation.

"What? Why?" Mom asked.

"If both our kids end up here, we should probably have a home base. We already have a pig and a puppy for grandchildren."

"It *is* a nice town," Mom agreed.

And just like that, Bootleg Springs reeled in a fresh catch.

———

We arrived back in Bootleg a scant hour before the wedding. I needed to fly through a shower and makeup and hair if I was going to make it before Cassidy walked down the aisle.

Dad pulled up in front of the Little Yellow House and turned off the car.

"Are you guys coming in?" I asked, already peeling my skin off the car seat and heading for the front porch.

"Bowie and Cassidy invited us to the wedding. We're your ride," Dad called. I was reaching for the screen door to yank it open when I noticed the roll of paper between the doors.

"What's that? A love note from Jonah?" Mom asked. "He's a keeper, Shelby."

My parents walked past me into the house and immediately went into grandparent mode, releasing Billy Ray from his crate and showering him with treats and kisses.

It was such a domestic scene. My parents making themselves at home in my house, playing with my dog.

But none of that registered.

Slowly, I unrolled the paper already knowing what I'd find.

It was a crude charcoal sketch of a woman with thick bangs and wide eyes. She had an upturned nose and a scar on her chest. She was naked.

"How did you find me?" I whispered.

Billy Ray jumped on me in sweet, puppy delight, and I scooped him up.

I looked over my shoulder and took my time studying every inch of the woods and yard.

Was he out there now?

Did he expect me to be as helpless as I'd been the last time?

He was going to be disappointed.

"Shelby," Mom called. "If you don't get in the shower now, we're going to be late!"

Chapter Fifty-One

Jonah

If Bowie's smile got any bigger, his face was going to split open. I'd never seen a man happier or more ready to march down the aisle.

"Did you see her? How does she look?" he asked me for the third time. My brother was referring to his bride.

"Yes, I saw Cassidy," I said again. I picked up the beer that Bowie kept putting down and handed it back to him. He needed something to do with his hands. "She looks—"

"Wait. Don't tell me. I wanna be surprised. Leah Mae made her dress," he said, imparting the information he'd mentioned at least sixteen times since I'd shown up.

Jameson growled at his tie in the mirror in the sheriff's den. Cassidy and the girls had commandeered the entire second floor of the Tucker household. The guests had taken over the backyard.

Gibson adjusted his suspenders, frowning.

There was a knock at the door. "Are you boys decent?" My mom poked her head in the door.

She was pretty as a spring day, as the town elders would say, in a blue and white dress that nipped in at the waist and fell away into a full skirt. Her short blonde cap of hair was accentuated with a sparkly headband.

"Hey, Jenny." Bowie greeted her with the full wattage of his smile.

"Oh my," she said, stepping inside. She gave my arm a squeeze before turning her attention to Bowie. "You look almost as excited as your bride." She brushed a hand over his lapels.

"I can't believe it's finally happening," he said softly.

"Are you nervous?" Mom asked him.

He shook his head emphatically then said, "Yes."

She laughed. "Okay. Then here's some advice. When the processional music starts. Close your eyes and count to five. When you open them, you'll be looking right at your beautiful bride. You want to remember every step she takes to you. You want to remember the second her hand touches yours and that first smile she gives you. Because the rest of the night is going to be a whirlwind. But you want to remember those moments for the rest of your life."

Well, hell. I had no idea my mom was such a romantic. It made my throat tickle.

Bowie nodded and swallowed hard. "Thanks for being here, Jenny. I know you're Jonah's mama and all, but I kinda feel like you belong to all of us."

My mom's eyes went damp. "I'm honored to be here with all of you boys," she whispered.

There was a lot of throat clearing and a few covert swipes at eyes with sleeves.

"Jameson, sweetheart, let me at that tie," Mom demanded, righting the damage he was doing.

She gave us all the once over, helping Gibson into his jacket. Tucking my boutonniere into place. Giving Bowie an extra squeeze.

The music outside changed. Checking her watch, she

peeked out into the backyard. "Well, boys, I think this is your big moment. Are you ready to walk out there and get your brother married?"

"Yes, ma'am," we answered.

"Good. Then get out there and have the best time," she said, shooing us toward the door.

Bowie paused in the doorway. "You'll sit up front, won't you?" he asked her. "You and Jimmy Bob? You can sit across the aisle from the Tuckers."

She pressed her lips together. "I'd be honored," she whispered.

We exited the den, and I dropped a kiss on the top of her head. "Thanks for being here, Mom."

"I love you, Jonah Bodine."

She was the second woman to tell me that today.

And it was the first woman I was thinking of when I took my place next to Jameson to the right of the trellis Gibs had finished in a burst of energy. Mayor Auggie Hornsbladt took his role as officiant seriously. He was wearing a shirt and tie under his best overalls.

Misty Lynn, the man-eating Venus flytrap, was dateless in the front row with her father and my mother. The way she was eyeing Gibson made me think there might be trouble later.

But I didn't have time to worry about Misty Lynn and whatever scene she'd undoubtedly cause. I was too busy looking at Shelby. I'd spotted her immediately a few rows back on the aisle next to her parents. Her thick bangs framed those watchful hazel eyes. The rest of her dark hair was pulled back in a low bun behind her ear. She was wearing a sunshine yellow dress and a smile that brightened my entire world.

Shelby gave me a little finger wiggle, and I returned it.

It was a good day. Not only was my brother tying the knot, but Shelby Thompson told me she was in love with me. And tonight I'd tell her that the feeling was mutual. That I didn't want this summer to come to an end.

"Here come the girls," Jameson hissed at me.

Reluctantly, I dragged my eyes away from my girl. Leah Mae, June, and Scarlett, eschewing the traditional aisle, saunter-strutted down the grassy expanse in blue. Scarlett blew Devlin a kiss when she passed him, and you'd have to be blind to miss the pride and love that beamed off him. My sister was loved. My brother was getting married. And I was starting my own future.

June, more dignified than the rest, gave GT a polite nod and the slightest of smiles as she passed him. GT looked like he wanted to jump up from his seat next to his mother and squeeze her tight. I had a feeling there was another engagement in the works there. Leah Mae, instead of taking her place next to Scarlett, be-bopped over to the man-side of the aisle and planted a kiss on Jameson that had the assembled guests cheering.

"Oh, what the heck," she said. She planted a kiss on me, then Gibson, and finally a resounding smack on the lips for Bowie.

Love was a physical presence here.

I'd been to weddings before. I'd watched brides and grooms share their vows over the murmured complaints of guests who didn't really want to spend their day celebrating. But today was different. Every single person in attendance was here because they loved Bowie and Cassidy and wanted to be here. To celebrate with them. To shed tears with them. To be there on the most special day of their lives.

The music changed, and I chanced a glance at my brother. Bowie's eyes were squeezed closed.

Cassidy appeared on the arm of Sheriff Tucker, a vision in blush and lace. She floated rather than walked to the head of the aisle. And when she arrived, when she paused to take in the moment, Bowie opened his eyes.

The moment was so powerful, so moving, I heard an intake of breath rise up from the chairs. Followed immediately by sniffles. Mayor Hornsbladt blew his nose noisily into a handkerchief.

When Bowie bent at the waist to catch his breath, I found Shelby again in the audience. Beaming through tears. I remembered back to when I thought maybe there was a possibility that I could see myself as the faceless groom in Rene's Pinterest vision.

This was different. This was real.

I wasn't some guy trying to fit himself into someone else's ideal. I was a man in love with a woman. And I wanted what Bowie and Cassidy had. What Scarlett and Devlin found. What Leah Mae and Jameson discovered. What George and June built.

And I wanted it all with Shelby.

Sheriff Tucker nudged his daughter forward, and they started down the aisle. Bowie was so excited he met them at the front row. The sheriff, with glistening eyes, let go of his daughter long enough to hug Bowie hard.

"Proud of you, son," he whispered.

They were words we all needed so desperately to hear.

Jameson cleared his throat next to me. Gibs was swiping at the corner of his eye with his jacket sleeve.

I looked for Shelby again. She was watching me.

I love you, she mouthed.

Chapter Fifty-Two
Shelby

The wedding was picture perfect. There wasn't a dry eye in the backyard when Cassidy and Bowie pledged their love to each other, and it wasn't just because the caterer had opened the bar early.

No, Bootleg Springs was as enamored with the happy couple as they were with each other. After the vows were spoken, the toasts made, and dinner served, I finally got a slow dance with Jonah.

"You look beautiful, Shelby," he told me as we swayed under strings of lights. I was barefoot in the grass in the arms of the man I loved under a starry summer sky.

"You look pretty great yourself," I said, plucking at his collar. He'd removed the tie, shed the jacket, and rolled up his sleeves after the pictures were taken. And looked even more delicious now with his suspenders showing than he had in the suit jacket.

"How you feeling?" he asked, swaying us in a slow tick-tock that made it feel like time was standing still.

"I feel…magical," I decided. That was the perfect word for what I felt.

"You're not too sore?" he pressed, pausing to dip me backward in a slow-motion arc. The lights and stars above us blurred in happy confusion.

I grinned as he pulled me back to standing, his arms banding around me. "I will be tomorrow and the next day and the next day."

"I'm so proud of you," Jonah said, leaning in to rest his lips on the top of my head. I was really glad I'd taken a second pass with the shampoo in the shower.

"I'm pretty proud of me, too."

"How did your parents take the 'hiding a diagnosis from them' news?" he asked.

I glanced over to where my parents were feeding each other cake. "Better than I expected. Though they still got in a parting guilt trip."

I wanted to tell him about the sketch. About what it meant. But the moment was so perfect. I selfishly held on to it.

"Speaking of parents," I said, nodding over Jonah's shoulder.

He turned us and spotted his mother dancing with Bowie.

"Everybody needs a mom," I whispered.

Jenny was laughing as Bowie spun her away from him. And then Gibson captured her other hand and took over the dance.

"This is what she always wanted," Jonah confessed. "A big, complicated family."

"It doesn't get much bigger or more complicated than the Bodines," I teased.

"Uh, excuse me you two." Jimmy Bob Prosser looked like his necktie was choking him. He was a big man with broad shoulders and work-roughened hands.

He was also sweating profusely.

"Hi, Jimmy Bob," Jonah said amiably, and I loved him just a little more for it.

"Hi," Jimmy Bob said. His Adam's apple worked in his throat. "I just wanted to, uh, tell you, well, reassure you that…"

He got that look that people got when the words they wanted to say up and evaporated right out of their head.

"Jimmy Bob, would you like a glass of water?" I offered.

"Oh, no thank you, Shelby. I'm just trying to work up the nerve to tell Jonah here how much I like his mama and how I have nothing but honorable intentions toward her," he croaked.

Love was in the air.

"That's good to hear, Jimmy Bob," Jonah said, giving the man a pat on the shoulder.

"She's one of a kind," the man continued. "And she and I have been talking some."

Judging from the flush on his face and neck, they'd been doing a lot more than just talking.

"Anyway, your mama's real special, and I was hopin'—"

"Hello." The woman in question floated into our little circle, a glass of champagne in hand and a lovely smile on her face. She pressed a kiss to Jonah's cheek, then turned and did the same to Jimmy Bob.

Jimmy Bob beamed at her brighter than the moon above. "Jenny, darlin', I was just tellin' Jonah and Shelby here how much I enjoy your company."

"Did you also tell them that I'm considering moving to Bootleg Springs?" she asked brightly.

Jonah stiffened in surprise next to me. "Are you serious?"

Jenny grinned. "Only if you don't mind."

"Mind?" Jonah laughed. He released me with a parting squeeze and picked his mother up in a bear hug. "Are you nuts? Are you sure?"

He set her down to see her face.

"Clarabell and her husband are thinking about retiring in a few years. They want someone they can trust managing Moonshine Diner." She shot a look at Jimmy Bob. "And I happen to like the company here."

Jimmy Bob looked like he'd just won Chicken Shit Bingo and the state lottery on the same night.

What Jenny didn't voice, what I wasn't about to bring up

since I was all about not ruining the moment, was the fact that she was probably also going to need to be available to a lot of questions from investigators. Callie Kendall was alive and out there somewhere. And someone was determined to make sure she stayed dead.

A shiver worked its way up my spine, and I felt as if there were eyes on me. I thought of the sketch folded up in my clutch. The shadow it represented.

As if sensing the chill, Jonah slipped his arm around my waist, drawing me into his side. I spotted my brother dancing forehead-to-forehead with June on the other side of the yard. Bootleg Springs had cast its spell on all of us, drawing us in and making us feel like we belonged.

I only needed to know if there was a place here for me with Jonah.

"I'm happy for you, Mom," he said gruffly.

"And I'm happy for you, son," Jenny said with a knowing tilt of her head in my direction.

"On that note, I'm going to whisk my girlfriend away to a dark corner of the yard for some necking," Jonah announced.

True to his word, he set a course and led me through the throng of jubilant celebrators. We were stopped a dozen times by friends and family.

Nadine Tucker's gardening shed, a charming little building tucked away behind the garage, appeared to be our destination.

Jonah paused in front of the door.

"About what you told me earlier," he began.

My pulse picked up. "Refresh my memory?" I said coyly, tapping my chin with a finger. I imagined nerd girls everywhere standing up and cheering.

"You said you loved me," he said, his voice whisper-soft and deep as the night that surrounded us here in this quiet little corner.

"Oh, *that*."

"I don't want you to leave at the end of the summer," he said. "I don't want to find a good home for Billy Ray. I want to keep him. And he and I will follow you wherever you go."

He was warming up for the big finish, and as much as I wanted to hear those words, as much as my soul was vibrating with the need to hear them, I had a few loose ends to tie off first.

"What about your mom? You can't leave Bootleg Springs if she's moving here. You have family here. A lot of family."

"And now that I know where they live, I can visit whenever it's convenient. I love this town, and I love my family, but, Shelby…" He paused and tilted my chin up so I was looking in those oh-so-tender green eyes. "I'd rather be next to you."

"Jonah," I sighed, savoring his name.

"Don't tell me you've changed your mind since this afternoon?" he teased.

I shook my head. "You'd follow me?"

"Wherever you go," he said, tucking a strand of hair behind my ear. Soft, intimate touches that were untying every knot in my stomach. "I can work anywhere. I can visit my family any time. But I want a hell of a lot more than a fling with you, Shelby."

Say it. Say it. Say it, the fifteen-year-old nerd in me chanted.

"Hmm, why is that?" I asked, dancing my fingers under his suspenders.

"I think it has something to do with the fact that I'm head over heels in love with you. Frankly, I'm surprised a smart girl like you didn't figure it all out weeks ago."

I poked him in the chest. "I've been a little busy."

"How's your schedule looking now?" he asked, leaning in and down, down, down.

"Wide open," I whispered. His lips were a breath away from mine, but I stopped him. "Jonah, wait."

He paused where he was. "What? Are you okay?"

His breath was hot on my skin. And I could feel the heat of his body through his shirt.

"I want to stay here. In Bootleg. Morgantown isn't too far.

And there are a handful of universities within a hundred miles. I might be able to work from home part-time like June. Or I'll just get good at long commutes. But my point is, I want to be here, with you and my brother and June and everyone else and—"

I was sure there were more words. And definitely a few not so pretty ones. I had to tell him about the sketch, and we had to talk to Sheriff Tucker sooner rather than later.

But for right this second, I was just going to kiss the hell out of Jonah Bodine on a beautiful, hot summer night.

His mouth closed over mine, tongue and teeth taking charge, and I welcomed it. He was who I wanted for my lifetime. We fit. We belonged.

"Shelby, honey, how much do you like that dress?" he asked.

"Not as much as I'd like your hands on me," I told him.

Chapter Fifty-Three
Shelby

The garden shed had the metallic tang of potting soil in the musky air. Dimly, I could make out shelves along one wall stocked with terra cotta pots and the like. The opposite wall was a puzzle of tools and gardening implements. And on the back wall, there was a long, skinny workbench.

Jonah carried me to it, settled me on it, and drew me to the edge.

He cupped my face in one hand, and I felt rather than saw him stare into me.

"My girl," he breathed.

I spread my knees wide and used my heels to drag him against me.

The bulge behind his zipper ground into me. I could feel the metal through the thin cotton of my thong.

The noise he made was primal. We were eye-to-eye as he flexed his erection against my opening.

I gripped the edge of the workbench, and the straps of my dress slid down my arms, hanging precariously. The scoop neck deepened to indecent. Jonah was bucking against me now, slowly, rhythmically. As if he were waiting for the dress to give up its battle against gravity.

Obliging him, I curved my shoulders forward and was rewarded with a gasp that I felt on my hard, furled nipples. He bent and dipped his tongue into the neckline of the dress where one areola peeked through. The rough flat of his tongue drove me wild. While he licked and sucked, I went to work on his belt and pants.

I didn't want him slow and sweet tonight. I wanted him wild with his own need. Desperate to have me.

I used my hands and my heels to shove his pants down just enough.

He sprang free, bobbing against my swollen clit, and it was my turn to gasp. Ignoring the fact that I was fisting the root of his cock, Jonah moved to lick over my other nipple. The dress was bunched around my waist from the top and bottom like a yellow tutu. My breasts were bared to his mouth while his hand slid between my legs.

He hooked a finger under the thong over the growing wet spot and then, with unfair patience, dragged the material back and forth over my cleft.

"I'm going to want you in this dress again and again," he growled.

He raked his teeth over my nipple, and I shivered.

"I'll want you bent over a table, your skirts pushed up, and your sweet ass on display. Just waiting for me to touch you." He slid the thong to the side and skated the tip of one finger through my seam.

I was balanced on the edge of the table and had nowhere to go. Forward would have me falling. Back would take me away from the cock I was trying to tempt with busy fingers. I stroked up to the top, my thumb dancing over the slit there.

"I'll want you to wear this to nice parties so I can lure you out into the woods and finger fuck you against a tree."

Jonah pumped into my hand and then slid two fingers into me.

I gripped his cock tighter. He groaned, nuzzling his cheek against my breasts before bringing his mouth to mine.

The kiss, that glorious filthy kiss, mimicked what we were doing to each other. Short, sharp thrusts of tongue, finger, cock. I ached for more, even as I felt my inner muscles dance. I could come on his fingers. But I wanted all of him. I wanted to seal this night and our promises the right way.

"Take me here, Jonah," I begged. I brought my heels to the edge of the table, opening my legs as wide as they could go.

"Fuck, Shelby. Who could say no to you?" He brought his forehead to mine, nipped at my lower lip, still pumping himself into my hand, still fucking me with his fingers.

Our breath mingled in the dark.

"Please, Jonah," I breathed.

"I don't want to hurt you," he whispered. "Your body's been through a lot today, and I'm worked up enough that I don't know if I can be gentle."

"That's exactly what I want. Don't be gentle with me. Trust me to take it, to handle it."

He growled low, fighting with his body's wants and his need to be careful with me.

"Show me you trust me," I demanded. I angled the head of his cock so it brushed between my wet, wet folds on his next thrust.

I saw the tightening of his jaw. He grabbed me by the back of the neck with one hand. "I'm going to be so pissed at you if you let me hurt you."

"We'll both deal with it," I promised, nudging my hips forward so he was notched in place. "Take me. Show me."

Without warning he drove into me, impaling me on the table. And then he was dragging his cock in and out of my slick flesh. Owning me. Claiming me.

He held me by the neck, keeping our foreheads pressed tight as he fucked into me.

"Stay quiet," he warned. "There are about fifty people right outside this door who could hear you scream when you come on my cock, Shelby."

I sobbed out a response, clinging to his shoulders as he used my body. It felt so decadent. Like my body and I were no longer strangers. Like Jonah had taught me how to find the pleasure my body could afford.

"Wider, baby," he grunted when my knees buckled, closing on his hips.

What a tableau we made. Fully clothed and rutting into each other. Gasping for breath. Begging for the undefined *more*. My breasts bounced as his thrusts grew more aggressive. I could name and describe the dozens of physiological reactions that were happening in our bodies right this second. But I couldn't for the life of me ascribe what I felt for this man to mere science.

It was elemental and magic. It was exotic and home.

My neck stung where his grip tightened. And I felt the first shimmers of what we were both chasing.

"Shelby," he bit out. That impatience, that need to satisfy me even though his own biological drive was leading the charge. It did me in. Jonah loved me. He would always want to take care of me.

And I did the same for him.

With his free hand, he found my exposed flesh, dancing pads of eager fingers over that tight bundle of nerves.

"Yes," I hissed. Again and again and again. Even after I broke. Even after he broke.

I felt him come. Felt the warm rush of his orgasm as it painted me from the inside.

He grunted softly and flexed into me again and again. I rode it with him, my hungry muscles opening and closing around him.

"I love you," he said, his voice ragged, his breath uneven. "I love you, Shelby. Say you'll be mine. I want a wedding like this. I want kids with you. I want the rest of my life to be spent at your side."

Of course. Of course. It drummed like my heart inside me, vibrating like a song.

"Yes, Jonah. Yes to all of it."

Chapter Fifty-Four

Jonah

That was the most Bodine thing I've ever done in my life," I confessed to Shelby as we tried to right our clothes. Shelby's hair was a "just had sex" disaster, and I fucking loved it. But her parents were outside, and so was my mother. And it was just bad form to strut on out of here looking like we'd just had the best pair of orgasms available to humans.

"What? Have sex in the town sheriff's garden shed during his daughter's wedding?" she asked smugly. "I feel a bit Bodiney myself tonight."

"Maybe it's the moon or the wedding or the gin. But Shelby, honey, I'm pretty excited about fall and winter and every other season I'm going to be spending with you."

She laid a hand over her heart. "You sure know how to make a girl feel special."

"How about you go get us a couple of gin and tonics, and I'll figure out a plan to get us out of here so we can go home and celebrate some more?" I suggested.

She answered by pressing a kiss to my cheek. "I'd be delighted, sugar."

Wearing a shit-eating grin, I went in search of the groom and found all hell breaking loose instead.

Gibson was holding Misty Lynn at arm's length, a look of abject horror on his face.

"Just give me another chance, Gibs," she wailed, eyeliner smeared under her eyes.

"Someone needs to tell that girl that desperation ain't attractive." Mayor Hornsbladt sighed into his sweet tea.

"How dare you try to ruin my brother and my best friend's wedding?" Scarlett snarled. "I knew invitin' your stupid ass was a mistake. But noooo, we had to be nice."

"Where are Bowie and Cassidy?" I asked Mayor Hornsbladt.

"The newlyweds had a distinct sparkle in their eyes and called it a night about five minutes ago. I think y'all's parents are waving them off out front."

At least the bride and groom weren't here to witness Misty Lynn's meltdown.

"C'mon, Gibs. It was always so good between us," Misty Lynn mewled. She was a drunken mess. Her dress was grass-stained, and her hair was exploding out of the prom updo she'd fashioned.

"Never gonna happen, Misty Lynn," Gibson growled. He let her go, but she latched herself to him like a needy barnacle on the indifferent hull of a ship.

"Jameson, Jonah? Wanna help a guy out?" Gibson asked through gritted teeth as he tried to dislodge her.

"Oh, I'll help you out," Scarlett said, striding over and grabbing a fistful of Misty Lynn's hair. "Now you listen, and you listen good, Misty Lynn. You ain't never gonna be good enough for my brother. And now that your daddy and Jonah's mama are gettin' serious, you can't try to lure him into your soggy sheets. You'll be kin if they get married. Brother and sister."

"It's not true!" Misty Lynn howled. Even drunk, she at least had an idea of how genetics worked.

"Stop making a fool of yourself in front of the entire town and grow some goddamn self-respect!" Scarlett said, keeping hold of the other woman's hair.

Misty Lynn took a swing at Scarlett but missed. Scarlett released her grip on the hair and watched her opponent sway.

"Y'all think you're so high and mighty. But you're not!" Misty Lynn slurred. "Your daddy was a murderer, and your mama was nothing but a loser. People feel sorry for you. They pity you," she spat out. "And you know what? They're all secretly scared that one day, someone is gonna push your buttons and you're gonna snap. Just like your daddy."

She did a slow turn around our circle until she faced me. "And you. Your daddy didn't even want you. Yet here you are beggin' for scraps."

"Misty Lynn, that's enough," Shelby said coolly. She had a drink in each hand.

"Oh, I'm just gettin' started," Misty Lynn sneered. "I'm just gonna keep tellin' the truth that everyone else around here is too scared to say. That Gibson always looks like he's five seconds away from murderin' someone. Or that Scarlett's gonna wind up with a drinkin' problem just like her daddy."

"Misty Lynn," Gibson said. His voice snapped out like the crack of a whip. "Hear me. We will never be together again. I regret every moment of my time with you when I was too young and too dumb to recognize that you were just a user."

She stumbled back like he'd struck her. "You don't mean that, Gibson Bodine."

"You don't even know what it's like to have real feelings for someone," Gibson said, his face twisting into a mask of frustration. "You string that poor bastard Rhett Ginsler along just to discard him when you get bored. That's not sexy. That's not attractive. That's fucking sad. You're fucking sad. I tolerate you because you're a Bootlegger. Because we grew up together. But you will never be anything more to me."

"Well, fuck you then," she shrieked. "Fuck all of you, dumb fucking losers!"

The music picked back up, and so did the conversations of all the witnesses. It wasn't the craziest thing Bootleg had seen at a wedding. Not by a long shot.

Misty Lynn turned and stumbled out of the yard. Shelby sent me an apologetic look and set the drinks down on an empty table. She headed in the direction Misty Lynn fled.

Maybe a good psychological talking to would help. I doubted it. But Shelby didn't like to see anyone in pain. Not even a man-eating monster like Misty Lynn.

I checked the front of the house first to make sure that Bowie and Cassidy were actually gone and didn't accidentally run down a drunken Misty Lynn on their way home.

I saw my mother in an embrace with Jimmy Bob under the oak tree. Sheriff Tucker and Nadine were wandering up the walkway arm-in-arm. No newlyweds, no Misty Lynn.

I ducked around between the garage and the house again, not really wanting to be the one to break the news to the parents that Misty Lynn had just caused an epic scene.

"Dinner and a show," Jameson said, appearing next to me. Like a good brother, he handed me a beer.

"Gibs okay?" I asked.

"Seems to be. He's used to her freak-outs by now."

I scanned the backyard for Shelby. I spotted her clutch on a table and the two drinks she'd left on another one.

"You lookin' for someone in particular?" Jameson drawled.

"Shelby," I said. "We're ah, kind of an official thing. Like permanently."

He clapped me on the back. "About damn time."

"Aren't men supposed to avoid commitment?" I joked.

"Only the stupid ones. 'Round here, we all know there's nothing better than pairing off with someone who's willing to put up with your shit for the rest of your life. So you're stickin' around?"

I nodded. "Yeah. Yeah, I am. Shelby, too. And my mom's thinking she just might take up residency, too."

"No, shit?" Jameson looked downright thrilled.

"Yep. She's in talks with Clarabell about managing Moonshine."

"Your mama?" Gibson approached from behind and joined the conversation.

"Yeah. Hey, have you seen Shelby?" I asked him.

"Not since she took off after Misty Lynn to soothe the she-beast," Gibs quipped.

I felt something. A little frisson of nerves skating through my gut.

"I'm gonna try to find her. I don't like her wandering around in the dark after what happened when she was on the bike."

Gibson frowned. "Call her."

"I'm probably overreacting."

"Call her," he insisted.

I pulled out my phone, dialed.

"What's going on? You don't think Misty Lynn would take a swing at her, do you?" Jameson asked.

I heard Shelby's ringtone and felt a fleeting second of hope before I realized it was coming from her clutch.

Gibson stepped off the deck and picked up the clutch. Opened it. He froze, then lifted his steely gaze to me. "Jonah."

I knew from the tone it wasn't good. I was off the deck, snatching the paper out of his hand before I could even formulate a question.

It was a sketch. Charcoal lines of a woman who looked a hell of a lot like Shelby. A naked woman. Scrawled across the bottom were the words "See you soon."

I started for the front yard, Gibson on my heels. Jameson on his. "What the fuck is wrong with you two?" Jameson asked good-naturedly.

That's when we heard the scream.

Misty Lynn holding a hand to her head, blood seeping through her fingers and turning her peroxide-blonde hair pink, stumbled into the backyard. "Call the cops, y'all. He took Shelby!"

Sheriff Tucker, Nadine, and my mother burst out of the back door of the house as pandemonium broke out in the backyard.

"What's the trouble?" the sheriff demanded.

But I was sprinting for the street.

Chapter Fifty-Five
Shelby

I had a two-bottles-of-wine headache, and the rest of my body felt like I'd gotten run over by the entire Bootleg Springs Fourth of July parade.

It smelled weird in here. Humid, close.

The garden shed? No. Good things happened in there. This was somewhere different.

So dark.

My head hurt.

Something was very, very wrong.

I tried to remember, struggled to fish out the memories. Jonah said he loved me. Bowie and Cassidy got married. Misty Lynn…something there. Something bad. She'd done something. But what?

I remembered the sound of glass breaking. Ah. She'd broken the window on Gibson's truck and was digging around inside it. Vengeance for the truth he'd told.

I'd tried to stop her.

I tried to move my arms, to rub the daze from my eyes.

That's when I realized I couldn't move them. But I was moving. Or rather my body was traveling through space. Movement.

A car? My senses slowly knit back together to deliver a still incomplete picture.

The pain in my head bloomed bright, and I knew it was no normal headache.

I could hear the rumble of an engine. Feel the rock of the vehicle as it traversed uneven ground.

I didn't know what had happened or where I was, but I knew I was in trouble.

There was a tired squeal of old, abused brakes and the rocking stopped. The engine cut off, and fear crawled its way up my spine.

I heard a metallic clunk and more screeching.

"Hello, Shelby."

Oh, God. He found me.

————

I managed to stay limp when he lifted me out of the trunk. I needed time to figure out how I was bound, where I was. How to escape.

I was not the optimistic, fresh-out-of-college, naïve social worker this time. No. I was Shelby Thompson, dissertation and triathlon finisher, Jonah-lover, dog mom, and Bootlegger.

I would not go down without a fight.

It felt like a zip tie binding my wrists behind me, and I focused on the hard plastic biting into my skin rather than the hand that was caressing the backs of my thighs as I was carried.

There were footfalls on wood and then a long slow creak. A door of some sort?

He flipped me over, placing me in a chair. Fear and adrenaline had my entire body trembling.

"I know you're awake, Shelby," the voice said calmly. And then suddenly there was light.

He pulled the hood off my face, and I saw him in the dull yellow light of a single bulb. He was older now and—God help me—even bigger. He'd always been a big kid. Now he was a big man.

We were in a cabin, a shack really. There were gaps in the walls and mismatched furniture that had seen better decades. It was hot and stuffy inside.

It stung when he ripped the tape off my lips. Lips that had said "I love you." Lips that had kissed Jonah and made promises just hours ago.

"Hello, Christian," I said quietly.

I paged through my rusty memory banks. Christian Harrell. Patterns of aggression, delusions, paranoia, and obsessive behaviors.

His family had been one of the first that I worked with fresh off my bachelor's degree. Diagnoses aren't usually made in the teens, but Christian had been showing early symptoms of schizophrenia. His diagnosis had been made officially at the mental health facility he was remanded to after he attempted to fatally stab his caseworker. Me.

Guilty but mentally ill. And as a juvenile, he'd been remanded to a hospital until he turned eighteen. My family thought I'd put the whole thing behind me, tucked it into a box and wiped my hands of it.

I preferred that they think that. But I'd kept tabs since. That's what you did when someone who tried to end your life still existed in the world. You watched, and you waited.

He'd moved with his family to Illinois where he saw a therapist regularly, and his medication was monitored. He worked in a grocery store. And now he was squatting in front of me, toying with a knife.

He liked knives.

"You've been a bad girl, Shelby." I flinched at the voice. He'd been a kid the last time. But he was a man now. "Hiding from me. Whoring yourself out. I've been watching. You know what I'm gonna do when I'm done with you?"

I didn't answer.

"I'm gonna find your roommate." He traced the tip of

the knife down my cheek. "He thought he could take you from me."

"How's your mother, Christian?" I asked suddenly. Keep him talking. Distract him from the knife. He'd always been close with his mother. She was his protector. "Does she know where you are?"

Did anyone know where you were? Where we were?

"Mom's stealing from me. She's taking money out of my room." He scratched the back of his head with the hand that held the knife.

Delusions. He'd always had trouble with thoughts about people taking things from him.

"Mom's stealing," he repeated.

"Does she know you're here?" I pressed.

He laughed, an unhinged, inhuman sound.

"Did you bring your medicine?" I asked.

He stood abruptly, shoving into my space, his forehead pressed against mine. "It's not medicine. They're trying to control me," he hissed.

He was sweaty and shaking, and I felt the first lick of despair. I couldn't talk him down from this. Couldn't appeal to him or make him let me go. I was going to have to fight for my life. He was mentally ill. And I was going to have to hurt him if I wanted to see the sunrise that was just starting to change the light through the shack's dingy window.

Something flickered outside. A shadow. Something moving.

Crap on a cracker. Were there bears up here? Was I going to have to fight off Christian and then a bear? Could a girl not catch a break?

He backed away and slashed the air with the knife, ranting incoherently.

Okay, deep breaths. He'd bound my hands but not my feet. That was a good thing. The zip tie was good, too. But I needed to get that knife away from him long enough for me to break the tie and unlock the door.

Difficult. Yes. But not impossible. I'd completed a damn triathlon today…yesterday? I was faster now than I was when I was twenty-two. Stronger, too.

He'd tried this before, and I'd won. I had to win again.

Dawn was breaking. The soft light chasing the dark.

I needed the light so I could see where I was running. *Focus on getting out of the cabin,* I told myself.

"We should have been together, Shelby. But you made me do this. You made me hurt you. And now it's too late," he raged.

He hit me with a backhand, which I'd always detested in movies. It felt insulting, degrading. It was both in reality, *and* it hurt like hell. My face stung.

I shook my head to clear my vision. The shadow was back at the window. But this time, it wasn't just a shadow.

It was a face peering cautiously through the dirty glass.

Henrietta VanSickle.

My heart lurched in my chest. I wasn't all alone. It wasn't up to just me.

What was she going to do? What was I going to do? I needed seventeen plans for all the contingencies. Was she calling for help? Was she creating a diversion? How did people in movie action sequences always manage to communicate their intentions?

God, my face hurt.

My thoughts were scrambling, and I did my best to slow them down. I needed to disable Christian temporarily, break the zip tie, and make it out the front door. That meant I couldn't be gentle, and I couldn't miss.

"How did you find me, Christian?" I said loudly. If things went bad, at least Henrietta would have a name to give authorities.

"The man," he said. "The man. The man." He was chanting it now.

"A man told you how to find me?" I didn't know what was delusion, what was truth.

"Why are you doing this?" I whispered.

"Why? *Why?*" he roared. "Because you always were mine, and you just kept fighting it. You couldn't just accept it."

He was back in my face. The knife pressed against my throat this time. I felt the tip of it prick my skin, felt the hot response of blood. He dragged the blade slowly, shallowly across my neck. I held my breath. One false move and—

The window shattered.

His head swiveled on his neck, the knife thankfully moving a few scant inches away from my flesh. I acted on instinct that would have had my self-defense instructor standing up and applauding. Leaning back, I snapped my head forward, connecting with Christian's face.

Oh my god. That hurt. If my head ever stopped hurting, it would be a miracle.

I lashed out with my foot. Where the hell were my shoes? It wasn't a good, clean shot. But it did the trick, sending the knife skittering across the floor.

My next kick was to his groin, and as he fell, I rose from the chair. My legs were jelly. But I managed to step out of his reach and cross to the door. "Run!" I screamed to my hero Henrietta through the broken window.

I reached for the knob, only remembering I was still bound when nothing happened.

"Damn it, damn it, damn it." I hinged forward, watching as Christian came up on his hands and knees. He howled like a wounded animal. I didn't know if I should kick him again to buy more time.

But I needed to get the door open.

I gritted my teeth and raised my wrists away from my back. Any shoulder flexibility I'd had previously was hindered by debilitating stiffness. I brought my wrists down against my back hard. God that hurt, and it didn't work.

Christian spit blood on the floor and started to crawl in my direction.

I slammed my hands down again, this time breaking the tie. My shaking hands made a mess of trying to unlock the front door, but I managed to open the door and slam it behind me.

I heard him hit the door a second later.

"Run!" I yelled again in case Henrietta was still in the area. I took off, jumping the two steps to the ground. My feet hit the ground as the front door burst open behind me. I didn't stop to look.

I just ran.

———

Q. Do you have a favorite Bootlegger?

Henrietta Van Sickle: While favoritism is not oft encouraged in relationships with friends, I would certainly be remiss if I did not mention Gibson Bodine. Neither one of us minds a good silence. He has a warm heart beating under the layers of gruffness and antipathy. You can count on him. And in the end, that's what matters most. Consistency. Loyalty. Gibson is the definition of always.

Chapter Fifty-Six
Shelby

I did not recommend running barefoot through unfamiliar woods with a mad man chasing me. Zero stars. Both thumbs down.

I had started down the drive but worried that Christian would appear in the car—the same damn car that had toyed with me on Mountain Road. So after about a hundred yards, I scurried off the path and into the woods.

Branches whipped me in the face, and I hoped to God I wouldn't have escaped only to lose an eye.

There was nothing ninja about my escape. It was either stealth or speed, and I opted for the latter. I barreled through the forest sounding like a herd of wildebeest.

"Someone help!" I screamed at the top of my lungs. "Literally anyone!"

I could hear him behind me. He wasn't as fast as I was, but the brush was getting thicker, and I was slowing down.

I dodged back in what I hoped was the direction of the drive. If he was on foot, maybe I could beat him on even ground.

It was still dim, too dim to see far enough ahead of me.

A fallen tree caught me mid-shin, and I went down hard.

All I wanted to do today was eat a bunch of dino nuggets and lay around watching horror movies. Was that asking too much? Instead I was hurling myself through the woods in a ruined dress and hoping to God someone would find me before Christian did.

I dragged myself up and limped over the log.

Something snapped behind me, and I could hear his ragged breathing. He was too close.

I started to run again. Something big and black moved in my peripheral vision.

On instinct, I glanced as I flew past. I caught a glimpse of fur and teeth, the glimmer of eyes.

"Holy fucking shit!" I screamed as the bear lazily turned its head in my direction.

The last of my adrenaline dumped into my system, and I turned into a sprinter. I hurdled another fallen tree, turning my ankle hard on the landing. But there was no way I was going to be a bear snack.

I ran on, the trees parting to reveal what looked like trail or driveway. I heard Christian behind me and poured on the speed. There was a roar.

And at first I thought bear, but somewhere a rational part of my brain identified it as souped-up pickup truck.

I ran toward the sound.

Headlights cut through the gloom of the woods. I was looking over my shoulder and didn't realize the trail turned.

I came to the turn nearly meeting the grill of the truck. It stopped so suddenly it stalled. I fell backward, and then Christian was on me. He hit me in the face again. Then his hands closed around my neck.

Things got blurry at that point. There were voices. Angry ones. I bit and clawed at my captor fighting for my life, and then suddenly he wasn't there anymore. The weight was lifted from my chest.

"Shelby girl, open your eyes and look at me!" Someone snapped out the command.

"There's a…" I coughed, trying to clear my throat.

"Are you okay? Open your eyes!"

I pried one eye open and realized the other one was glued shut with blood or sap or a combination of the two.

Gibson was looking down at me. GT pushed in on my range of vision.

"There was a bear," I murmured.

"Did she say there was a fucking bear?" GT demanded.

"Henrietta," I rasped.

"She called me," Gibson said. "That's how we found you."

"She okay? The bear didn't get her, did it?"

"We'll find her," Gibson promised.

"Where's Jonah?" I asked, trying to sit up.

"He's taking care of some business," Gibson said, looking beyond us.

"You stay right where you are," GT insisted. "You almost ate grill." He tapped the bumper of the truck.

"He's sick," I whispered. "Christian. He's mentally ill."

"Shelby, sweetheart? You okay?" Jameson came into my watery frame of vision.

"My head hurts real bad, and I'm so hungry. My feet hurt, too. I think I stepped on every burr in the woods. Where's Jonah? Where's the bear?"

"Jonah's just fine," Jameson promised.

"Where is she?" I heard Scarlett's shriek and more car doors.

"Scarlett!" Devlin called.

I heard sirens then. A lot of them. Morning arrived with flashes of blue and red. And I realized the Bodines had raced law enforcement and won.

The faces above me jostled, and I was staring up into Jonah's green eyes.

"Hi," I said softly.

He cupped my face in his hands. His breathing was ragged. There was rage and panic and fear in those beautiful eyes of his.

"Why are your hands bleeding?" I asked.

"Why is your head bleeding?" he countered.

"Oh. I couldn't tell if it was blood or sap. Do I still have both eyes?" I asked.

"Yeah. Two of the prettiest eyes I've ever seen." Jonah dropped his forehead to mine.

"Ow." I winced.

"Sorry, Shelby honey," he said, gathering me into his arms.

"I head butted him," I said, sighing into his chest. He was still wearing his groomsman shirt and suspenders. There was blood melting into the white. I wasn't sure whose it was. "Then there was a bear."

"Can we get some EMTs over here?" Gibson yelled over the ruckus of sirens and new voices. "Think our girl's got a concussion."

"Hey, Jonah," I said.

"Yeah, baby?"

"Thanks for making me so fast."

"You scared the hell out of me, Shelby Thompson," he whispered in my ear, gently brushing my hair back from my face.

"Scared me a little bit, too. Henrietta saw me. She broke the window. Then you saved me."

"Gibs almost ran you over."

"Wouldn't that have been ironic? Survive a kidnapping and murder attempt, a bear, and then get taken out by a pickup truck." I gave a half-hearted snort-laugh.

"That's not gonna be funny for the next thirty years or so. So don't be trying to joke about it."

"Excuse me, sir." A burly woman in uniform came into my line of sight. She set an official-looking medical bag down next to me.

"I'm a ma'am," I insisted.

Jonah gave a weak laugh. "She's talking to me, Shelby. She wants me to give her a little room so she can get a look at you."

"Don't leave me," I demanded, clinging to him.

"I'm not going anywhere."

"Where is he?" Sheriff Tucker sounded weary beyond his years, and I realized there was a whole heck of a lot we had to tell him.

"He's over there," Jameson said. "He's not goin' anywhere."

"Is he…" I didn't want to finish the question. I didn't really want the answer.

"Just let the nice lady look you over, Shelby. We'll worry about everything else later," Jonah advised.

I thought that sounded really smart.

Chapter Fifty-Seven
Jonah

I rode with Shelby in the ambulance on the way to the hospital. The EMTs assured me about fifty-six times that she was okay. That the blood was mostly from her head wound. That the cut on her throat was not life-threatening.

But my hands were still shaking.

They bandaged my raw knuckles, and Shelby and I sported matching ice packs over blooming black eyes.

I didn't know if I'd ever stop seeing that moment when the man tore out of the woods and fell on her. Intent on removing the woman I loved from this world. That was going to take a long time to get past, to not see every time I closed my eyes.

But it helped to look at Shelby smiling up at me like I was her hero.

I'd pulled him off her, dragged him away, and unleashed the rage I was feeling on him.

He'd got in a few lucky shots, but it wasn't an even match. Jameson dragged me off him, though I wasn't happy about it at the time. But Christian was still alive and now in police custody.

He wasn't answering questions like how he found Shelby, but I had a suspicion that I wanted to run by Sheriff Tucker.

They wheeled Shelby into a room in the emergency department, and I planted myself in a chair in the corner while the staff poked and prodded her and asked her a million questions. I held her hand between tests.

The verdict: A concussion, a ton of bruising, and residual soreness from her triathlon.

"Shelby!" James and Darlene paused in the doorway, looking at their daughter on a gurney.

"Hi, guys," she said cheerfully.

While the Thompsons fussed over Shelby, I spotted Sheriff Tucker outside and excused myself.

"Had a long conversation with your mother about an hour ago," Sheriff Tucker said mildly, handing me a cup of coffee. "She had some interesting theories regarding an ongoing investigation."

"I've got a few theories of my own," I said, taking a sip. "It was a sealed record," I told him. "How many people have access to sealed records?"

"Shelby got into a sealed record," the sheriff reminded me. "Can't be that hard."

"But add it to the rest. Someone took out Abbie Gilbert. Someone scared Cece Benefiel enough to make her recant her statement and now leave her house. Those remains are not Callie Kendall, but someone changed the report. Harrell said a man sent him. I think that man was Judge Kendall. Maybe he didn't do his own dirty work," I said before the sheriff could argue. "Maybe he has people who don't mind getting dirty."

Sheriff Tucker peered into his coffee as if he were looking for the answers. "The kid was off his meds. Hallucinations and delusions are common for his diagnosis."

Frustration brought my blood to a simmer. "Look, I know that we have a mountain of suspicion without a scrap of real evidence. But that's your job. You connect these dots. He screwed up somewhere, and you need to catch him."

"If any of this is true—" The sheriff leaned in and lowered his voice. "Any one piece of it, we're dealing with a very dangerous individual. And I am counting on you and the rest of your family to stay real quiet while I look into this. If we're going to get this bastard in a cage, it's gonna be because we crossed every T and dotted every I. We're not getting a confession out of him. We're building a case piece by piece until that cell door slams shut, got it?"

Sheriff Tucker believed us. He believed my mom. And for the first time, I believed that everything was going to be okay.

Unbelievably grateful, I nodded. "I give you my word. My family won't throw a wrench in this. We've got a lot riding on the truth."

"Good. Now, a word of warning. Gibson and Scarlett aren't gonna make it easy on you. They're hot-headed like their daddy. You're gonna have to impress upon them how important it is that this doesn't leak. Because if there's even a whisper of the truth, whoever sent Christian Harrell after Shelby will try again."

I nodded. I would do whatever it took to keep Gibs and Scarlett in line if it meant Shelby would stay safe. "I won't let anyone do anything to jeopardize her safety."

"You're a good man, Jonah. Just like your brothers," he said.

"Sorry for ruining the wedding for you," I said.

His mustache twitched. "My daughter married the love of her life last night. Far as I can see, nothing got ruined 'cept maybe Misty Lynn's designs on your brother."

I'd forgotten all about her hissy fit. "I have a feeling she'll survive."

"Appreciate your time, Jonah," he said, all business again. "Now, why don't you get your girl and take her home? Word on the street is she's gonna be discharged within the hour."

"Thank you, sir."

———

True to the sheriff's prediction, Shelby was discharged an hour later. She had a concussion, a lot of bruising, and a very empty stomach.

"All things considered, I feel pretty good," she chirped as I buckled her into the car.

"All things considered, you look pretty good, too," I said, leaning in to kiss the tip of her nose. She looked awful. Her eye was swollen and purple. Her throat was bandaged. There were bruises all over her arms, and she winced every time she moved.

Scarlett arrived with a change of clothes for Shelby, shorts and an Enjoy the Journey t-shirt. The rest of us were still in our wrinkled, bloodied wedding gear.

"My parents said that Gibson got a hold of Henrietta Van Sickle, and she's okay," Shelby said. "She saved my life. I'm so glad she wasn't eaten by a bear."

"About that bear—" I began.

"Jonah, I am starving," she complained. "I barely had anything for dinner last night thanks to the sex in the shed— did I tell you I had to confess that part to Sheriff Tucker? Talk about embarrassing. And I know you just want to drag me home and tuck me in bed, but if I don't eat something soon, my body will go into starvation mode and start hoarding fat, and it'll probably trigger a flare."

I sighed, dropping my head against the seat. I was so tired. But a sit-down with the family might be what we both needed.

I cracked open an eye and looked at the clock on the dashboard. "We've got enough time to make the wedding brunch."

"Yay!" she said. "Ow."

"We'll stay long enough for you to eat, and then we're going straight home, and I'm not leaving your side for at least the next six years."

"That sounds fair," she said, lacing her fingers through mine.

Chapter Fifty-Eight

Jonah

The Brunch Club restaurant put us in the back room tucked away from curious eyes. The whole town woke to the news that Shelby had been abducted from Bowie and Cassidy's wedding and then escaped, heroically injured.

I imagined the rumors would reach their peak by evening.

I settled her in on the padded booth and took the chair across from her. Jameson and Leah Mae were on our left. Scarlett and Devlin on our right. Gibson strolled in with a frown on his face.

"What's with the face?" Shelby asked.

"Someone broke into my truck last night. Wallet's missing."

"Brunch is on us," Jameson promised.

"I think it was Misty Lynn," Shelby announced. I nudged her water glass toward her. "My memory's a little foggy since I was conked in the head. But I remember following Misty Lynn out to the street. She broke your truck window with a paver from the Tuckers' flower bed and was rummaging around inside."

My focus was on Shelby, but I noticed that Gibson's expression went stony.

"I think we're gonna need Jayme," he said quietly.

"Already called her around six this morning," Devlin said, glancing at his watch. "She should be here—"

"Now what disaster have you inserted yourselves into, Bodines?" Jayme, our family attorney, strutted into the room in city black. She tucked her designer sunglasses into her designer bag and made a beeline for the coffee carafe.

George and June entered behind her, my mom on their heels.

"You're gonna need something stronger than that," Mom announced, whirling in and wrapping Shelby in a gentle hug. "So glad you're okay, sweetie."

"Thanks, Jenny," Shelby said, hugging my mom back. "Me, too. You should be pretty proud of your son."

"I am every day," she said, leaning in and hugging me hard.

"You two can't scare me like that ever again," she said, switching into mom mode.

I laughed.

"Jayme, I need to talk to you," Gibson said, trying to drag our attorney's attention away from the caffeine she was mainlining.

Reading his expression, my mom rose and went to him. "What is it?"

"My wallet was stolen last night," he said. Something seemed to pass between the two of them.

"One crisis at a time," Jayme insisted. "Let's start at the top with the abduction and assault."

"Actually there's a bigger crisis," Shelby said. "You're definitely going to want liquor."

"Mr. and Mrs. Bodine are here for breakfast," Cassidy chirped from the doorway. She strolled in hand-in-hand with Bowie, both beaming in newlywed bliss.

"Well, what in the hell happened to all of you?" Bowie asked, gaping at us.

We were quite a sight to take in. Shelby looked exactly like an attempted murder victim. I was bruised and bloody. Jameson and Gibs were still in the rumpled pants and shirts from last night. The girls had last night's makeup on and what was left of their hairdos.

"Y'all either had one hell of a fight or one hell of a party without us," Cassidy pouted.

Shelby was the first one to start laughing, and the rest of us fell in behind her.

"Would someone please tell us what the hell happened?" Bowie said, drawing his wife into the room.

"Imma get us a round of Bloody Marys," Scarlett decided.

We waited until we had our drinks and our meals before dishing the dirt.

"I missed a Misty Lynn meltdown?" Cassidy complained.

"Don't worry. I'm sure someone got video," Scarlett promised.

"Okay, so, Misty Lynn throws herself at you, gets rejected for the millionth time, and flips out?" Bowie clarified.

Jayme rolled her eyes. "This is the weirdest fucking town."

"So she storms out, and Shelby follows her," Leah Mae said, picking up the thread. "This was after she and Jonah had sex in your parents' shed, by the way."

"Wedding reception sex, nice," Cassidy said approvingly.

"Anyway, Shelby went after Misty Lynn and caught her breaking into Gibson's truck," Jameson continued.

"About that—" Gibson said. But nobody paid him any attention.

"The next thing we know, Misty Lynn is screaming her head off, sayin' someone took Shelby," Scarlett said.

The retelling, now that all the parties were safe, was mildly entertaining…to everyone except me.

"I remember trying to pull Misty Lynn out of your truck," Shelby said to Gibson. "And she was crying and yelling about teaching you a lesson. Then it all just goes black."

"According to Misty Lynn's statement, a man appeared out

of the shadows and pushed her down. She struck her forehead on Gibson's truck. He grabbed you and knocked you unconscious," Jayme said, reading off her phone.

"How did you get your hands on the report already?" Devlin asked.

Her painted lips curved. "I have my ways."

They told Bowie and Cassidy the rest of the story in fits and starts.

"I can't believe we were so busy having hot newlywed sex that we had no idea any of this was going on," Cassidy said, pushing her plate away. "I need to get into the station and get the scoop."

"Before you go," I said, eyeing Shelby. "There's something else you guys need to know."

Mom straightened her shoulders and took a fortifying gulp of her Bloody Mary. Gibson's foot was jiggling where it crossed his knee at the ankle.

"What the hell are you all up to?" Scarlett demanded. She wasn't a fan of being left out.

"This doesn't leave this room," I insisted.

"You're starting to make me nervous, Jonah," Devlin admitted.

Shelby squeezed my hand. "I got this," she said. "Okay, it all started when I asked June to take a road trip with me…"

―――――――――

Ten minutes later, the room was dead silent except for the slurp of Bloody Mary glasses emptying.

"So Callie's alive?" Scarlett asked finally in an uncharacteristically soft voice.

"As of last year, yes," Mom said carefully. "And I told Sheriff Tucker all of this after they found you this morning, Shelby."

"What about the report? The dental records matched?" Leah Mae asked, leaning in.

"We suspect the report was doctored," June spoke up.

"This is a lot to take in," Devlin said.

"I'm gonna need like six more Bloody Marys," Jameson said.

"So Dad didn't…hurt her." Scarlett stared down at her plate of forgotten waffles.

"Your father saved her life," Mom said softly.

"You think it was the judge that did that to her?" Cassidy asked. I could see the cop in her warring with the girl who'd lost a summer friend.

"It's the only thing that makes sense," Shelby said. "Callie was adamant about not going home. He's in a position of power. He had access to Christian's sealed file. I'm sure he's got people willing to do dirty work for him. And he loses big if Callie comes strolling back into town telling the truth. He could kiss that federal judgeship goodbye. It's better for him if she stays dead."

"The important thing to remember is, everything is circumstantial right now. We have to be patient and let law enforcement do their job," I insisted, remembering the sheriff's warning.

"Oh, 'cause they've done such a bang-up job so far?" Scarlett snapped. "No offense, Cass. I'm just processing a whole lotta feelings right now."

"Understood." Cassidy nodded.

"Sheriff Tucker believes us. This is more than anyone has known about the case since Callie disappeared," I reminded them. "We'll nail him for it somehow."

"And when we do, maybe Callie can come back," Mom said softly.

"Speaking from a place of not nearly enough vodka for this," Jayme began, "I'm going to strongly encourage you all to listen to Jonah. Do *not* interfere with this investigation in any way. If you see Judge Kendall buying sticky buns downtown, you paste a nice-as-fucking-pie smile on your face. Because if any one of you acts up and tips him off, I swear to my red Ferragamos that I will personally destroy your life. This man has gotten away with actual murder—allegedly. And it's possible he went after

349

Shelby through that boy—allegedly. If one of you fucks up and he stays free, his next alleged victim is on you." She pointed a sharp, red nail around the room, making eye contact with everyone.

"Yes, ma'am," we chorused. Jayme was a terrifying woman. I was very glad she was on our side.

"On that note," I announced, rising from my chair. "I'm taking Shelby home."

I held my hand out to her and helped her up. I heard her whimper of pain and knew we'd pushed our luck. She was going to bed and not getting up until I said it was okay.

I slipped my arm around her waist, a show of affection to everyone else but a stabilization for her.

She paused. "Oh, Scarlett? We need to talk about some real estate options," she said.

"Oh yeah?" My sister perked up.

"Yeah," I agreed. "Shelby and I are staying in town, permanently. We're gonna need a bigger house."

"Billy Ray needs more space," Shelby said, beaming up at me.

"And Shelby's gonna need dedicated office space."

I knew we were battered and bruised and there were emotional scars that would take a long time to heal. But looking into her eyes right now, I felt our future stretch on in front of us. Her monster was going to jail. And soon, the shadow that had fallen over the Bodines would be lifted forever.

"Let's go get our puppy," I told her as she leaned into me.

"Where is he?" she asked.

"Millie Waggle has him and Katherine," I told her.

The door to the dining room opened, and Sheriff Tucker stepped in alone. He didn't look happy.

"Sheriff Tucker," Jayme said, standing up to position herself between my family and the law. "What can we do for you?"

"It's a good thing you're here, Jayme," he said, toying with his hat in his hands. "If you wouldn't mind accompanying Gibson down to the station with me, I'd be much obliged."

The only one who didn't look surprised in the room was Gibson.

"What is this regarding?" Jayme asked, all scary business now.

"Gibson's wallet was turned into the station this morning by a citizen concerned about the contents," he said vaguely.

Judging by Gibson's expression, he knew exactly what the sheriff was referring to.

"What in the hell?" Scarlett burst out. "Did that damn Misty Lynn steal his wallet and then get mad about the condoms he's not usin' to protect himself from her herpes flare?"

"I'd rather discuss this at the station," the sheriff insisted, looking more uncomfortable than a cat under a rocking chair.

"Dad," Cassidy said, her eyes implored him.

"It's gonna be fine. It's just some questions."

Gibson's jaw ticked.

"My client and I will meet you at the station, sheriff, as soon as we're done with our breakfast," Jayme said, hands on hips, as if daring the man to make a demand.

"Much obliged," Sheriff Tucker said. "Swing by the station when you have a chance, Cass, and I'll catch you up about last night."

He left, and the room stayed completely silent for about ten seconds.

"Well, what in tarnation was that all about?" Scarlett finally demanded.

Everyone started talking at once.

"Let's get this over with," Gibson said to Jayme.

He left without saying a word.

"If Misty Lynn turned up dead and they try to pin it on Gibson I am going to burn this town to the ground," Scarlett said, picking up her drink.

"Scarlett, what have we said about making threats in public?" Devlin asked, patting her thigh under the table.

She sighed heavily. "Not to."

Chapter Fifty-Nine
Shelby

I woke to a cacophony of smells. Glorious, greasy smells.

I cracked open an eye and stretched. Billy Ray grumbled in his sleep next to me on Jonah's bed. Our bed. Jonah had carried me upstairs and, after another shower, tucked me into bed with instructions not to move for at least two hours.

A bleary glance at the clock told me I'd been out for almost four.

My body sang a chorus of aches and pains. I was due for another round of anti-inflammatories washed down with a big glass of wine…or a Mountain Dew.

Fantasizing about a two-liter bottle, I limped down the stairs into a fantasy land.

"Am I hallucinating?" I whispered.

Every flat surface in the living room was covered with takeout containers and junk food.

Jonah sat on the couch eating a fried chicken leg. "Surprise!" he said with his mouth full.

"What is all this?" Onion rings and cheese sticks and an

entire tray of dino nuggets crowded the coffee table. There was a six-pack of Mountain Dew in a bucket of ice on the floor. The table I used as a desk now held a greasy bag of fast food burgers. There was an entire apple pie and more fried chicken sitting on the TV stand.

"It's a pig-in," Jonah said cheerfully. He crossed to me and gave me a gentle kiss. "How are you feeling?"

"Like I don't know what to dive into first," I said, reverently.

He handed me a plate. "You once asked if I ever ate garbage."

"I didn't mean an entire convenience store and fast food restaurant," I laughed.

"Every time I finish a big event that I trained hard for, I treat myself with a pig-in."

"I didn't think it was possible since you saved my life and all. But I think I love you even more right now than I did before I fell asleep," I whispered, sniffing the fried chicken.

"Have at it, honey."

He grabbed the pain meds while I loaded up a plate and fished out a can of soda from the bucket.

"I am so happy right now," I said, biting the head off a stegosaurus nugget.

"There's also some regular nuggets and a bunch of sauces in that bag," Jonah said, pointing with an onion ring to another bag.

"I can't believe you did this for me," I said, feeling way too emotional for this to be just about junk food.

"It's all about balance," he said, with his mouth full.

"You're really sexy when you gorge yourself," I told him.

He grinned at me, half of an onion ring hanging from his lips. I laughed.

"How are you really?" he pressed.

I grabbed a burger, unwrapped it, and took a bite. My eyes rolled heavenward. "I feel like so many weights have been lifted that I might float away," I confessed.

"I talked to Cassidy," Jonah said. "Christian was treated at the hospital and taken to a secure mental facility where he'll be evaluated to see if he's fit to stand trial."

"He won't be," I guessed.

"He's not getting out again, Shelby," Jonah said. "Not even if he stays on his meds. His mother wants to talk to you when you're up for it. She feels responsible."

"She's not," I said, shoving a few French fries into my burger bun.

"She probably just needs to hear it."

"What about Gibson? What was all that about this morning?"

"Cassidy was pretty cagey about that. But I managed to drag some info out of her playing the 'my girlfriend was abducted from your wedding' card."

"Mean."

"Yeah, well. You're my girlfriend, and Gibs is my brother."

"So what did Misty Lynn find in his wallet?"

"A picture of Gibs and Callie together."

The burger stuck in my throat, and I coughed. I took a swig of soda. "Like from before she went missing?"

He nodded.

"What kind of a picture?"

"It was one of those photo booth deals. A strip of pictures. They were making faces."

"I didn't know he even knew Callie," I said, going for another nugget.

"No one did. That's the problem. He never said a word in all those years, so naturally the cops have some questions."

"Where is Gibson now? Did they let him go?"

"He was released after a formal interview. Now he's back to playing hermit. He won't talk to anyone."

"No charges, at least. That's good."

"For now. We'll see what happens next. The judge is going to know that Gibs was interviewed. The why is gonna come out."

"Maybe he'll stay away? If he did turn Christian loose on

me, wouldn't he want to stay out of Bootleg for a while? Keep his hands clean?"

"If he knows what's good for him, he'll steer clear," Jonah said stonily.

"You Bodines and your Bootleg Justice," I sighed.

"This will end with him in a cage," he promised. "And it's all going to be okay."

"It will be," I said, reaching for his hand and bringing his bruised knuckles to my lips. "What next?" I asked him.

"We wait for law enforcement to sort the shit out, I guess. Keep our mouths shut. You and I are gonna do some house hunting. You'll do some job searching and schedule your dissertation defense and an appointment with your rheumatologist to head off the flare that's probably headed in your direction. And after your brother proposes to June in a few months, I'm gonna start ring shopping for you. We Bodines take turns."

I gaped at him. "First of all, I meant what are we eating next? Secondly, I forbid you from proposing for the first eighteen months of our relationship. We're still in the honeymoon period. We need more time to make sure you don't turn into a jerk."

"Oh, definitely the pie. There's whipped cream in the fridge," he said, ignoring my demand.

He got up and loped into the kitchen. Returning with a spray can, he paused in the doorway and sprayed a dollop into his mouth.

"Jonah, I've seen you sweaty and shirtless. I've seen you do pull-ups until the veins in your arms tried to explode. I've seen you completely naked and wet in the shower. But I have never been more attracted to you than I am right now."

He grinned. And when he kissed me, it tasted sweet and full of promises.

Billy Ray bayed from upstairs. There was a thump when he threw himself off the bed and stampeded down the stairs, barking accusatorially.

"We're right here, buddy," I assured him. He nosed at the

food on the table. "You may have one dino nugget. But that's all I'm willing to share."

"Hey, how many kids do you think we should have?" Jonah asked, picking up the remote control. "You like kids, right?"

I let out the air that had trapped itself in my lungs. "I like kids," I said carefully.

"I think it would be cool to have a family here, surrounded by family. They'll have cousins and aunts and uncles."

I felt a warm gooey sensation in my stomach.

He settled on the couch and arranged me between his legs so I could lean back against his chest. Outside the birds chirped, and the sun shone. Neighbors poured sweet tea and gossiped. My parents walked their grandpig. Jonah's mama snuggled up to her boyfriend at the ice cream shop.

And everything felt just about perfect.

"Hey, did I tell you about the bear I saw?"

Epilogue
Shelby

I was pedaling my butt off, sweat beading on my arms and dripping from my chin. Jonah was next to me in the darkened studio. It was just the two us. The music thumped off the walls, reverberating in my bones. I could see the last mile ticking down down down.

"Almost there!" He flashed me his heartbreaker grin in the dark. "Keep going!"

My legs were burning. A white-hot fire under the skin had consumed the muscle and was now devouring bone. And I kind of almost sort of didn't hate it.

"Go, Shelby honey, go!" Jonah crowed as the screen on the far wall clicked over to fifty.

I slumped over the handlebars in relief.

"No, you don't. Keep moving. Bring the heart rate down slowly," he said, stepping off his bike. He rested his hand on my neck, his thumb brushing the scar I bore there. A reminder of how close we came to nearly losing it all. A reminder that every day together was precious.

But the past was officially the past. Never to haunt us again. And the future stretched on in front of us like an endless happily ever after.

"How come you get to stop?" I huffed, but I managed to make a wobbly revolution of the pedals while I complained.

He crossed the room and grabbed two fresh sweat towels off the shelving system next to the festive fake Christmas tree and returned to me, still grinning. "Fifty miles, Shelby. Not bad for a little ankylosing spondylitis."

I took the last of the resistance off the bike and let the momentum carry my legs around and around.

"That century ride isn't going to know what hit it," I predicted breathily.

Jonah and I had signed up for a romantic 100-mile bike ride through Canada this coming summer, and we were spending the cold West Virginia winter training in his new gym space.

He changed the music on his phone from hard-driving, celebratory rock to a slow, sweet country ballad. It was adorable how Bootleg Springs had claimed yet another victim.

"How you feeling?" he asked as I took a swig from my water bottle.

"Tired but good," I said. "I promise."

He looked…nervous? Excited?

"What's going on with you?" I asked pointing a finger in the direction of his handsome face.

My flares had been few and far between since meeting Jonah, and when I did get knocked down by one, I had my handsome, pushy boyfriend to pull me back up. I was thriving. *We* were thriving.

Jonah's new gym was a bustling gathering place year-round for townsfolk trying to work off a few extra pounds during the holidays, for summertimers trying to maintain lake bodies. To his loyal elder following who mostly just wanted to gossip and watch his back muscles flex.

With my PhD hot off the presses, I'd landed a research professor gig at the nearby Buck State University where I was heading a decade-long study on the opioid crisis in communities. My survey was also being rolled out as a nationwide initiative to identify, among other things, loneliness within communities and potential solutions. And I was working on a book. The story of how Bootleg Springs claimed me as its own.

Billy Ray was now almost full-grown, though he still acted like a puppy. Fortunately our paper towel consumption had finally returned to normal.

Best of all, we finally had a home. We'd saved and searched, weighed our options and overthought. And then on Thanksgiving Day, just last month, crowded around the huge table in Scarlett and Devlin's new home, the Bodines had handed Jonah a set of house keys.

The keys and deed belonged to the Bodine childhood home, now stripped of old, sad memories. Refreshed and renovated. Ready for a new family. Our family.

"Jonah, I—" I lost my train of thought immediately.

Jonah Bodine, my boyfriend of a year and a half—scratch that, my boyfriend of exactly eighteen months—was on bended knee in front of my bike.

"Shelby Thompson."

"Jonah Bodine," I whispered back. My feet froze in the pedal cages.

"It's been exactly eighteen months since you and I first decided to start this summer fling," he began. "And as you instructed me, couples shouldn't even start talking about the future until they've survived eighteen months."

"I do recall imparting that information," I said, bringing my fingers to my lips. My hand was shaking. My vision was blurring, and I had the distinct suspicion that it wasn't sweat.

"It's been eighteen months and one wild ride. You were there with me every step of the way through everything my family went through. You were by my side when things seemed like they were at their darkest. You stuck."

I pressed my fingers against my lips harder as his words hit bullseye after bullseye dead center in my heart.

"You showed me what a partner is supposed to be. You let me in. Let me fix things on occasion. And Shelby, honey, I can't wait for the next eighteen months with you. The next eighteen years. The next forever. I'm ready. Are you?"

I nodded, blinking back tears. And kept nodding.

"Good, 'cause I've got something real important to ask you." He revealed a small black box, and I held my breath while he opened it.

It was a simple oval solitaire that glittered like a thousand stars on a delicate gold band.

"Dr. Shelby Thompson, would you do me the great honor of being my wife? Running herd on a bunch of loud Bodine kids. Riding through Canada and running through everywhere else. Growing old here so we can cause a ruckus at The Lookout. Would you do all that with me?"

I could barely get my feet off the pedals. I launched myself at him, mostly out of joy but also a little because my legs weren't working yet.

He caught me. *Jonah always caught me.*

"Is that a yes?" he asked, his voice muffled by my sweaty hair.

I nodded and kept right on nodding. "It's the biggest, loudest yes you've ever heard in your life."

We laughed, fumbling in the dark studio for the box, the ring, the kiss.

It was salty and sweet and everything I'd ever dared dream of. And so was Jonah.

My parents were going to be thrilled. Hell, the entire town was probably going to throw a party.

"This isn't going to interfere with Gibson's wedding, is it?" I asked.

Jonah laughed. "My brother and I already discussed it. It's all good."

"It's better than good," I said, watching the diamond wink on my finger. The sparkle blurred before my eyes. "It's perfect."

"We've got about twenty minutes before my phone starts

ringing off the hook with Scarlett demanding to know if it's official yet and insisting we come over to celebrate. She's making dino nuggets for you."

I snort-laughed and covered my mouth. "Twenty minutes? We can get into a whole lot of trouble in twenty minutes."

"I've got a bottle of champagne on ice in the locker room. What do you say we pop the cork and get cleaned up?"

The way those green eyes sparkled, brighter than the diamond I wore, I knew exactly what he meant.

"Jonah, you are going to be everything your father never had the chance to be. You know that, right?" He already was. The good man. The generous neighbor. Now, he'd be the dream husband. The wonderful father he never had.

He cupped my face in his big, warm hand. "That's the plan, Dr. Bodine. And you're everything I ever wanted."

Acknowledgments

Smooshyface Clairebear Kingsley for writing this series with me and being a super cool human.

Dawn, Jessica, and Amanda for those eyeballs.

My BRAs for being forever wonderful.

Cleo for shedding all over my desk during edits.

Joyce and Tammy for watching endless Queer Eye episodes with me. Oh and doing all the work, all the time.

My secret street team that came together accidentally and made beautiful magic together.

Winston the free-range patio pillow for turning me into the neighbor other neighbors avoid.

Mr. Lucy for remaining devastatingly handsome.

Panera for feeding us when I'm on a deadline and can't be bothered to cook.

Tacos for always, always making life better.

About the Author

Lucy Score is a #1 *New York Times*, *USA Today*, and *Wall Street Journal* bestselling author. She grew up in a literary family who insisted that the dinner table was for reading and earned a degree in journalism. She writes full-time from the Pennsylvania home she and Mr. Lucy share with their obnoxious cat, Cleo. When not spending hours crafting heartbreaker heroes and kick-ass heroines, Lucy can be found on the couch, in the kitchen, or at the gym. She hopes to someday write from a sailboat, ocean-front condo, or tropical island with reliable Wi-Fi.

Sign up for her newsletter by scanning the QR code below and stay up on all the latest Lucy book news. You can also follow her here:

Website: Lucyscore.net
Facebook: lucyscorewrites
Instagram: scorelucy
TikTok: @lucyferscore
Binge Books: bingebooks.com/author/lucy_score
Readers Group: facebook.com/groups/
BingeReadersAnonymous Newsletter signup:

Printed in the USA
CPSIA information can be obtained
at www.ICGtesting.com
LVHW050052101024
793434LV00034B/540